'The
Where burning Sappho loved and sung.
'Lord Byron'

SAPPHO SINGS

A fictionalized biography of Psappha*
The Poetess of Lesbos

Peggy Ullman Bell

* [suh-FAH]

Peggy Ullman Bell

SAPPHO SINGS

All Rights Reserved © 2008, Peggy Ullman Bell

ISBN1438214316
EAN-139781438214313

No part of this book may be reproduced or transmitted in any form or by any means, graphic, electronic, or mechanical, including photocopying, recording, taping or by any information storage or retrieval system, without written permission from the author.

Although based on what is known and rumored about The Poetess , this book is a work of fiction. Names, characters, places and incidents are either products of the author's imagination or are used fictitiously. Any resemblance to actual events or locales or persons, living or dead, is entirely coincidental.

Cover design © 2008, Peggy Ullman Bell, executed by Pauli Driver Smith, Lady of The Lake Graphic Designs [ladyofthelakedesign.com]

Rainbow Fire graphic © 2006, Associated Press

Portions of SAPPHO SINGS appeared in PSAPPHA, a novel of Sappho, UpStart Publishing, Y2K

To

Daughters

And

Generations

Of

Daughters

Peggy Ullman Bell

[page deliberately left blank]

Acknowledgements

Thank you to librarians everywhere, without whom historical novelists could not function. Thank you to all of those who encouraged my attempt to add to the body of literature that surrounds this remarkable woman.

My appreciation to Bliss Carmen, Canada's former poet laureate, whose work with the fragments (Sappho: One Hundred Lyrics, Boston, 1903) provided inspiration for this book and to Henry Thornton Wharton, for the research and motivation behind Carmen's insightful interpretations. (Sappho: Memoir, Text, Selected Renderings and A Literal Translation 1885; 2nd. ed. 1887)

Thanks to Algernon Charles Swinburne whose use of the extant lines drove me to take on this project. (Poems and Ballads, London, 1866)

Special appreciation to Paul Roche and his publisher, for granting permission to include his translation of "Please," which fit my plot so perfectly, I did not have the heart to paraphrase.
(The Love Poems of Sappho, Prometheus Books, 1999)

To these and to the many and various others who have translated and interpreted the bits of Psappha's nine books that remain available to us, thank you for keeping her voice alive.

Thank you also to Sonia Johnson for granting me permission to open chapter thirty with her poem.

Bouquets of gratitude to my editor, Tricia Bush, whose patience and editorial expertise gave me the courage and the tools to "get it right." Without her, Sappho's Song would not have proper "seasoning."

To those who say I should've included the fragments I say, "They're here."
To those who know Sappho well enough to spot them I say, "Blessed be."

Peggy Ullman Bell

[page deliberately left blank]

Sappho Sings

Book One

THE LESVIO*

---
* Lesvoi (a citizen or citizens of Lesbos)

Peggy Ullman Bell

[page deliberately left blank]

"*Psappha*, as she called herself in her soft Aeolian dialect, was born at Eresus, on Lesbos*"
The Life of Greece by Will Durant'

-- I --

On the opposite side of the island from her birthplace, on a hill above and somewhat south of Mitylene, Psappha leaned her back against the outside of her stepfather's garden wall and stared across open water. The mainland shore remained in shadow as Dawn dressed ancient mountaintops in brilliant white. Soon the sun would move higher to grace the twelve mainland Aeolian cities with early morning light. Near the second to last, a thin column of smoke wafted upward. Whatever vessel had the signal fires ablaze throughout the night was getting closer. *It should reach Mitylene by noon.*

She edged into the shadows as her mother's husband exited the main gate. His robes drew a dark green line across dew-drenched grass as he hurried toward the oleander-shrouded path that led down to The Lady's Park and from there to the beach, which would soon be crowded with people headed into the city of New Mitylene to learn what news the night fires foretold.

Despite her mothers repeated warnings of what could happen to her afoot in the city "now that you're almost all grown up", Psappha followed Eurigios*, being careful to not let her former nursemaid catch her. Praxinoa* would make her use her mother's sedan chair.

---

* Psappha (Suh-FAH)
* Eurigios (you-ri-GUY-aus)
* Praxinoa (prax-in-NO-ah)

"Its curtains will protect you from prying eyes," Praxinoa would have said. *They'd also hide everything interesting from me,* Psappha secretly replied.

She peered between towering oleanders to catch fleeting teasing glimpses of the twin cities beyond The Lady's Park. When she stepped from between the hedges, Old Mitylene displayed itself before her. *Like a jade and ivory cameo, tied with two golden-ribbon bridges to the teeming young city on the shore. A jewel in a crescent of noise,* Psappha thought as a poem began to form. Before she went to bed, she would inscribe it into the wax tablet that lay always ready on her dressing table.

The ancient city of mansions and gardens rested on an island in the middle of the bay. In the near harbor, the fishing fleet nestled like a flock of many-colored ducks. In the deep harbor beyond the bridges, a black-sailed trireme strained at anchor. *A great, chained panther its three rows of oars like claws reaching skyward.*

On the farthest shore, The Lady's sacred olive grove stretched away from the beach with young leaves shimmering in dawn-light. *Like a thousand needles sewing up the sky.*

Eurigios spoke and the next line of some future poem escaped her. "Where do you think you're going, young lady? And where's your chair?" Eurigios stroked his neatly cropped blond beard in a pretense of age and authority. "Your mother will never forgive me if I allow you to stroll about the city like a street urchin."

Determined, Psappha squared her shoulders to accent small, pointed breasts beneath a clinging Egyptian linen peplos. The ribbons girdling her trim waist held her skirt just above her unpainted toes. "Please," she said, in a studied imitation of her mother's most seductive tone.

Eurigios blinked. "But . . . ." His uncertain demeanor advertised his youth.

Scarcely ten years older than Psappha, Eurigios was born a scant year before her brother Charaxos*. *Maybe that's why Charaxos chose to study with Pythagoras in Croton instead of joining Mother and I in exile: Or was it because his birth twin Alkaios* left to rent his sword to King Neccho* of Egypt? A pity. They used to all be such good friends.*

Eurigios paid a high price in friendship to gain my mother's hand. A shame he never gained her love. Then nobody does-- except maybe Charaxos.

Eurigios moved onto and across the grass at the beachside edge of The Lady's Park. Psappha hurried to follow. Enveloped as she was in bitter childhood memories, she failed to notice the marble bench half hidden in a cluster of azaleas. It nearly toppled her.

"O-o-oh," she moaned as she collapsed onto the bench. "I've stubbed my toe."

Across the glade, a giggle of girls danced among the trees, following a lithe young woman whose ivory-cream skin and long, silver-gold hair perfectly defined the generally accepted concept of beauty. *If only Mother could have such a child.* Long-legged, graceful, creamy-skinned and golden-haired, the dancer was the embodiment of everything Psappha considered beautiful in a human being: The opposite of her abbreviated, olive-hided, dark-haired self. "Who is she?"

"Who?"

"That marvelous dancer, who is she?"

Eurigios arched a brow, then shrugged and said, "I don't know much about her but if you'll stop dawdling I'll tell you what I do know as we walk."

Psappha hurried ahead of him then turned and walked toward the city backward. "Tell me."

---

* Charaxos (KAY-rah-khaus)
* Alkaios (Al-KAY-aus)
* Neccho, Pharaoh of Egypt (609-593 bce)

"Most suppose she is Athenian or an Aeolian from the far country. Her coloring is Athenian, like your mother's, but she knew no Hellene when they found her."

"Found her? Where? What is she called?"

"Turn around, Psappha' and walk beside me before you stumble again and fall. Here. Give me your hand. They found her in some wreckage on the beach. That's why they call her Atthis*."

"Is she really Atthis, Goddess of the Rugged Coast come to live among us?"

"I don't know," Eurigios said. "She could be I suppose. Who knows? From the way Poseidon-Earthshaker raged that day, she must at least have his protection."

"Oh, yes." Psappha skipped a step to keep pace with him. "I remember. A few weeks ago, Earth trembled greatly as she repulsed Poseidon's advances."

Eurigios nodded. "They discovered Atthis on the beach the next morning."

"Atthis," Psappha whispered. The name tickled her palette.

"Come, Psapph'. You're dawdling again."

The marketplace on the beach in New Mitylene was a wonder of riches from throughout the world and Psappha loved every noisy, stinking inch of it. She would have dashed ahead but for his firm hold on her hand. Fascinated by the crowds, colors and varying smells, she barely noticed the shabbiness of the booths that lined the filthy street.

"Here, little lady, sir," a hawker whined, "the finest wines of the house of Judah. Sweet wine fit only for so beautiful a lady."

"No, no, friends," another pleaded, "only the moon-kissed dates of Libya are sweet enough to pass the lips of so fair a child of Aphrodite*."

Psappha laughed at their exaggerations. *Fair indeed. Ha!*

---

* Atthis (AT-this)
* Aphrodite (one of The Lady's many names.)

They brushed by another merchant dressed in gaudy foreign garb, his voice dripping honey. "Pay no attention to them, good sir. No wine or dates can compare with the sweetness of Apollo's succulent, golden globes. From the Sun's own sacred groves I bring you the biggest and the sweetest of his blessed fruits."

Psappha edged through a crowd near the temple of Zeus, pulling Eurigios with her. In the shop there, amid bins of figs, nuts and dried grapes, a dark little man displayed rough gold disks.

"These are what Achaeans use for trade," he said, stroking his small, dark beard. "See the fine image of Aphaea* by which they mark them. No more must merchants spend their days in idle bargaining solely to end up with more goods for still more bargaining. Now you can pay us in gold coins and with them we can purchase only that which will sell quickly."

"But, where would we get them?"

Psappha turned her head enough to see who spoke. Near the edge of the crowd, a muscular peasant stood, arms akimbo, eyes prancing.

"From me," said the merchant. "Sell me goods I want and you'll soon have a supply of gold coins."

"Where would I carry them?" the man scoffed. "Do you expect me to carry a basket like a woman?"

Psappha giggled at a mental picture of the huge ruffian with a basket on his head.

The bearded merchant was not amused. "Where else but in your mouth?" he snapped. "I'm sure you could carry a fortune there."

The bleating of a trio of goats being driven into the temple caught Psappha's attention. Their perfect beauty reminded her of her distrust of priests and gods who, unable to bleed painlessly themselves, murdered Gaea's sacred creatures to appease their jealousy.

---

* Aphaea (a [as in at] FAY-ah)

A grubby merchant in desert robes insinuated a small, jewel-encrusted mirror in front of Psappha's frown.

"Ah, sir," he proclaimed, addressing Eurigios. "It is for such beauty as this that my master makes his magic glass."

Psappha turned away from him in a huff and confronted her own image, full-length in a magnificent piece of standing glass.

"Eurigios," she exclaimed bringing her palms together sharply. "You must buy this for Mother."

"I doubt she would like it much right now."

"I know," Psappha admitted; her enthusiasm dampened, "but the reflection is so much clearer than in her polished-copper one. You could save it and present it to her as a birthing gift."

"Perhaps it is you who would like it," he teased.

She crinkled her nose. "I have no use for mirrors. Even if I did, I could not let you buy me presents."

"Why not? You are my wife's daughter and you will marry my brother when he returns. Why should you feel shy with me?"

Psappha hung her head and scuffed the dust with her shoe. How could she tell him that she hated the thought of Alkaios's return? How could she tell that after seven years his beloved younger brother had become a stranger: *A stranger to whom our parents betrothed me at birth: A stranger to trap me in a life of sedan-chairs and babes. I want more.* Unsure as to what that something more might be she decided that hurting Eurigios would be pointless. Instead, she smiled and walked quickly on.

They made their way through the crowds, passing booths bright with fabrics from unknown lands, brought to Mitylene by Phoenician traders -- stalls overflowing with figurines and presided over by stiff-bearded Egyptians -- open corrals filled with bellowing cattle. Eurigios hurried her past a refinery where naked slaves stirred great vats of boiling fleece. Psappha sidestepped huge jars of lanolin. She ran past slaughter pens swarming with green flies and held her nose before swine pens deep in slime.

She dawdled near stalls of rare oils, tables strewn with exotic herbs, brocade-bedecked bins of rare spice. Eurigios tugged her hand and they stepped onto the quay. Psappha paused once more to admire the sleek, black trireme. *A fitting tribute to the shipwrights of Tyre who built her.*

Such contrast, she thought as a flamboyant Egyptian dragon ship slid past the black trireme.

"Come, Psapph'. The Egyptian will have news." Eurigios's grip tightened but Psappha held her ground.

From here she could see her ancestral home in the old city, tucked close by the citadel's south wall, close beside the seat of power. *As was my father. The House of Scamandronomous* should belong to me! Not Charaxos. He left. Our father would want me to have it. And, not this new babe Mother's expecting. Let Eurigios provide for his own.*

Eurigios tugged her hand and pulled her along as he hurried the length of the wharf. The pleasing scents of incense, spices and rare oils quickly gave way to the stench of rotting fish and sweating stevedores. The dock nearest the dragon ship gabbled with people. At the very end, a man shouted from atop a bale of papyrus.

". . . on the west bank of the river Euphrates, near its westernmost bend. We camped behind the city. From our fires, we could see Neccho's encampment.

"The enemy arrived at night. Their fires lit most of the riverbank. We did not find out who they were until after the battle. By then, they had pushed us south into Judea. We camped again near Jerusalem.

"The Chaldeans* must have been fat with victory. They left us to make our way back to Egypt as best we could: Nipping at our heels to keep us moving."

"What of the Lesbians?" someone called from the crowd.

---

* Scamandronomos (Skam-an-DRO-no-maus)

* The 11th dynasty of the Kings of Babylon (6th century BC) is conventionally known to historians as the Chaldean Dynasty.

"They fought bravely and well," the man said. "Those who did not fall at Charchemish have earned their wages."

"Where are they now?" another in the throng shouted.

"Many elected to remain in the Pharaoh's new city for Greeks called Naucratis*," the man said. "The rest we brought home with us."

Eurigios did not wait to hear more. Psappha ran to keep pace with him.

"Wait!" she gasped.

"I'm sorry," he said when she arrived at his side breathless and panting. "I thought Alkaios might have returned and I forgot everything else."

"It doesn't matter." She sighed as her breathing slowed. "I know how much you love your brother."

They had re-entered The Lady's Park. The stone path crackled beneath their sandals. The dust of the street fell softly from their feet. Psappha glanced over her shoulder, holding Mitylene in her gaze until the trees blocked her view.

"Hurry, Psapph', your mother will be worried."

No, she won't.

Eurigios took the hill in sure strides. Psappha's legs seemed to grow shorter the longer they climbed. The way seemed rougher than it had in the morning.

They reached the house to find the outer gate already bolted for the night. Eurigios called to the guard and the gate squeaked open. "Word has come from your father's house," the gatekeeper announced. "Your brother has returned."

Eurigios danced an impromptu jig that ended in an exuberant hug. "I must greet him," he said as he let her go. "Don't look so glum. I'll tell Praxinoa it's my fault you're late." *But not before she's boxed my ears.* "Torches," he shouted into the darkness. "Tell your

---

* Naucratis (gnaw-KRAT-tiss) Egypt

mother where I've gone. I won't be long," he called over his shoulder as he hurried away. Two torchbearers ran to precede him.

Psappha slumped through the gate. A large dog growled softly then ambled toward her as she entered the garden. Turquoise-black birds scattered in his wake.

Psappha knelt to scratch Gruff's long, drooping ears. Nuzzling his neck while his tail whipped up dust clouds, she watched the strange new birds. They glistened in the sunlight. Their excited clucking tickled her belly. She chuckled softly, not wanting to disturb the old gardener who puttered near the kitchen door. She smiled an apology as he approached.

"The Minorcan who sold them to us claimed their eggs finer than duck eggs," the old gardener said.

"I doubt we'll ever convince my mother. Though they're the whitest eggs I've ever seen."

The old man nodded agreement. "The merchant said they rival those of the peahen. Perhaps you could have some prepared without telling her."

"Nothing in this house goes without her notice." *Except me.*

"I suppose you're right," the old gardener said. "But, if that he-bird doesn't stop waking Dawn, I'll wager he gets eaten before the eggs."

Psappha returned his grin. "I don't think I'll take that wager."

Most of her understanding of passing events had come from overheard conversations between this wily old man and her nursemaid, Praxinoa.

As if conjured by a thought, the front door creaked and Praxinoa's presence filled the doorway. Psappha's hands sprang to protect her ears.

"What kept you so late? Don't plug your ears when I'm talking to you. I had a terrible time getting your mother to rest."

"I'm sorry." Psappha lowered her hands and picked at the folds of her peplos. "I was with Eurigios."

"Of course you were. Eurigios left half an hour ago."

Psappha breathed in as much false confidence as her chest would hold. "I was in the garden trying to find the right words to tell Mother that he's gone to welcome Alkaios. I didn't want her to be angry with him."

"It's you she's displeased with. I had to tell her where you've been all day. This will be your last childish jaunt, I'm sure."

Psappha hung her head.

"Change your dress and wash the city from your feet before you see her."

~ ~ ~

Psappha's satin slippers made no sound as she slipped into her mother's chamber. The room was huge and trimmed throughout with precious purple and intricate 'broidery. A great lavender-veiled bed dominated one corner; an orchid draped chaise at its foot.

Klies* reclined upon it, the back of one hand shading her closed eyes while a servant-girl brushed pale hair that glistened like sun-drenched sacred spider-webs. The sheer violet linen of her gown parted below her distended abdomen to frame long, slender legs. A second slim, perfectly manicured hand lay over her voluptuous breasts. Psappha remembered when her mother's nails had been cracked and broken, when, in the bad times following Scamandronomos's death there was no time for pampering and the purple dye had been too dear. *Was that when I failed her? Did she turn cold because she needed rest and all I did was cry for her to hold me?*

She took a step closer to the chaise, silently catching the servant's attention.

"Mind you don't wake her," the girl whispered as she passed Psappha the brush. "To awaken a pregnant woman is to endanger the life within."

Psappha perched on the edge of the servant-girl's stool. *Superstitious nonsense*, she thought as she continued the brushing of her mother's hair without missing a stroke. The long, moon-gold tendrils

---

* Klies (KLEE-ace)

entwined her fingers like gossamer silk. Strands of downy hair draped themselves across her lap. She wished that she could weave a kiton of them and walk forever with its kiss upon her skin.

After about ninety strokes, she decided Klies was asleep. Silently signaling the girl, she whispered, "Come for me the instant she awakes."

Klies's azure-blue eyes opened wide and threatening. "Must you come in here chattering like a blue monkey every time I try to rest?"

"I'm sorry," Psappha choked through a hidden sob. She had broken a primary rule. Klies was not to be upset, yet Psappha invariably managed to do exactly that. In a fluster of movement, she sprang to her feet and fluffed Klies's cushions. "Eurigios sent me. He told me to tell you his brother has returned."

"I know."

Psappha sighed. *I should have been first with the news.* "He said to tell you he'd return soon."

"With the dawn no doubt. No matter. It will give us time to talk. Here. Come. Sit by me. That's better," she added as Psappha returned to the servant girl's stool. "It's time to plan your wedding."

Psappha flinched. "Can't we do that tomorrow?"

"Now that Alkaios has returned, there's no reason to wait. Your marriage has been postponed far too long already."

Psappha felt as if her mind was on fire. An emotional fever ran through her veins as she tried to recall his face.

"Psappha, you're shivering, dear. Run lower the tapestry over the window."

"I'm not cold," Psappha responded honestly, and then went to lower the tapestry.

The moment she returned, Klies continued. "We must set a date,"

"Yes, ma'am. I s'pose we must."

"By Aphrodite's sandals, Psappha!" Klies swung her long legs off the side of the couch and sat up. "One would think you'd be pleased."

"Why?"

"Why what?"

"Why must I marry? I have my songs. I could hire myself out to sing at other people's weddings."

"You're much too old to waste your time plucking your lyre & longing for fame that will never come. You'll have enough glory in Alkaios's shadow, if he'll still have you. Every woman needs a husband."

"Why?"

"Why to raise your children of course."

"I don't need children."

"Of course you need children. Every woman needs children."

You don't need me. Psappha hung her head, avoiding the impatience in Klies's eyes. *What good to be the daughter of kings when my own mother thinks I'm ugly? I'd rather be a golden-haired goose-girl.* She blushed as she remembered things overheard from goose-girls and shepherd boys while hidden in the orchard.

"Don't you want to be loved?"

"Of course but why must I marry?"

"Why? Because. That's why."

"I will not marry just because."

"You will marry whom and when you are told."

"I won't!"

Klies slapped her. Psappha jumped to her feet, threw the brush across the room and kicked the stool after it. "I won't! I'll weep and wail and cut my hair."

"You'll do no such thing."

"I will. I will." Psappha paced the room, keeping just out of view, measuring her thoughts. "I'll wed when and if I'm ready or I'll go to my marriage bed veiled in black with hair no longer than a robin's tail. And -- I won't wed a stranger; Eurigios's brother or no. I'd rather spend the rest of my life in The Lady's temple. I saw what happened to Dika. She married against her will and she's not played or sung a note since. The Lady revoked her gift."

"That's enough, Psappha. You will marry Alkaios and that's that. It's what your father wanted."

Psappha plunked her hands on her hips and glared. "That's not fair. Everything I don't want to do is 'what your father wished'. My father didn't wish to die but it didn't stop him."

Klies looked as if Psappha had hit her. *Now I've done it. What was it the girl said? Too awaken... but she's already awake so maybe it's all right.* In a fluster of fear for her unborn sister, Psappha hastily fluffed Klies's cushions and eased her among them. "I'm sorry," she said and this time she meant it. "I'll go. You need to rest."

"No." Klies restrained her with a light touch on her arm. "Stay. We can talk about weddings another time."

Must we? "Can't it wait until after my sister is born?"

Klies smiled. "Sister?"

"Of course a sister." Psappha retrieved her mother's brush. With the hairbrush once more in her hand, she resumed her brushing as deftly as she sometimes stroked the strings of her lyre.

The lyre Alkaios made me after Charaxos failed to teach my immature fingers the secrets of his kithara. She remembered the day he gave it to her. That was the day she decided she'd be a notable in The Congress of Poets someday. She couldn't wait to tell Alkaios but when she did, he laughed. "Only men receive invitations from that exalted bunch." *We'll see,* she remembered thinking. *We'll see.*

She had once shared her dream with her mother but Klies had scoffed. Now, she shyly shared another. "The child you carry will be a beautiful little golden sister who will grow up looking just like you."

"For shame, Psappha. Such flattery. You shouldn't defy the gods. They'll get jealous."

"It isn't flattery when it's true. You're beautiful. I can't wait to see you dance at the summer festivals. Oh-h-h," she groaned with exaggerated grief. "I can't possibly marry without you there to dance."

Klies sniggered. "Perhaps you're right. Perhaps we should delay the wedding until after the birth. I have but one daughter. I will want to dance at your marriage feast. Perhaps Alkaios will agree to wait for the youngest guest." She cast a wry smile toward her abdomen.

Psappha fought to hide her exultation. *The child is not due for weeks. There's ample time for everyone to change their minds.*

~ ~ ~

Later, in her own chamber, Psappha devoured the fresh fruit and nuts that Praxinoa had left for her. Praxinoa had prepared her for sleep since before she could remember. This night, Psappha was glad she wasn't there. She needed time alone to sort her thoughts. Her mind was a maze of questions she preferred to ignore. Determinedly, she covered her doubts with Praxinoa's habitual evening queries. *What did you do all day? Did you study your Homer? Did you make any new songs?*

When that no longer worked, she left her clothes in a rumple on the floor and snuggled into bed where she hugged her goose down pillow and scrunched her eyelids tight. However, Morphios was busy elsewhere and his dream-evoking son Hypnos was nowhere to be found.

Toward midnight, she got up, took up her lyre and went to perch, nude, on the sill of the open arch that served her as a window. At first, her touch on the strings was automatic; her throaty alto voice doleful as she sang, "Maidenhood, maidenhood why wouldst thou fly from me? Golden-tressed Lady-of-the-pure-and-beautiful where is thy compassion? Electrum-crowned Majesty, have mercy," she sang to Aphrodite but it was Klies she envisioned on the peacock throne. "I am to wed a man I no longer know."

After a time, her music brought her calm and comfort and finally, inevitably, joy. Her fingers danced upon the sacred strings; composing; creating prayer-songs of such beauty and power that she was herself amazed by The Lady's gifts.

The heavy throb of a kithara vibrated through the night and she missed a note. A moment later, she joined the unseen kitharist in an ode to Eros that caused her pulse to quicken. Each note blended with those of her dulcet lyre.

The tempo increased as the kitharist led her into a rousing paean to Pan. She recognized the melody. She had heard it often as a child. She blushed, remembering the day Alkaios taught her the paean's naughty words. She sighed almost with relief when the irreverent paean strummed to a close.

Her rest was brief. A moment and then the twang of martial music stormed the night. The composition, an intricacy of trills and patterns designed to defeat the skill of a lesser artist was one Psappha had never heard but she quickly rose to the kitharist's challenge then followed with a new piece of her own. The kithara quieted, as if the kitharist had faltered. Not so. When she finished her piece, the challenger continued.

Psappha picked up the next tune with little effort. This time she recognized the song. It was a toast to wine and roistering, played as only Alkaios could play it. She recalled the first time she heard it. She was nine. A week later, he was gone.

Now, as their duet carried her back to childhood -- yesterday -- when encumbering responsibilities had been a distant illusion she set aside her distaste for his martial compositions, his fascination for war and wine, and heard only the interwoven harmony. Alkaios was her teacher and her friend. She had forgotten that she missed him.

As she matched his kithara with her grown up lyre, perfect harmony brought back the beauty of his face. It was a boy's face. *But -- he is no longer a boy!*

Peggy Ullman Bell

[page deliberately left blank]

> *"A lovely being, scarcely formed or molded,*
> *a rose with all its sweetest leaves yet folded."*
> 'Lord Byron'

-- II --

The next day, Psappha posed beside a mirror pool in the orchard above the house. Eurigios and Alkaios's family home was farther up the hill. *Wherever he chooses to go, he'll pass this way.* Her fingers tested the strings of the lyre on her lap. When she heard footsteps, she began to sing her newest lyric.

"Oh, Lady Earth, with bright-feathered birds singing in your hair, how tenderly you draw your hills of embroidered green velvet around you. The Sea stretches strong arms to embrace you. The pulsating voice of Poseidon joins Gaea's song in a passionate duet to life."

While she sang, she studied Alkaios's reflection in the pool. He lounged against an ancient apple tree, seeming a part of its strength. The plume on his worn helmet reminded her of the Minorcan he-bird's roguish tail. *He's more handsome than Eurigios,* she decided, *and that's not an easy thing to accomplish.* Sunbeams added burnished highlights to the reflection of his silver-blond hair. His fine square jaw was bare as an Athenian's and tanned as dark as an Egyptian's. His eyes, accented by bronzed skin, looked pale as a perfect blue sky, their whites as clear as milk, the luxuriant lashes shading them were palest gold.

He wore a simple, abbreviated tunic, belted at the waist. She averted her gaze from the leather-sheathed sword and concentrated instead on the pale down that covered his well-muscled, darkly-tanned arms and legs. His limbs and his bared right shoulder glistened with oil. The breeze shifted and her nose twitched in reaction to the sharp, cinnamon smell of him, her nostrils flaring in response to his beauty. *Soldiering has rendered him more fit than his sedentary brother.*

"S'pha," he said. "I've brought you a present."

His voice flowed through her like the hot honey and ginger with which Praxinoa battled the winter cold. She turned her head slowly. The urge to spring to her feet and run to him was strong, but she resisted. *It would be unseemly. A woman must maintain her dignity.*

"Don't you want to see it?"

Calling up every scrap of poise she owned, Psappha rose and strolled toward him, being careful that her hips did not cause any sway of her skirt.

"Well," he drawled, "if you're not interested . . ."

He swung his arm and tossed the gift away.

In her rush to rescue it, Psappha tripped on her hem. Baritone laughter convulsed around her. She stood before him, so angry with herself she trembled.

"What is it, child? I didn't mean to frighten you."

Child is it? I'll show him who's a child. Psappha planted her fists on her hips and stared up at him. "Open your eyes, Alkaios. I'm no more a child than you are. You let my size deceive you."

Psappha's spirit shrank beneath his scrutiny. *Why did I ask him to look at me? He'll see how dark and ugly I am. Oh, Aphrodite, Gracious Lady, I must wed this man. Please make me lovely in his sight.*

Alkaios took both of her hands in his and drew her closer.

The doeskin of his vest kissed her cheek and its leathery smell relaxed her. She took a step back. Determined to impress him, she raised herself on tiptoes and reached as if to remove his helmet. Instead, she used the helmet straps to pull his head down. Her curious lips met willing response.

Alkaios molded her body to his. When he released her, he held her at arms length and whispered, "No, Psappha, you are no longer a child."

The sensations of the kiss intrigued Psappha. She longed to pursue them just to see where they led. Alkaios retrieved the ebony chest then held it out to her. The wood felt warm and damp from his hands. Her fingers tingled as she opened the lid. Inside the little box, a painted figurine reposed on white silk. Psappha lifted it out with a thrill of recognition.

The Ophidian's bare-breasted, seven-tiered gown seemed molded to fit between her fingers, the ivory warming quickly in her palm, as if the ancient goddess still lived and wrestled her up thrust snakes to invoke a special blessing just for her.

Psappha felt a blush rising and hurriedly replaced the statuette in its silky nest. She snapped the lid and thrust the tiny chest toward Alkaios. "The time for fertility goddesses will come soon enough," she said, hoping the artificial chill in her voice would cover her sudden embarrassment. "Perhaps you should keep your gift until then." Afraid to trust herself to say another word, she left him.

Halfway home she plunked down under her favorite apple tree. "How could I have acted like such a child?" she asked the blossoms above her head. *A silly simple child. He is so beautiful and I am such a goose. Thank Zeus our parents pledged us as children. If our parents hadn't set our troth, he wouldn't have me and I'd stay a Maiden forever.* Without warning, the terror of becoming a social outcast replaced her fears of marriage and lost freedom. It was fame she sought, not notoriety.

"Hera, thou wicked. Why could you not make me blond and beautiful like my mother?"

She sniffed and snuffled until the crying stopped, then trudged home, smudged and crumpled.

Eurigios stopped her as she stepped inside.

"Have you seen Alkaios?"

"Your brother is a blind, arrogant bull."

"Oh, so you have seen him."

"Yes, I've seen him. I made such a fool of myself I'll never be able to face him again."

Eurigios chuckled.

Psappha flinched. "Don't laugh. He thinks I'm still in swaddling and I proved I should be."

"It can't be that bad, S'pha."

Psappha parked her fists on her hips and glared up at him. "You've been talking with him about me."

"No, Little One, Alkaios and I had more important things to discuss."

"Don't lie! Why else would you call me 'S'pha? That's his secret name for me." She stared at him until he offered a penitent smile.

"All right, yes, we talked about you after your moonlight duet last night. He was understandably curious after all this time. You were a child when he left."

"In his eyes, I still am," she said. "I just proved it."

"Psappha stop. Alkaios couldn't help seeing how lovely you are."

"Lovely? By Cyclops's eye, Eurigios, you must be blind as your brother."

Eurigios shook his head. "It doesn't matter. You'll have to face him soon in any case. He's joining us for dinner."

"I'll stay in my chambers."

"No, you won't. Your mother's not feeling well. That's why I waited for you. I need you to preside at dinner in her place."

"I won't."

"You will. We have guests."

"I won't, and that's the end of it."

"Be reasonable, Psappha. Now that Alkaios is back, your mother's pregnancy is all that postpones your wedding. People will expect to see you at his side. Did you know he arranged for construction of your home before he paid his respects to our mother?"

"The soldier's life has made him anxious to fill his bed."

Eurigios roared with laughter. "A full bed is probably the one thing Neccho's troops didn't lack. From what I've heard, Nebuchadnezzar* captured more women than soldiers when he overtook them. Now go and prepare to serve our guests."

Psappha hesitated a moment more to establish her maturity then she slowly turned to leave. Eurigios swatted her bottom and she scooted toward her waiting governess.

Praxinoa had cleared away all the clutter left from morning. A purple kiton laid spread upon her bed. On the table next to it, in its normal place, was her lyre. Next to the lyre, as if it had always been there, stood the ivory figurine. Psappha stomped across the room and snatched it up. "How did this get here?"

"A servant of the master's brother brought it," Praxinoa said. "Should I send it back?"

"No. Leave it." Psappha placed the statuette in a more prominent position on the table then turned away. "I don't have time to think about it now. I have to take Mother's place at dinner." As she crossed the room, she released the scarabs at her shoulders and the kiton she'd been wearing fluttered to the floor. She caught a glimpse of her naked form in the mirror above her dressing table and she frowned. Still frowning, she slipped into the waiting tub, closed her eyes and imagined herself caressing the dancer in the park. Blossom-scented steam caressed her blush. Her breasts pinked from the heat of the water then swelled as she imagined Alkaios's sun-dark hands against their virgin olive oil tone. Her thoughts made her skin itch. She ran small, strong hands over her body and wondered if there was any way to make the itching stop.

Eurigios burst into the room like a storm-borne leaf, all red, and gold and crackly. "Psappha, do hurry."

Psappha jumped to her feet. Eurigios grinned as Praxinoa hastily shrouded Psappha in dry linen. "Hurry, beautiful one, our guests are waiting."

---

* Nebuchadnezzar (Nabu-kudurri-usur) king of Babylon 604-561 bce

"Stop teasing. I'm almost ready."

"I'm not teasing. You are beautiful and when you sing, the sky opens for the Olympian's applause. You should sing for Alkaios."

"I'll never sing for your haughty brother again. He'd probably pat me on my head and send me back to Praxinoa."

"Not if he glimpsed you as I just did."

Psappha's hairbrush barely missed his ear. He chuckled softly then ducked out of her room. When she was sure he was gone, she donned the purple kiton, checked the scarabs at her shoulders then braided the last of the season's lilacs into her hair. She could not sit, as Klies did, and let another fool with her hair. The thought of it gave her goose bumps. "Ready?" At Praxinoa's nod, she hurried to the banquet hall, with a fast detour through the kitchen to give the cook her final instructions.

Once within the banquet hall, she had not a minute to herself. She threaded her way between the couches as one guest after another commanded her attention. The women among them pretended not to notice when their companions reached to caress the nude cupbearers, raising a squeal or mock protest from the handsome boys with a well-placed pinch.

Eurigios rose to greet her when she reached the dais. "Good health and welcome milady."

From the couch at his right, a man she did not recognize seemed to look through her dress. Eurigios intervened. "You dishonor the daughter of my house, Pittakos.*"

Pittakos! Psappha spat the name in her mind. *What business does Eurigios have with Pittakos?* Her guess churned her stomach. She spoke with painful courtesy.

"It's been many years since you've graced this family with your presence, Pittakos."

Eurigios looked puzzled. "You've met before?"

---

* Pittakos (Pit-ah-KAUS)

"Not exactly, Stepfather. I remember the name from my childhood."

The man she held responsible for her father's death rose to unsteady feet, a gleaming goblet spilling in one hand. Taking her hand with the other, he turned it over and slurped a kiss into her palm. Bowing to her breasts, he said, "I, Pittakos, beg your forgiveness milady. I'm afraid I mistook you for one of the dancers. One forgets that Eurigios heads so mature a household."

Psappha felt his voice enclose her in an unwelcome embrace.

"Will you share my couch?"

The question was so loaded she hung her head in confusion then peeked up at Eurigios. From the corner of her eye, she could see that Pittakos's slur had stung him. Before she could decide her next move, she felt an arm encircle her waist and she cringed. Then, glancing up, her eyes met Alkaios's smoldering gaze and her distaste subsided. "The Lady Psappha will dine with me.

Like the others, Alkaios was nude to the waist, his body sweet and sleek with scented oil, his hair glistening with pomade. As she took her place beside him, he caressed her cheek then laid her head against his chest. She snuggled into the crook of his arm and tried to ignore her surroundings. The men's voices hummed in her ears like distant bees.

"... and so, Eurigios, the time is near when . . ."

"I know, Pittakos, but . . ."

Psappha forced herself to focus on the food and disregard their conversation. She selected a bit of fresh vegetable from the bowl on the small table beside Alkaios's couch. She licked herbed vinegar and olive oil from her fingers. Alkaios tucked a bit of roast duckling into her mouth and wiped his kithara-string calluses on a chunk of steaming barley bread. Psappha crinkled her nose with pleasure and smiled her thanks as servants replaced their bowls with plates of anchovies fried with nettles and cloves; a special favorite of hers that improved the already superb flavor of the bread.

Silence prevailed while Eurigios ceremoniously watered the wine. When he finished, Pittakos resumed his argument.

"Do you really believe the lives of your family will be worth anything if we allow Melanchros to continue turning Lesbian law into a misbegotten mire of an imbecile's mental abortion?"

"They will be alive." Eurigios countered tiredly.

"You are a fool!"

Alkaios snatched his arm from behind Psappha and sprang to his feet, glaring at Pittakos. "How dare you insult my brother over his wine? I realize you're a common-born lout but even you should know better than to abuse your host. If Melanchros is an ass in armor, he's your ass in armor. You originated the coup that set him over us and cost us our fathers."

Pittakos scrunched his brow. Standing, he still had to look up to meet Alkaios's eyes.

"I came here to ask for help. I intend to rid Mitylene of a jackass, to borrow your analogy, with your help or without it."

"Another invitation to death Pittakos?"

Psappha had not intended to speak. Now that she had, she wished she were a turtle and could pull in her head.

"Do you find politics intriguing, milady Psappha?"

She winced. His disdainful tone hurt. "I try not to think of politics at all but yours appear to threaten those dear to me."

Pittakos slumped onto his couch and raised his goblet for a refill.

Psappha took his posturing as a deliberate attempt to nullify her importance.

Alkaios reseated himself, hugged her close and grinned, apparently amused by the novelty of having a young woman further his argument for him.

Psappha seethed with resentment. She didn't like patronization nor did she appreciate being someone's personal entertainment. She would deal with Alkaios later. As for Pittakos, she knew he needed the old families to lend respectability to his disastrous plans. He dared not let the subject drop. She formed arguments in her mind as she waited. Soon he continued in a more conciliatory tone.

"You think do you, daughter of Scamandronomos that I am a threat?"

"You? Certainly not. But, the course you suggest can hardly lead to peaceful living."

"Life has been peaceful for you, milady. You are most fortunate. You've been sheltered, Lady Psappha. I suspect you always will be. Some of us have not found life so pleasant."

"Well protected? Was I well protected when you and your ideas cost me my father and my proper home?"

"You're too young to understand."

"But not too young to suffer from his loss," she countered, angry and insulted by his obvious disdain. "Because of you and your precious politics, I lived an orphan in ugly Pyrrha* while my betrothed enlisted in a foreign war and my brother ran off to study elsewhere. Even now, strangers enjoy my rightful home. How can you be sure your precious politics won't bring me further pain?"

"No one can be sure of that. We can only hope."

"And while you are hoping, men die."

"Yes, men die. Men will always die for what they believe to be right."

"For what who believes to be right? One man? A few men? You? Or the men who will do your fighting? Men with families? Mother's sons? Women's husbands? Fathers will fight and fathers will die. For what, Pittakos? Will their fatherless daughters appreciate your better life if they must live it alone? I can tell you I didn't. Not then and not now."

"Men must fight . . ."

"...and women must wait. What drivel. Do you think to console anyone with that?"

---

* Pyrrha (PEER-ah) a town on the southwest coast of Lesbos
  rumored to have been swallowed by the bay of Kaloni.

Pittakos reached for another flagon of wine. "It is not my place to console anyone, milady. I will try to build a better life for the people of Mitylene, and for all of Lesbos, in whatever way I can."

Psappha could sit no longer. She jumped to her feet and, in two strides, stood glaring down at him; her fists pushing at her hips; her nails gouging her palms.

"It's not your place to console anyone," she hissed through clenched teeth. "Then whose place is it? You want to stage a re-assumption of power in which many will die and yet you expect to come out of it pure and beautiful with no responsibility for the pain you've caused."

All eyes had fixed themselves on Psappha but she saw only Pittakos. She shouted down him. "I cannot understand how bloodshed can be the answer to anything. War is nothing but the greed of one man pitted against the greed of another."

Pittakos appeared undisturbed. His next words and the trace of pity in his tone increased her agitation.

"I do not expect you to understand the true situation, milady. You have been sheltered from the deplorable conditions in Mitylene, as you should be."

"You do not expect me to understand. You do not attempt to explain. Then how, pray Zeus, do you expect the people to understand?"

She was beginning to tire from the searing force of her own anger. A deeply drawn breath helped her to continue.

"You say that conditions are terrible. Surely, nothing could be so bad that destroying Mitylene is the only way to fix it. What do the people think? They are the ones who must fight your battle. Have you asked them if they want change? Are yours the changes they want? Have you asked them for their help?"

She noticed tiny beads of sweat piercing the oil on his forehead and she laughed. From the corner of her eye, she saw Alkaios raise his goblet. "Gentle friends and guests, Lady Psappha suggests that Pittakos go to the people for aid. What say you?"

Psappha blinked as the hall erupted with noise. Goblets clattered to the floor. Chairs and couches screeched on the tiles. She had forgotten him. In her anger, she had forgotten all of them. Now she retreated, her courage scared away by mass confusion. She did not resist when Alkaios pulled her down beside him, placed her head again on his shoulder and continued taunting Pittakos.

"Come, my fine man-of-the-people," he drawled. "Shall we put the question before your public? Shall we ask the populace if the husband of Dracon*'s sister shall be their choice of leaders?"

Raised voices blended into a babble of bawdy aspersions as the diners gathered behind Alkaios. Pittakos looked like a man about to be stoned. His wife was a known and some said unrepentant porna. His words came out cracked.

"I came here to solicit your help for the sake of the city," he said. "I did not expect unanimous acceptance, nor did I expect ridicule. Eurigios? Are these your sentiments also? Or, does your insolent young brother speak only for himself?"

Eurigios glanced at Alkaios. "It's never the intention of this household to insult a guest," he said reprovingly. "My brother's betrothed is young," he added as if to give Psappha a reprieve based on immaturity. "Nevertheless, I must admit the young ones have a point. Perhaps the common people should have a voice."

Pittakos seemed to wilt. Minute beads of sweat grew to rivulets that trickled toward his beard.

"Very well," he said; his gravel-tone voice barely audible. "I will ask the people."

"And if the people decide against you?" Psappha regretted -- a little -- her part in creating his embarrassing predicament, but, since the situation already existed, she saw no reason not to pin him down. "Will you give up your dangerous plan if the people refuse to follow you?"

---

* Dracon (c.659-c.601 B.C.E.) introduced the first written legslation to Athens.

Pittakos seemed unaware of the sweat that dripped from his beard to join the meat juices stuck to the mat on his chest.

"Yes, milady, before this company, I give my word. If the people reject my leadership, I will not press it on them."

"What good is your word?" Alkaios put in. "Our fathers had your word, but you chose Melanchros over them. Now that you see your mistake, you expect us to trust you. We aren't the fools you think."

Pittakos's dark smile came nowhere near his eyes. "The people will decide."

Alkaios hugged Psappha approvingly and whispered, "That was something."

Psappha sighed. "It was not intended as a joke. When he fails to rally the people, we'll hear no more of war until the next idiot evolves," she said more to convince herself than Alkaios or anyone else who might be listening. The two of them had gathered more than their share of attention. She shivered when Alkaios echoed her uncertainty.

"He may not fail. What he says about Melanchros is true. The mercenaries may decide that returning to be ruled by a donkey is intolerable."

"He must fail. No matter how bad things are, the people will choose peace. What good can it do Mitylene to tear her apart?"

"I hope you're right, S'pha. Our position will be unpredictable if he succeeds."

"Surely Pittakos will behave honorably toward fellow aristocrats," she whispered behind her hand, "even those who disagree with him."

"That's just it, lovely eyes. Old crack-toes is no aristocrat although he tried to become one by marrying Dracon's sister. Everyone knows what a porna she is. That's why my jest cut deep. Truth is the most deadly weapon. I don't think Pittakos will be gentle if he gets an opportunity to avenge tonight's humiliation. If war comes, look to yourself. In either case, there is danger. If

Pittakos loses, Melanchros is sure to hear of it and assume a conspiracy. If he wins, it could be worse."

Bright costumed acrobats, jugglers and dancers filled the hall.

Alkaios winked at her. "Enough of intrigues for now. Relax. There is no end to talk that leads to nothing."

Psappha did not respond. Her thoughts were elsewhere. She stared toward the center of the dancers where Atthis's willow-wand form swayed hypnotically. She saw little else. Her palms grew moist and tingly; a tingling embarrassingly echoed elsewhere. Atthis dance closer. *Like an osprey circling over its prey.* A warm glow built deep in Psappha's gut. Atthis swayed. The glow took fire. Atthis whirled, her kiton clinging to long clean limbs. The fire sent sparks through Psappha's inner thighs. Atthis circled close and the sparks coalesced into a cauldron of molten lava on the altar of Aphrodite.

Psappha glanced quickly at Alkaios. Had he noticed? She would perish from embarrassment if he knew. Is this how she was supposed to feel when she kissed him? She was given no time to decide.

"She is lovely, isn't she?" Pittakos's voice reeked with ownership. "She is my ward."

Psappha cringed. She realized that, as an orphan, Atthis would be someone's ward but, Pittakos? Her small body trembled with rage.

Alkaios stroked her hair. "Are you afraid of Pittakos? You wouldn't need to concern yourself if you'd let me look after you."

Psappha spoke without taking her eyes off Atthis. "How can I not let you look after me? You will soon be my husband."

"That's not exactly what I had in mind, S'pha." His long fingers traced the joints of her spine. "I want to be more than a husband to you."

"You're already more than a husband," she said without glancing his way. "You'll always be more than a husband, Alkaios. You're my friend."

Atthis twirled from the room and the spell was broken.

As the entertainers retired, bearers appeared outside the archway and guests with female companions escorted them out. Psappha rose distractedly. Alkaios took her hand and placed it on his arm. She smiled at Eurigios and glided from the hall. As she walked, she felt Pittakos's eyes upon her and she edged instinctively closer to Alkaios.

The stroll down the corridor unnerved her. Her earlier words, spoken thoughtlessly, echoed in her mind. The memory of Pittakos's expression made her intensely aware of Alkaios's protective presence. At the entrance to her chamber, he stopped and bent his lean frame just enough to gather her to him. Her feet dangled inches above the tiled floor as he kissed her with practiced skill. New sensations stirred her. Not as strong as those she felt for Atthis, but no less good.

She felt boneless. When he lowered her enough for her to stand, she hid her face against him fighting to catch her breath. Had he released her immediately, she would have crumpled to the floor.

When he did release her, he leaned down, bestowed a fraternal kiss on her forehead and said, "Good night, gentle friend, may Morpheus bring you quiet dreams."

Watching his back as he strode away, Psappha thought she could understand Helen's madness. *If Paris was as straight and fine as Alkaios, Helen could have done naught but have him for herself. As I will have him*, she thought.

Alkaios joined some guests who were also on their way back into the banquet hall and, as they passed from sight, Psappha went into her chamber aching with a hunger she could not define. She tried to visualize their wedding night, but her imagination failed her. She brushed half-formed images from her mind. *Such thoughts are more suited to cupbearers.* She scolded herself but she was more reconciled to the concept of marriage than she'd ever expected.

> "Before the beginning of years
> there came to the making of man
> Time with a gift of tears; Grief, with a glass that ran;
> Summer, with flowers that fell;
> Remembrance fallen from heaven,
> and madness risen from hell;
> Strength without hands to smite;
> Love that endures for a breath;
> Night, the shadow of light,
> and life, the shadow of death."
> 'Algernon Charles Swinburne'

-- III --

Psappha passed the days that followed strumming her lyre in the orchard above the house. Lilacs slowly gave way to roses as she munched first citrus then apples while providing accompaniment for the ribald songs of the workers in the fields. The goats sometimes came to her for apple cores.

From her favorite spot beneath a gnarled, old apple tree, she could see across the water to the cities of Ionia. They lay along the coast like crystals in a Phoenician glass chain, faceted and multicolored, outlined and accented by the rising sun.

Just below her, on the side of the hill, her stepfather's house seemed an amphitheater stage. She followed its activities in her mind while watching those that took place out of doors. Whenever Pittakos visited, she stayed in the orchard until he had gone.

This morning, she had scarcely settled beneath her tree when he roared through the gate, hollering for Eurigios, lumbering through the garden like a great clumsy ox. *He'd have made a fine Cretan priest.*

There would've been no need of an ox head mask to make him look like a Minotaur.

Pittakos stayed all day while his horse munched dill by the kitchen gate. Eventually, the setting sun warned Psappha that time to linger had passed. Her lyre seemed unusually heavy as she trudged downhill. Upon reaching the house, reluctant to enter while Pittakos remained, she sat on the threshold and cuddled her great cat. Stroking the soft Persian, cooing to him, listening to him purr, she failed to hear the door open behind her. A shaft of candlelight crept across her lap and the cat leaped off into the night.

"Well, Lady Psappha."

The sound of his voice crawled up her spine. She brushed nonexistent scorpions off the back of her neck.

"What are you doing here in the dark?"

She almost told him. However, whatever else he was, he was a guest. *No wonder Alkaios calls him crack-toes. His feet are dirty.*

Rising slowly, struggling for composure, she prepared to ease past him into the house. He blocked her way. "You are so beautiful, little Psappha." He laid his rough hands on her shoulders.

Psappha stiffened. "I'm sure you will excuse me, Pittakos. It grows late." Venom dripped from her tone despite all effort to remain polite.

"Don't spurn me, lovely lady. It wasn't by my wish that your father died. Must you punish me forever? Don't you know he could have refused to join me?" The hands stroked toward her elbows and she ground her teeth. "One smile, Psappha and you'd soon be living in your father's house beside the citadel."

I don't want it at that price! She wrenched free of his grasping hands. "It's late."

She drew her skirts aside, ducked beneath his outstretched arm and marched into the house no longer caring if she'd sufficiently hidden her revulsion.

"Later than you think, Miss Arrogance." Pittakos's grumble reached her through the door.

She fought her churning stomach all the way down the corridor, passing her mother's chamber almost at full run. Through the heavily draped windows of her bedroom, she heard the wind skipping over the trees. *Like a thousand squirrels outracing a fire.* The sound suited her mood.

Praxinoa snored softly on a low stool beside a cooling bath. Psappha undid one of her own sandals and dropped it to the steam-dampened floor. Praxinoa started awake, frowned reprovingly then knelt before Psappha to remove the other sandal. "You've missed supper," she said as she rose.

Psappha sighed. Her stomach grumbled quietly as Praxinoa unclasped the scarabs at her shoulders and whisked her falling kiton onto a pile of laundry in the corner. Psappha stepped into her bath confident that there'd be something to snack on later. The remains of tension dissipated when Praxinoa began stroking her forehead with rose oil. As the gentle pressure spiraled toward her temples, she let her eyelids close. The familiar ritual soothed her spirit. All thought of Pittakos' arrogance and personal liberties faded as Praxinoa sponged the day from her body as she had done every evening since before Psappha could stand on her own. When she finished, Psappha stepped from the tub and stood quietly while Praxinoa wrapped her in soft, Egyptian linen. Moments later, at her dressing table, she devoured the soft fresh bread she found there. Her wrap fell away. Moist linen dropped from bench to floor as she released and brushed her hair, holding it at half-length to reach the ends. The warming oil on the brazier near her bed filled the chamber with attar of roses.

Psappha watched Praxinoa's reflection in her polished copper mirror as she moved the warmed oil aside then placed a flagon on the grill to warm. Psappha finished re-braiding her hair. Then, Praxinoa filled a small China cup with steaming, amber liquid and held it toward her. Psappha sipped gratefully. The heady infusion of chamomile and honey caressed her from the inside while its musty scent delighted her nose. When the cup was empty, she let Praxinoa lead her to the turned-down bed.

She squelched a pleased moan when Praxinoa's familiar hands massaged her budding breasts then worked down the length of her arms to snake oily fingers around and between her own. She drifted deeper into the ritual-induced trance where Praxinoa's hands became the touch of Alkaios. She envisioned his eyes peering into hers, his hands stroking – molding - lifting her on blazing tremors toward Olympus.

The down-filled bed rearranged itself beneath her as she obeyed the urging of a playful twist on her right great toe. The disembodied hands circled and shaped her buttocks, invoking odd sensations not unlike the strange lava flow of feeling that had overtaken her all unexpected when she watched sweet Atthis dance. She lifted her hips toward their arousing touch and -- the dream changed – Atthis was not there -- Alkaios was gone and in his place -- Pittakos -- his leer turning her nudity to nakedness. She felt herself fall -- falling -- crashing into the waiting arms of Father Poseidon. She sat up, shaking dreams from her mind. A long, drawn out scream startled her to her feet. Praxinoa urged a robe on her as she ran through the torch lit corridor. Eurigios barred Klies's door.

"This is no place for you, Psappha. She is well looked after. You -- Praxinoa -- take your young mistress to my brother."

When Psappha continued to push forward, he added, "Go, Psappha -- go."

"But . . ."

"Go!" he punctuated with an outstretched arm, one resolute finger pointed toward the front of the house. Another scream came from the chamber and he rushed inside.

Psappha stared after him. "It's not fair! I'm nearly a woman. Why should I be kept from this, the most womanly time of all?" She sloughed off Praxinoa's restraining hand and followed a newly arrived priests' assistant into Klies's chamber. Someone had shrouded the bed with heavy curtains. Psappha eased through an opening and stopped, stark still.

Her gaze darted wildly over the scene then focused on the havoc around her mother. She had expected The Lady's priestesses. Instead, the area around Klies overflowed with men; brightly-robed Asklepian priests*, each with at least two male servants at his elbow. Candle-smoke clashed with the reek of unfamiliar incense. Klies writhed on the bed looking painfully alone. A stubby birthing stool squatted beside the bed. In her haste to reach her mother, Psappha tripped over it. On her knees, she inched between the hovering priests and pried her mother's hand open to press its palm against her cheek. "Mother, I'm here now. I'll help you."

Klies's face was a distorted caricature of its usual beauty. Her eyes seemed glazed. After several moments, they glittered with recognition. "Great Hera's girdle, Psappha, get out! Go! Go at once! You are not needed here." She waved her daughter toward the door then turned abruptly to the wall and unleashed another scream.

"This you must not see," Praxinoa whispered; her hands gentle on Psappha's shaking shoulders. When Psappha tried to shake her off, Praxinoa hauled her to her feet and shoved her through the surrounding curtains.

Psappha slogged from the room thinking, *perhaps this time she'll get a daughter she can love -- or a fair son The Fates will let her keep*. Reluctantly, she thought of her mother's second son, the stillborn infant Eurigios II, born to Klies less than a year after her father was murdered. Closing her mind to painful memory, Psappha thought instead of Atthis. *What if she were my sister?* For a fleeting instant, she wondered why the thought displeased her.

"Come, Psappha," Praxinoa coaxed. "Come with me as your stepfather instructed."

---

* Asklepian (Ask-LEP-pean) priests of Asklepios god of medicine.

Psappha balked. "She needs the midwives. "Praxinoa -- send for The Lady's midwives!"

"No, Psappha. I tried, but your mother's husband forbad it. 'The priests will take care of her', he said. Now, come, little one. We must go."

Psappha followed numbly. Her pulse pounded in her head. As the torch-bearing guards led the way up, through the orchard, to Eurigios' family home, she prayed for the life of her Mother. Alkaios's mother greeted her in the doorway but Psappha did not speak. The wind stole through cracks in the hallway shutters as she led Psappha to a sleeping chamber. Its raging drowned the sound of the crackling fire that awaited her but all she heard was the terrified beat of her heart.

She huddled in the strange bed, shivering. Each crash of thunder seemed to strike with increased fury. Visions of ghosts unbidden wandered through her mind, specters from another time. Whenever sleep came near, the stampeding thunderbolts jarred her awake, refusing to let her rest, refusing to let her forget. Dawn's soft drizzle, dreary remnant of the storm, lulled her into fitful sleep.

She awoke to find the shutters open. Cool air floated in, bringing the vibrant purity that only a violent storm can impart. Kneeling on the elaborately carved chest that stood beneath the window of what might be Alkaios' own chamber, Psappha's eyes strained to see her mother's home.

The day dragged by almost without her notice. Silent servants brought meals and then returned to carry them away untouched. Late afternoon sun peeped beneath thick clouds. Evening shadows lengthened and all but disappeared in darkness before she saw Eurigios plodding up the path. His shoulders hung. His step faltered.

She met him at the gate.

"Mother?"

"The child lives," he informed her tonelessly.

Psappha slumped against the arch.

Eurigios turned and retraced his steps. Psappha followed him down the hill. *Now I'll never be able to make her love me,* she thought as her small body bent more from sorrow than from the gusting wind.

Peggy Ullman Bell

[page deliberately left blank]

> "O wise among women, and wisest,
> Our Lady of Pain."
> 'Algernon Charles Swinburne'

-- IV --

Psappha wandered the garden. The house rumbled with people but she refused to hear them.

"It is time, Psappha." Praxinoa wrapped her in Klies' deepest-purple cloak.

Psappha braced herself for the walk to the front of the courtyard where Eurigios waited. He looked as though he had accepted neither food nor drink in days. *Do I look that bad,* she wondered. As she took her place beside him in the procession, she decided she didn't care. For the first time in her life, she had let Praxinoa do her braids. They formed a womanly coronet atop her head. Sharp Mesopotamian hairpins held the braids tight upon her scalp. An insignificant hurt compared to the pain inside.

Klies's pyre awaited them in the back of the orchard, just beyond the laurel hedge, with an open grave close by. Psappha kept her eyes down and concentrated on the dust kicked up by the bier-bearers who walked immediately in front of her. When they reached the gravesite, the bearers set their burden on the pyre and stepped away. Eurigios handed Psappha his knife. Her fingers trembled as she pulled the pins from her hair. Tear-blinded, Psappha stepped past the gaping grave then lifted a hank of hair and slashed it just below an ear. The crowd hushed as she built a mound of fawn-roan tresses on her mother's breast. When she'd shorn all of her hair to the nape, she stepped back and Eurigios lit the pyre.

The professional mourners wailed. Their false piety insulted her senses. Their keening death chant cut into her spirit and she screamed. Their approving nods penetrated her consciousness and she laughed -- and laughed -- and laughed.

Alkaios' palm resounded against her cheek. She stared at him in shocked disbelief then gratitude as tears rushed to her eyes, unchecked. Throwing herself to the ground, she cried her childhood onto the breast of Earth; the only real mother she'd ever had if she'd dared admit it.

After the pyre collapsed, after the diggers had closed the grave, Psappha allowed Alkaios to lift her to her feet. She sagged in the shelter of his shoulder. She did not remember him leading her back to the house. She thought it odd that the servants bowed as she approached. Praxinoa stepped forward.

"Your instructions, mistress?"

Psappha instinctively looked around expecting to see her mother behind her.

Alkaios took her hand. "Not now, Praxinoa. It's too soon."

Praxinoa nodded, signaled the servants back to their respective duties and led Psappha to the front chamber, Klies's chamber. All of Psappha's things were there. She would miss her tiny quarters next to the kitchen.

~ ~ ~

The running of the household left Psappha no time to think. Eurigios spent most of his time with Alkaios, rarely coming home before morning. When he did come home, he closed himself away from everyone, including Psappha.

Desperate for company other than servants and slaves, she found herself increasingly drawn the nursery and to the babe, a perfect, golden boy. The time for his dedication came and went. He neared his third month, when Psappha decided his naming could wait no longer.

One blustery day in late autumn, she lingered in Eurigios's empty chambers throughout the day. Toward midnight, she heard Alkaios' inebriated, "Good 'morrow." Moments later, Eurigios stumbled into the anteroom, nearly knocking Psappha off her feet in his rush to enter his private rooms. She did not let him close the door. When she refused to leave the doorway, he tossed his cloak at a chair, rubbed his hands together over the glowing brazier, slumped into a chair, reached for the nearest flagon and said, "What are you doing in here, Psapph'? You know I want to be alone,"

"What you want is unimportant to me right now," she said as gently as she could manage. "In your infatuation for Dionysus, you've forgotten my brother."

"I haven't forgotten Charaxos, Psapph'. I sent for him. He should be here soon."

Psappha grabbed his shoulders and shook him. "Eurigios! Pay attention! I'm not talking about Charaxos. We had word from him weeks ago. He's not coming. He saw no reason to interrupt his studies for a funeral that is long past. You've forgotten your own son! You have a golden son who deserves a name!"

"My son has a name," he said after a while. "His name is Eurigios. Just like mine." He giggled drunkenly then his eyes hazed again. "But my Eurigios is dead." He looked so desolate it hurt to see him. He lolled in his chair, his drink spilling in one hand while the fingers of the other twisted the tassels on the damask tablecloth. "My little Eurigios was born dead, Psapph'. Don't you remember?"

Psappha knelt beside him and took his head upon her shoulder. With effort, she freed her mind of foggy pictures of the small grave near Pyrrha, replacing them with a clear vision of the beautiful babe in the nursery.

"Surely you remember that you have a new son," she murmured soft and motherly. When he did not react, she slapped him. "Eurigios! Give me a name for my brother! He is without a god's protection. Tell me to whom he is to be dedicated."

"Don't shout at me, Psapph'. Go bother your mother."

Psappha crammed her fist into her mouth and ran from him. *Alkaios! Damn you! Why haven't you helped him? Dionysus, thou charlatan!* She prayed. *Why do you deceive him so? Psyche, beautiful Psyche, beloved of Eros return thy gift of reason to Klies' husband. Let him not wander like Echo, forever unable to love life for love of Narcissus.*

In the adjoining chamber, she threw herself onto her mother's bed, buried her face in a Klies scented cushion and gave in to a rattle of sobs. Eventually, her reservoir of tears ran dry, the trembling stilled and she succumbed to the stupefying power of Hypnos and Morpheus, his nightmare-creating son.

By morning, she knew what she must do. She dressed quickly and quietly, covered her shorn head with a purple scarf and went to the large chest behind what had been her mother's dressing table. A flurry of dust fluttered from the lid as she opened it. Beneath bolt after bolt of various fabrics, she found what she wanted -- a length of exquisite white-on-white brocade. Stuffing it under one elbow, she slammed the chest and dashed to the nursery where she thrust the fabric into Praxinoa's hands.

"Swaddle the boy and come with me."

~ ~ ~

The Temple of Apollo adorned the crest of a low hill. Its alabaster columns rose toward the midday sun as if reaching to embrace Him. Apollo's own laurel bordered frost-wilted gardens. Faded flowerbeds lined each winding path upon which Apollo's priests had sown mint and thyme. Each herb-crushing step released a symphony of scent as Psappha marched toward the open-air temple. Praxinoa followed in her wake, the babe in her arms.

As she strode forward, Psappha berated herself for having delayed so long in the vain hope that Eurigios would rally in time to do the dedication, as custom dictated he should. *My brother should not have gone five months nameless.* Eurigios's negligence left the choice of patron to Psappha. She chose Apollo partly because Apollo was Alkaios's patron. *Any god who can safeguard that rapscallion is very good at his work.* And partly because it was Apollo's golden light that shone in the baby's hair.

The altar stood at the exact center of the temple in order to catch the sun's rays every day of the year. Psappha took the swaddled babe from Praxinoa and laid him on the smooth stone. Kneeling, she lifted her face and arms to Apollo and recited an invocation composed in the dark small hours of a fitful night.

"Mighty, brilliant, sweetly-smiling, sweetly-singing Apollo, accept, if you will, this child. Grant him thy protection. Guide his steps with thy light, oh Phoebus Apollo, though he may falter. Shield him forever with thy warmth. Lend him thy voice, Apollo Musicos, that he may better sing thy praises. Save him an honored place near thy altar.

"Grant, Oh Apollo, this petition for Larichos, son of Eurigios, son of Aegeus, son of Zeus harvest-maker. For Larichos, I beg thy patronage, Divine Apollo. For Larichos, son of Klies, daughter of Ariadne, daughter of Minos, son of Poseidon Earth-shaker, by Theseus son of Ericthos, son of Poseidon Father of Ocean, I beseech thy blessing.

"Pay heed, Oh Apollo, to this invocation from Psappha, child of Aphrodite, child of Scamandronomos who dwells with Klies upon Elysian Fields. Hark, Oh Apollo, to Psappha, sister of Larichos who, by thy will, shall this day become thy child."

Psappha lowered her supplicating arms, gently freed the infant from his wrappings and lifted him with hands clasped around his sturdy ribs. Rising, she held him high above her head. Together thus, with four quarter-turns, she presented her small brother to each of the four winds. Then, with him cradled in her arms and her back turned from Apollo's altar, she silently invoked for him the protection of Unseen Artemis. Her heart throbbed with tenderness as she turned and laid her small brother naked on the patch of bare soil at the foot of Apollo's altar. Once again, she raised her hands to Apollo.

"Hear, Exalted One. Behold thy son, Larichos, in the arms of his only living mother, Earth. Guard him well thou Golden One that he may serve thee with greatness and grace."

She reached to Praxinoa for glittering brocade then re-wrapped Larichos and rubbed her cheek against the golden down on his head.

"You are truly Apollo's son," she whispered in response to his bright smile.

Psappha braced her feet as the floor of the temple shook, standing as a sailor might on rough seas. "Don't be afraid," she crooned more to the frightened woman beside her than to the smiling child. "It's just Father Poseidon reminding us that we have his inherited protection, but that he can withdraw it anytime he chooses. See. It was only a warning. He's quiet now."

Placing Larichos ceremoniously into Praxinoa's outstretched arms, she said, "Guard him tenderly, sweet Praxinoa, as you have guarded me. He will have need of your gentle strength."

> "The sky is changed, and such a change!
> Oh night and storm,
> and darkness! Ye are wondrous strong,
> yet lovely in your strength,
> as is the light of a dark eye in woman!"
> 'Lord Byron'

-- V --

Winter passed without event and spring brought Psappha no joy until the day her sunny little brother took his first wobbly stem. She hurried to knock on Eurigios' door, anxious to share her excitement. Hearing Alkaios inside, she let her hand fall to her side. His tone kept her from turning away.

"I tell you, brother dear, Melanchros goes too far. We must be rid of him."

"Quiet Fool! The darkness hides a thousand daggers ready for such carelessness."

"I tell you, it's overdue. We can succeed if all in our party keep quiet. The populace decided to let Pittakos lead but can we trust him?"

"He's as fond of his head as you are of yours, little brother."

"Perhaps more so but can he be trusted? What assurance do we have that he won't sell our heads to save his own? He has no fondness for aristocrats. He's proven that before."

Psappha heard them nearing the other side of the door and she slipped into the adjoining chamber, closing that door behind her. A moment or two later, she heard Alkaios in the garden. "All right, Eurigios, go on drowning yourself in wine, but remember -- he who has wine as a chain around his wits has no life at all. In the morning, we go to trap a fox. If you would be with me, be early."

"I'll be there."

When the sound of his footsteps died away, Psappha hurried into the court-yard garden. She caught up with Alkaios as he reached the outer gate. "I'll be with you tomorrow."

"What?"

"I'll be with you. I heard you talking inside."

"Tomorrow's work is not for little girls, S'pha."

"I turned sixteen months ago in case you didn't notice. Must I sit with my 'broidery, waiting for word that I'm truly an orphan? Or, that I'm widowed, without ever having been a bride?"

"Nothing can happen to the betrothed of Poseidon's fiery daughter."

"Don't patronize me, Kios. I am no longer a child. You told me so yourself."

"That was in another context and you know it." His gentle smile belied the gruffness of his tone. "No one dies from what you're old enough for; not with the help of a bit of clean sheep-gut anyway."

"Stop teasing. We weren't talking about childbirth and there's nothing amusing about death. There'll be danger on the morrow and I will be with you."

"No you won't. You'll wait here. I'll come to you as soon as it is done."

"But . . ."

"You'll wait," he said, with a finality that allowed no further argument.

He bent to kiss her. She let his lips brush her cheek.

~ ~ ~

Psappha slept fitfully then awakened to a house that was much too quiet. Her first instinct was to run to the nursery. It was empty. The floor abounded in scattered toys. One of Larichos' miniature chairs lay toppled by his bed. She ran to Eurigios' chamber, bursting in on him unannounced. He stood by his dressing table, with one foot on a stool, buckling his greaves.

"Where is Larichos?" she shouted at him.

"Who? Oh -- the boy -- I sent him to Antissa. He'll be safe there. My sister went with him. She'll take care of him."

"But, why? Don't you trust me to look after my own brother? I've done all right so far." She caught herself before she said without you.

Eurigios looked at her but his thoughts were elsewhere. "The boy is safer with his aunt in Antissa, Psapph'. If -- Great Zeus forbid -- If Alkaios falls today, you must go there too. Our mother and her servants are too old to protect you."

If Alkaios falls, I'll fall beside him. "Where will you be?" she asked. Her contempt for him hung in the air unspoken as she snatched up the flagon he was reaching for and pitched it into the corner beside a broken goblet. Shards of pottery floated in the spilled wine.

"What'd you do that for? You'll have to clean it up. Praxinoa isn't here to do it for you."

"*You* clean it up!" she growled, turning away.

"I won't be here either, after today."

She spun to face him. "You're going with Alkaios?"

"Aye. I'm going. But I'll raise no hand against my lawful Tyrant."

She studied his desolate face. "If you go and don't fight, you'll die. Is that it? Do you plan to die?"

Eurigios edged by her and lifted an ancient shield from the window chest. Psappha grabbed his arm and spun him toward her. "Answer me! Do you plan to die?"

His eyes left hers and focused on the bed he had shared with her mother.

Following the direction of his gaze, Psappha said, "You can't find her by dying. She's already begun another life."

"She's dead," he said pulling away from her to adjust his helmet. "There's no other life. She's just dead."

"That's not true, Eurigios. The Lady's cycles never end. Death is but a doorway to a new beginning. My mother, your wife, is in a new life and it is a good life. The Lady rewards her own."

"Don't try to fill my head with womanish drivel, Psapph'. If your Lady is so great, why'd she let your mother die?"

Psappha wanted to remind him that he was the one who'd called the priests and not the midwives, but now was not the time. "Please, just believe me. She wouldn't want you to die."

"When life is over, it's over and I need to be free of this pain." He shook off her restraining hands and lurched from the room.

"Wait!" she shouted, rushing after him but by the time she reached the garden, he was gone.

Not knowing what else to do, Psappha went to the storeroom next to the nursery to raid one of her older brother's trunks. It took only moments to strip out of her kiton and into one of Charaxos' outgrown outfits. Rummaging through another chest, she found a pair of worn buskins that could not have fit him since childhood. They were stiff and scratchy but she had no time for oiling. She snatched a short, leather vest from yet another chest and then hurried to the great hall where she yanked her father's double bladed sword from the wall. It fell to the floor with a resounding clank, too heavy for her to hold. His great shield was out of the question so she left it and went to her mother's chamber which was now her own.

A small bronze labrys decorated the wall above the dressing table. Alkaios had brought it to her along with the little goddess from Crete. Psappha snatched it down and ran from the house.

The garden gate stopped her. Someone had locked and bolted it both inside and out. She shouted for the gatekeeper but no one came. Furious, she flung the labrys over and beyond the garden wall. In a heartbeat, she scrambled up after it. Dropping to the grass outside, she rolled several meters and crawled several more to retrieve the labrys before brushing herself off and heading down the path.

Dirty and disheveled, the labrys clenched in her fist, Psappha passed through The Lady's Park unnoticed. The marketplace seemed deserted, the hawkers silent or subdued. The wharf was crowded. Near the approach to the south bridge to Old Mitylene, she joined a small group of men and boys and made her way across with them. At the east end of the bridge, she climbed atop the balustrade to survey the crowd for Eurigios or Alkaios. She didn't see them. The fact that she didn't see Pittakos either didn't worry her. *Perhaps it should.*

Men shouted near the citadel but they were too far away for her to hear their words. After a time, she spotted Alkaios. She jumped down from the railing and barged through the crowd with warning of his brother's intentions. If anyone could stop Eurigios, it would be him.

She pushed and bumped her way through the throng of shouting men. When she elbowed aside, he cuffed her then, with a good-natured laugh, he swung her onto his shoulders. "Will ya look at that, young sir? Ain't he the feisty one?"

From her perch, Psappha saw Eurigios mount the citadel steps, unarmed and seemingly unafraid. The great doors stood tightly closed. A cheer rippled through the crowd when Pittakos emerged from the building through a secret door. He raised his hand as if to call for quiet. Mounted troops burst forth from each of the side streets, their javelins flying before them. One of them skewered Eurigios.

Before Psappha could react, the citadel's great door burst open. Archers spilled onto the portico. The crowd ran in every direction at once. She lost sight of Alkaios in the confusion. Her benefactor reached up, lifted by her ribs and set her onto her feet. When someone knocked her over for the third time, she decided to stay down. Crawling, she inched forward neither caring about nor stopping to help the fallen men she passed. The sacred labrys, still clutched in her hand, seemed to burn for a taste of Pittakos' traitorous back.

She scrambled onto a mound of bodies and looked dazedly around. She saw Eurigios, pinned to the great door. Her revulsion fed her rage. Pittakos had compounded his share of blame for her losses. She fingered the handle of the labrys seething with hatred for him. The corners of her mouth turned upward in an expression no one could ever mistake for a smile. Scrambling down from her grizzly vantage point, she elbowed her way toward the citadel.

It was a slow, bruising journey. She did not feel the blow that felled her.

~ ~ ~

Psappha awoke hours later on her own bed with no idea how she got there. Her head hurt. Tentative fingers located a painful lump just above her right temple. Hearing Alkaios' hushed voice in the corridor outside her room, she quickly swung her feet to the floor. Shaking off her dizziness, she stripped to Charaxos' short tunic and kicked his gore-splattered buskins under the bed. She was brushing caked blood from her hair when a servant tapped politely on her door.

"Milord Alkaios wishes to speak with you, milady."

"In the garden," she said without getting up, "in a few minutes."

From her window, she saw Alkaios exit to the garden. He was dressed for battle, although his helmet and shield were gone. He looked like he had been over Styx and been rejected. Bloody muck stained his legs hip high. She paused by the door to give him more time to collect his thoughts. As she neared him, she saw that dried blood covered one arm and stained his sword. She stopped when he refused to meet her eyes.

"Beautiful Psappha," he rasped. "I have something I must tell you, but I cannot find the words."

He shifted from one foot to the other, staring at the ground. Psappha adopted an overly formal tone to divert his obvious anguish and her own nervous guilt.

"If what you have to say is proper and your tongue is not preparing something evil, shame would not prevent you, you would speak out."

He slumped to his knees before her and leaned his head on her bare thigh. She laid her hand on his tangled hair, holding her breath and fighting not to reveal that she already knew what he was about to say.

"What is it, Kios?"

"My brother's dead," he whispered without looking up. "I let them kill him."

"You would have prevented it if you could," she said, not expecting his guilt. *Why should he feel guilty? At least he fought. He must have.*

Alkaios buried his face in the folds of her brief tunic. "You don't understand. I could have prevented it. I knew Pittakos wasn't trustworthy."

She combed his matted hair with her fingers. "You warned him," she crooned, trying to comfort herself, as much as him. "I heard you warn him, Kios. What more could you do? It's not your fault he wouldn't listen." She pretended not to know he was crying.

"They were waiting for us." He said. "When Eurigios reached the top of the citadel stairs, I saw Pittakos come from inside the palace and give the signal. They came at us from all sides. They pinned Eurigios with a javelin. I saw you atop a mound of bodies and I threw away my shield and ran to you. I could think of nothing but your safety. I didn't even check to make sure my brother was dead."

Psappha bent forward over him and hummed softly as if he were Larichos. After a while, he raised tear-ravaged eyes and said, "You must come to my mother's house."

"I can't just pack up and go. Who'd protect Eurigios' house? Praxinoa isn't here."

"S'pha, you have to listen to me. Eurigios is dead. This house will be forfeit as your father's was and mine. Pittakos murdered Melanchros. Mitylene's in chaos."

"But, if Melanchros is dead, the nobles rule. The daughter of Scamandronomos is safe."

Alkaios slowly rose, leaned forward and clasped her shoulders. "No, daughter of royalty, you are not safe," he said in measured tones as if to imprint each syllable upon her mind. "After killing Melanchros, Pittakos set himself up as Tyrant. We have lost the ass and gained a bull. Mitylene's still ruled from the stables."

Psappha stood, pulled free and walked a few paces down the path.

"You must be misinformed," she said, turning back. "The people would not accept a murderer as Tyrant."

"It's true," he said. "Pittakos has betrayed us just like he betrayed our fathers and because we trusted him he knows which of us poses the biggest threat. Many will go to prison this day. I heard on my way here that there's a price on my head. Old Crack-toes isn't wasting any time."

"But, why? Why you, Alkaios? It's been nearly a year since the banquet. Surely the frivolous gods won't let you be struck down with your best songs as yet unsung."

"It's my songs that put me in the greatest danger, S'pha. Remember what I said about truth. Even though Dracon's sister is a porna, Pittakos can't afford to tolerate public insult to his wife, especially not now."

She leaned against him. He reeked of death and vomit. She pushed him away. "Why couldn't you have been quiet?"

"I sang the truth," Alkaios insisted. "But, I don't think you're in any danger. Pittakos will need aristocrats to keep him in power. He won't risk angering them more than necessary by killing a girl much less one of Mitylene's favorite poets."

"You must flee - quickly. You've already lingered too long."

"Not until you promise to go to my mother's house."

"Oh – all right – all right -- just go."

She refused the brotherly kiss he would have given her, urging his hasty departure yet aching to cling to him, to hold on to someone – anyone if only for a moment longer.

When he was gone, she went to the nursery where she shoved an army of toy soldiers off a chair and plopped into it. Forcing thoughts of the day aside, she pictured her small brother romping on the floor. She thought of the adorable way he waddled when he tried to walk. At less than a year, he knew how to hum most of her favorite songs. If she concentrated hard enough, she could hear his out of tune plunking on her childhood lyre.

Her mental vision of the lyre reminded her of Alkaios. *Be safe, my friend. Be safe.* Trembling fingers wound themselves in the remnants of shorn braids. There's nothing left for another funeral bier, she thought as she gathered all the toy warriors one by one and placed them neatly upon a shelf. When she had ordered the nursery to her satisfaction, she climbed the worn stone steps to the roof from which she could see a corner of her father's house. *You won't steal another home from me, Pittakos. I won't let you.*

Peggy Ullman Bell

[page deliberately left blank]

> *"The thorns which I have reaped are of the tree*
> *I planted; they have torn me, and I bleed.*
> *I should have known what fruit would*
> *spring from such a seed."*
> *'Lord Byron'*

-- VI --

The roof steamed in the moist afternoon despite the damp chill in the air. Psappha hoisted herself up onto the parapet to get a better view of her father's house. The flight of a graceful bird caught her attention. The bird hovered above the city then dropped from sight just as she realized it was probably a vulture.

A dust cloud moved along the winding road from Mitylene. As it got close, Psappha saw a pair of dappled gray horses drawing a two-wheeled chariot. *Who?*

Whoever it was stopped at her gate. Psappha started toward the stairs. The Gatekeeper would see to the horses and the house servants would show their driver to the main hall and make him welcome. There was no reason for Psappha to hurry. Nevertheless, she didn't pause until she reached the entrance to the banquet hall.

Her guest hunched over meat left from the night before. His tunic was naught but wrinkles, his cloak lay in a heap on the floor and he sucked on fingers well greased with mutton. Psappha's nostrils flared in disgust. The incongruity of such a man driving so fine a team rang through her mind like the discordant clang of a sacrificial gong.

"You wish to see me?

He turned his head, not putting the mutton aside. He spoke with grease oozing from the corners of his mouth.

"Are you Psappha?"

"I am Lady Psappha."

He put the stripped bone on the table and spoke without wiping his chin.

"You're under arrest."

"For what? I've done nothing." The feel of a desperately wielded labrys flashed through her mind.

"You'll have to ask Pittakos about that. All they told me was to bring you to the citadel. You wanna go like that?"

Puzzled by his insolent stare, Psappha glanced at the brass mirror in the corridor behind her. A vision of Charaxos stared back at her. She still wore his outgrown tunic. *Kios must be as numb as I, else he would have noticed.* "You will allow me time to change," she stated, rather than asked.

"Sure," he mumbled. "Why not?" He was midway through his second flagon of wine before she reached the archway.

~ ~ ~

Psappha dressed slowly and deliberately, cultivating anger and indignation as she bathed. Whatever her situation, Klies's daughter would not appear before her antagonist in less than her finest attire. She cast aside several lengths of cloth before selecting a deep-violet silk that Eurigios had presented to Klies upon the birth of their first son. It seemed appropriate somehow.

Psappha recalled that among other special occasions as she draped the silk over one shoulder, crossed it at her side, wrapped it over and under itself and brought the ends together above the original cross at her waist. Her fingers trembled, almost poking themselves with the pin as she secured the cloth with Klies' jade and ivory broach. The color went better with Klies' fair skin and golden hair but it would have to do. *I'd look better in armor,* she thought as she fluffed what was left of her hair.

Before returning to the main hall, she massaged musk oil onto her bare shoulder, remembering ugly Pyrrha, remembering Klies' forbearance through all of it. Tears clogged her throat as she let her mother's inheritance of strength fill and steady her. Propriety and resilience guided her steps as she went to rejoin her uninvited guest.

The respectful expression on his face assured her that the time and care spent on her appearance had been worth the effort. He retrieved his wrap from the floor, bowed awkwardly and allowed her to precede him from the house.

They rode in silence, the driver busy with the fractious team, Psappha clinging to the rim of the vehicle, her legs aching as she fought for balance. The New City streets were deserted. Smoke spiraled from abandoned stoves. As they approached the bridges, the noise grew louder and the press of the crowd soon blocked their way. The driver tossed the rains to an urchin who clasped them importantly. He dropped a few coins into the lad's outstretched hand as he stepped from the chariot. "Return the team to the citadel stable as traffic permits. You'll be well rewarded," he told the boy as Psappha dismounted.

On foot, it was worse. For each step forward Psappha had to pause until her captor forced a passage for her. She thought she saw Alkaios in the excited, somewhat fearful throng. *He wouldn't be that foolish.* She tried to dismiss the thought but was unsuccessful.

Guards blocked egress from the bridge to all but a few. One of them licked his lips as Psappha passed. She felt his lascivious stare on her back as she and her escort walked the white-cobbled way to the citadel. As they passed her father's mansion, the grumble of the crowd seemed to fade behind them. For an instant, her mind filled with visions of a happier time. A few steps farther along they faded. *I can't remember his face.* She wanted to weep. Pride forbade it.

She recoiled from the citadel steps then climbed them, careful to avoid the many bloodstains. A jagged scar marred the elaborately carved door panel on her right. She cringed from the dark, irregular stain that surrounded it. Burning with her need for vengeance, she would have marched directly to the audience chamber had a sentinel not barred her way. When he directed her toward a bench-lined wall, she chose a spot at a distance from the others waiting.

She perched on the edge of a splintery plank, back straight, chin up and eyes front. Every few minutes someone was ushered through the guarded doors. From time to time, one of them would come out and scurry away. Psappha refused to wonder what happened to the others.

After what seemed like hours, a trio of servants lit bright torches around the edges of the room. Psappha's bottom had gone numb but she dared not stand and rub it. It would be too undignified. Instead, she wriggled her seat for a second then leaned her aching back against the wall. The cool marble warmed to her presence and she let her eyelids fall. Dark imaginings filled her heart with dread.

"S'pha?"

Her eyelids snapped open and she gasped. "Kios, you fool! What are you doing here?"

"I came as soon as I heard you'd been arrested. It's me he wants, not you."

"You should have gone away," she said, fear for her own safety lost beneath her concern for him. "He won't harm me," she said, but she didn't believe it. "What can he possibly fear from one small girl?" she asked, hoping she sounded brave.

"Pittakos is capable of anything, S'pha. You baited him rather efficiently last summer."

"I wasn't nearly as rude as you," she countered firmly, though her daring was slipping. "Get out of here before you're recognized."

"Too late."

He was right. The guards were coming. As they approached, the sentinel motioned for Psappha. The crowd in the long corridor buzzed as she strode forward without looking to see if Alkaios followed.

Inside the audience chamber, she stopped at the foot of the dais with her head high and her shoulders firm. Pittakos sat above her.

His disdainful glance beyond her said, 'yes', Alkaios, fool that he was, had followed her. Her bravado wavered. She sighed.

Pittakos smirked. "Nice of you to bring your lover with you, Miss Arrogance. Saves me the trouble of tracking him down."

"She didn't bring me, Crack-toes. I came here on my own."

Psappha was glad to note that Alkaios' pride was still firmly in place, but she wished he would curb his attitude.

Pittakos ignored him. He stalked back and forth before Psappha, his thumbs hooked in his belt, his dingy hair contrasting sharply with his gleaming breastplate. His sheath swung restlessly, as if searching for a real weapon to replace the ostentatious toy it contained. Rich court greaves topped buskins stained with what looked like the grime of a million battlefields.

Revulsion slithered up her spine as he spoke. "You seem to have changed your mind about mixing in politics. You should have fled to Antissa with your aunt."

Psappha's eyes widened with anger. "As I told you before, milord pretentious, "I never involve myself in politics, though they insist on involving themselves with me."

"My reports say differently," he said, stepping from the dais. Hands behind his back, he circled her, passing between her and Alkaios. Alkaios opened his mouth. Psappha shook her head at him as Pittakos continued to circle her. "I'll wager this silk becomes you better than the battle tunic in which my messenger found you," he said, stopping before her, appraising her from top to toe. "You seem to have had an interesting day, Psappha. Several of my prisoners swear they fought beside you in this morning's business. I have one who even claims you as his leader. Quite a task for a wee bit of a girl armed only with a ceremonial labrys." His smirk had widened into a leering grin.

Psappha considered warily before she replied. *What wild fantasy might I weave in the torturer's embrace?* "Any story can be obtained in the dungeons," she said. "Webs woven of fear are flimsy. As for my accuser, let him know his own terror and not attempt to add to mine."

She could not help remembering the evening he caught her petting her great cat on the stoop. *He opposes me now because I refused him. This is his revenge.* His continuing lascivious surveillance chilled her. She couldn't help but feel relieved when Alkaios drew his attention from her.

"Leave Psappha out of this, Shuffle-foot. She took no part in this morning's business, as you call it, but I did. Say what you will to me. My opinion of you is well known."

Pittakos's lip curled away from stained teeth as he growled, "Your opinion is too well known, Street-poet. You will leave Lesbos on the first ship out of port and take your lady-in-greaves with you."

Psappha stumbled backward. *Leave? Leave Lesbos? Leave Mitylene? Again?* "No!"

"Yes, Miss Arrogance," Pittakos hissed. "You will leave Lesbos. I've had my fill of singers and songs."

The sibilants spurted onto Psappha's stricken face. Her fingers felt numb as she wiped away spittle and furious tears.

"You will leave," Pittakos repeated, obviously quite pleased with himself. "There's a ship in the harbor set to sail for Tyre, by way of Samos and the Cyclades. You and your mouthy betrothed will be aboard."

Alkaios pushed Psappha behind him.

"You pot-bellied old fool! It is I who dared sing the truth. Yet you, you ignorant alley-urchin, choose to exile the fairest flower of Mitylene. Must you create a cultural vacuum to suit your lack of breeding?"

Pittakos took a half-step sideways and continued talking at Psappha.

"I understand your brother is studying with Pythagoras. Perhaps you will see him while the ship reloads on Samos."

Psappha affected a poise she did not feel in order to reply. "Your information is out of date, Man-of-the-people. The fact that

Charaxos is in Egypt has been common knowledge among aristocrats for quite some time. I'm not surprised you hadn't heard."

Pittakos sputtered as if about to retort. Alkaios robbed him of the opportunity.

"Banish me if you wish, Tasteless-one, but let Psappha stay."

Psappha stamped her foot, grabbed Alkaios' arm and thrust him aside.

"I can speak for myself, thank you."

Facing Pittakos, she drew herself up almost to his collarbone and spat in his face.

"There, thou brainless tool of a graceless goat. That is what I think of you. Look to your mirrors, Pittakos. Good men died for you, but you're not worth a porna's scorn."

She pivoted and marched toward the door, her grief-cropped hair snubbing him as artfully as the saucy tail of the Minorcan rooster in Eurigios' garden.

Oh, Terpsichore, blessed dancer, please don't let me trip.

[page deliberately left blank]

> *"Oh love, Oh lover, loose or hold me fast.*
> *I had thee first, whoever have thee last."*
> *'Algernon Charles Swinburne'*

-- VII --

Psappha clung to a mooring post; all pretense of maturity and poise consumed by dread. Alkaios touched her hands. She tightened her grip, afraid that, if she let go, she would disappear.

Alkaios tried to pry her hands apart. "Don't do this, S'pha. Let go. You're getting hawser grease all over your best kiton. ... Remember who you are, Psappha. Don't let Old Crack-toes see how much he's hurt you."

Psappha gulped gall and glanced behind her. Pittakos stood amid his simper of sycophants, seeming oblivious to her and her hatred. Three days without seeing him had done nothing to diminish her anger. She wanted to claw the satisfaction from his face. He appeared to taunt her by possessively stroking his young ward's silver-gold hair.

Atthis! She must not remember me like this! She stumbled to her feet. Her knees felt nonexistent. She swayed.

Alkaios caught her by her elbows. "Don't faint. See how he awaits the chance to gloat?"

Psappha clung to him.

He whispered near her ear. "Stand proud."

She wrapped herself in affected poise.

He honored her with a shallow bow then stepped aside to let her precede him to the end of the pier.

The waiting dinghy rocked as she stepped into it. *I won't let Pittakos silence me*, she vowed as she fought for balance. The instant she took a seat in the prow, she leaned over the starboard side and heaved her breakfast into the harbor.

"It will be better aboard the trireme," Alkaios said as he eased his lean frame onto the seat beside her. He pointed toward where a sleek, black Tyre-built merchantman strained at anchor and a line of unrecorded poetry echoed in her mind.

Like a chained panther with three rows of shipped oars pointing skyward like misplaced claws. She didn't want to think of ships and sails, and sorrow. "Be quiet! She told her anguished soul but her resentment refused to hush. *I'm past sixteen. I should be in The Lady's Temple learning the joys of sensual love, not puking my guts out in this wallowing bathtub full of stinking oarsmen.*

The dinghy skirted beneath the prow of the trireme then bumped against the side of a squat, red travesty of a ship. A rope ladder snaked downward.

"I should have known Old Crack-toes wouldn't let us sail off in luxury."

Psappha turned her back on the trireme, grabbed the grungy ladder and began to climb.

"That's the spirit. I'm glad you're feeling better," Alkaios prodded.

Psappha scowled down at him then hoisted herself over the bulkhead and onto the ship's rough deck. Once aboard, she leaned forward over the scarred outer railing, her gaze straining toward her home. *Mitylene, Ancient city, Thy citadel stands at thy center like a sentinel guarding a dream.* She smiled as her mind birthed a new poem despite, or was it because of, her misery.

The boat bobbled. She grabbed the rail so tight she rammed a splinter into her palm but the pain was nothing compared to the ache in her heart. She remembered the scent of exotic herbs and spices and a terrible loneliness filled her. *How can I leave? How will I bear it?* The air around her stank of dead fish and stale grease, but she smelled hyacinths and roses. Sun-baked oarsmen squinted at her from their benches. She noted their chains and she shivered. *Nothing Pittakos orders will ever surprise me again.*

She didn't realize she was crying until Alkaios brushed tears from her cheeks. "We'll be back," he said.

She wanted to believe him. She tried to drill his words into her brain as she stared at her beloved island storing pictures in her mind. Sunbeams danced on the water and sparkled on the marble bridges that connected the old city and its citadel to the audacious upstart on the shore. As the late afternoon sun sank behind the island it cast the markets into shadow while sending golden beams streamed through a break between the hills where they passed gently over the home Alkaios had planned for her and sharpened olive-leaf needles in The Lady's sacred grove. A stiff breeze brought the odor of spoiled vegetables and blood but Psappha remembered perfume vendors and she sniffed to catch the fragrance.

Alkaios gathered her to him and whispered, "We will return."

"Yes," Psappha agreed. *I will return some day, when sages recite my verses and every beggar in the marketplace knows my songs.*

Her bravado faded with the sun. She remained secluded in her cabin throughout the evening. She heard someone bring, and then carry away, her supper but she did not care. *What's to become of me*, she wondered as the acrid smoke of the old oil in her lamp drove her onto the rolling deck. Mitylene was but a silhouette against the darkening sky.

The moon drew silver chains on the water. A light breeze touched her with memories as she strolled along the quiet deck. At the prow, she turned to see Alkaios exiting his cabin. She had forgotten him. Now, she found herself needing his company more than she ever could have imagined even a single day before.

His mist-moistened back glistened in starlight as he leaned over the bulkhead. He didn't look up from the water as she approached. When she laid her hand on his arm, he glanced at her. She thought she saw hunger in his eyes. Her pulse quickened. She wanted him to do something -- anything -- to fill the aching void inside her soul.

"'Kios?" She reached and gently stroked his soft, golden beard. "Alkaios."

"He had no funeral," he said hoarsely.

"What?"

"Eurigios. We gave him no funeral."

Psappha realized how badly she had misread his expression and she blushed. His brother, her stepfather, was murdered and he grieved deeply while she stupidly cried for the loss of a city and an unrealized love. *Mother was right. I am an ogre.* Embarrassed beyond words, she placed both hands securely on the railing before them and leaned forward to hide her face. The breeze caught at her kiton. It fluttered as if playing tag with the loose folds of his robe. He was her only link with home and she needed him, more desperately than she could ever let him know.

"Don't look so sad, S'pha. We'll be back."

"I wasn't thinking about Mitylene."

"Then, what is it that troubles you, child?"

"There you go calling me a child again. I may be small Alkaios, but I'm less a child now than I was last summer. Nevertheless, right now I feel terribly alone."

"You're not alone, little one. I'm here." He folded her into his arms and kissed her lightly on the forehead as any gentleman might kiss his younger sister. Psappha wasn't feeling sisterly. His bare chest scorched her cheek. *Oh, Aphrodite, help me*, she prayed. *Make him quiet the aching hunger The Fates have caused me.*

She wriggled loose, taking care that her up thrust nipples maintained contact with his chest. "Do you still think me a child, 'Kios?"

"I told you long ago that you were no child," he reminded her thickly. "Relax. There's plenty of time."

"Time? Time? There is no time, 'Kios. What if pirates seize the ship? What if the crew decides to sell us to Trojan slavers? Anything could happen and probably will. The Fates are cruel." With that, she reached into his hair and drew his head down. The touch of his lips came as spring rain when what she wanted was midsummer heat. With her fingers firmly tangled in his hair, her tongue became a serpent determined to destroy his will.

Alkaios pushed her away. "Behave, S'pha. You'll remain a maiden until you are my bride, but not a moment longer, I promise you."

Psappha put every ounce of her affronted dignity into her stare.

In return, she got a puzzled frown. "Forgive me," he said. "I didn't mean to offend you."

"Didn't mean to offend me? Didn't mean to offend me? You fool! You refused me. What greater offense is there?"

"Stop it! I didn't refuse you, you little idiot. I choose to wait 'til you are my bride. How is that refusing you?"

"Bride!" she shrieked. "When, Kios, where? There are no brides or bridegrooms here. There may never be another time of brides. You save me to feed your pride with a public display of stained cloth. Don't you understand that all of the public that matters has been left behind us?"

He glowered at her and growled through clenched teeth. "You dare speak of pride? Where's yours, S'pha? What makes you ask this of me? It isn't love for me I see in your eyes. I would take you here and now if I thought you truly wanted me but you don't. You've come to womanhood untouched. Remain so until you are my bride or find another bridegroom. I will not be your teacher."

Oh, you won't, won't you? His refusal had made her want him and now his anger inflamed her. She found herself wanting him for himself, and not just as her last connection to Mitylene. A scene once witnessed between her mother and Eurigios flashed through her mind and she took the hint. She heaved a huge sigh then wilted against him as if in defeat, making sure that her breath stirred the fine down on his chest. Through his robes, she felt his unsheathed sword of life brush hard against her thigh. Shivering with satisfaction, she nuzzled closer, her blood pounding in tune with the rapid beat of his heart. Turning her head slightly, she tickled his alert nipples with her lashes.

Alkaios shoved her roughly away.

Psappha returned undaunted, determined to have her way. She brushed against him with enough swivel of hip to leave no doubt as to her intention. He grasped her shoulders and shook her like a disobedient child. "Stop it, Psappha. You're behaving like a porna."

She defied him with a giggle. "Porna am I, Milord Righteous? And, would thee smite me with that sword which presses so valiantly against thy robes? Or, would thee rather place it in a sheath designed to hold it?" She reveled in his weakening resolve. The sword she had alluded to rose still further in answer to her challenge.

"The desecration of a virgin is abhorrent to the gods."

"Which gods, 'Kios? Surely not Zeus. His penchant for rape is astronomical. The only gods we might offend are those who teach that men own everything. What they think abhorrent is that The Lady's Maidens own themselves. The gift of sensuality is mine to do with as I will."

"A bride must be above reproach," he said, but she could sense his resistance slipping.

"And who's to marry us, Kios? The ship's captain or some renegade priest in whatever rat hole Pittakos decided to stuff us down?"

She fought against showing her delight as his hands loosed their grip on her shoulders and slid softly down her arms. A tiny victorious sigh escaped her lips as he scooped her up and carried her toward his cabin. He released the remnants of a growl as he kicked the door.

She dropped her scarabs on his cabin floor and untied the ribbon from her waist. Her kiton fell away when he placed her on his berth, leaving her displayed before him but she yearned to be astride.

Despite her yearning, despite a night of kisses and caresses, the way to Aphrodite's most sacred altar stayed firmly locked. Psappha wanted to scream with frustration each time Alkaios hesitated, reluctant to break through. Toward dawn, she wrapped her legs around his slim hips, gripping tightly. With her ankles crossed, she pushed against his buttocks with her feet and, with a single determined heave; she forced his entry into her personal temple.

~ ~ ~

When she awoke the next morning, she was alone. Mitylene lay shrouded in a low fog. It was as if the city mourned their going and had clothed itself in sorrow for the event. Psappha cried when the doleful throb of the drum began and long oars dipped into dawn-dark water to draw her away from everything she'd known and loved. Mitylene was gone. No more would she stroll through the marketplace amongst wonders of strange and exotic places. Never again would she sit in The Lady's Park and watch Atthis dance among the children. Lovely Atthis was forever lost to her.

"Where are we going?" she asked when Alkaios joined her from the Captains mess.

"He won't say. Claims he's under orders not to. Guess you'll just have to settle with sailing off to paradise in my cabin."

Psappha remembered their night together. Then she recalled her reaction to Atthis. Then she laughed, wildly, hysterically, tears streaming unheeded on a face past due for grief.

~ ~ ~

As the ship carried them ever further from Mitylene, Psappha attended the school of Eros with Alkaios as her tutor. The days drifted by like the tiny islands that dotted the horizon. Her conquest of Alkaios now complete, Psappha allowed herself time to think of Atthis. Impudent Eros reigned supreme while Mighty Poseidon napped.

They were less than an hour out of Samos when great billowing clouds swirled above them like smoke caught in a whirlwind. Gusting east wind held the ship stationary in spite of the straining oarsmen. Psappha had been on deck to watch their departure from the port. She ducked into her cabin when the rain began.

Thunder rattled the boards beneath her feet. Lightning flashed past her porthole. "Oh, Mitylene, thou lovely Mitylene," she wailed. "Never shall I see thee again. Lesbos, thou pure and beautiful jewel of the Aegean, no more will Psappha walk thy cushion of green, nor dance among the flowers on thy breast."

What seemed hours of lonely terror passed before Alkaios burst into her cabin clad in a rower's loincloth. "Are you all right?"

"No. I'm not all right. This excuse for a ship can't hold out against the anger of the gods. We're going to die."

"No one's going to die, S'pha. I'm here." He took her hands and bent to kiss her lightly on the forehead. It was hardly enough considering the storm, and what they'd shared but there was no time for more.

Psappha clung to him. He smelled of salt and wind. Outside, The Nubians among the crew began a keening death-chant more terrible than the thunderbolts that split the tormented sky.

"I must go," he said. He extricated himself from her desperate grip and was out the door before she could protest.

Psappha followed. The rising wind tossed the clumsy vessel about and no amount of prayerful singing could blind her to their danger. She shuddered as the first of the cargo splashed into the sea. *Why bother to lighten the load? There's nowhere to run aground!* The storm determinedly blew them away from port. She pretended she could still see Samos through the driven rain but she knew it wasn't real.

Alkaios stumbled toward her, shouting, but the wind stole his words.

"Here!" she yelled. "I'm here, Kios! Here!" A huge wave hurried toward them. "Look out!" she yelled pointing. Alkaios glanced over his shoulder then continued his struggle toward her. Wind whipped her kiton against her legs. Rain and salt spray stung her eyes. The ship slid into a trough. The wave broke over their heads. Psappha slid toward the bulkhead, then, just as she was certain Poseidon had decided to claim her life she felt a firm fist grasp her ankle.

"Go back inside!" Alkaios ordered the instant she had her feet on the deck. "I don't have time to look after you. I have to help man a pump!"

"I can pump!" Psappha screamed above the thunder.

"Nonsense," he shouted back. "The pumps are bigger than you. If you won't go inside, I'm tethering you to the mast."

"What about you?" she asked. "Look to yourself you always said."

"No time," he boomed. Securing the knot at her waist, he turned to go.

"Kios! Stay with me!"

"I can't! Be brave, Psappha! We have a wedding to attend!"

The sway of the lumbering vessel wrenched her from side to side. The mainmast to which he'd tied her chaffed her back. Her throat ached from shouting. Wind sucked moisture from her skin as rain blurred her sight. Waves scoured the deck, curling around her ankles like fingers trying to pull her from the ship. Wet rope choked her waist and left her gasping. The yeoman's drum throbbed in her gut. Twenty oarsmen took up the beat. She bit her lip as she watched Alkaios struggle toward the belly of the vessel. She screamed when a spar broke free and smacked him to the deck. Tears of relief joined the salt spray on her cheek when he arose and continued toward the pump.

The ship wallowed in ever-widening circles. Curses resounded all around. She would have joined them but her teeth chattered so much from cold and terror no words could get past them. Wave after wave drove at them then came one as huge as the clenched fist of Poseidon. Psappha tried to shout a warning and got a mouthful of salt water for her trouble. From above and behind, she heard the sharp crack of splintering wood and saw the aft mast tumble into the sea. She searched for a glimpse of Alkaios. She saw him hunched over the aft pump in apparent safety and she began to pray. *Oh, Hera, Hera, look thou, Hera! Protect Alkaios from thy angry husband!*

The mainmast cracked then snapped. Poseidon grabbed it with a watery fist and flung it into the storm. Psappha whirled with the spinning mast. *Poseidon! Poseidon! Blessed Father – no -- I can't die now. No one will remember my name!*

Book Two

THE LADY OF LESBOS

Peggy Ullman Bell

[page deliberately left blank]

> *"She walks in beauty, like the night*
> *of cloudless climes and starry skies;*
> *And all that's best of dark and bright*
> *meet in her aspect and her eyes;*
> *Thus mellowed to the tender light,*
> *which Heaven to gaudy day denies."*
> *'Lord Byron'*

-- VIII --

Psappha regained consciousness in an unknown world. She moved her hands and felt fine cotton sheets. *Egyptian,* her fingers told her. Recognizing the clink and rasp of rigging, she knew she was on a ship. The bunk on which she lay rocked with the gentle roll of waves. *Was it all a dream?*

Memory swamped her euphoria. She thought of the squat ship upon which she began her hated exile, but the soft linen told her she was no longer there. Terror and grief rushed at her in expanding waves.

Her eyes clenched against reality, Psappha pounded the bunk with raw, cracked fists. *Kios is gone!* She raged at offending gods. *Capricious charlatans, why weren't you watching? Oh Lady Mother, do you delight in my torture? Do you take pleasure in my suffering, Aphrodite? Your bastard son inflamed me then you let Poseidon snatch me from the ship.*

Distorted rainbows filtered through her closed eyelids. Her bones ached. The air around her smelled of sweat and stale oil. Peeking cautiously through her lashes, she saw polished teak walls and massive mahogany furnishings instead of rough sea chests and unfinished bulkheads. Through the porthole, she glimpsed vast sails.

The ship was huge. She hoped they built it better for the journey than the scruffy craft upon which she had embarked from Mitylene.

Stretching, she moaned. She felt skinned and salted. Her fingers rasped across sun-scorched flesh as she searched for broken bones. Realizing she was naked, her hands flew back, dislodging her covering. She grabbed at it and felt other hands tuck it around her. She peeked and thought she saw Pittakos of Lesbos standing over her. She scrunched her eyes shut and rolled toward the bulkhead in terror. *Where am I?*

Someone spoke. She rolled toward the sound ready to rise and flee. *Flee to where? Fool!*

A soft cloth touched her forehead. *Pittakos would not be so gentle.* Her eyes slowly opened. She looked up into smoky, cobalt eyes. Ebony hair framed the man's face. In coloring, he resembled Scamandronomos, her father although he was sun-bronzed to the point of seeming to be of a different race. His hook-tipped nose pointed to wide, full lips, visible in his thick beard only because they displayed an ivory-toothed smile. Gold and emerald rings dressed his ears. *Extravagant booty for a crewmember, even on as large and profitable a merchant ship as this appears to be.*

She avoided the sight of shoulders broad enough for a Minotaur. Instead, her gaze followed the arrow-tail of crimped black wool that splashed over his chest and shafted downward out of sight beneath a simple kilt. *He looks like Hades.*

When he spoke again, his voice was softly soothing but his words hovered just beyond her understanding.

"Who are you?" she asked. "Where are the others? Did you find Alkaios?"

He crimped his brow.

"Were there other survivors?"

He shrugged.

"Answer me, damn you!"

He smiled.

My Lady witness, he thinks he is Hades! Father Poseidon to what vengeful brother hast thou delivered me? "I am Psappha of Lesbos," she said, pointing to herself. "You will answer me at once."

The dark man grinned and turned to leave.

"Wait! Damn you, wait. Who are you? Where are you taking me? Were there other survivors? Where is Alkaios? Alkaios of Lesbos, you must have heard of him. Come back here!"

Tears of frustration scorched her salt-scoured eyes as she poured a small libation from the tray the dark man had left her. With determination born of pain, she fought to believe that Alkaios was also safe and dry somewhere. *Well dry anyway*, she thought as she lifted her glass in prayer, "Lord Dionysus, don't fall asleep over your cups and allow such a dear worshiper to get away."

~ ~ ~

They must have put poppy juice in the wine Psappha thought when she again awakened. Her limbs felt heavy, her head light. It hurt to move. Nevertheless, she knew the longer she stayed in the wide bunk the stiffer she would get. It took several nauseating tries, but she managed to stand. The massive mahogany furnishings lent support as she searched the cabin for some form of clothing. Finding nothing better, she settled for a length of rough sailcloth, which she knotted at one shoulder, using a bit of rope about her waist to hold it around her and off the polished deck.

She wished the dark man would come back. *What good would that do? He doesn't understand a word I say.* The scruffy old seaman who brought her breakfast was no better. When she spoke to him in flawless Hellenic, he merely shrugged. Throughout the day, she listened intently to garbled conversations beyond her door. By nightfall, she realized they did indeed speak Greek but in several odd and varied dialects. By evening, she was able to translate most of what they said into her own soft Aeolian dialect.

She saw nothing of the ship's neglectful captain. *What sort of man would fail to greet a lady no matter in what fashion she came aboard his vessel?*

Feigned indignation did not help. She trembled, remembering Hades' image in the flesh. What sort of man could control such a one as he, so handsome in a gruesome way? She shivered. The challenge of meeting the vessel's captain was intoxicating yet terrifying in his power over her fate. *How did I come aboard? What happened to Kios?*

"Who are you?" she asked the youth who bustled into the cabin shaking rainwater from his cap of russet curls. Although his face was hairless as a babe's, he looked to be a year or two older than she was. *A bit mature for a cupbearer*, she thought. Yet that is what his attire proclaimed him. The emerald tunic that pretended to cover his lean body matched intelligent green eyes. Maybe she would finally get an answer to her most important question.

"My name is Lycos*," he said in rich, proud tenor. "How may I serve you?"

"Were there other survivors?"

He arched copper brows. "Survivors?"

"Yes, survivors, you simpering fool," she almost shouted from frustration, "From my ship. Was anyone else saved?"

"There was no ship. Only you and a log and a lot of seaweed."

No ship! Had it sunk? No! She refused to believe it. Alkaios was alive. *Dionysus would not let him die. But, if he is not dead, he let them sail off without me.* Anger fought with grief. Had he not seen her fly from the ship?

"Kerkolos* spotted you from the lookout," the boy continued unaware of her thoughts. "He slid down the mainmast and fished you out of the sea with a cargo net. You should have seen him. He hauled you aboard all by himself, broken mast and all." His voice was soft and merry.

---

* Lycos (LIE-khaus)
* Kerkolos (KARE-kaw-laus)

His smile infuriated her. "What are you grinning at, you rude boy. I don't see anything funny about the loss of an entire ship and everyone aboard."

"Not everyone," he said. "You're here. Maybe others are somewhere else."

"Others are probably dead," she said, her voice drenched in misery, "and all you can do is grin?"

"I'm still picturing Kerkolos plucking you from the sea like a hooked sturgeon."

"Who is Kerkolos?"

Lycos's bright eyes went wide with astonishment. "Kerkolos of Andros, you met him. The captain, didn't he tell you?"

"I haven't seen him."

"Of course you have. He sent me here."

Psappha felt blood rushing to her face, realizing he could only be referring to the dark man. *The image of Hades is the captain!* She had subconsciously watched him as he left her cabin. His upper body had seemed a miracle of muscles but his legs were bony and bowed. To her shame, she had dismissed him as an oarsman despite his wealth of jewelry. "Why didn't he identify himself? If I had known it was he who rescued me, I could have thanked him."

"That's probably why he didn't tell you."

"Are you the one who undressed me?" She had to know. She could not bear it if it had been the dark one.

"Nothing to undress. Old Poseidon stripped you clean."

Psappha wanted to cry. She visualized a leering crew. *No wonder Kerkolos smiled so much.*

"Don't worry," Lycos said, as if privy to her thoughts. "The African whisked you out of the net and into Kerkolos's cabin so fast nobody got a good look at you."

"The African?" Psappha frowned, picturing some heathen oarsman daring to touch her naked body.

"She wouldn't let anyone get a good look at you," Lycos said.

"She? There's another woman aboard?"

"Not just another woman," he said, beaming, "A queen."

Psappha frowned. "Don't lie to me, boy. Pharaoh would not allow his wife to sail on another man's ship."

"Oh, the African is no man's wife," he said, chuckling as if the idea was amusing. "And she's no pampered Egyptian either. The African is a warrior."

A warrior? A savage. The glow of respect in the Lycos's eyes said that either he liked savages, which was unlikely given the delicacy of his appearance, or the African was something else; something more interesting. "I would meet this African," she said.

"Oh, she'll come by -- if she chooses."

~ ~ ~

The African strode through the cabin doorway the next afternoon. Taller than most men with skin as richly hued and lovely as the cabin's teak walls, the woman filled the cabin with her presence.

Psappha succumbed to an unexpected shyness. Suddenly half past sixteen didn't seem so worldly after all. "If it pleases you, I'd like to know your name," she said her voice tremulous and inexplicably timid.

"I am called, Gongyla*, milady."

"You needn't call me milady. I am Psappha." Awed by the magnificence of the woman before her, she left the aristocratic 'of Lesbos' off her introduction.

Gongyla's deep chuckle warmed her like the sun that appears suddenly on a blustery day.

"How came you here, oh, queen?" Psappha asked, wanting to hear the vibrant voice again.

Gongyla's patrician face saddened. "There was a war, little dove. My people fought bravely. I, myself, killed many of our enemies with my bow, but victory gained us nothing. My people were hungry. If

---

* Gongyla, Gyla (Gone-GUY-lah, GUY-lah)

not for Lord Kerkolos, my people would have sold themselves to the slavers. I could not let them be sent to the market beyond Tyre."

Psappha shuddered. She had heard of the market beyond Tyre. Rumor had it that no one ever returned from there: The men went to the mines to die slowly, the women to brothels to live, though their souls were dead.

"Tell me of thy country, oh Queen," she said, hoping to coax a smile.

Gongyla seemed to stretch her head higher on her long, arched neck. ""My land is far: A green land, past a white land, behind the land of the Carthaginians; near the birthplace of the river Niger." There was sadness mixed with the pride in her resonant voice, her tone rich with feeling. "My people are as free as eagles in flight. The women are strong and fleet of foot; the men as gentle and watchful as the great cats with whom we share the hunt.

"There are birds in my country with plumage brighter than Egyptian brocade. And small animals like creeping children that fill the air with endless chatter like gynakeoni."

Psappha's brow furrowed. "Gynakeoni?"

"You will see," Gongyla said, smiling softly.

Psappha answered the smile by touching Gongyla's long, tapered hand. "What of thy gods, thou hunter, are they gentle like the little animals or fierce like thyself?"

"We worship no gods, Ivory-one. We worship only Cybele, whom you call Queen of Heaven."

"You know The Lady," Psappha joyfully exclaimed.

"What lady?"

"Not lady, Oh queen. The Lady; Cybele, Isis, Asherah, Astarte, Artemis, The Lady of a Thousand Names, The Lady by whatever name. My mother was her priestess.

"I, too, am a priestess," Gongyla said, "and what of you?"

Psappha shuddered, ashamed before such majesty. "I'm an exile," she whispered, head down.

"Oh?" the queen murmured deep in her throat, reminding Psappha of the great cats so recently mentioned. She tried to imagine Gongyla striding through a jungle on the heels of a leopard. *No, not on its heels; beside it; almost a cat herself: silent and dangerous in the undergrowth.* "How came you here?"

The question pulled Psappha from her reverie. "I spoke when I should have stayed quiet," she almost whispered. "I challenged a gutter-rat who became a king." Her voice cracked. Her mind reeled with visions she would rather forget.

"Don't think about it if it hurts you," the African said in a voice that whisked through Psappha like a spark in the woods flashes through the undergrowth.

"I poked a snake and lost my home," she said. "I should've known I was pushing him too far and now Alkaios is dead because of it."

"Alkaios?"

"My betrothed," Psappha said, the words flowing like a river of tears.

"He is not dead," Gongyla said; her voice as sure as winter rain. "You will see him again. But not for a long time."

"And you know that how?"

"I know." The beautiful African spoke with the authority of a queen and Psappha believed her though she knew not why. "Now tell me more of this confrontation of yours."

"All eyes in the hall were on me, I realized later, but at that moment, all I saw was Death and His messenger.

"He dared to say he did not expect me to understand, but he expected the people to understand. I demanded that he ask them, thinking that would end his death-creating schemes, but I was wrong. The people chose regicide and he obliged them. "Why couldn't I have just kept quiet?"

"Because, it wasn't in you," Gongyla suggested, a hint of a smile lifting the corners of her sensuous lips.

Psappha nodded glum agreement. "Alkaios and I are poets and being quiet isn't part of that." *A poet with no audience and the finest of us is gone.* A tear rolled down her cheek.

Gongyla caught it on her finger. "Don't worry," she said. "You <u>will</u> see him again. Meanwhile, I've heard Kerkolos has a fine gynakeon*."

---

* gynakeon (guynah-KHEE-ahn)

Peggy Ullman Bell

[page deliberately left blank]

"I live not in myself,
but I become portion of that around me:
and to me high mountains are a feeling;
but the hum of human cities torture."
'Lord Byron'

-- IX --

"What in the name of any of The Lady's thousand names is a gyna-whatever?"

"Guynah-KHEE-ahn," Lycos pronounced for her, seeming amazed by her question. "A gynakeon is the secluded and well guarded women's quarter of all fine homes."

His accepting attitude infuriated her. This gyna-whatever sounded like a golden prison. "I grew up in a fine home," she said. "A fine home in the world's finest city, Mitylene. I enjoyed total freedom in all of both, not just in a quarter of a single house."

Lycos gawked. "There are places where decent women wander as freely as boys?"

"On Lesbos, boys don't wander anywhere," she lied. "They mind their manners and speak when spoken to."

Lycos surveyed her face then sat on the edge of the bunk to join her giggles. An icy breeze stopped their laughter. Kerkolos spoke from the open doorway.

"It appears you approve of my choice of servants, milady."

Psappha gulped a giggle and sat up straight. "A fine choice," she said with all the dignity she could muster. "But not a servant, Master Kerkolos -- a friend."

Kerkolos' dark eyes swept over the two of them. Psappha blushed, remembering he had seen her naked. Lycos also blushed and that made her curious. *But now, is not the time to pursue it.*

"So, you know my name," Kerkolos said, his full lips widening into a ready smile. "What else has this scamp told you?"

"Very little." She winked at Lycos. "He was attempting to explain why a proper lady should confine herself to a prison within her own home."

"Gynakia," Lycos injected nervously.

"Gynakia are hardly prisons," Kerkolos said. "Most gynakeoni enjoy their privacy, although some of their customs may seem strange to those from less sophisticated cultures."

Psappha bolted to her feet. "Lesbian culture was advanced when Athens was still a suburb of Mycenae! How dare you call us unsophisticated? Lesbian women live free while Androsans apparently can't trust theirs in the company of men. Or is it that you fear they'll run away?"

"So," the dark one said with an infuriating chuckle, "the little fish can fight. Save your fury, small fry. When I've decided what to do with you, I'll let you know. Meanwhile, I'll leave you children to your games."

"Isn't he wonderful?" Lycos bubbled the moment Kerkolos was gone.

"Wonderful? He's a monster. He's pompous. He's . . ."

"A sphincter," Lycos supplied and Psappha's resentment got lost in laughter.

When their giggles subsided, she picked at the sailcloth robe she had fashioned for herself. "Do you think you could find me something better to wear?"

Lycos scampered out like an eager puppy and was back with an armload of fabric before she had time to miss him. She picked through the assortment while he added oil to the braziers. When he finished, the cabin was so warm -she didn't hesitate when he signaled her to strip. For reasons she had not yet defined, she felt as comfortable with him as she would have felt with a female attendant.

Lycos stared but said nothing.

"What ails you, boy? Surely you've served women before?"

"I've served lots of women but--"

"But what?"

"You look different from the ladies of the Gynakia."

"I'm ugly?"

"Oh, no, milady, you're not ugly. You're beautiful, but you -- you're--"

"I'm what, you fumble-tongued whelp?"

"You're hairy."

"I'm what?"

"You're hairy, milady."

"What're you talking about? Hairy? Are these gynakeoni of yours all so disfavored they've no badge of womanhood to break the monotony of flesh?" She could not imagine being without The Lady's sacred symbol. *Still, if the African . . . ?*

"They would be as hairy as you if their hair were not removed. Hair does not go well with the diaphanous clothes they all wear. When they bother to wear any," he added with a giggle.

Although nude, Psappha found it hard to imagine diaphanous clothing with wind and rain raging outside. *Will it never stop,* she wondered as Lycos unfolded an odd-looking padded table from the leeward cabin wall. Following his gesture, Psappha climbed onto it, rolled onto her stomach and stretched. *This is better for massage than my bed at home.* "How do they do it?"

"Do what?"

"Remove the hair, of course." She had noticed when he dropped formal address but curiosity had made propriety less important than answers. "How do they remove the hair?"

"With creams."

"Do you have such things?"

"I have them." She saw his satisfied smirk from the corner of her eye, but she chose to ignore it. "Would you like me to use them?" he asked, rubbing the tension from her shoulders.

"Does it hurt?"

"No."

"You're sure?"

"Yes. I'm sure. I could do it while you sleep." He smacked her bottom. "Roll over."

Psappha did as instructed. The touch of his hands on areas of her skin that usually started her dreaming felt friendly, sisterly and not at all erotic.

"Shall I fetch the creams, milady?"

"Oh, we're back to 'milady' now are we? Well, since you are no bigger than I, and will not conduct yourself as a proper slave, you can call me Psappha but not when your master can hear."

"I'm no slave, Psappha. I can serve you well enough, but I am free-born."

His pride pleased her. She ached for friendship never truly found.

"Shall I fetch the creams, Psappha," he repeated with emphasis on 'Psappha' and with thumbs bearing down on the muscles of her inner thighs.

"M-m-m-m-m-m."

~ ~ ~

Conditioned from birth to allow massage to lull her into deep sleep, Psappha awoke to a shining new world. The transformation was astounding. Lycos had changed everything. Stark teak walls bore filmy lavender draperies. Soft, sheer violet curtained the bunk. A down-filled comforter covered her and most of the massage table. Her tortured skin felt cool beneath the silk. Wriggling contentedly, she let her hands explore her body. Her fingers touched The Lady's mound and darted toward her navel, startled to find The Lady's most precious temple naked of adornment. *Yet, it feels strangely sensuous.*

"It pleases you?" Like a fox guarding a henhouse, Lycos perched on a stool nearby, delight and mischief competing on his impish face. Bright green eyes sparkled between his freckles and his flame of hair.

Psappha blushed then smiled. "Yes, Little Fox, I think it pleases me."

"Someone else used to call me that."

"Oh? Who?"

"My mother," he said but she could tell that he was lying.

She chose not to pursue it. Instead, she gathered the comforter around her and went to the newly acquired chaise. Lycos dragged his stool to her side and reached for her hand. When he scowled, she yanked the offending hand away and tucked it beneath her. He fished her other hand from beneath her covering and began filing her cracked and broken nails with deft strokes of the pumice.

I must look horrible. "Lock the door. I don't want anyone else to see me."

Lycos flashed a self-satisfied grin, reached beneath the couch then held a hand mirror before a face she barely recognized. "I don't wear paint!" Psappha protested, trying to wipe it off.

Lycos grabbed both her hands in one of his, being careful to avoid the injured wrists. "Look again," he said. "Lycos knows." With his free hand, he again raised the mirror, moving it back and forth when she tried to look away.

Unable to avoid him, or it, Psappha gave in and studied her new image. He had platted her hair into myriad braids interwoven with russet ribbons that added interesting highlights to what she had considered its fawn drabness. Her eyes, their lash-lines darkened with kohl, stared defiantly at her from the flawless glass.

Not bad, she decided. Even with her nose crinkled, the overall effect was gratifying. As she relaxed, the aspect changed. Her eyes shone like huge amethysts. Her full, red lips invited kisses. She puckered at herself and chuckled. "All right, Little Fox, you can let me have my hands now."

He jerked away and dropped to his knees beside her.

"Forgive me, milady, please," he pleaded, a faint smirk belying his mournful tone. "I didn't mean to hurt you. Please don't tell Master Kerkolos. I won't do it again."

Psappha laughed until her eyes filled with tears.

"Stop! You'll ruin all my work."

"What would Kerkolos do if I told him?" she asked when she caught her breath.

Lycos shrugged and shook his head. "Not a blessed thing. He's a kind and gentle man, Psappha."

I wish.

~ ~ ~

Lycos became Psappha's constant companion. They walked on the open deck together every sunny afternoon. At first, her worn and beaten condition made her dizzy. She often felt faint as she watched the African's daily routine.

Every time the African climbed the mast, Psappha's breath hung in her throat. Sleek as an Asian panther she was, climbing swiftly, graceful beyond imagining. Poised at the edge of the crow's nest, wearing only in a narrow swath of amber cloth around her loins her oiled body glistened in the sunlight like polished mahogany. The beauty of her captured Psappha's breath. When she dove, Psappha's breath released slowly, her chest deflating almost painfully. Psappha never tired of watching her. Gongyla knifed the water like a glistening black swan, wings folded; neck arched to meet the foam. *A glory worthy of The Lady Cybele and a distant throne*, Psappha thought as Gyla paced the ship with strong sure strokes. Her fear of strange shores and guarded houses seemed manageable, whenever the African was nearby.

As the days grew shorter, wetter and cold, she and Lycos spent more time in her cabin defeating each other at sennet. When, after a few weeks, she was able to walk without swaying, she no longer needed Lycos' hand at her elbow, but he seemed to like having it there, so she let it stay.

"When will we reach Andros?" she asked him one chilly afternoon, antsy in the chair he had provided for her on the sunny afterdeck. She couldn't see the mast from here.

"We're not going to Andros," he said. "Kerkolos's family home there is no longer fit for habitation. We're bound for Syracuse. In fact, we should have sighted it two days ago, but the wind threw us off course. That's why we don't usually sail these waters in mid-winter."

"Let's walk," she said. "It's even too cold for swimming," she added when a turn around the deck didn't produce the desired vision of Gongyla.

Kerkolos stood at the tiller commanding his crew with crisp shouts. "He looks like Hades staring across Styx in hope of fresh victims. When <u>he</u> decides what to do with me? The nerve of the man!"

Lycos giggled.

She spun toward him. "What are you laughing at?"

"You, you're captivated by him."

"I am not!"

"Then why are you so upset? He's done nothing to earn such anger. You wouldn't care so much if you didn't half love him."

"Don't be absurd. I have to care about him. He owns my destiny."

"Look!" Lycos shouted.

"Where?"

"There," he pointed. "That bit of white on the horizon below the clouds. Can you see it?"

She nodded. "What is it? Another ship?"

"No, it's Sicily."

Psappha marveled that the ship didn't nose under as the crew rushed to the prow, their eyes straining toward the horizon. She, too, watched as the speck grew larger, turned gray, brown, green and brown, and slowly disappeared in the gathering darkness. "How long?" she asked Lycos as the men returned to their posts.

"Dawn, I think."

She shivered. The air had turned cold the moment Helios dropped out of sight, but that was not what troubled her. While Lycos went to light the braziers in the cabin, she worried about her reception in Syracuse. Kerkolos had practically ignored her since he hauled her aboard. *Will that change when he has me among his women?*

The only light she could see was the bow lantern and a faint glow that extended a mere inch or two outside her cabin door. A sliver of moon peeked from between thick clouds. A stout breeze pushed the ship toward her unknown future. She gathered her cloak tighter and stared toward the hidden horizon, her eyes burning from tears and salt.

"We'll dock soon after first light tomorrow," Lycos said when he returned to fetch her. "Kerkolos sent the longboat ashore to announce our arrival."

The cabin warmed quickly after Psappha closed herself inside. Nevertheless, she trembled as she removed her clothes and loosed her hair. A proud glow filled her as it cascaded onto her shoulders. "What awaits me in this place?" She whispered into the near darkness. *How will I survive? What sinister plan does the dark merchant have in mind for me? Am I to disappear into a gynakeon, never to have my verses heard?*

Her mind protested the thought of becoming unknown. Lost ambitions taunted her. *We were to be famous together. Alkaios, if you live, how will you find me?* She flinched when someone called to her from beyond the cabin door.

"Psappha," Kerkolos called again.

Thinking he needed something from the cabin, Psappha threw on an extra robe and opened the door.

Kerkolos gave no indication of wanting to enter. Instead, he shifted slightly on his bandy legs, took her into his massive arms and kissed her. Then, before she could decide whether to respond or not, he released her and left.

"What manner of man is this?" She grumbled at the walls as she closed the door. "How dare he march in here and kiss me as if I expected it?" With a startled gasp, she touched her fingers to her lips. "I did expect it," she whispered. *I wanted him to stay. Am I that afraid?*

Peggy Ullman Bell

[page deliberately left blank]

"I stand a wreck on Error's shore,
A specter not within the door,
A houseless shadow evermore,
An exile lingering here."
'Adah Isaacs Menken'

-- X --

Breakfast was late and when Lycos brought it, it was only cold barley-cakes and honey. Psappha took a nervous bite of honey-dripping cake then gathered what belongings she had into a small wooden box. There were only the few garments Lycos had sewn for her, an onyx-backed boar-bristle brush on loan from Kerkolos and a pair of carved ivory combs she had not seen before.

Lycos shook his head when she held them out to him. "No," he said. "They were never mine. I removed my cosmetics while you slept."

Wondering who had made her a gift of the delicate combs, she tucked the box under her arm took a last look around the cabin. It looked as it had when first she saw it, stark and masculine. No trace of her remained.

Oh, Lady, guard me in this new place she prayed as she stepped from the cabin and breathed deeply of crisp morning air. The familiar conglomeration of harbor smells filled her mind with pictures of Lesbos, but the city that sprawled before her was not Mitylene.

Sweetly-smiling Aphrodite, she prayed, *guard me in this foreign metropolis. Protect thou me, Oh Mother of Tenderness. I am so far from home.*

She saw Kerkolos coming toward her and hastily added. *If I must fill his bed, Sweet Lady, I pray thee fill my heart.*

Kerkolos paused near a group of seamen. Under his direction, they quickly untangled the ropes they had been struggling with and he continued along the dock.

"Lady Psappha," he said when he reached her, "you are welcome to the comforts of my home until you can return to your own."

"Your gynakeon, Kerkolos?"

"My gynakeon is already full, milady, and is presided over by my mother. She sent you this."

Psappha flinched internally when she followed his gesture toward a sedan chair, heavily draped in magenta velvet. She sniffed in distaste. Such mundane use of precious purple dye seemed the grossest form of ostentation. She thought she detected anger in the set of his shoulders as he turned and strode down the gangway without another word. She stomped her foot and would have flounced back into the cabin that was no longer hers but Lycos stopped her with a suspicious chuckle.

"All the comforts of the captain's home," he said with a hint of warning in his voice.

"His gynakeon you mean."

"A gynakeon is not a prison, Psappha, but it can be dangerous. Beware of the presenter of gifts," he added with a gesture toward the chair and its handsome bearers.

Psappha entered the deeply cushioned chair with a resigned sigh. *I wonder what Kerkolos' mother thinks about having two more women dumped on her without warning.* Lycos's vague warning crossed her mind but she dismissed it. *What danger could there be in a satin prison occupied only by women?*

The chair rocked upward. From behind its curtains, Psappha imagined Eurigios's home as her destination. Tears filled her eyes when she remembered it was not.

The chair tilted forward as the bearers started down the gangway. The purple draperies fluttered open and Psappha saw sights that bore no resemblance to her beloved Mitylene. Instead of cerulean twin harbors, a single greenish bay stretched to and under an immense bridge.

White buildings glared at her with a thousand black eyes. Most were larger than the citadel on old Mitylene. Row upon row of them on terraces that extended upward until the canopy on the chair blocked them from her view.

She scrunched the gap in the curtains as tightly closed as she could get it. *Oh, Beloved Lady, guard your frightened daughter in this vast metropolis. Protect me, Oh Mother of Tenderness. I am so far from home.*

Psappha was cold even with the curtains closed. She felt every sound as the bearers bore her through noisy streets and alleys. After what seemed like an interminable time surrounded and bombarded with shouts and petitions in a dozen languages, a thousand garbled dialects the racket stopped. The way became quiet. Every other turn led to a hill, and the swaying of the chair nearly lulled her to sleep before the bearers paused.

Hearing the sound of grating metal, Psappha stiffened, trembling as heavy gates clanged shut behind her. *Where is Lycos?* She wondered. *Where is Kerkolos?* It seemed hours since she had heard a familiar voice. Nervously, she shifted on the cushions and parted the drapes behind her. Only then did she realize there were two chairs. Gongyla lounged with curtains wide, grinning at Kerkolos. "A worthy prize to present your mother," she said.

Kerkolos nodded. "Aye. A prize well worth an off-season sail."

Psappha seethed. *A prize indeed.* She tried to get angry enough to squelch her fear. She didn't know whether to be relieved or peeved when he walked away without speaking to her. She let the curtain fall shut. *The Fates landed us here together. Why can't I enjoy the adventure of it, as she seems to, instead of wondering how they plan to torture me next?* She feared Kerkolos might choose to exercise his power over her by selling her, an idea that had not occurred to her till now. *Gongyla does not seem afraid. Perhaps I should not be.* She was not given long to ponder.

"Psappha," a woman commanded her attention. Psappha shifted to her other hip and drew the curtain aside. A warm smile rose to her face. The woman was enormous —the perfect image of The Lady -- Great Mother of all. Psappha stepped from the chair prepared to love this beautiful woman as she loved The Lady but all resemblance to The Goddess faded when the woman spoke.

"My son instructed me to make you welcome," the woman said through pinched, thin lips bordered by rouged lumps that grew with her artificial smile. She waved a bejeweled hand attached to a bangle-bedecked arm and the bearers hurried off. "Come, your quarters are ready." She turned and stomped toward the whitewashed stone house with no further word. Psappha stood forgotten, confused and terrified until Gongyla stepped forward and took her hand.

Their hostess paused before a pair of ornate bronze gates, which she unlocked with one of the keys almost hidden among the folds of fabric at her waist. Each clink of keys added to Psappha's impression that she was on Persephone's journey and that Hades waited at the end of the passage.

Gongyla bowed Psappha inside. Their hostess frowned at them over her shoulder then led them down a long warm corridor with closed doors along either side. At the end of the corridor, a tiny iron grille opened in the top of a heavily ornate cedar door. The woman whispered briefly before the door creaked open. A gush of near jungle heat chased the last of winter's chill away.

They entered a corridor lined with small sleeping cubicles. Each contained but a single soft, almost washed out color, no one quite like any others. *Thus might the girl's barracks in the House of the Labrys have looked before the Mycenaean invasion.* Psappha felt like a sacred heifer expecting sacrificial bulls to rage toward her at any moment.

The corridor opened upon one side of a large pavilion. Lush vines reached upward from marble planters to spread on trellises suspended from the ceiling, above them, a large clay pipe. Water gushed from the pipe to a pillar of rock over which it cascaded downward, drenching small clusters of scented herbs growing in the crags, tumbling from rock to rock then gurgling amongst a web of floating lotus in the six-sided pool at the center of the room.

Gongyla took one look then shed her clothes and shallow dove beneath the flowers. Moments later, she surfaced then skimmed through and under the water like a playful dolphin. Around her, on cushions placed to avoid splashing, women whispered in quiet pairs. Others stood near the great pillars that supported the roof. More sat on the edges of the marble planters.

Psappha knew it was impolite to stare, but she could not resist. The gynakeoni's complexions ranged from the bluish-white of skimmed milk to the warm, rich shine of polished teak. Each wore a different color. She recognized none of the pastels from the corridor. These more vibrant hues matched glimpses of curtains visible in three additional corridors that fanned from the hexagon pavilion. "There are so many," she whispered in awe.

"There were more when I came."

Psappha started. She had disremembered the woman at her side. "Forgive me. I know better than to stare like a pagan and ignore my hostess."

"It is expected," the woman sniffed. "Come."

Blushing with embarrassment, Psappha followed her hostess around the pool. A hint of smoke called her attention to unlit torches set in bronze sconces on walls and pillars. Sunlight streamed through a large arch directly opposite the corridor through which they'd entered. Kerkolos's mother led her past it to a curtain of amethystine beads that completed the sixth side of the vast pavilion. "My son insisted you be given this chamber. I hope you appreciate it. My husband had this built for me. Please don't blow your nose on the drapes."

The insult was so direct Psappha could not speak. Instead, she stepped quickly through the tinkling beads. The chamber beyond was even richer than she expected. The floor of the chamber consisted of crushed and bonded limestone, set with the priceless iridescent mollusk shells from which men obtained the precious purple dye. Shades of purple decorated the entire suite, from the translucent amethyst of the curtain beads to the faint lilac-pink of the thick silk drapes that bracketed the window arches. Violet tassels on heliotrope hangings accented the ebony bed, and, through an arched doorway opposite the beaded curtains, she could see a tiny garden, dead now except for a few wilting asters. Even so, the effect was sumptuous beyond a Sybarite's wildest dream, disgustingly alluringly ostentatious.

"It is truly lovely," Psappha said as meekly as she could. "Thank you."

"Thank my son. He kept the workers at it all night." Gold bracelets jangled as she swept the air with a bejeweled hand. "This is nothing. My son could afford better. He finds more purple mollusks in a season than his father did in a lifetime." A bit of drool at the corner of pursed lips and the blades in yellowish eyes made Psappha take a step backward, sure the woman was about to spit in her face. Nothing about the woman's holy resemblance to The Lady could prevent Psappha from detesting her.

"My son wished that you call me Adriana*." The look she gave Psappha said 'you do, and I'll bite off your nose'.

Then, like her exasperating son, she left the room without giving Psappha time for retort.

Moments later, Adriana came back dragging a wisp of a girl by the wrist. She thrust the child forward with enough force to send her sprawling. "This one will see to your comfort," she said, as Psappha dropped to her knees beside the child. "You'll have to break her in yourself. She's stupid and ugly and I don't have time to train her."

Won't take the time is more like it. Psappha brushed a wisp of hair from the child's forehead. The girl looked back through vibrant purple eyes set in dark, sunken circles. "She's not ugly. She's hungry."

---

* Adriana (AID–ree–ah–nah)

"Hardly," said Adriana sourly.

Psappha clasped the girl child's hand and was surprised to note that her own was smaller. "You've nothing to fear from me," she whispered. "It's I who am afraid. I've never been in a place like this before." The girl's enormous eyes widened, although Psappha had not thought they could. "You must help me get used to it." In a somewhat louder tone, she added, "My name is Psappha. What's yours?"

Adriana spoke before the child could answer for herself. "Her name is Lyneachia*." Psappha crimped her brow. "Lyn-nay-ah-KHEE-ah," Adriana impatiently pronounced. "See how well her eyes match my chamber."

Psappha shot her a questioning frown.

Adriana snorted. "A momentary lapse. The chamber is yours now as is this worthless one. A stowaway from one of my son's ships last season. He gave her to me knowing my love for the exotic. She's a shiftless piece, but she does go well with the new decor. If you don't want her, I suppose I can take her with me. My husband's brother is building a house in Sybaris. She can serve in the guest chambers when it's finished. I suppose she'll pass in the dark."

Angry past caution, Psappha glared up at her.

Adriana sniffed and gazed down the length of her nose. "Do you always kneel to slaves?"

Psappha got to her feet but held tight to Lyneachia's trembling hand, helping her to rise, warning with her eyes and a squeeze of her hand that she must not attempt to kneel in turn.

Adriana grunted her disapproval and decamped.

Psappha immediately sent Lyneachia to scout the kitchen. She returned with enough varieties of fresh baked bread to please The Lady, in all her thousand incarnations. Behind her, other servants brought trays heaped with winter vegetables and fruit. Still others offered dishes both hot and cold the likes of which Psappha had

---

*Lyneachia (Lyn-nay-ah-KHEE-ah)

never seen on such short notice. She quickly ate her fill of fine-textured bread and young collard leaves bathed in herbed vinegar and olive oil.

One thing is certain. In this, my new abode, I shan't lack for fine cuisine. She smiled as Lyneachia polished off much of the remaining food.

"Where did you come from?" she asked when they were again alone.

Lyneachia studied the floor and muttered, "I don't know."

"Where were you born?"

"In a gynakeon."

"But, Adriana said you were a stowaway."

Lyneachia brightened. "I was. I crawled out through a hole in the wall."

"What wall? Where were you?"

"I don't know. It was a bad place. They were going to sell me to a procurer. I heard the eunuchs talking. I ran away. Adriana was ready to do the same. You heard her. But it's all right now. Now I belong to you." She ran her fingers along Psappha's cheek. "I'm not afraid anymore. Not with you here."

Psappha wished she could feel as sure. She didn't like having so little control over her own fate or Lyneachia's.

"I'll do what I can for you but I won't own you."

"But you do own me." Lyneachia's purple eyes were full of fear. "If you reject me she'll put you out of these fine quarters and sell me for a porna's price."

"Don't worry," Psappha said with confidence she did not feel. "She answers to her son. You and I will be friends, Lyneachia, but no one will own you unless you want them to. Now tell me about the others. Are they also slaves?"

The child's thin face scrunched in a worried frown. "Not all but most. Are you going to free them too? They've no place to go."

"I can't free them," Psappha admitted with regret. "I lack the power. There are so many. How did they all get here?"

Lyneachia brightened. "Many belonged to the old lord, Lady Adriana's husband. He built his reputation on the number of beauties in his house. Milord Kerkolos brought the free women here, just like you, but all they got was a cubicle in the bright corridors."

"The bright corridors?"

"Oh yes." Lyneachia bounced onto the bed. "The light corridor, the one you came in through is for slaves only. The others, the ones with all the brightest colors belong to free women and girls here to be cared for and protected by Lord Kerkolos."

"Protected mostly from his mother I suspect." Psappha sat on the bed and hugged Lyneachia to her side. "If they're not slaves, why are they here? Why do they let themselves be locked away like this?"

"Why did you?"

"I had no choice," Psappha replied. When she realized she had answered her own question, she returned the child's impish smile, but her laugh was rueful. Tension gripped the muscles of her neck and shoulders.

"Lord Kerkolos is very kind," Lyneachia said. "Though he ignores us all once he's seen to our care."

"If he ignores you, why does he take in so many?"

"I've been told there are not as many as there were when his father was alive. I also heard his father did not ignore them."

Psappha gave her a conspiratorial wink. "But why does Lord Kerkolos collect so many?" she repeated.

"Because he's kind. There is much hunger and sadness in the world, milady. He accepted many in trade for food for their people. The new one, the one who came with you is a queen who gave herself to save her people, though she could have sent another in her place. Lord Kerkolos would not have minded."

Psappha felt a sharp pang at the thought of Gongyla being a slave. "I'm sure the Lady Adriana enjoys having a queen for a slave," she said, rubbing the back of her neck.

"The African is no slave. Lord Kerkolos would not allow it. Word flies fast among gynakeoni. Rumor has it Lady Adriana is sorely vexed because of it, but Lord Kerkolos is not the sort to enslave a queen," Lyneachia said as she led her new mistress to the tiled bath in a nook off the bedroom. "The African is much too proud. Like you," she added with a smile. Psappha frowned. *Pride and prison do not mix.*

Lyneachia clapped twice. Moments later, two serving women hurried into the chamber bearing amphorae of water, one hot, one not. Lyneachia sprinkled autumn jasmine into the tub. The fragrance of its petals rose with the steam. The closet filled with scent. She tested the temperature with her elbow before beckoning Psappha.

Psappha stepped into the bath. She gasped at the coldness of the water. Lyneachia dumped the contents of the second amphora over her head and she nearly cried out from the heat of it.

Lyneachia grinned broadly. "The priestesses of Iphis* will think you a tantalizing offering."

Her words meant nothing to Psappha. She listened to the gynakeoni through the beaded curtains. Their laughter mystified her, considering their situation. They clapped their hands in rhythm with a song. The music reminded her of a dancing golden girl-child and a wave of homesickness, apprehension and grief flowed through her, adding to her tension -- tension that gynakeon-born Lyneachia soon relieved with an educated talent Lycos could not have imagined. *The child has skills she chose to hide from Adriana.*

Psappha sighed and stretched belly-down on the lavender massage-table.

~ ~ ~

For the next several weeks, Psappha confined herself to her rooms and their adjacent garden, unready to give her being over to the prison she believed the gynakeon to be.

---

* Iphis (EEE-phis)

I am a poet, she protested. *When I die, my words must live after me.* The lack of lyre and tablet could not keep her from composing.

One predawn, disgruntled because the poem she attempted would not behave, she threw a pitcher at what she thought was a carpeted wall. The pitcher did not break. She watched, amazed as it slide safely to the floor. Belatedly curious, Psappha investigated and found a narrow flight of stairs behind several layers of heavy tapestry.

At the top of the hidden stairs, she found her own secluded section of roof. *I should have found this sooner. It's wonderful!* Dazzling houses crowned the slope above the house, looming over the pretentious dwellings of new wealth like disapproving parents.

Pipes joined the house above to this one, and then ran from Psappha's side of the roof to the next and to the next and so on down the landscaped terraces, making a continuous viaduct. The homes and estates of the current elite stood on either side of the house and on the next terrace below. Other women gathered on their roofs to share cool morning air.

Far below, riotous Syracuse lay splattered along the shore. Dawn's shadows dressed the hovels on the outskirts, almost creating beauty.

Helios soon covered the roof with a steamy glare. Moisture trickled from her brow, but she did not retreat. Instead, she loosed her hair and shook it to catch the wispy breeze.

Directly below, Lyneachia picked irises in a tiny courtyard. It was spring again and Psappha ached for her lost home with its sweeping lawns and fragrant, unbound orchards. She longed to run again on the glistening beaches of Mitylene. She heard a ripple of female laughter and felt a sharp pang of longing for her mother, gone now for almost a year. She ached for the gentle beauty of children dancing in The Lady's park. A fleeting vision of Atthis, suppressed before pain had time to rise.

The gurgling of the fountain in the gynakeon filled Psappha with an ache she could neither explain nor dissipate. She longed to join them but doing so would mean acceptance of circumstances she was not ready to embrace.

"Psappha."

Her hand jumped to her throat as she turned. Only one man could gain access to this roof.

"Must you always sneak up on me?" Even as she snapped at him, her mind chastised her. *Why must I always snarl at him? He's been nothing but kind.*

"Psappha," he said, melting her perplexity with a warming smile. "It is my wish that you become my wife."

Psappha studied him. He seemed calm and assured. There was no hint of teasing, no hint of desire, nothing in his cobalt eyes to remind her of Alkaios' gentle blue. She wrapped herself in the same affected poise she had used upon Alkaios' arrival home. That hadn't worked well. *But I'm older now.* Chin up and haughty, she eyed him up and down and said, "Did it occur to you to ask? No. I suppose not," she answered her own question, recalling his earlier words. 'When I decide what to do with you', he had said. Apparently, he had decided.

She turned her back on him. *Now why did I do that? He could kill me. No one would ever know.* She glanced warily over her shoulder. He was gone. She had not seen, nor heard, him go. She shivered in the warmth of a midday sun.

The scent of lilacs floated up to her as she crossed the roof toward the stairs leading down to the central garden. The enclosure below resounded in cheerful chatter. Kerkolos' garden, however beautiful, seemed but a walled-in flowerbed, the women strange and frightening, yet, in her loneliness, she felt drawn to the music of their gentle laughter. *He can't be all-bad. Listen to them. They're happy.*

Amid and above the incoherent chatter, she heard a voice that drew her down the three steps to a lower roof. Beyond and below, in the women's garden, tiny silver and gold fishes chased each other in a small shaded pool. Women and girls clustered around a huge arbor dripping with wisteria.

"There once was a young man of great cleverness," one of them prompted.

"Once, in his travels to Egypt, he stopped at an inn," said a low-voiced storyteller from deep within the arbor. Recognizing Gongyla's vibrant tone, Psappha strained to hear.

"The inn-keeper had a wife and two sons and two daughters. At dinner, they brought five pigeons to the young guest to serve. He gave the innkeeper and his wife one bird. To the sons he served one bird, also to the daughters. To himself he served two birds and ate with relish.

"The innkeeper was surprised but, when they brought in a fat fowl, he again asked his guest to cut and serve, as the rules of hospitality demand. The guest served the head of the fowl to the innkeeper and his wife. To each son he served a leg, and to each daughter, a wing. The rest he kept for himself."

"Why, Gongyla?" a musical voice cut in.

"That is what the inn-keeper wanted to know," the storyteller continued, "so, he asked the young man, just as you have asked me, and the young man told him, 'I have done the best I could to be fair.

"You and your wife and one pigeon make three, as do two sons and a pigeon, and a pigeon and two daughters. Three, also, are two pigeons and I. As to the fowl, the reason is simple. You and your wife are the heads of your family and as such should have the head. Your sons support the family so, of course, they should have the legs. To your daughters, I served the wings since they will soon marry and fly away from your home. The body resembles a ship so I kept it for myself since it was on a ship that I came here and on a ship that I hope to return.'"

Psappha giggled. A bevy of faces turned upward. The dark-haired storyteller leaned from the arbor and called, "Did you enjoy my story?"

"A most clever young man," Psappha called, and then drew back, cursing The Fates for their twisting of her life. The women sounded happy. She knew she would enjoy their company if given a choice, but no one had given her a choice, and that galled her. She was afraid that, if she allowed the women entry to her heart she would never escape to sing the praises of The Lady for the world to hear.

Nevertheless, she edged toward the stairs leading to their garden. Each step downward seemed a step toward oblivion, but she kept going. As she approached the fishpond, the women and girls scampered into the pavilion. She regretted their going but she understood. By assigning her the purple chamber, Kerkolos had set her apart, and she compounded it by hiding there.

The lilacs smelled sweeter when she neared them. *At least I have the bees for company.*

Gongyla sat deep within the wisteria-shrouded arbor, her head thrust slightly forward on her swan-like neck. "Did you think I would not wait for you?"

Psappha said nothing.

Gongyla's hair lay close to her scalp like sheared black fleece. Her face inscrutable, perfect, as if chiseled by a master's hand. "Come," she invited, patting the bench beside her. "Sit with me."

"Do you wish to return to your home on a ship like the young man in your story?" Psappha ventured shyly.

"You are not of the gynakeon, Psappha, or you would have no need to question. You have kept to yourself so far, but you have months ahead with only memories to sustain you. One day, loneliness will bring you to the Sisterhood and we will gladly welcome you into the Temple of Iphis."

The name sounded only vaguely familiar until she remembered Lyneachia's use of it. "Who is Iphis?" she asked. She had not been curious before. "And, where is this temple?"

"Iphis rules the gynakia where no man, not even a god, may enter."

"You confuse me. No one can keep Kerkolos from the gynakeon, not even a goddess. He owns it, just as he would like to own me. Explain yourself!"

"No, Psappha. You will come to know Iphis when you are ready to know the gynakeon."

"By Aphrodite's eyes, I know the gynakeon. I've seen it all. It squats like a fat toad waiting to devour me."

Gongyla's soft jungle eyes offered comfort, driving chinks in the armor Psappha had wrapped around her heart. "Your temper spoils the beauty of your eyes, Psappha. You have seen Lord Kerkolos' gynakeon, that's true, but you have closed your Self away from its spirit. I've watched you when you thought yourself alone. I've heard you, too. Your soul cries through your music. Eventually, you will come to us. I hear it in your songs."

Psappha slumped. She tried not to cry, but Gongyla's arm felt warm around her shoulders. "What would you have me do?"

"I want nothing from you, Psappha, only that you open to what life brings. When you want to know the gynakeoni, you will come to us. Only then can you be initiated into the rites of Iphis."

Gongyla's tender, black eyes promised comfort, but Psappha refused it. "Life in a gynakeon is a luxurious trap, a bright hole that brings obscurity. You may be content to use your stories for the entertainment of imprisoned women, but I am Psappha of Lesbos and I <u>will</u> be remembered."

[page deliberately left blank]

> *"It [marriage] happens as with cages:*
> *the birds without despair to get in,*
> *and those within despair to get out."*
> *'Michel de Montaigne'*

-- XI --

"Who is Iphis?" Psappha asked when Lyneachia brought their dinner.

Lyneachia set down her tray. "Iphis is not for you."

"What?"

The girl straightened slowly then repeated, "Iphis is not for you."

"Why not? You were the first to mention her."

"That was a mistake. I've since learned that Lord Kerkolos has other plans for you."

"To Hades with his plans. Who is Iphis?"

Lyneachia's enormous eyes filled with tears.

"Oh, stop that! Nobody's going to hurt you if I can help it," she said, knowing she was powerless even to protect herself. Whatever the dark merchant's plans, Pittakos had left her no choice but to acquiesce - eventually. Taking a deep, calming breath, she said, "Tell me."

Lyneachia settled, cross-legged, onto the Persian carpet. "All right," her lower lip trembled, "I'll tell you. But you have to promise never to tell anyone how you know."

"I promise," said Psappha as she settled beside her. "Tell me.

"Iphis lived long, long ago," Lyneachia began in a hushed and nervous tone.

"It is said that, before Iphis was born, her father extracted a hateful promise from her mother," Lyneachia whispered, her gaze darting to the beaded curtain that separated the chamber from the gynakeon. "Iphis' father made her mother vow that, if the child she carried was born female, it would be left in Zeus' cave to die. But, when the time came, his wife could not bring herself to kill their daughter.

"Instead, she swaddled the girl-child and told her husband he had a son. When he presented the infant to the gods, he named her Iphis…"

"And?" Psappha prompted.

"And, his wife felt great relief. By giving the child a name that has no gender, there was less chance of offending the many gods.

"The girl-child, Iphis, grew into a very beautiful boy. Or, so her father thought," Lyneachia said with a merry twinkle in her eyes.

"At the proper time, her father announced that his son, Iphis, was now adult and that the beautiful Ianthe* was to be his bride."

At this point, Lyneachia forgot she was supposed to be quiet. Her voice became stronger as she continued. "Iphis and Ianthe were much together, as befits a betrothed couple -- and it was not long before Iphis fell hopelessly in love.

"Iphis and her mother did not know what to do. If they told the father the truth, the mother would surely die. If they did not, they both feared Ianthe's reaction on the wedding night."

"So? What happened?"

"It is said that, on the eve of the wedding, Iphis' and her mother went to the Temple of Io to pray. It is said the mother prayed for forgiveness, while Iphis prayed to be released, either from her masquerade or from her burning passion for Ianthe. But, in truth, Iphis prayed hardest to be allowed both."

"And?" Psappha prompted.

"And . . . after a time, Iphis and her mother left the temple. As

---

* Ianthe (EE-an-thay)

they walked away from the altar, Iphis grew stalwart and handsome. Some say that, to this day, there is always a gift at the Temple of Io from the youth, Iphis, who came to the altar a beautiful woman and walked away a proud young bridegroom."

Psappha sighed, finding it hard to imagine a love strong enough to make the gods pay heed. "But, if Io transformed Iphis into a man, why do you and the African speak of him as female? And, why did Gongyla call Iphis a goddess if she was mortal? Does she still live?"

Lyneachia cast a cautious glance behind her. "Please, milady, no more questions. Let the gynakeon keep its secrets. Lord Kerkolos has special plans for you." That last was softer than a whisper, as the child scrambled to her feet and hurried through the beaded curtains.

Psappha could hear talking and laughter, but she could not bring herself to follow. Homesickness nibbled at her. Loneliness ate her spirit. Lyneachia's story had reminded her of both Alkaios and Atthis. An inferno of feeling smoldered in her veins. No amount of pillows over her head could shut out the happy chatter of the women beyond the beaded curtains.

When at last she drifted from sheer exhaustion into sleep, she tossed and turned, tormented with sensuous dreams. Fire, incompletely formed and banked too long, flared and raged unchecked. In her dream, Psappha saw Ianthe. No, not Ianthe -- Atthis -- golden, flawless Atthis, dancing -- swaying -- tantalizing -- forever unreachable. The dream changed and she saw Kerkolos -- dark, stern, ugly, beautiful face -- his deep, haunting eyes -- shining halo of ebony waves. She felt Alkaios -- Olympian body molded for her touch. Her heart saw Atthis' steps quicken. Her mind heard Kerkolos' heart keeping the beat. The fantasy brought his face close to hers. She awoke naked in her own sweat.

Get up! Your stubbornness is a tighter prison than the gynakeon could ever be. Get up, and share the cool refreshment of the pool.

She slipped into a robe then pushed through the beaded archway. Surrounded by painful silence, she dropped her robe at the edge of the pool and stepped into the fragrant water.

Lyneachia popped up in front of her, kissed her then disappeared beneath the lotus leaves. By her impulse, the child evoked a flood of memories. Psappha's mind transformed the pool into the placid Bay of Mitylene. The women became her beloved companions. Her homesickness floated away in the midst of their splashing play. They passed her merrily from one to another as if she were a water ball, swimming in circles around her, kissing her as they passed. They formed a ring and gestured for her to swim by them.

Psappha swam in ever-widening circles hoping to see The African but she was not among the women who let their hands flow along her back as she skimmed by. There were more of them with each pass and still Gongyla was not there. Eventually, women rimmed the entire pool, caressing her beneath the water.

To tired to swim, but unwilling to leave, Psappha walked around the circle, pausing to kiss each woman and girl lightly on the cheek. They were not all beautiful, although some were amazingly so.

"I'm so glad you're here," Lyneachia said when Psappha returned to her starting point.

"Do you wish to join the Sisterhood of Iphis?" asked one of the elders.

Judging by her welcome into the pool, Psappha guessed the nature of the sisterhood, and it went against everything she had been trained to expect in her life, although she was not sure why. The men had their cupbearers, but they were young boys in need of a mentor; they grew out of it. Most of them, she reminded herself, thinking of Lycos.

"I don't know," she said.

"Perhaps it is too soon?"

Psappha looked up to see Gongyla standing nearby, nude, arms folded beneath her breasts, long, strong legs set straight and tall. "Perhaps," she whispered, her voice stolen by the magnificence of a queen.

Gongyla nodded to Lyneachia, who got out of the pool, picked up the robe Psappha had dropped and held it for her, giving Psappha no choice but to leave the pool, don her robe, and return to her lonely chambers.

~ ~ ~

Laughter filtered through the beaded curtain day and night. The fragrance of lotus wafted through from the scented pool, but none of this had any effect upon Psappha. She had attempted to join the women. Gongyla had sent her back.

One warm evening, she sat before her mirror, studying her reflection, her mind awash with discontent. "I look like a peeled olive," she grumbled at her reflection.

"I like olives," someone said.

Psappha's hand jumped to her throat. In the glass, she saw the purple wall-hanging move.

Kerkolos untangled himself from the tapestry and said, "I'll be glad when we can take this down."

"Why wasn't I given a key to the door back there?"

"You have the key whenever you chose to use it," he said. "The door leads to my chambers."

So that's why Adrianna was so unpleasant. She knew his plans from the beginning, but why wouldn't she? She said these had been her quarters. Oh, Hera help me, why didn't I make the connection?

To make matters worse, Kerkolos confirmed it. "You were given adjacent quarters because I intend to make you my wife."

"You intend, do you? And, of course your intentions are to be obeyed."

"My dear lady, I am paying you a compliment." His tone reminded her of Pittakos. "Will you marry me?"

"You're more than a little late with the question. What will you do if I say no, put me up for sale?"

"You're not a slave, Psappha."

"Women are all slaves here, are they not?"

She studied his reflection in the glass. He stood with his bandy legs planted as if on a rolling deck. His sinewy arms folded over his massive chest.

"Will you marry me?"

In the glass, she saw desire flare in his eyes as she brushed her hair. "If you want me, I can't stop you," she said. "As for marriage …" She turned to face him. All trace of emotion vanished from his eyes. His expression seemed cold, empty, his attitude haughty, disapproving and an echo of his mother.

"Will you marry me?"

"No."

His eyes flared again, burning into hers. *Like volcanoes of indigo flame.* "You will be mine," he said with the mocking arrogance that she found so infernally aggravating. Then, he picked her up and marched through the doorway behind the tapestry then dumped her onto a huge mahogany bed. "You will be mine."

Psappha rolled over, jumped up and scooted past him, to and through the gaping doorway, slamming the door behind her. "In a pig's eye, I will."

~ ~ ~

Weeks passed with no further exchange between them. Psappha avoided the women more completely than before. It embarrassed her that they had all known his intentions. It perturbed her that no one had told her.

In the evenings, she heard their laughter and imagined Kerkolos enjoying their charms. *Not that I care, but he did propose.* She wished she had not rejected him so rudely. *What will the bandy-legged oarsman who turned out to be richer than Croesus do with me now?*

"Oh, maidenhood, maidenhood," she sang softly to herself. "Where have you flown from me? Where are your sweet, cool dreams – your innocent nights of restful sleep?"

Kerkolos could take me any time he chose. It's all Pittakos' fault. Left alone, Alkaios and I would have been safely married now – at home in Mitylene -- where we belong.

Her mind filled with memories of Alkaios and squandered innocence. *I seduced him so why am I suddenly so shy?*

Oh, Lady, help me, I prayed. Make him quiet the aching loneliness the

Fates have caused me. So who's to quiet that loneliness now?

Find yourself another bridegroom, he said, but I don't want another bridegroom. I don't want any bridegroom. Not if it means I must be silent.

The Lady's Maidens own themselves. I told him that, but is it still true? Do I still own my self in this place, this prison of purple beads and flowers?

Nevermore will you come to me, maidenhood nevermore will you come.

~ ~ ~

"Does my mistress wish me to send a message to my master," Lyneachia asked first thing the following morning.

"Send a message? Where is he? Has he left Syracuse?" Psappha was surprised at the sinking feeling the thought invoked.

"No mistress. My master is aboard his ship in the harbor. He thought you might be more comfortable with him out of the house, but he has not yet left port."

"Is he so busy that he has no time to visit his mother?"

"The Lady Adriana is not here, mistress. She too is aboard Lord Kerkolos's ship awaiting her removal to Sybaris where she will reside with milord's uncle." The nostrils of her small nose had flared, expressing her opinion of Sybarites in general and Lady Adriana in particular.

Psappha seethed. "So that's it. His offer of marriage was nothing but a way of meeting the demands of society."

"No mistress."

Psappha winced. She had not intended to think aloud. Lyneachia's soft denial intruded on her private thoughts. *I want it to be more than that,* her rebellious mind demanded. *Aphrodite, thou cruel and vicious harlot, you allowed Alkaios to be snatched from me by thy scaly sisters-of-the-deep and now you would present me to a man who wants me because he can't think of anything else to do with me. Do you intend to force me to give myself to Athena? If that is thy plan, thou jealous bitch, I shall not let you fulfill it.*

"Lyneachia send word to your master that Psappha of Lesbos bids his attendance at once." Lyneachia smiled but did not move. "Well? Go on. What are you waiting for?"

"What you said before..."

"What that I said before? I said a lot of things." *Most of which were irrelevant.*

"What you said about marrying my master..."

"I didn't say I would marry your master. I merely guessed why he had asked me, but I thought I spoke only to myself."

"You spoke to yourself, mistress. I'll never say anything but..."

"But what, child? Are you still afraid of me?"

"No mistress." Lyneachia grinned. "It would be easier to be afraid of a kitten."

"Kittens sometimes scratch." Psappha forced her voice into its smoothest tone. "What are you trying to tell me?"

"What you said about society. You're wrong. Maybe on Lesbos you could have been right, but not in Syracuse. Syracuse doesn't care how a man takes care of his women, Syracuse cares only that he does. Even if that were not so, Lord Kerkolos would not be led by society's demands."

"How do you know? You're merely a slave."

"In Syracuse, slaves are freer than their mistresses, milady. Much is said in front of slaves that would not be said in the presence of friends, or even servants. Slaves are not always confined to gynakia. There is a slave on the ship who tells me things when I go to the market."

"What has your friend told you of Kerkolos? What manner of man is he in his world of men?"

"He is as you see him."

"As I see him? I see him as an illusion that appears and disappears when least expected."

"And, in your dreams, milady, how do you see him then?"

Psappha blushed. Lyneachia nodded.

"It is as I said, milady. Kerkolos is as you see him. He doesn't have to marry you, but he does have to take care of you and since he wants you the best way for him to do that is through marriage."

"He has more than enough women."

"He isn't like his father, Psappha. He hasn't touched or been touched by any of the women since he reached full manhood."

No wonder they worship Iphis. "I've heard him among them at night."

"You couldn't have. He's been here only long enough to speak with you then leave. Should I take your message now?"

"Tell me the way out and I'll deliver it myself."

"You can't do that." Lyneachia trembled. "It would dishonor the master if anyone saw you on the street. He would be very angry."

"He can get as angry as he likes. What more can he do to me?"

"Nothing," Lyneachia said. "But, he could return me to his mother and she'd beat me. She likes that."

Horror chased disappointment from Psappha's mind. *How could I let the thought of temporary freedom rob me of good sense? They can do as they wished with me but I won't be the cause of harm to Lyneachia.* "You go, Child. Tell him I wish to speak with him."

~ ~ ~

Psappha primped, paced and prepared. It seemed hours before what she saw in her mirror became vaguely satisfying. She looked less dark in the red-violet kiton she'd chosen. Through its diaphanous folds, her nude body hinted of gold. The amethysts on her girdle matched her eyes. Her Phoenician glass necklace caught their color and multiplied it. Still she was not pleased. "Why couldn't I have been born all pink and gold?" she argued with what the mirror showed her. "Why couldn't I be glorious like my mother or the girl-child Atthis instead of looking like a throwback to some Minoan warrior's romp in a field?"

"Even so fine a glass as the one before you now can't show you how beautiful you are."

She didn't turn. He had come through the hidden doors and stopped just inside the drapes behind her. She saw him clearly in her mirror. "I didn't expect you so quickly, Kerkolos."

"I came as soon as I received your summons. Is there something you need? Would you prefer other quarters? Your girl tells me you have stayed apart from the women. That you bathe while they are in the garden and only go to the garden when you can be there alone. You have joined them only once and she fears you have been lonely."

Psappha adjusted the crocuses in her hair. "I need nothing," she retorted haughtily. *Great Artemis's anger, why do I keep doing that? He owns my future whether they call me slave or free.* She modulated her voice and continued softly. "I have been quite comfortable, thank you, milord. I merely wished to inquire if there is anything I can do in return for your hospitality."

"You can become my wife."

Is he serious? Of course he's serious, but why? Does he love me? She could not be sure. He looked like a statue. However, as she continued to study his reflection in the glass, the arrogance with which he always wrapped himself seemed to relax. The ice in his eyes melted, turning to amber fire. *He wants me!* It flared from his eyes as he watched her, supposedly unseen. She turned.

His expression shifted, becoming unreadable marble. "You have not answered my question, milady. Will you marry me?"

Psappha studied his face intently, her thoughts racing. *He wants me. Why won't he say so?* She needed some sign, any sign she could interpret as a declaration. She could not bring herself to accept him without one. Even if what Lyneachia said was true and society did not care, she cared. *He wants me. If he declares it, I will accept him.* "I can't answer you," she said. "If I answered you now, I'd have to say no again. There's nothing between us to build a marriage on."

Kerkolos loomed over her like a thunderous cloud. When he spoke, his voice throbbed with checked emotion. His eyes burned into hers. "You will be mine," he said.

As he stalked from the chamber, Psappha's soul cried. She felt the trap grow tight around her and she knew of no way out.

~ ~ ~

Adriana flounced into the purple chamber less than an hour later, startling Psappha and causing Lyneachia to drop the sponge into Psappha's bath water.

"So," she growled without benefit of greeting. "You dare refuse my son."

"I didn't refuse him," Psappha said as she slid beneath the bubbles. "I merely refused to answer him."

"It's the same thing," Adriana declared. "I don't want you here," she hissed. "This was all red while my husband lived," she said with a wave of her arm. "I knew my son's intentions the instant he ordered the color changed. I didn't want him to marry -- Ever! But, I will not allow an ignorant, uninitiated chit from nowhere insult his generosity. You will accept him, graceless one, or you will never enjoy another day."

Psappha shrank from her ire. Friendless in a foreign land, she depended on Kerkolos generosity for survival. Mitylene was lost to her forever. Nevertheless, she did not wish to marry a man she did not love. Even if love between husbands and wives was considered unlikely and unnecessary, she had loved Alkaios. *I still love him. It's as Gongyla said. I'm alive so there's no reason to think he's not also. He has to be alive. I love him!*

You wanted him, her thoughts taunted her. *Love or want. It is the same. That doesn't matter now*, she decided, chaffing at her own thoughts, realizing that her justifications applied to Kerkolos as well. She sighed.

Adriana mistook Psappha's sigh for acquiescence. "So," she sniffed in triumph, "you will accept the high honor my son wishes to bestow upon you." She obviously considered her victory complete when Psappha nodded. "Very well," she said, "I will inform him his foolishness will not go unrewarded."

Before she left, she turned and leveled an evil glare. "After the ceremony, as is customary, I will leave this house to you. You will be mistress here -- while my son lives."

[page deliberately left blank]

> "*A thousand hearts beat happily; and when*
> *Music arose with its voluptuous swell,*
> *Soft eyes looked love to eyes which spake again,*
> *And all went merry as a marriage bell.*"
> 'Lord Byron'

-- XII --

Lycos marched through the hidden doors, destroying the pre-dawn quiet: In his wake, a score of burdened servants in close-order.

"Wake up. Wake up, you lazy girl. It is your wedding day."

Psappha groaned and rolled over, nuzzling her pillows, trying not to hear his cheery voice or Lyneachia's outrage.

"How'd you get in here, you preposterous little man? You are a man, aren't you?"

"Of course I'm a man and you needn't bar the way so futilely little girl. I've no interest in gynakeoni. I'm here to prepare Psappha for her wedding. Now be a nice little girl and I might let you help."

He nudged Psappha. "Everything is ready but you, lazy one."

I'll never be ready. Oh, 'Kios why couldn't we have stayed silent? But then -- if we had -- I'd be marrying you -- wouldn't I? Marriage is a deeper prison than these abysmal Syracusian gynakia. I just want to go home.

When Psappha did not appear to respond, Lycos yanked her covers off. "Up, up! There's no time to waste." He pulled her to her feet, waved Lyneachia away, stripped Psappha of her nightdress and marched her to and through the beaded curtains, into the central pavilion.

The gynakeoni clustered around her, pouring warm, scented oil from ornate carafes onto her breasts, her shoulders and her back as they hustled her toward the pool with Lycos hovering close rattling off wedding plans. "I've arranged everything. Since you have no family here, this house will substitute for your father's house until after the wedding. Kerkolos is aboard ship. The wedding guests will escort him here for the feast.

"Adriana will remain here long enough for you to settle into your new duties. Then she will give you her keys and leave to take up permanent residence in the home of her brother-in- law, Lord Kerkolos' uncle. You'll see. It'll all work out just fine." He loosed a satisfied sigh as Lyneachia scraped the oil off with an olivewood strigil then shed her own garments as she led Psappha into the water. Gongyla was conspicuously absent.

Psappha's thoughts whirled too fast for her to catch them. The languor she usually felt when she bathed was not forthcoming. Tension ruled. *I must endure -- but how?* The answer did not come. She stepped from the pool exhausted, not invigorated. She drooped as Lycos wrapped her in virgin fleece and hustled her back to the purple chamber where he dressed her in a whisper of pale rose silk. Over that, he draped translucent veiling the color of an April sky. The layers fluttered in a fantasy of lilac as he conducted her to a three-legged stool that had not been there the day before. *This is all wrong. Oh, Kios, where are you?*

Nerves already strained zinged in protest as Lycos fussed with her hair. She ached to snatch the brush from his hands. Instead, she twitched on the small stool and endured. Lycos stroked her arm. "Hold still a little longer, Adelphi. I've nearly finished." Psappha sighed and leaned her shoulder against his thigh but she did not relax. She couldn't; not while he worked on her hair. "Behold," he commanded long minutes later.

Psappha fingers tingled as she took the proffered glass. *What can even Lycos' mastery do for me? I will not look.* She returned the mirror.

Lycos shrugged and waved an arm toward Lyneachia. "You -- there – girl, where are milady's sandals?"

"Right where you kicked them, milord jackal. You've lost them in all your fussing. I should have taken care of my mistress myself. See how you've tired her, charlatan."

Lycos sniffed disdain. "You'd have had her painted like an oriental vase. She is the bride of Kerkolos of Andros. She must outshine all the beauties of Syracuse."

"How can she outshine anyone, thou dullard? You've done her up plain as an empty temple."

"That's what you think, you impudent snit. Psappha needs neither paint nor jewelry. She's beautiful as she is."

"Have mercy, you two. You're giving me a headache."

Lyneachia grumbled. "Forgive me, milady. It's not me giving you a headache. It's milord prissy's braids. I could've told him weaving all that horsehair in would make them too tight."

Lycos bowed his head, lower lip protruding. "I did the best I could with stubble," he said, referring to Psappha's shoulder-length hair.

Psappha sighed. The last thing she wanted to think about was her mother and the little brother she'd never see again. "Behave," she said. "Let's get on with it."

Lycos resumed his normal foxy grin as he led her past the tapestries into the teak and mahogany chamber where he took her by the shoulders and spun her toward Kerkolos's floor to ceiling Phoenician glass. "Look!" Psappha looked away. He shook her.

Lyneachia attacked him from behind and Lycos shrieked in protest. "Yiiee! Let go!" Small hands stayed locked on his russet curls. He loosed Psappha to reach back to rid himself of the banshee in his hair.

Psappha wrapped her arms around Lyneachia's waist and pulled. "Stop it! Let go! Step away. He means me no harm. He thinks he's talented enough to create beauty where none exists. Settle down. Both of you and I'll look: Just for the sake of quiet."

Mirrors cannot lie. This one did. He had braided thick fawn-copper strands into her hair to create a high coronet that acted as a dry vase for a cluster of violets. Other than the flowers, her only ornaments were her enormous amethyst eyes. The effect was not at all displeasing but Psappha remained unconvinced.

~ ~ ~

Adriana met them in Kerkolos's private courtyard, her bulk encased in brocade, her keys half-hidden in the folds that overlapped her waist. The moment her eyes met Psappha's she turned her back and preceded them into the public areas of the house.

Psappha's head reeled. The great hall threatened to explode around her. *All of Syracuse is here.* People peered at her as if she was a gem presented for appraisal. Some squinted as if they had forgotten their jeweler's lens.

She looked into Kerkolos's eyes and saw Poseidon's Ocean waiting to drown her. She posed at his side while her spirit ran like a trapped deer. The vintage Chianti in the marriage cup tasted of bitterness, but she sipped it anyway.

Servants placed one marvelous dish after another before them. They all tasted like wadded papyrus to Psappha's nervous palate. Hyacinths, piled in huge mounds on all the tables, smelled like spoiled celery. Just when she dared hope for prompt release from her public misery, a parade of servants entered bearing a burnished platter resplendent with the traditional peacock of Hera, roasted full feathered and surrounded by fresh, ripe fruit. Psappha pretended to pick up something from the floor when instead she deposited her wedding supper there.

When, at last, the ceremonies ended, the newly wedded couple sat together and endured the ribald teasing of the guests, a universal torture in which Adriana took particular delight. Psappha hid her face against Kerkolos' shoulder, weak with embarrassment. To her immeasurable relief, he carried her from the hall amid a riotous chorus of cheers and coarse jests. She kept her face hidden until the doors of banquet hall swung shut behind them.

Kerkolos stood her on her feet in the main corridor, which she had not seen since the day she arrived. Lycos draped an embroidered violet robe around her shoulders. Psappha raised the hood, keeping her thoughts to herself.

Kerkolos whisked her from the house and down the many terraces to the docks. Her hood fell away as he carried her into the cabin that had been hers for a little while. He had covered the wide berth in white satin and fur. The traditional quince, supposed, when shared by the bridal couple, to insure sweetness of speech, waited in vain on the bedside table, ignored in favor of richer fruits.

He did not speak, nor did she want him to as he loosed the flowers from her hair and combed his fingers through her braids. Psappha sighed. The braids were indeed too tight. She desperately wanted to scratch her head. *It feels like the horsehair was full of fleas.* But she had no time to dwell on her discomfort.

Kerkolos removed the clasp at her waist and let her double kiton flutter off the tips of his calloused fingers to spread around her ankles in a froth of pink and blue.

The ship rocked against the wharf. She heard the wedding guests clamber aboard, singing and chanting ribald jokes beyond the cabin door. Kerkolos whispered something as he drew her closer to the fur draped bunk but all Psappha heard was Adriana's shouted suggestions. She remembered why they waited so noisily and she trembled. *Oh, Aphrodite, thou weaver of wiles, I've lost it. There will be no blood. He will surely cast me out, denouncing me as a porna.*

Kerkolos eased her onto the satin with a tender kiss. He entered her slowly then forcefully.

Psappha shrieked then loosed an exultant chuckle. *Oh, Eros, thou precious, you've mated me to a giant! He'll never know.*

Triumphant, she let Aphrodite's fires rage unchecked. Her limbs became liquid, serpentine, twining. Her small body arched to meet his every thrust; deep recesses of her being flexed, relaxed, reached and gripped. Her lips turned molten, fluid, expanding, devouring. Her luxuriating body trembled and throbbed in glorious celebration of Kerkolos -- son of Zeus -- Heracles – woman-bound – enslaved by a depth of passion she didn't feel.

~ ~ ~

Next morning, after a brief dreamless sleep, Psappha sat by a mahogany-framed, polished copper mirror absentmindedly brushing her hair wondering why she felt so detached from what had happened in the night. He had touched her in places and ways she had not imagined could lead to such ecstasy yet she felt nothing once her body cooled. She studied his reflection and knew she ought to feel blessed. He lay on his side facing away from her. She caressed the curve of his hip with her eyes and decided he was beautiful. Laying her brush aside, she spun toward him on the polished bench and winced. She'd forgotten he'd torn her. It was only a tiny tear, but it was enough. She smiled, remembering her bridegroom's triumphant grin when he tossed the stained sheet to the impatient wedding guests. In tenderness and pride, she went to where he lay and kissed the hollow where his hip blended with the muscles of his back.

He awoke and drew her to him; his voice was throaty and warm as he whispered in her ear. "I wish that spring could last forever."

Psappha snuggled closer, knowing that the end of spring would separate them.

Later, in the afterglow, as she rested in his arms, he said. "You've been too much alone. When next I sail, go again to the gynakeoni. This time all will welcome you."

"Why should your women welcome me? Especially now when I've taken you from them?"

Kerkolos laughed. "They're not my women and I wouldn't be surprised if they thanked you. I was never attentive to household needs until you came. I left all that to my Mother. Didn't she tell you?"

"If they're not your women, why are they here?"

"Oh, they're mine all right: Mine to feed, house and care for. Many belonged to my father."

"I heard he used them," Psappha said then covered her mouth in immediate regret.

Kerkolos cocked a brow at her then continued unabashed. "My mother arranged marriages for many of them since my father's death. They do well enough, considering the smallness of what dower she allowed them."

Psappha lowered her eyes. She refused to let him see how much his casual mention of dowries hurt her. *My father's house was to be my dower.*

"The rest are merchandise," he said. "No, no, water nymph. Don't look at me like that. I don't intend to sell them, much to my mother's horror. Most of them are from destitute kingdoms, traded to me for food and rough clothes. The queen you so admired traded herself when she could have traded others. I accepted, out of pity for her people. To refuse would have taken her pride. I couldn't do that. Overall, they're quite difficult to maintain although, pride be considered I'll admit that having the best of many tribes grace my house hasn't harmed my reputation: Quite the opposite in fact."

Psappha teased the crimped black mat on his chest. "Perhaps you sampled others in your travels."

"Who? Me? I'm innocent as a newborn babe."

"Don't try to fool me, thou leopard-fleeced wretch. Somebody taught you."

"Shall I show you more of what I learned?"

He lunged. She dodged. They fell, together in a merry heap. The braziers crackled, glowed, smoldered and went out.

~ ~ ~

Kerkolos expected his mother to teach her domestic management. *As if I'm some backwoods peasant with no training whatsoever. I'm an aristocrat, for Hera's sake. I know how to run a house.*

Nevertheless, the scope and confusion of Kerkolos's lifestyle had her questioning Lycos and Lyneachia from dawn 'til dusk. Adriana refused to teach. Under her auspices, Psappha became a showpiece for the entertainment of an endless stream of guests.

Conversations soon forgotten filled her evenings. Adriana typically excused her early to await Kerkolos's pleasure in their chamber.

On the day of the fleet's departure, she sat on the edge of the bed and folded her hands in her lap, palms upward watching Lycos helped Kerkolos pack already bulging sea-chests. "May I keep Lycos with me?"

Lycos glanced her way, shrugged and continued packing. Kerkolos came and drew her to her feet.

"I need Lycos with me. My mother is leaving."

Thank Gaia for that. She treats me like a glorified porna while teaching me nothing I need to know.

"Try not to think too harshly of her," he said as if privy to her private thoughts. "She was the fifty-seventh daughter of a Persian king, trained for nothing but opulence and self indulgence. Sybaris with its hedonistic style will be the perfect place for her. But you'll have the gynakeoni for company. You promised. Remember?"

"I'll keep that promise, but I want Lycos with me."

"Why?"

Psappha stared at their joined hands. "We're to have a visit from Hera," she whispered so that only he could hear. She felt his fingers tremble. He released her hands and tipped her chin with a single finger. She raised her eyes. He looked stunned. She wanted to giggle.

He went to his knees before her and laid his cheek against her waist. "A child? When?"

"After the leaves fall, I think."

"I'll tell my mother she must stay to look after you."

Psappha fought a wave of nausea unassociated with her condition. "Oh no! I'll be fine without her."

"Adriana has delayed her voyage much too long already," Lycos said.

Thank you, my friend. She smiled up at him when Kerkolos laid her, like an infant, on the great bed. "Your mother loves Sybaris and Lycos can teach me what I need to run the house."

Kerkolos covered a sigh with a grin. "I can't fight both of you. He can stay." Leaning over her, he held her palm against his cheek and said, "You must wait until I return."

Psappha laughed. "Hera waits for no man, you great black bear. She comes at her appointed time."

"She will wait for me."

Psappha ruffled his hair. "Of course, thou bear, since you decree it, so shall it be."

He bowed his head in mock repentance. She lifted his face between her palms and kissed his nose.

Peggy Ullman Bell

[page deliberately left blank]

> "On with the dance! Let joy be unconfined;
> No sleep 'till morn, when Youth and Pleasure meet
> To chase the glowing hours with flying feet."
>   'Lord Byron'

-- XIII --

Psappha had not expected to miss Adriana, but she did. When full management of the household fell to her, she quickly came to rely on the older servants. They trained Lyneachia and Lyneachia taught Psappha what she needed to know in order to establish a comfortable routine.

The feel of Kerkolos' hands seemed branded on her flesh. Daylight and dark, her body mocked her. She filled her days directing the servants in binges of unnecessary cleaning. At night, she tossed on the great bed with banked fires smoldering in her veins, a throbbing being with no one but herself to bring her quiet sleep.

Then came a night when nothing she could think or do brought even a modicum of peace. Muggy, stale air clogged the great bedroom and soaked her sheets with sweat. Rising, nude, she donned a loose, thin robe and returned over the roofs to the garden. The night air was fresh and fragrant. Torch-glow filtered through the curtained arches of the pavilion like a beacon in the fog of her mind. Walking slowly toward the light, her mind sang a new song.

Night, you bring all that Dawn has scattered, the sheep you bring, and the goat. You bring every child to its mother, and me you bring out of darkness into light.

A hush fell over the women when she entered. The effect was ethereal. It felt as if all the nymphs of Olympus had gathered to examine her.

Torches, blazing in their sconces on the pillars and walls, sent billows of smoke high into the vines overhead, pulling the heat with it and creating a pleasing draft when combined with air from the open arches.

Lyneachia stepped from between the islands of light.

"Have you come to the Temple of Iphis, Psappha?"

"Why are they all so quiet?"

"They are afraid," Lyneachia explained softly. "They do not understand why you have avoided them, or why you come here now."

"They have no reason to fear me. I am small and they are many."

Lyneachia chuckled then frowned. "That is not the sort of hurt they fear, Psappha. You are their mistress now. You could sell them."

"Why would I sell them? This was their home before it was mine."

"Lady Adriana wanted to sell them. Maybe they are afraid that you, too, would think them too expensive to keep since you have no need for them."

"It is for my husband to say if they are needed or not. I think, perhaps, their number increases his reputation in this city." She looked around.

The women looked back. Expectant faces reflected both curiosity and caution. There were not as many as Psappha had thought. She decided that many of those she had seen about the house had been servant wives. She did not see them here now. Nor did she see Gongyla. *Perhaps she went with Adriana.* Disappointment sank to the pit of her stomach and soured.

The water gurgling from the conduit high in the wall was the only sound until Lyneachia spoke again.

"Why are you here, Psappha?"

"I would know more of Iphis," she admitted timidly, made nervous by the silence.

"Have you come to join the Sisterhood of Iphis?"

"I have come to join the Sisterhood."

As suddenly as the gynakeon had stilled, it burst into sound, dozens of voices all at once in almost as many languages. Psappha hardly noticed when Lyneachia's deft hands peeled away her flimsy robe. The women chattered like all the ports of the world. Their voices battered her already frazzled nerves. Rather than waiting for someone to lead her, she dove beneath the surface of the pool, swimming in underwater circles until the ache in her lungs overruled her shyness.

She burst to the surface. Good-natured laughter greeted her sputtering. Abandoning her loneliness, Psappha joined their frolic. She swam in ever widening circles, thoroughly enjoying the game. On the third pass, Gongyla shot up from beneath the lotuses to entwine a blossom in her hair. Suddenly, and with little splashing they were left alone in the pool. *As if the flower was a prearranged signal.*

The Nubian's lithe form undulated through the water toward Psappha. Before she had time to react, Gongyla enfolded her in satiny arms, lingeringly kissed her and then released her as promptly as the kiss began.

Psappha stood wet and stunned as the dark beauty knifed beneath the water, surfaced a few feet away, smiled then rolled to and floated on her back, conical breasts and patrician nose pointing toward the greenery high above. Psappha almost reached her before she swam away.

Psappha followed, swimming strongly, but Gongyla continued to elude her. If she went underwater at one side of the pool, staying down until her air was gone, the lustrous Amazon was breathing calmly at the other. Finally exhausted, Psappha stood, breathless, near the waterfall. Gongyla propped her elbows on the opposite edge, sent droplets flying with a quick shake of her short, black curls, then winked and dove beneath the lotus yet again to surface inches in front of Psappha, her smooth, sinewy body glistening beneath a sheath of water.

"Melahrine,*" Psappha whispered in silent wonder, "Melahrine." At last, she understood the word. When Kerkolos had applied it to her and told her it meant darkly beautiful, she had scoffed and called him color-blind. "A dark woman cannot be beautiful," she had told him, thinking only of herself, forgetting the sight of Gongyla diving from the mast. Now, she remembered and the reality stole her breath.

Gongyla regarded her with wide, slightly tilted, almond shaped eyes. Her head graced her long, arched neck as if chiseled from flawless cedar by a master artisan. Her full, sensuous lips curled slightly in a hint of a smile. Her breasts, full and firm as pomegranates, rose and fell with her breathing, the nipples like mahogany inlaid on cinnamon. Lotus scented water dipped into a tiny navel set like a jewel in contoured, supple, oiled leather. There was no hint of Atthis here.

As if tired of Psappha's scrutiny, Gongyla crinkled her perfect nose, tilted her head in invitation and they swam together to the marble stairs where Psappha was lifted and carried, limp and dripping, from the pool to the purple chamber.

The women crowded in around them, giggling as the beautiful cousin of Pharaohs sat Psappha on her massage table and wrapped her in fleece. The women arranged themselves on the floor, their multicolored, diaphanous kitons spread around them. *Like a field of wildflowers.* Gongyla flashed a confident grin and a wink and the women rose as one and fluttered from sight. Then she ambled away, leaving Psappha bewildered, speechless and wanting, without being sure what it was she wanted. The vision of a muscled back and long, strong legs stayed in her mind long after Gongyla had gone.

---

* Melahrine (mel-ah-REEN)

She scarcely noticed Lyneachia brushing her hair dry. "I wish they would all trust me as Gongyla seemed to," she ventured as Lyneachia put the brush aside. Without urging, by long established habit, she shrugged off the fleece and reclined, face down, on the table, being careful to put no pressure on her slightly expanded womb.

"She is a queen," Lyneachia whispered, kneading scented oil into the tense muscles of Psappha's back, "A queen and fearless, but you can make the others trust you."

"In the name of Aphrodite, how?"

"In the name of Aphrodite."

Lyneachia forestalled further questions by bearing down on relaxing tendons, working the oils as if she wished to drive them into the bones themselves. Her hands eased only a little as she anointed Psappha's feet, rubbing the oils between toes that wriggled beneath her touch. The pressure of her busy hands became more insistent, almost painful.

"Tell me more about this Sisterhood of Iphis," Psappha implored as Lyneachia dug her fingers into firm young buttocks.

"The customs of Iphis are better learned than explained. Tradition forbids foreknowledge. I can tell you only that initiates of Iphis have no need to sing their nights away in loneliness. Will you allow the initiation?"

"I already said I would," Psappha mumbled sleepily. "Now, leave off the unnecessary digging."

Lyneachia's touch gentled instantly.

Psappha drifted into the nether world of erotic visions. She felt the hands plying the muscles in her calves, caressing the tingly hollows of her knees. There was an almost imperceptible moment of neglect and then the feeling changed.

Lyneachia's hands seemed larger somehow, the fingers' purpose more pronounced.

Tender, sense-evoking fingers whispered over her thighs, sending fiery messages to every follicle. Strong hands circled and shaped her buttocks, invoking sensations familiar yet subtly strange.

Psappha lifted her hips toward their arousing touch. As the gentle pressure spiraled toward her heels, she squirmed with delight. At the gentle urging of a playful twist on her right great toe, she rolled over in the darkness without rousing from her sensuous euphoria.

Disembodied hands began their journey from her ankles, massaging their way upward, finding and stimulating every erotic nerve they passed. Psappha reveled in the tongues of flame that radiated from the searching fingers; fingers that wandered over her taut and slightly rounded abdomen, tracing nerve lines to delicious delirium. Her own hands had never come close to arousing such wild sensation.

Maliciously long nails delicately teased her engorged breasts. Like serpent's tongues, they warmed and cooled the tender tips, then trailed slowly down the length of her arms. Oily fingers snaked around and between hers sending torrid shivers to her groin.

The moist touch of a flicking tongue on alert nipples added dimension to her dreams. Warm lips and cool tongue revisited all the places the fingers and the nails had found, blazing trails of breathy coolness on molten skin. She moaned and wriggled away from their delicious torment then writhed toward it again repeatedly.

Relentlessly, the persistent tongue invaded Aphrodite's most sacred temple, sending rivers of magma coursing through distended veins. The fever of veins erupted like lava from the mightiest of Poseidon's volcanoes, filling her brain with honeyed fire. The child in her womb stirred and stretched as wave after wave of aftershocks trembled through her body. *This is what The Lady Earth must have felt when She birthed the mountains.*

Slowly, ever so slowly, the lapping tongue eased away frustration's fire and led Psappha gently over diminishing canyons of desire, leading her tenderly from unsteady earth and lava pools to deep and dreamless sleep.

~ ~ ~

Psappha drifted awake, stretching languidly, enjoying the luxurious fluidity of her satiated body. Eighteen and what a birthday gift the night had been. She let her mind linger in the afterglow of sensuous dreams. *It was no dream!* She pushed herself up with her hands. *My mind can't imagine what it never learned. But, who?* The question rang cracked bells in her brain. The echoing bells were themselves echoed by the jangle of coins. Psappha worked her way into a sitting position.

Gongyla stood just inside the curtains clad in cinnamon-satin skin and a tiered collar of gold disks. A smile played at the corners of her lush mouth. Psappha stared in spite of all of Praxinoa's careful training. The woman was more glorious in the soft light of morning than she had appeared by torchlight or in the bright sunlight of a shipboard afternoon. *If she weren't smiling so broadly, she could be a carved and polished cedar statue of Artemis. She speaks.*

"And how does my lady feel this morning?" The husky, possessive tone of her voice evoked Psappha's dream, in vivid detail.

Psappha flushed apace with her racing pulse. The nudity in which she had luxuriated a moment before became an embarrassment of nakedness beneath the slow appraisal of dark jungle eyes. "You need not call me milady. I am Psappha."

Gongyla glided toward her, gazing at her through eyes so dark they seemed to have no iris. When she spoke again, Psappha could see the vibration of sound on the surface of her swan-like throat.

"You are my lady," Gongyla said.

Feeling near to drowning, Psappha sensed that, yes, for the moment at least, she was indeed Gongyla's lady. She felt protected and completely bedazzled. Her fingers reached like curious kittens. At the touch of heated flesh, they darted back to her lap. Unable to delve into jungle dark eyes, she focused on the bit of intricately carved bone that habitually protruded from Gongyla's hair. "I am to be initiated into the Sisterhood of Iphis," she bragged, proud that she had something to say which might interest an African queen.

Gongyla's deep chuckle warmed her. "I made thee a servant of Iphis last night, thou innocent and gentle-voiced monkey. Do you now wish to become her equal?"

Psappha's face flamed. She hung her head, remembering the dream that was not a dream. *To be the equal of Iphis? No, not here, not now. Not ever*, she realized, remembering that she could never return to Mitylene, to Atthis. *But to be Iphis' obedient servant . . .? Yes*, she thought, *judging from last night, being the servant of Iphis has advantages.*

Chagrined, yet intrigued as never before, Psappha wondered what it might be like to perform such delightful ministrations on radiant cinnamon-hued skin. Again, inquisitive fingers reached. This time, when they touched flesh, they hesitated but they did not withdraw. They walked over cinnamon-hued silk skin like gulls treading hot lava sand.

Gongyla did not move. She waited, her breath controlled, her eyes bemused, as Psappha's curious fingers strolled the sinews of her body. Her expression encouraged Psappha's exploration.

In her heart of hearts, she yearned for Atthis, but, in the here and now, she willingly accepted Gongyla as her sovereign.

"Gyla," she whispered as she slid from the massage table and stepped closer. Her nostrils flared to the scent of sweet musk as she ran her fingers over wing-tipped brows then down over wide, high cheekbones, across lips as soft as rose petals to stroke Gyla's long, sleek neck. Breathing more quickly, she drew the stoic warrior nearer with her lowered gaze.

Gongyla embraced her prize and laid her among the cushions on to the floor. Their bodies intertwined as they settled among the cushions. Their hungry spirits melded tighter with each shared caress. Hungry fingers found forage on each other's bodies, in pastures long familiar on their own.

Psappha's hands wandered Gyla's body, in echoes of touches on her own. The alien sameness evoked a tempest in her senses, emotions rampaged anew, matched, now, by another, becoming a

Sappho Sings

cyclone of sensation feeding upon itself until, at last, it was consumed and, like vine and tree, they slept.

[page deliberately left blank]

"Pleasure is nothing else but the intermission of pain."
John Seldon'

-- XIV --

Summer danced in splendor. Mornings were an unending frolic. There were long afternoons during which the elder gynakeoni showed Psappha from whom Kerkolos had learned the tricks he knew. Gongyla filled hot summer nights with lessons the gynakeoni had withheld.

In the evenings, while Psappha composed verses with her stylus, Lycos dozed and Gyla whittled. She kept her long-bladed skinning knife honed so sharp Psappha was sure she could have shaved the down from a day old gosling without causing a peep. Most evenings, she alternated between a Lydian style lyre for Psappha and a bow she wanted for herself, while teasing Lyneachia until she revealed her secret escape route.

After that, Psappha and Gongyla spent most afternoons exploring Syracuse hand in hand, ignoring Lycos's dire warnings of disaster. To hide her identity, Psappha dressed in Lyneachia's clothes before joining Gyla at the vine–hidden postern gate.

They found a treasure trove of Cretan relics in a tiny out-of-the-way shop. They returned to the gynakeon loaded with Ophidian statuettes and a large sacred labrys that gravely frustrated Gyla because it would not take an edge.

With the enthusiastic help of the gynakeoni, they dismantled one of the vacant cubicles and installed dozens of tiny snake priestesses surrounding the polished but unsharpened labrys. Behind the shrine,

Gongyla constructed a passage to the public rooms hidden even from friendly Lycos.

"Just in case," she said, but she never bothered to explain.

~ ~ ~

One morning, a week or two after the autumnal equinox, Psappha concealed her advanced pregnancy with a heavy cloak that also served as protection against a brisk wind. Only her servant's sandals showed as she and Gongyla slipped out for another try at finding a statuette of The Lady as Mother to grace their makeshift temple.

They returned at sunset, empty-handed, and found the little gate barred from the inside. Gongyla shooed Psappha into a recess in the wall. "Wait here," she whispered.

A thousand possibilities raced through Psappha's mind and none was welcome.

It seemed like hours later when Lycos came to fetch her. "Psst!"

"I'm here," Psappha whispered in a panic. *If Lycos is here, where's Gyla? Did the wind bring Kerkolos to port? What will he do? How will I keep him from punishing Gyla?*

Lycos offered no clues. "Put these on," he said, handing her a bundle of indoor clothes.

"Here?" *How can I change clothes here?*

"Yes, here," he said. "Unless you want to face your husband in servant's garb. He was furious when he couldn't find you. Lyneachia told him you went to see the Asklepian priests about your condition."

"I would never do that," Psappha protested. "Men know nothing of Hera's work."

"Argue theology later, Psappha. You barely have time to change. Kerkolos arrived at noon. We were all terrified until Gongyla scaled the wall and told us where you were. He must never know you went out, on foot no less."

"Change quickly, Psappha! I've got to hire a chair."

Psappha scrunched as far into the nook as she could; trembling without noticing the cold. She changed her dress beneath her cloak, struggling to control her fears. When Lycos returned, she stepped from the shadows into the seclusion of Adriana's old chair.

By the time the bearers set the chair down inside the main gate, Psappha had managed to control her breathing and compose her face. Lyneachia was pretending to assist a very weary expectant mother into the house when Kerkolos spotted them.

"You should not have left the compound," he growled. "What if you had been seen?"

"I wasn't."

"But you could have been." *He sounds too much like his mother.* "Give me your keys."

"I need the keys to manage the household."

"I've seen how you manage. Give me the keys. From now until I sail, I'll do the managing. After that, Lycos will carry the keys. I will not have you wandering Syracuse like a husbandless porna."

Psappha handed them over, feeling like a scolded child.

"Go to my quarters," Kerkolos ordered as if to magnify the effect.

When she reached the master's suite, she found the door to her purple chamber locked and bolted. *Thank The Lady he doesn't know Gyla was with me.*

Peggy Ullman Bell

[page deliberately left blank]

> *"There was the door to which I found no key.*
> *There was the Veil through which I might not see.*
> *Some little talk a while of me and Thee*
> *There was -- and then no more of*
> *thee and me."*
>
> *'Omar Khayyam'*

-- XV --

Two days later, it was as if Hera had indeed awaited the master's return. Psappha tossed in a stiff-backed birthing chair, straining against straps that cut into her wrists and ankles.

Kerkolos paced and growled. Late arriving Asklepian priests tiptoed past him. Lycos retreated as far as the doorway where he stood, a poised fox unsure of which way to pounce. The priests of Asklepios eyed him caustically. *They consider him an intruder. They're the intruders! Where are The Lady's Crones?*

Psappha screamed and sobbed. Visions of her last visit with her mother crowded her mind. Now, as then the smoke of torches, braziers and incense filled the room. *Eros, you lascivious bastard what have you gotten me into? -- Lady, Lady, -- Mother of All help me now in my hour of need. Let go, Poseidon! -- Misbegotten Eros, you traitor -- your aim was faulty. You mated a doe with a stallion and expect her to birth a horse.*

Her body stiffened with each spasm, arching, straining against her bonds, bashing her head against the unresisting birthing chair. Her hair hung in loose, limp tangles as she screamed as much in anger as in pain. *Oh heartless Fates, where are The Lady's Crones?*

After a while, the priests forgot to turn the hourglass. Instead, they clustered around her shaking their heads, stroking their beards, mumbling unintelligibly among themselves then shaking their collective heads again. Kerkolos slumped into a chair, his strength wilted into an ocean of helpless tears.

Psappha's scream cut the air and hung there, rising and falling with each contraction, never completely dying away.

Gongyla burst into the chamber, a minuscule loincloth her sole concession to the priests. With bared teeth, she shoved them aside like yapping puppies. When one grabbed her arm, he landed in a corner.

Psappha shrieked and arched again. With vision blurred and senses exhausted, she watched Gongyla stride toward the birthing chair. She felt the straps rip loose. She went limp as Gyla picked her and laid her on the great mahogany bed.

Psappha groaned as Gyla peeled the sweat-soaked gown from her pain-ravaged body. She sighed when her knees were pushed up to provide the Priestess a clearer view of the birth canal. *Blessed be The Lady, Cybele.*

Gongyla drew the carved bone ornament from her hair, held its thin sharp blade in the torch-flame until it glowed then with one deft stroke, she punctured the sacred membrane. Psappha cringed with embarrassment as warm fluid soaked both Gongyla and the bed.

Gyla ignored the drenching. Psappha cringed only slightly as The African reached with gentle hunter's hands to turn and then draw forth a slippery squalling scrap of female indignation.

~ ~ ~

Awakening in a soft, clean, perfumed bed, Psappha took several minutes to reorient herself before noticing her feet, beautiful feet, wonderful feet that she could see while lying flat on her back. *I've missed you, feet,* she thought as Lyneachia placed a swaddled bundle in her arms.

She gazed down upon a minute red face framed with wispy yellow down, and she trembled. She held her breath as she folded back the final cloth. "Beloved Mother, thank you," she whispered as anxious fingers examined tiny hands and perfect toes. She had a daughter. *A perfect golden girl. Blessed image of Larichos and our mother.*

In memory, she saw a giggle of girls danced among the trees, following a lithe young woman with ivory-cream skin and long, silver-gold hair. Un-awakened, she had not recognized her feelings. Now that she did, the pain of exile deepened.

The lovely girl-child, Atthis danced in her memory as her newborn daughter sought her breast. She remembered the girl-child's golden hair and a glow began deep within her gut. She recalled the moment Atthis whirled near, her kiton clinging to long clean limbs, and the glow took fire. The infant found the nipple and with firm sure grip sent sparks through Psappha's inner thighs.

"A lovely and expected payment for the pain of motherhood," Lyneachia said in response to the new mother's startled blush.

~ ~ ~

Lyneachia easily transferred her loyalty to the infant. Lycos served the Master's chamber. Psappha's confinement passed more quickly with his tales of pirates and princes to fill the days. He reminded her of the months she remained in the purple chamber, holding herself aloof from the gynakeoni, haunted by the siren call of their laughter. Now, she ached for the sound. Her spirit fumbled toward it as her infant daughter fumbled toward her distended breast. However, gynakeoni chatter did not reach the master's chambers.

She ached for Gyla but was afraid to send for her with Kerkolos in the house. Winter's first storm howled outside the day she decided she'd played the invalid long enough. After much discussion, she convinced Lycos to let Lyneachia help her dress. Kerkolos found her on her feet prepared to serve his dinner. He refused to allow it. With Psappha seated on a wealth of cushions, he watched her every move as she nibbled her way through a tasteless dinner. She scarcely waited for the servants to finish removing the dinner tables before she began pacing the overly warm room.

Kerkolos stretched on the bed and patted the space beside him.

"Come here. It's too soon for you to be up so long."

Psappha made a great show of stirring the embers in the brazier.

She puttered with her jars and repeatedly sorted her jewels.

"I said come here."

"I'll be there in a minute. I want to straighten this tray."

"Leave it. The servants will do it -- if it still needs doing. Now -- come here."

Psappha perched on the edge of the bed; her fingers busy with the scarab on her shoulder as she searched for words. When he touched her, she fell back onto the bed without having opened the pin, her feet still on the floor; her eyes fixed on the canopy.

Kerkolos leaned over her to kiss her forehead. "What is it? What's bothering you? Why are you so on edge? You need to stay clam for the infant's sake. Are you only pretending to be strong, little water bird? Are you ill?"

"I'm fine. A little tired is all."

"Then what's the trouble? You're acting as if Olympus were about to fall. Is the child imperfect?"

Psappha bolted upright and glared. "Imperfect? She's the meaning of perfection. There never was perfection until she was born."

"All right, all right, she's perfect." He folded her into his arms, fell back onto the pillows with her and maneuvered their bodies until they were lying in the middle of the bed with her head cradled in the crook of his shoulder. "If the child is perfect -- no -- don't scowl -- tell me what's troubling you."

"The gynakeon," she whispered.

"Do we go through that again?" He raised himself onto one elbow and turned her face toward him. "I have told you that the gynakeoni are as nothing to me. Do you still disbelieve me?"

"I believe you but, what about me?"

"What about you? You are my nightingale, my song."

"What about me and the gynakeon?"

"I have told you. You can ignore the gynakeon or spend all of your time there. It doesn't matter to me, as long as you're here when I want you."

She whispered. He leaned closer. She whispered again, each damning word struggling toward expression. "I'm a servant of Iphis."

"You are servant to no one."

She tried again. "I'm an initiate on the Sisterhood."

"Of course." He yawned.

Psappha stared in amazement. She had expected a variety of reactions to her confession. Indifference wasn't one of them. "You're not angry?"

"Why should I be angry? What you do with your summers is nothing to me."

"You don't mind?"

"Of course I don't mind; not as long as I have your undivided attention while I'm here. The rites of Iphis are older than time out of mind. They keep women content when men have other things to do."

Psappha tried not to be angry. She had expected rage, had primed herself to counter it. Now, he left her speechless.

"If it weren't for Iphis you'd be dead," he said. "And I would have no daughter. Your warrior queen brought the babe when the priests of famed Asklepios were ready to forfeit your life to Hera."

"My life can't be forfeit to Hera," Psappha said, grateful for a topic she could understand. "I'm destined for Poseidon," she told him. "But, tell me more about Gyla?"

"Gongyla." His eyes darkened slightly as he emphasized The African's formal name. Then they softened again as he continued, "Gongyla, magnificent savage that she is, stormed in here like a demon fresh from Hades, sent Asklepians flying into corners and punctured the stubborn Membrane of Hera with one jab of that lethal hairpin she wears. She delivered our child from your tortured body with the inborn skill of one tuned by nature to the love of helpless animals."

Psappha sighed, remembering the strength of tender hands.

"She loves you," Kerkolos continued. "My poor almost broken

toy, she loves you -- as greatly, I think, as I."

There followed a long discussion of philosophical differences and constraints.

~ ~ ~

It took Psappha several days to absorb the fact that Kerkolos loved her despite everything. *A Lesbian husband would be furious*, she thought. *Imagine the damage to his pride.* Then she remembered Lesbian gentlemen fondling cupbearers and decided such an attitude on their part would be hypocritical.

Although she avoided Gyla while Kerkolos was in the house out of respect for her marriage vows, she felt neither guilt nor remorse. She composed their daughter's dedication alone in the purple chamber, being careful to fashion it in accordance with what she now knew of Kerkolos's traditions and beliefs. When she finished, she hurried through the connecting door to seek his opinion.

Kerkolos had his back toward her.

Psappha giggled at the sight of Lycos who, with a mouthful of pins, was trying to fit an ordinary sized toga around Kerkolos' massive chest.

"Such a proud father," she teased, "so swollen with pride his clothes don't fit."

Kerkolos yanked off the unfinished garment and tossed it over Lycos. One glance at Lycos's struggles to free himself and Kerkolos doubled with laughter, his hands on his knees. Psappha kicked his bare bottom, shoving him toward the garden. He turned and gathered her into his arms.

"You overgrown bear," she protested. "You'll get me all mussed. Stop it." She squirmed as he nuzzled her neck with his beard. "Stop it!"

He stopped, stood and started toward the discarded kiton. She ran after him and grabbed at him but there was nothing to get a hold on so she dashed in front of him, snatched his beard and jerked his head down hissing, "Oh no you don't, thou despoiler of innocence, You started this. Now finish it."

He did. Too quickly, but there was no time for instructions. It was their daughter's dedication day and they were keeping everyone waiting.

~ ~ ~

A half hour later, Kerkolos' strode from the house, his furs flaring as he walked, his buskins making convenient indentations in the early snow. He charged the hill below Aphrodite's temple as if it were a bastion to be conquered. Lyneachia followed, stretching her legs to step in the hollows he had made with his feet, all the while holding the fleece-wrapped babe tight against her breast.

Psappha shivered from the icy wind, thinking that today her husband really looked like the great bear she sometimes called him. Hearing a soft crunch off to the side, she smiled over her shoulder at Gongyla, who had abandoned the slippery path to march in self-made tracks at the edge of sight, every curve of her body straining against soft doeskin.

How different this is from when I dedicated Larichos. There were no flowers peeking up around Aphrodite's temple. The gardens lay hidden beneath a thick blanket of snow. The inside of the temple was bright with torches that gave no heat. Psappha clutched her mantle and yearned for summer. *Is it only the sun's warmth I crave?* Before the thought took root, Kerkolos began reciting the dedication she had composed. She half-listened. It was similar to Larichos's dedication except that the invocation was to Aphrodite instead of Apollo and her daughter had a father to deliver it.

"..., Oh Illustrious Aphrodite." Kerkolos put his huge hands around his infant daughter's ribs and lifted her nude from the fleece. "Behold Klies, daughter of Kerkolos of Andros by Psappha of Lesbos," he recited as he held her toward the altar.

Psappha gulped. Until that moment, she had not known what name he had chosen for their daughter. She felt warm inside despite the chill wind whistling through the open temple.

"Accept her, Bountiful One, as you accepted her earth-born mother. Gracious Aphrodite...."

Kerkolos presented their tiny Klies to the each of the four winds. Psappha puffed with pride. Her brave little daughter did not cry.

Kerkolos raised Klies high above his head to invoke the guardianship of unseen Artemis. Psappha stepped forward. There was only one line left. The one with which he presented the child to The Fates in her mother's arms. She gaped when Kerkolos prayed instead to Artemis in words she had not written. "Take heed, Dark Lady, and watch her well lest The Foam-Born One and her cohort Iphis lead her into mischief."

Psappha wasn't sure if his impromptu prayer was for their daughter or for her. Nor did he explain. He simply finished the dedication according to script and headed home, giving her no choice but to follow.

As they approached the inner gate, he picked her up, Klies and all, and carried both wife and daughter into the gynakia.

~ ~ ~

Later that night, Psappha slipped from her husband's bed, lifted her daughter from her cradle and hurried through the secret tunnel to Gongyla. Together, they collected every spare lamp in the gynakeon and placed them around the makeshift temple. The tiny shrine was rich with the fragrance of incense and spice scented oil. The little Cretan goddess's ruffled skirt glinted many colors in the flickering light.

Gyla removed tiles and bonded limestone from the floor to bare a small patch of Earth's breast for Klies to lie on.

"Dear Lady, behold your daughter, Klies," Psappha began as she placed her daughter before their tiny altar. "Accept her, Gracious One, as you accepted her earthly mothers. Daughter of Psappha is Klies, granddaughter of Klies, your priestess."

The Lady demanded no more. She knew the rest. Psappha, however, was not finished. Picking up her daughter, she carried her to the garden and lifted her high overhead. "Behold! Artemis, Queen of the darkened moon, I pray thee accept Klies, daughter of

Psappha, brought to life by a hunter's blade. Take heed, Divine Huntress, Lady of Wild Things, and guard her from all who would harm or imprison her."

Turning, Psappha laid her nude and wiggling infant into Gyla's hands. "Your spiritual daughter," she said. "May The Lady Cybele protect and keep us all."

"I will guard her well, my lady, as I will forever guard you."

~ ~ ~

Klies filled much of her parent's time throughout the long winter. Her first real smile was for her father. She was barely out of swaddling the day he stripped her down and tossed her into the gynakia pool.

"No!" Psappha dashed to the rescue. Kerkolos stopped her at the edge.

"Relax," he said. "She was in water when she came. Watch and learn. She hasn't forgotten."

Psappha felt herself about to drown as her daughter coughed and spurted. Lyneachia walked into the water, got a firm grip on Klies' ribs and held her with her tiny feet dangling inches below the surface. Klies gurgled and her father roared with laughter.

"Stop!" Psappha jerked away from his restraining hand and rushed into the water, angry when her kiton slowed her down.

"What a way for Poseidon's daughter to behave," Lyneachia whispered.

"She must swim," Kerkolos insisted. "Do you want her to drown the first time she meets the sea?"

"She's not going to sea," Psappha snarled, clutching her struggling infant close.

"Hush," Lyneachia cautioned. "Be still and let me remind her of what she knows."

Psappha knew Lyneachia would not harm her child but, as she handed her back, she considered her young friend as dictatorial and demented as she thought her husband.

Minutes later, she stared in awe as her pudgy little girl paddled around the pool like a jubilant puppy, never more than a few centimeters from Lyneachia's protective hands.

~ ~ ~

Unlike their busy days, Psappha's nights became a puzzle of loneliness. In her husband's bed, she found a measure of peace that vanished seconds after passion's final flare. When he slept, she lay awake, wondering why she felt so incredibly detached.

Would it have been this same way with Alkaios, she wondered, thinking of another lifetime: A time when she spent long afternoons beneath an apple tree above her home in Mitylene, listening to the shepherd's ribald tales. She recalled yearning for the peace of the orchard the day Pittakos ordered her arrest. She remembered shielding her eyes from the mid-day sun as she watched a dust cloud move along the winding road from Mitylene. In her mind, she relived the precarious ride into the city, clinging to the rim of the chariot, her legs aching as she fought for balance.

She remembered asking, "What can he possibly fear from one small girl?" *Oh, the naïveté of youth.*

"Pittakos is capable of anything," Alkaios had warned, but she had not truly listened.

She shivered remembering the moment when Pittakos stepped down from the dais and stalked back and forth before them, appraising her with his beady pig's eyes. Even now, far away from him his scrutiny made her feel unclean.

Psappha gagged as she relived her feelings from that moment. She remembered thinking she would rather die than leave Lesbos. Leave Mitylene? "No!"

"What is it?" Kerkolos inquired groggily.

"It is nothing," Psappha lied. "Go back to sleep." Soon he snored softly but she still could not sleep. Every time she closed her eyes, she saw Mitylene receding. She could not forget the way the sunbeams dressed the bridges in gold as she boarded the squat travesty of the ship Pittakos had chosen for their journey into nowhere. She remembered clutching the railing until her knuckles ached. Tears dampened her pillow as she recalled the sound of oars dipping into dawn-dark water, drawing her away from everything she knew and loved. *Except Alkaios. Oh, Alkaios, beloved poet, where have The Fates deposited you and your irreverent songs?*

~ ~ ~

Psappha's discontent grew. She wanted to feel close to her husband, but she couldn't. She yearned for Gyla but dared not be near her. Each night, she stayed in her purple chamber as late as she dared, listening to the music of gynakeoni laughter and looking toward spring as if it were a beacon in the dark.

In the spring, she was dumfounded when Kerkolos sent his ship to sea with Lycos at the helm.

As summer progressed, Psappha found her fondness for her husband growing in proportion with his fondness for their child. She continued to hunger for Gongyla but she respected her husband's wish to let him monopolize her time.

Together, he and Psappha watched through the summer as their little daughter learned to swim from lotus to lotus like a pink and golden water nymph.

During Klies's second winter, Psappha taught Kerkolos the intricacies of Sennet while Klies built imaginary roads on the hearth. Whenever he grew tired of losing, he let Klies steal a die and end the game.

Klies' second spring arrived and she crawled, toddled then ran after her father one minute, Lyneachia the next, while Psappha laughed from the comfort of the arbor. It was as if the child's secret name was hurry. Lyneachia found it hard to keep her still long enough to dress her in the morning and she often simply ran out of breath and fell asleep amid the garden flowers.

Kerkolos declared himself unable to trust his fortunes to hirelings for another season, despite his inexplicable faith in Lycos. Psappha fought to hide her relief as he prepared for his voyage to the trading centers of the Aegean. She didn't want to think of him as her jailer although he was despite his proclamations otherwise. At his side, she felt lonelier than she did during his brief journeys into the city.

On the morning he was to sail, Klies rode to the docks on the front of his saddle, waving her chubby arm at everyone they passed. *She'll be talking before he returns.* Psappha regretted all that he would miss even as she looked forward to the freedom of his absence, disregarding the dangers of dancing with Poseidon. *One birthday in peace is all I ask.*

~ ~ ~

With Kerkolos at sea, warm nights drifted by in Gyla's willing arms. Hot days brought a whiney daughter ever pestering for her father. Klies's misery became so intense that Psappha found herself welcoming the rains of autumn as a herald of his return.

She stood by her window one day, watching the wind drive multicolored leaves westward, listening to the click of dice behind her where Gyla and Klies raced dotted chariots across the hearth. She did not look around when Klies' merry chatter stopped.

The scrape of a chair and a sharp intake of breath made her turn. Lycos stood two steps inside the room, his face as dark as the impending storm. Lyneachia hustled Klies away as Lycos opened his mouth to speak.

Psappha clamped her hands over her ears. Her eyes begged him to say nothing. Without the words, the truth she read in his eyes would not be real.

Gyla rushed to enfold Psappha in strength.

Psappha pounded Gyla's back with her fists. *Kerkolos is dead,* she raged at offending gods. *He is dead, thou capricious charlatans. Why weren't you watching? Aphrodite, thou fickle, thou false, you send me lovers, then you snatch them away. Do you delight in tormenting me? Do you take pleasure in my suffering?*

No, no, Sweet Aphrodite, gentle beauty, great have been thy gifts. The glory or the gods has been my heritage. The mating of gods my gift, but Kerkolos is gone, thou porna. You stole Alkaios from me then you then lent me Heracles' image only to snatch him away and bestow him upon your sisters of the deep.

Why must they get my beautiful ones to warm their scaly beds? Twice now my lovers have drowned, thou bitch. Surely, I will take my gifts to Hera. She robbed me of nothing but my maidenhead and she gave me a golden daughter in exchange.

Quieter now, Psappha began to sense the warmth of Gyla's flesh against her own. Her eyes stung from lack of tears as she drew comfort from the tender strokes upon her back. It took all of her emotional strength to pull away.

Blessed Aphrodite, forgive me. Poseidon has captured my soul. Where were you, Hermes, protector of traders, when your salty uncle stole my protector? Were you sleeping, God of Commerce, while my daughter's father drowned in some greedy mermaid's pool?

Poseidon, my father, is this the price you place on my life? It is too high. Better you had taken me than leave my daughter fatherless.

You sent me to a safe harbor, Father of Ocean, now you've claimed the harbormaster for yourself. I will accept no more of your temporary gifts. They cost too much.

[page deliberately left blank]

Book Three

THE

POETESS

Peggy Ullman Bell

[page deliberately left blank]

> *"Grief can take care of itself, but*
> *to get full value from a joy*
> *you must have someone to divide it with."*
> 'Mark Twain'

-- XVI --

Psappha lay alone with her husband's spirit, twisting her bedraggled hair. She hadn't brushed it in days, much less braided it into her usual coronet. *What would be the use? I'd only have to take the braids down every night. I should have cut them off. To what end? Kerkolos had no pier on which to burn them. No funeral, no wailing mourners, he had naught but the hungry sea.*

The Lydian lyre gathered dust in the farthest corner: a sad reminder of the days when Gyla carved its intricate designs. Psappha hadn't allowed Gyla near her since Lycos brought the news, not because she didn't want her. She kept Gyla away because Kerkolos had wished it and because she wanted her too much.

Psappha swung her legs over the edge of the bed and sat up as the doors to the purple chamber burst open. Lyneachia stood between them, wide-eyed, out of breath and pointing wildly toward the gynakeon. "What?"

"Adriana..." the nursemaid managed before collapsing in tears against a doorjamb. Two-year-old Klies, who had been playing quietly on the hearth, began to wail.

"Tend to her," Psappha said over her shoulder as she ran into the purple chamber. Beyond it, the pavilion was a chaos of screams and harsh male voices. As she emerged through the curtain beads, a burly man marched past with the arm of a struggling woman in each hand. Psappha rushed at him but ran into Adriana's bulk instead. "Stand back!"

"Stand back? Why would I?"

Psappha tried to push her mother-in-law aside. *It's my gynakeon*, she raged, despite never having wanted to lay claim to it before. "Leave them alone!" She yelled at the men-at-arms who continued to round up young women and girls and herd them toward the exit as if she had not spoken. She moved to the side to get around the wall that was her former mother-in-law. Adriana grabbed her wrist. "Let me go! This is my home. The gynakeoni are mine. How dare you bring strange men among them?"

Adriana's grip tightened. "It may be your home, but, it is no longer your house and the slaves were never yours. They belong to the owner of the house and since Kerkolos did not return, all that was his belongs to his uncle. You can thank him for the roof over your head. He convinced me that the pleasure of denouncing you was not worth the damage to my reputation."

"I don't care a fig for your reputation."

Adriana sneered. "You made that clear with your behavior. I know all about your jaunts into the city while my son was absent. He would have put you and your bastard on the street if I'd told him."

Psappha gaped. "Klies is your grand-daughter."

"Sheep dung," Adriana said. "My grandchild would be a boy and he wouldn't have piss-colored hair. No doubt, some wine-sluggard you and your black bitch found in a gutter sired your spawn."

"Klies is Kerkolos's daughter and your grand-daughter, more's the pity. How long do you think it takes a seed to sprout?"

Adriana snorted.

Psappha was not impressed. Having reminded herself of Klies, she looked around for her. Seeing her safe in Lyneachia's arms, she continued her interrogation of Adriana: Calm as ice despite Adriana's punishing grip on her wrist. "What brings you here now, old woman? You didn't come when your son's child was born. You were too busy chasing pleasure in Sybaris to attend her dedication. Why do you come now that Kerkolos is no longer here? By what right do you say this is not my house?"

"Women cannot inherit and, since your only child is female, all of my son's property passes to his nearest male relative which happens to be my late husband's brother."

"But that's ludicrous. On Lesbos, the gender of a child has no bearing on inheritance."

Adriana huffed. "Sicily is not some backward island."

Before Psappha could form a retort, a shuffling of feet and muffled curses attracted their attention to a cluster of Adriana's minions milling around, mumbling among themselves near the entrance to the exit corridor as if unwilling, or unable, to proceed.

"Call off your men, Adriana. If, as you say, this is not my house, I am still a guest here and as such deserve respect. Kerkolos told me the prime rule of hospitality holds sway even in Sybaris."

Adriana dropped her affected airs but held tight to Psappha's wrist, which had become quite numb. "No disrespect intended, my dear. I merely came to oversee the collection of my brother-in-law's property. The slaves could have been removed to my brother-in-law's house in orderly fashion if not for -- well -- see for yourself." She waved her free arm and the largest of the men stepped back enough to let Psappha to see into the head of the corridor.

Gyla stood with long legs spread and braced, strong white teeth bared, nude except for the ostrich plumes that crowned her crimped hair and hid the skinning knife Psappha knew was there, her drawn bow the only thing blocking the men's full view of her from fire-spitting eyes to firmly planted toes. A full quiver leaned against the wall nearby.

She looks so small, compared to them, Psappha thought with a shiver of apprehension. *Only her beauty protects her.*

"You men are imbeciles," Adriana growled. "Shall we return to your master and tell him a mere woman stopped you from completing your assigned task? Get on with the removal."

Gongyla bared her teeth. The men took a step backward. Gongyla glowered at them and they retreated farther.

Psappha saw the gleam in Gyla's eyes and she sighed. "Gongyla protects what is mine," she informed her sputtering mother-in-law.

"The slaves are not yours." Adriana pulled a sealed scroll from her sleeve and handed it over.

Psappha let it fall to the floor. She watched through tears as the frightened younger slaves trailed past her. She had promised to protect them, yet here she stood, helpless. "What will you do with them?"

"They will be sold, of course."

"No," Psappha protested.

"You have nothing to say about it," Adriana said. "My husband's brother has more than sufficient slaves and, unlike my son he is not willing to keep those whose sale could bring him profit. He will have enough added expense maintaining this house and those who are not slaves until suitable husbands can be found for them."

Psappha flinched, afraid that Adriana numbered her among those in need of husbands.

"Fortunately," Adriana continued. "Most of the slaves are or will be breeders. They'll bring good prices."

"You've been planning this."

Adriana shrugged. "As you please. Nevertheless, we will sell the slaves and marry the other breeders off to whoever will take them without dower. Don't worry, helpless one. There are enough old and ugly ones to insure your comfort. Regardless of paternity, the house is part of Klies' dower and will therefore have an adequate staff as propriety dictates until such time as I find a husband for her as well."

In a pig's eye, you will.

"The purple-eyed one is yours," Adriana added with obvious regret. "She was deeded to you when my son ordered you assigned the bridal chamber. It's on the scroll I gave you." She licked her lips as if clearing a bad taste from her mouth.

Psappha reveled in her tiny victory. Over the past three years, Lyneachia had grown from a scrawny girl-child to the loveliest of women. She drew a modicum of satisfaction from the sense of substantial loss of profit written on Adriana's face.

"Will you order the Nubian to at least clothe herself so the men will get on with their work?"

"But, Adriana," Psappha said with feigned innocence, "No one owns Gongyla. Why would you expect her to obey?"

Adriana harrumphed at Psappha then gave the men a wilting stare. All four of the mercenaries suddenly remembered their trade and rushed the warrior queen as a group. Gyla met their assault with a cat-like snarl. Her bow-string twanged and one of the men fell back, an arrow quivering in his neck. Two others threw themselves at her, tearing the bow from her hands and pinning her arms. As she struggled, the fourth man ran at her. He fell back screaming when her foot connected with his balls.

Gongyla's laughed. The men holding her shifted to tighten their grip. She used their movement as a device to free herself, breaking the nose of one in the process. The fourth man stepped out of range, eyeing her as he might any other wild she-cat. Adriana screamed in futile rage. Adriana's brawny chair-bearers rushed into the corridor from the courtyard.

"Gyla! Behind you!"

"Get her!" Adriana shrieked.

Fresh men-at-arms rushed into the pavilion.

Adriana's palms gleefully smacked together. "Take her! She's worth ten of the others. Earn your pay!"

Five men grabbed Gongyla from behind and wrestled her to the floor.

"Bind her!" Adriana growled. "Use the chains!"

Gyla a slave? Never! Psappha wrenched free of Adriana, grabbed the votive labrys from their makeshift shrine and charged Gongyla's captors.

"Psappha, no!" Gyla shouted.

Psappha paid no heed. She hit one of the men on his hip but was not strong enough to sink the blade. He snatched the labrys with a snarl. When she lunged for it, he bashed her nose.

She awoke on the floor with Lyneachia holding a slab of raw beef to her eye while Klies wailed nearby, unattended.

"They're gone?"

"Yes."

"Everyone?"

"Yes."

"Gyla?"

Lyneachia nodded and Psappha wished she were still unconscious.

> *"None shall part us from each other,*
> *one in life and death are we;*
> *All in all to one another – I to thee and thou to me!*
> *Thou the tree and I the flower – Thou the idol;*
> *I the throng – Thou the day and I the hour –*
> *Thou the singer; I the song!"*
> *'William | Schwenck Gilbert'*

-- XVII --

Psappha brooded in the arbor oblivious to the fading roses all around her. The garden seemed as barren as she felt. Sunbeams slanted through multi-colored trees. Klies scampered among chrysanthemums and asters. Lyneachia approached carrying the Lydian lyre. Psappha winced as she waved the instrument aside. Her wrist was swollen and painful but it was for her heart that she wanted to cry. All thought of rejecting Gyla had vanished the moment she learned of Adriana's ultimate betrayal. *She was no slave! She was born to be free. The Lady meant her to be here with me.* She hid her hands as Lyneachia put the lyre into her lap.

Lyneachia found Psappha's hands and laid them gently upon the strings. "You must sing."

Gradually, as if directed by someone else, Psappha's practiced fingers found a melody. The chords came uninvited. "Black is my world," Psappha sang a metered dirge. "In shadow I walk but I do not move. I see but do not look. My light, my life, my sight is gone. Alone I cease to be. Time is …"

Lyneachia grabbed Psappha's uninjured wrist. "That is not your song, Psappha. Look at your daughter." Psappha raised her head to meet tear-flooded baby eyes. Klies invariably took her cues from her mother. If Psappha cried, Klies must cry, though she did not know the reason. Psappha felt a twinge of guilt. She forced a smile as a new song came to mind. "I have a little daughter," she sang. "Like a perfect flower is Klies, fair mirror of her father. No ribbons have I for her shining hair. It needs none. It glows on its own. No ribbon could add to the beauty that is hers. A sparkling bubble of music is Klies, blessed by sweet Thalia, kissed by Polymnia, gifted by Terpsichore, beloved of all the rose-armed muses and beloved of her mother."

Klies scrambled onto her lap, wriggling a place for herself between her mother's softness and the magical lyre. She stretched her small fingers on the strings as if imagining it was she and not her mother playing.

Psappha chuckled.

"Now, that's what I like to hear."

Psappha dropped the lyre, sat Klies on the bench and bolted to her feet, running before she shouted, "Gyla! How?"

Gongyla shrugged. "A little swim," she said as she grasped her lover close.

"A little over two leagues," said Lycos, strolling toward them.

"You, too," Psappha exclaimed from her vantage off the ground in Gyla's arms. Looking at him over a warm shoulder, she thought he looked a bit less arrogant than when last she saw him. "How did you escape?" she asked Gongyla.

"Quit climbing Gyla as if she's a tree and I'll tell you," Lycos said.

Gyla chuckled, unclasped Psappha's arms from around her neck and eased her to the ground.

Psappha's eyes widened the moment she was on her feet. "You're hurt!"

"It's nothing," Gongyla grinned.

"Nothing! They cut your beautiful face."

Gongyla touched a finger to the festering gash above her eye. "Hmmm, so they did."

"It's a mess," Lycos said with a touch of amusement.

"A mess! Is that all you can say, you donkey? Gyla, sit so I can reach you. As for you, you grinning incompetent, go find a physician."

"She doesn't need to be physicked," he said. "All she needs is some soured wine and a bandage. Oh, don't ruffle up so, Psappha. Take a good look at her."

"I am looking at her, fool. She has an oozing wound."

Psappha tore a strip from the end of her kiton, dipped it into the fountain then reached to dab dirt from the wound. "Lyneachia fetch some spoiled wine from the kitchen."

Gyla shrugged away from her hands. "Leave be, Kitten. You'll spoil the scar."

"Warriors," Psappha huffed, hurting from the thought of a vicious mark on Gyla's beautiful face.

Gyla quieted her anger with a smile. "Come, Little-one, sit. Your daughter is weeping and Lycos is tired."

"I'm tired," Lycos scoffed. "You're the one who should be tired."

When they settled in the arbor, Gyla took Klies onto her lap then consented to having her wound cleaned while Lycos explained. "I was at the docks. When I saw Adriana and her henchmen with the women, I sneaked aboard her ship. About two leagues out the witch caught me and decided I should serve her tea, which was a big mistake. I took the old porna her tea well laced with crushed poppies. As soon as she nodded off, I slipped out and undid Gongyla's locks.

"Gyla kicked two of her guards overboard and dove in after them. I volunteered to use the dinghy to recapture her and here we are."

"She'll come back," Psappha worried.

"And miss the social season in Sybaris? Not likely. We're safe 'til spring. What's for supper? It's been a long row."

~ ~ ~

Winter in the near empty gynakeon seemed long and spring came late. Gyla took Klies into the garden on the first warm afternoon. Psappha brought her 'broidery and watched from the edge of the fountain. Klies rode Gongyla's shoulders with her golden hair fluttered behind her like a warrior's headdress. After a while, Gyla stood the child on the ground and handed her a miniature bow. Psappha picked up her basket and went to where Lycos gathered flowers. She dropped hyacinths in the basket as quickly as he handed them to her while watching the archery lesson from the corner of her eye.

"You are too much alone," Lycos said.

"I'm not alone. I have Klies." *And Gyla*, she thought but was not sure how much she should tell him.

"You are alone," he persisted. "The child does not occupy your mind."

Psappha left him and returned to her place by the fountain where she put down the basket of hyacinths, took up her embroidery and retreated to the wisteria-shrouded arbor.

"Stop avoiding me," he grumbled as he joined her. "You are a woman and need more than a child's company."

"What would you suggest? Would you have me walk the streets of the city in search of company?"

"Psappha, you are my heart's own but sometimes you make me want to leave you forever. Either you're sailing the sky, or you're lost in the depths. Try the ground. Open your home to the young ladies of Syracuse. There is much they could learn from you."

Psappha punched the needle through her 'broidery and into her finger. "What a fool you are," she said more to herself than to Lycos. She stuck her punctured finger into her mouth and headed for the rose arbor. Lycos followed. "How can I open this house to guests when I've barely enough servants to care for us?" she asked when he settled once more beside her.

"Not guests, Adelphi*, pupils: Pupils who will bring their own servants. Say the word and I will fill the gynakeon with the daughters of respectable families. They will come eagerly to learn from you and will bring a sizable tuition with them.

"Your house and your purse are empty. Fill them. Teach your music. You make a lyre defy the gods. Why keep your skill to yourself? You string words together like gems on a bracelet. Are you so selfish you must keep your jewels in a cask, hidden from thieves?"

"How do you propose I open a school when I'm forbidden to open my gate? How could I find students in a city that imprisons its women and drives them to Iphis?"

"What do you know of Iphis?" he asked, glancing uncomfortably toward where Gongyla was restringing Klies' tiny bow. "You were born for men," he declared.

"As were you?"

He drew back his arm as if to strike her. She caught his wrist. "Don't you see, dear friend, we're not so different, you and I. As Apollo loved Hyacinthos, so you loved Kerkolos. As Ianthe loved Iphis, so I love Gyla. How can we be enemies, Little Fox, when we are so much the same?"

"You will go no more to Iphis?"

"I will go again and again to Iphis as you would go to Kerkolos if he were here and called to you." His bleak expression told her Kerkolos had never called. She wanted to comfort him but had no words for that. "You, better than all others, must know that no man can offer me anything of value that I have not already owned. Kerkolos cannot live again, nor can Alkaios."

Lycos veiled his eyes. "Alkaios?"

"You did not know him, dear heart. He was with me on the ship."

---

* Adelphi = close female friend

"You should have told me."

"You knew him?"

"I knew him."

"From his poetry?"

"From his poetry," he said but she could tell that there was more. There was a deepened sadness in his voice when he added, "You think he drowned?"

"I don't know. Perhaps. Perhaps not. I'm here safe. Perhaps he is safe somewhere as well."

His brow crimped with emotion she could not define. "There may come another."

She shook her head. "For you there may come another, Lycos. You merely loved him. I was loved by him. I have no need to look for another. I know there are none to be found."

"You may return to Lesbos one day. Is there no one there for you to love?"

"Perhaps I could have learned to love Alkaios, but he was lost before I got the chance."

"Was there no one else?"

"No," she said then, on second thought, she added, "that's not quite true. There might have been someone – perhaps. I don't know."

"Tell me about him."

"Not him, Little Fox, her."

"But you knew nothing of Iphis before you came here."

"Lack of such knowledge did not keep me from appreciating the wonder of a beautiful golden child when I was but a child myself. The feelings existed long before my exile. They frightened me. It took Iphis' priestesses to define them and teach me to accept. Enough talk of Lesbos. Lesbos and Atthis are far away. Pittakos will never allow me to return to Mitylene."

"Nor do you need to. She's probably a fat matron by now anyway," Gyla said, letting Psappha know she had heard too much of their conversation.

"Dancers seldom run to fat."

"Nor do hunters."

"Peace," he pleaded. "Peace." His gaze darted from one to the other like a fox cornered by a brace of bitches. Psappha couldn't keep from laughing. Gongyla's smile took more coaxing.

A ball bounced in front of the arbor and rolled under the bench. Klies scampered after it. Gongyla swatted her plump little rump as she dived between their legs. *Klies never has trouble making Gyla smile.*

With one eye on the child, the other on the mother, Gongyla poured herself onto the grass in front of the arbor and rolled onto her stomach, stretching like a great, dark cat. She propped her chin on her fists and grinned as Klies scrambled into her mother's lap to play with Psappha's lips as Psappha resumed her conversation.

"Tell me, Lycos, how could I gather pupils for such a school as you propose?"

Gongyla frowned. "School?"

"Yes, a school," Lycos said. "What did you think I would propose? Another temple?"

"Hush," Psappha said. "Peace," she echoed his plea of scant moments before. He hung his head sheepishly, but she could see the corner of his smile. "Now, tell me, Little Fox, aren't all women of family confined to gynakia?"

"They may travel under proper escort," he explained. "Gynakia women are permitted to reside for a time in the homes of friends, or family. They would be allowed to live and study with a teacher of high repute."

"I am a stranger here. Their families know nothing of me. I've seen no one outside these walls since my wedding and I remember little of that."

"Syracuse may be strange to you, Adelphi, but you are not without standing. Kerkolos had a fine reputation. The city still bristles with the shame of Adriana's treachery. The people's sympathy is with you. Just leave the details to me. You have only to consent to teach those who arrive."

"Very well, Little Fox, but you attempt the impossible."

~ ~ ~

Soon they heard a public crier's voice from beyond the wall.

"Come, thou, gentlemen of Syracuse. Bring your daughters, the sisters of your heart, to Psappha of Lesbos that she may instruct them in the graces.

"Daughter of Agamemnon is Psappha, also of fair Minea. Guarded by Mighty Poseidon is she, beloved sister of the Muses, widow of famed Kerkolos, blessed daughter of Aphrodite.

"Lovely are her songs, oh lords of Syracuse, great are her many gifts. Make haste, gentlemen of Syracuse that The Lady of Lesbos may have time for thee."

And, the daughters of Syracuse's best families came, a few at first, a trickle, a stream, then a flood of vibrant girls who filled the house with beauty and laughter. As the need arose, Psappha discovered rooms she'd never imagined much less seen.

Her fame spread, season by season. Wealthy merchants throughout the trading world sent their young women to The Poetess, some from as far as Cathay.

They became so many that, in the third year, Gongyla relinquished her post at the gate to an accommodating eunuch and began assisting with the teaching.

I must tell Lycos to dismiss the crier soon, Psappha reminded herself late on an autumn afternoon. Her garden overflowed with merry maidens. They fluttered to her and settled onto the grass before her arbor like a fountain of multi-shaded rainbows more dainty than rosebuds.

"Come, milady. Sing for us." Two of them clasped her hands and drew her along the path to where Lyneachia waited with her lyre.

Psappha accepted the lyre but rejected the inviting pile of cushions in the rose-shaded arbor in favor of the broad base of a purple-draped window-arch. Gyla saluted her from across the garden then returned her attention to the cluster of maidens she was teaching to use the long bow.

The girls arrayed themselves on the grass near Psappha's feet like iridescent peacock feathers. She patted the windowsill and five-year-old Klies came to sit beside her. Lyneachia hovered near, but not so near as she had when Klies was younger. Gongyla paused to smile as Psappha began to sing.

"Mitylene, thou lovely, Mitylene, thy daughter's eyes strain vainly toward thy sun-burnished citadel; thine orchards where once she walked when her girlhood was all flowers; thy bubbling streams in winter, singing their way to spring; thine air so pure, like crystal, adorning an azure sea; thy cliffs of pure and beautiful delight, kissing Poseidon with joy. Even thy raging winds and trembling mountains, would I welcome to be once more with thee.

"But, no more shall Psappha see thy fragrant hills dressed in spring's gay 'broidery; no more Earth's brocade pajamas on thy frosty trees; no more thy snow-sheeted snoozing beneath a wintry sky. Call no more to Psappha, sweet island. Psappha cannot come."

As the last note died, she brushed a tear from her cheek and relinquished the lyre to her best pupil. Only then did she realize that Klies was no longer near. Scanning the garden, she saw her daughter perched on a rock like a curious gull, near the far corner of the garden where Gyla posed like a willow in a flowerbed, demonstrating her skill for disinterested maidens.

Gongyla pulled the bowstring easily, sending a winged arrow to the center of the target then she handed the bow to an inattentive, dark eyed girl. Laughter rippled through the garden as the maiden drew the string and released it, sending the arrow up -- and down. Psappha couldn't help joining the merry response. Gongyla covered the distance between them like a gazelle fording a brook.

"Don't laugh, Psappha. They try."

"But they look like puffs of wind trying to blow down a mountain."

Gyla leaned threateningly over her. "Can you draw my bow?" she whispered.

"No," Psappha returned, "but I can pull your hair."

"Who will protect you if you do?"

"I wouldn't need protection if I picked the right time."

"And what time would that be, little bird?"

"When you are my playful cub, thou feline." Psappha purred mockingly. Reaching up, she stroked Gongyla's hair. "Where is thy fierceness now, thou cat who is my kitten?"

Gongyla slung her over her shoulder. Psappha laughed with mock protest. Gyla carried her up onto the sill and through the arch. She stalked through the purple chamber and into to the mahogany one beyond where she dumped Psappha onto the bed. When she would have joined her, Psappha rolled away.

"Not now," Psappha said, casting her eyes toward the twitter they had left in their wake.

"Now," Gongyla insisted with a firm, gentle grip on her shoulder.

"They'll know," Psappha whispered. Her lover's responding chuckle against her neck tickled her from hair roots to toenails.

"Of course they'll know," Gongyla mumbled against the nerves just below Psappha's right earlobe, her fingers busy with the stubborn scarab-clasp on Psappha's kiton. "They were born in gynakia -- hold still. . . ." She sprawled onto the bad empty-handed as her captive wriggled away and darted for the doors.

"Hold still, indeed," Psappha defied her from a relatively safe distance. Having gained her freedom and trying to regain her dignity, she reached for the pull cord to call Lyneachia.

"Touch that and pay the price," Gongyla challenged, rolling luxuriantly onto her back.

"Price? What price, thou queen?" Psappha surveyed Gongyla's sleek body, her eyes filled with a reverence. Smiling, she released her kiton and stepped away from it to stand nude on the small Persian rug inches from the carved and polished bed. Gongyla crooked a finger and Psappha dove into her arms.

> *"Once more upon the waters, yet once more!*
> *and the waves bound beneath me as a steed*
> *that knows it's rider!"*
>
> *'Lord Byron'*

-- XVIII --

Psappha sat on the edge of the mahogany bed, brushing her twelve-year-old's unruly hair. *She's grown so tall I'll soon have to stand to brush her.*

Klies fidgeted.

Psappha loosed an impatient sigh. "Be still!"

Klies's adolescent face scrunched into a belligerent frown but she stopped wiggling for half a second. Her long amber hair flew to meet the brush, the waves springing tighter with each stroke.

Psappha glanced into the mirror opposite and was struck by Klies's growing resemblance to her namesake. *Golden and beautiful like Atthis. How proud Mother would have been to see her flower.*

An unexpected uproar sounded from another part of the house and Klies was gone before Psappha heard Lycos shout, "You cannot enter here!"

Dropping the brush, she hurried to follow Klies to the public courtyard where Lycos stood in a tiny circle of torchlight, growling through the small lookout in the solid ironwood door. "Take your nefarious business elsewhere, Soldier. The House of The Muses is inviolate. We have no pornas here."

"I'm not looking for a porna, you evil minded mound of dung," a strong male voice called from beyond the door. "I bear a message of great importance to the daughter of Scamandronomos."

"I don't care whose daughter you have a message for," Lycos said. "You can't come in here at this hour. Come back in daylight and maybe I'll let you in."

"Open the gate," Psappha told him. "I'm the daughter of Scamandronomos. I'd like to hear what he has to say."

Lycos shook his head. "Let him put the message through the lookout."

"Open the gate."

Lycos again refused. "What if it's a trick?"

By this time, most of the household had aligned themselves behind Psappha and Klies. Gongyla hadn't bothered to don a kiton despite the cooling weather. She stood braced in her usual skin and quiver attire with an arrow notched and centered on the entrance. "Open it."

Lycos complied. The gate swung open and the visitor stepped into the tiny circle of light. Psappha's hand shot out to stay Gongyla's arrow. She stared, mouth gaping and mute, unable to believe her eyes. The beardless youth who stood before her in Lesbian armor wore a younger version of Alkaios's mocking grin.

"Has the daughter of Scamandronomos no welcome for the son of Eurigios?"

Psappha's whisper was tentative. "Larichos?"

"Yes, little elder sister. I'm sorry I startled you but that fool over there wouldn't let me in quietly." He glanced toward Lycos, his azure eyes so like their mother's that Psappha forgot to breathe.

She came to on a couch in the main hall, with Lyneachia holding a damp clothe to her forehead and Gongyla warning others away with a dark eyed glare. Lycos leaned on the doorframe with a protective, restraining hand on Klies's shoulder. Her adored baby brother grown tall stood nearby.

"I've come to bring you home," he said as he stepped closer.

Psappha paid no heed to his words. She ached to touch him, hold him; caress him to see if he was real but his bearing did not welcome gushing emotions. Her eyes brightened when she recognized the shield he carried as the one she'd intended to use against Melanchros. "How'd you find me?" she asked, for lack of something better.

"Your fame is great, little elder sister. My master heard of your work here . . ."

Psappha disregarded his teasing tone. "Master?" she echoed, coming to her feet strengthened by an inherent pride. "How comes the son of Eurigios to a master?"

"A master in name only, noble Psappha: A patron actually. I've been cupbearer to Pittakos since I turned thirteen – last year."

Pittakos! Psappha stared mutely, waves of anger-born nausea cramping her stomach. *What vile purpose could induce Pittakos to bestow such honor upon the brother and nephew of exiles?* Terrified of any possible answer, she swayed. Gyla stepped forward. Psappha restrained her with a gentle touch. "He's my brother."

"A brother at whom you're angry."

"No, sweet champion, it is not Larichos who draws my anger." Forcing calm, she again asked Larichos, "How'd you find me?"

"As I said, my lord has heard of your work here and sent me . . ."

"Your lord? How dare crack-toes call himself lord over the scion of the first house of Lesbos?"

"'Tis but a figure of speech, thou phoenix."

"A figure I wish erased."

Larichos continued as if he hadn't heard. "Pittakos heard of your great success and begs that your return to your home. It is said that your pupils come to you from all the greatest households."

"Hardly all," Psappha said.

"Even so, we've heard that many begin to call my tiny elder sister The Poetess, peer of Homer." His familial pride was obvious and echoed by Klies.

"We have seven from the ruling house of Persia and two of Croesus's granddaughters," she bragged.

Larichos eyed his gangly niece. "And who might this bright young woman be?"

Klies blushed and ducked behind her mother.

"She's my daughter. Klies, say hello to your uncle."

"Greetings, Niece." He honored Klies with a courtly bow, much to Klies' obvious delight.

"She is named for our mother and she grows more like her every year."

Larichos smiled and winked. Twelve-year-old Klies dashed from the room with Lyneachia at her heels.

Psappha sighed. "You'll have to excuse her lack of manners, Larichos. She's seen no man except Lycos and eunuchs. Lycos will explain," she added in response to his arched brow.

"In that case I'll leave you to consider your decision. If someone will show me where I can divest myself of the grime of travel?"

"Forgive me, dear brother. I let surprise supersede manners." His eyes told her no apology was necessary. "Lycos, have the guest room in the gatehouse prepared." Lycos nodded. "Good," she said, "When you're refreshed, we'll have a late supper."

As Lycos ushered him out she thanked The Lady for the cook who arrived with the Persians. Until then, they had fended for themselves, having been unable to find a cook who was both free and capable of meeting Lycos's exacting palate.

She used the walk through crackling leaves and crowded corridors to compose her thoughts. *Pittakos wants The Poetess to add luster to his ignoble rule. He's a pig who wants to profit from my fame. Why do I care why he summons me? He's nothing to me. I can't let my loathing for him keep me from my home.* By the time she settled into her favorite Abyssinian chair in the main parlor, she had things pretty much sorted out. Three and a half Olympiads in Syracuse had not made it home to her. Her ears hummed with the remembered sound of surf on The Lady's Beach. She glanced up just as Lycos and Larichos entered.

"...but would she be safe," Lycos expressed his worries.

Gongyla, clothed in an abbreviated kiton stood with her back to the mantle studying Larichos. "This Pittakos person may have already changed his mind."

Larichos answered both while addressing Psappha. "You will be honored there as you are here, Psappha. There is no risk. Others have already returned."

"Others? Alkaios?"

"No - not yet - but soon," he answered sadly but with hope. "The Insurrection is long forgotten."

"Insurrection?" Klies was too curious by nature to remain in hiding for long.

Larichos offered Psappha a playful smile. "Didn't you tell her you were exiled at my age for trying to sink a labrys in Pittakos's back?"

Klies arched her brows in wonder.

"Some try," Psappha scoffed. "I got knocked cold while accomplishing nothing. Just like I did in the gynakeon," she added, nodding apologetically to Gongyla. Then, to change the subject, she said, "I can't abandon my students."

"They'll follow you," Lycos assured her.

To which Larichos added, "There are new pupils awaiting your return. Many had made plans to sail for Syracuse when Pittakos published your amnesty and bid me escort you home."

Psappha smiled as her understanding grew. *He'll tolerate my presence to prevent the exodus of Lesbian maidens. But will Poseidon permit me to reach Lesbos?*

Later, as she walked Larichos to the gatehouse, her hand tucked possessively in the crook of his elbow, she found it hard to believe this tall young man was scarcely three years older than Klies. At the gatehouse door, he bent nearly double to kiss her cheek.

"Good night, little elder sister," he said, smiling like Pan at a picnic.

Psappha turned away in an affected huff.

Startled to see a tear on Gyla's mask-like face, she brushed it tenderly away. "Be happy, please, my cinnamon soldier. We go to lovely Mitylene!"

~ ~ ~

Next morning, Lycos greeted her with a sad expression. "You'll sail in the spring?"

"We'll sail in the spring," Psappha corrected. "It will take that long to get things together and you must come with us. How would I manage without you?"

"You have your young brother to look after your interests," he said.

"How could you think that would make a difference? We are friends, you and I. Nothing could change that."

"You would feel differently about me on Lesbos." He stared at the fire, shuffling his feet. "I thought perhaps I would go home myself."

"You have no home to go to, Little Fox. Why are you trying to deceive me?"

"I don't want to be a burden to you. Things are very different on Lesbos. You must remember some of the outdated ideas you had when you came here. Our friendship would seem strange to your people."

"My dear sweet friend," she said, holding her arms out to him. "You are a part of me. The love I have for you is no burden." He came to her and knelt, snuggling his head against her as she wove her fingers into his unruly hair. "When I first saw you, it was as if the loveliest of Lesbian cupbearers had appeared before me. You will always find welcome in my home and you'll love Mitylene."

She stroked his back until the muscles relaxed then she urged him to his feet. "There is much for you to do. All the travel arrangements must be made and who but you to make them? You'll be my business manager in Mitylene, just as you've been here. No proper school can function without its chief administrator."

"Of course, of course," he warbled officiously. "The criers must be informed that The Poetess will be in Mitylene next season. The pupils will need time to prepare."

Psappha laughed as he scurried from the room. Turning, she saw Lyneachia watching her with veiled eyes. "What is it, my purple-eyed friend? Surely you don't think I'd leave without you."

"I hope that you do, milady. I want to stay here. Please, milady, don't look so hurt. I don't want to be apart from you, but I think I should stay here."

"Nonsense. You'll come to Mitylene with us. Klies still needs a governess and Praxinoa was growing old before Larichos was born. I need you to look after Klies' interests."

Lyneachia hesitated a moment as if unsure how to proceed. Gongyla flashed her disapproving glare. She squared her slender shoulders, turned to Psappha and said, "It is in Klies' interest that I wish to stay. This house is Klies' dower. She must have a representative in residence or Adriana will sell it out from under her."

Psappha acknowledged her point. She had deliberately forgotten about Klies' greedy grandmother. It pleased her that Lyneachia put Klies' interests above her own. She smiled appreciatively, knowing how much the girl would miss the child.

"You may wish to use the house again yourself one day," Lyneachia suggested. "It would be best to keep it open."

Psappha shook her head.

Lyneachia returned the gesture. "When you came here, you thought you would never return to Mitylene. You may come back to Syracuse one day. Your home will be ready to receive you when you do."

"Very well, Lyneachia. If you really want to stay behind, you shall be my steward. Tomorrow I will prepare scrolls putting Klies' dower into your hands." Hugging the happily weeping girl, she thought, a steward should not be a slave. *I will set her free*, she decided. *All my remaining slaves shall be as free as Gyla has always been.*

~ ~ ~

A few days later, Adriana's screech interrupted the family's breakfast. Psappha motioned for the others to stay put and then she hurried to head her off.

"You are forbidden to leave Syracuse," Adriana growled when Psappha met her at the outer gate

Psappha was glad she'd changed every lock in the house. "You can forbid all you want but I will do as I wish."

"You're not coming?" She had not heard Larichos come up behind her. He looked stunned.

"I am," Psappha assured him. "And Gongyla's coming with me."

"That's part of why I'm here," said Adriana, handing Psappha another officious looking document. "The African is mine and the purple-eyed one is yours only so long as you remain in Syracuse. If you leave she reverts to me."

It was Psappha's turn to be stunned. "Gyla was never a slave."

"She is now," Adriana insisted. "Read."

"I don't need to read your stupid documents. She's free and if Lyneachia chooses to come with me, she's free too."

"You can't free either of them. My brother arranged to have title to them transferred to me."

"I don't have time for your nefarious manipulations, Adriana. I am Psappha of Lesbos and I'll do as I please. I'm The Poetess," she added, recalling Larichos's claim. "Return to your brother, before my brother throws you out."

"Your brother? Why didn't you tell me your brother had yellow hair?"

"So did my mother," Psappha replied. "But I didn't think it was relevant."

"Relevant? You back woods tart. If both your mother and your brother have yellow hair then Klies really is my granddaughter and you will not take her from me."

"Stop me." Psappha slammed the gate.

"You can't leave," Adriana called but Psappha kept on walking.

~ ~ ~

Psappha didn't need to summon a magistrate. The magistrate came to her.

"Your mother-in-law's documents are clearly forged," he said. "You are free to do as you choose."

"Would you file this for me," she asked, giving him the document making Lyneachia guardian of Klies's inheritance.

"Of course. I regret whatever inconvenience your late husband's mother may have caused you. Unfortunately, the slaves she stole before cannot be retrieved."

Inconvenience, Psappha thought after the man had left. Sadness permeated her spirit. She thought of the women and girls she'd lost to slavery and her tears flowed unabashed.

~ ~ ~

Winter crawled on ancient knees. Psappha packed and repacked a hundred times before the first crocuses finally broke through. They would sail within the week. Of those who were going, only Gongyla had no trunks to pack. She had tucked the minimal clothes she seldom wore into a corner of Psappha's smallest sea chest.

Lycos had acted strangely ever since the day Psappha signed the emancipation scrolls. His agitation seemed to increase after Larichos sailed on the first ship of the season to take word of Psappha's decision to Pittakos lest some Lesbian maidens depart Mitylene for Syracuse before word reached them that The Poetess was coming home.

Watching him pace the room, Psappha pretended not to notice until he dragged over a stool and sat beside her.

"Adelphi," he began in an unusually serious tone. "Is it true that women walk freely in Mitylene?"

She loved to see him pout. The years seemed to melt from his face when he pouted, reminding her of their early times together. The more serious he became, the more he pouted and the less she could resist teasing him.

"Women do," she said. "Boys mind their manners."

Lycos ignored her jibe. "If women are free," he said, "Gongyla must come with us."

Psappha fixed her gaze on her hands to cover her surprise. After a momentary pause, she grabbed the opportunity for further teasing.

"Be sensible," she said. "Gyla is free. She does not have to stay with me any longer. She can do as she pleases." She almost choked on the effort needed to keep a fixed expression in the face of his perplexity. "Gyla would not be happy in Mitylene," she said. "Lesbian women mingle freely with men. Iphis would not find so ready a welcome there."

"Iphis finds welcome wherever women are," Lycos pronounced indignantly. "She no more confines herself to gynakia than Eros fails to fling his arrows outside of the marriage chamber. Like him, she is everywhere, though she may not always be called by name."

He began his irritating pacing again. Psappha chose to ignore him while she considered how to respond to his unexpected change in attitude.

"Look at me when I'm talking to you, Psappha. I insist that Gongyla come with us. Why is she not packed?"

"You insist, do you?" She got up, took his shoulders and nudged him into a chair. Fists on hips, she stood over him, challenging, knowing she had carried the joke too far but unable to stop herself. "You insist? You were the one who was so against my devotion to Iphis. I thought you would be glad if I forsook her. You seem to enjoy ordering me around so much, why aren't you smiling. If she is not happy, she can go home. The famine there is over. Isn't a separation what you've always wanted?"

"Gongyla's home is where you are and you know it," he said. "She has no home but you."

"Now you're making more of me than I am, Little Fox. Gyla is my friend, my companion, yes, all right, she is my lover but we do not depend on each other for life. We would not die if we were parted."

Lycos glared. He stood and faced her squarely. "Perhaps she doesn't need you to live, thou heartless she-goat, though I think she would rather die than be without you."

He didn't ordinarily call her vile names. Watching his eyes, Psappha realized that somehow, without her noticing, he had come to care more for Gyla than he intended. His evil expression added to the tenderness she felt for him.

"What are you grinning at?" he snarled. She dropped her tiny smile.

"Did you really think I would abandon my champion, Lycos? Would any respectable woman travel without a proper guard? Who would protect me on my journey home if not Gyla? Who would defend my honor? You?"

Lycos glared, grimaced, smiled halfheartedly and then shook his head.

"Psappha, Psappha, what am I to do with you?"

"You, worker of wonders, are going to design a wardrobe for Gongyla. She can't sail in what she doesn't wear here. The crew might like it, but we might never reach Mitylene."

"There is nothing to design," he answered thoughtfully. "You call her your champion, dress her that way. Have Lesbian armor made for her. I'll make the molds myself."

"You will not," Gongyla said, having come in without either of them noticing. "You may be a womanish fop, Lycos, but you aren't a woman yet. I'll make the molds myself. If I have to cover myself, sir maiden, I'll do it with my own designs."

Lycos ruffled slightly then smiled. Psappha chuckled.

"She is not insulting your ability to create beauty, my cagey fox. Only what's left of your masculinity. Let her do as she wishes. Whatever she decides upon, she'll be magnificent."

~ ~ ~

The day of departure dawned balmy and clear. Psappha paced the front hall. Lycos had gone to the ship the day before to see to the stowing of their trunks. Lyneachia waited in the sedan chair with

Klies. Psappha's meandering thoughts kept pace with her footsteps. I am not sad to leave this place. What is taking her so long? The ship is waiting. Mitylene is waiting. Where is she?

"Do hurry, Gyla," she called. Her voice echoed through the nearly empty house. Gongyla marched toward her and she sucked in her breath.

From doeskin buskins to jaunty white ostrich plume, Gongyla was radiant. "Hadn't you better close your mouth, my love? You've always known I was beautiful."

"You are!"

"I know, pokey one. Now come on. The Poetess must not miss her ship."

Psappha felt like she was brimming over with bubbles. "You're going to love Mitylene. You've never seen it's equal. The old city sparkles on its island like an emerald cameo. In spring, The Lady dresses the hills in flowers. In winter, her winds sing Zeus' songs, both terrible and marvelous.

"We'll walk among her trees, you and me. The apples with their pastel garlands, olives with moonlight-bladed leaves that look like they're trying to stitch the sky and oaks so tall a hundred squirrels could nest in them without getting in each other's way. We'll stroll together in the marketplace with no need for disguises. We'll have our school, but we won't lock it behind garden walls. Our pupils will roam the scented hills and valleys as free as the clouds of grazing sheep. They'll gaggle in open fields like the many flocks of geese already there. You'll see. You'll hunt the woodland game and fish in crystal streams. Just you wait."

Gongyla tightened her arm around Psappha's slim waist as if to help contain her effervescent happiness.

"It sounds like my green land, tender one. Such liberty was known where women ruled, but men will not permit such freedom."

Psappha's mind cautioned her with a memory of the curtained sedan chair she had rejected the day Alkaios returned from Neccho's war. She thrust the thought away. *The Poetess is not some snit of a girl intimidated by outmoded custom.*

"Students will come," she said. "Mitylene is the center of the world."

"Will they not be shamed to walk so openly?" Gongyla asked as they climbed the gangway onto the waiting ship. "Will their families send them to so lax a teacher?"

"They will not be shamed, beloved warrior. The girls of Lesbos do not fear being seen." Psappha stifled her misgivings by telling her, again, about watching Atthis dancing in the park

Gongyla's brow crinkled. "She is the one who calls you?"

"She is one I might have called," Psappha said.

"Will you call her to Iphis?"

Psappha hedged. "Iphis does not reign in Mitylene."

"Iphis reigns wherever women are." Gongyla's thunderous eyes forbid further discussion.

Psappha let the subject drop, but it hung like a threatening storm between them as she gripped the rail with one hand, shaded her eyes with the other and stared at the horizon.

Peggy Ullman Bell

[page deliberately left blank]

> "And the best and worst of this
> that neither is most to blame,
> if you have forgotten my kisses
> and I have forgotten your name."
> 'Algernon Charles Swinburne'

-- XIX --

A shout from the rigging of the graceful trireme turned all faces north. Psappha ran to the bow, straining her vision, struggling to see the speck that was Lesbos. As the ship drew nearer to the city, her impatient eyes blinked as Helios kissed the citadel with morning, his light resting there in an extended caress. She saw squat white houses dozing within alabaster walls. Streets yawned in the crisp spring air.

Mitylene slowly awoke. By twos and threes, men stumbled along the quay. Merchants raised tent flaps and began setting out their wares. Psappha's pounding heart echoed the coxswain's drum. The seamen's chant, as they furled the sails, rang anthems in her heart. From behind and below, she could hear the oarsmen straining. She watched and listened as; to duet of stevedore and boatswain ship and dock were wed.

~ ~ ~

Psappha glided down the ramp draped in purple, adorned with gold, ivory, copper and onyx. Pittakos bustled to meet her. Except for looking older and a bit shopworn, his appearance had not changed. He still combined the splendid with the shoddy to create a grotesque parody of grace and leadership.

"Welcome, Lady Psappha," he bellowed for the sake of the crowd. "Your city proudly welcomes you home."

"Proudly, Pittakos? Has so much changed, since last we met?"

"Nothing has changed so much as you, Lady Psappha. You have grown lovelier in your absence."

Psappha fought to modulate her voice. "An absence you caused, sir satyr."

Pittakos responded beneath his breath. "An error I have come to regret." He smiled to please the crowd.

"Such gallantry must tax you, Pittakos, or, has the burden of your office stolen the sting from your tongue? You didn't send for my because of my beauty. My ability to attract trade and taxes prompted you. You would have let me rot in Syracuse if I had not become too famous to ignore." *If he is to exile me again, I don't want to leave this dock. I'd rather die here and now in Mitylene's embrace.*

"You wrong me, Psappha," he said in an undertone. "I have no quarrel with you."

"Quarrel enough to have kept me in exile for almost fifteen years."

"You would have been sent for long ago had your whereabouts been known. It was assumed you had perished when swept overboard."

He still spoke for the crowd, apparently gracious, but Psappha saw the tautness of his neck. Taking a deep breath, she called up her singer's voice and said, "Do you expect me to believe that the daughter of Scamandronomos is renowned in Babylon and unheralded in Mitylene?"

His face reddened as he continued his political charade. "We heard long ago of the Illustrious Sappho of Lesbos. As soon as we learned she called herself Psappha, your young brother was dispatched to discover if The Poetess was indeed our Psappha."

His tone sent a familiar shiver the length of her spine. For the world, Pittakos looked like a merchant trying to sell something wonderful at a bargain, but Psappha saw his anger and she smiled. Her quiet voice dripped disdain. "Is it that you no longer fear my innocent verses, crack-toes, or has my small success softened your resolve to deprive me of my home?"

"It was not from fear that I sent you away, Psappha," he said, his lecherous eyes confirmed her earlier suspicions. "There seemed no logic in allowing you and your mouthy betrothed to stay here worrying at my heels in troubled times."

"Have you forgotten that I am no cur-pup to worry at anyone's heels? I was never a danger to you, gutter climber, yet you sent me away. Now you deign to welcome me with honor. Why?"

"Perhaps I missed the sharpness of your tongue," he hissed as the throng tightened around them.

"I doubt that." She obliged him by keeping her voice hushed. "More likely your greed for fame drove you to reason in spite of yourself."

His porcine eyes flickered. "You could have returned at any time."

"Somehow, I doubt that, Pittakos." With a gracious wave to the throng around and behind him, she stepped off the gangway into the shade of a stack of baskets.

"It's true," he admitted. "Some of our best maidens were preparing to journey to Sicily. However ..."

Psappha nodded to the sycophants in close array. "If you will excuse me, I would like to get under cover before the sun gets much higher."

Pittakos bowed before her, his scraggly beard brushing his dusty feet. "I will escort you," he said. "I've taken the liberty of having your father's house prepared for you."

Psappha suppressed a gasp. *Living in my father's house seemed so important.* Now, she realized she no longer wanted to live in the shadow of the citadel. She released her breath slowly under firm control. "I will reside in my brother's house, thank you."

"Your brother's house is quite fine, but it is hardly fitting for a teacher of your stature. Surely your pupils would feel more at ease among the upper aristocracy."

"My students will feel at ease with the simple pleasures of earth and sun -- or they will not be my students. As for me, I am an aristocrat wherever I reside, and, I do not choose to have any of my luster rub off on you."

"As you wish," he said in a tone so low it was barely audible above welcoming cheers. Then once more proclaiming loudly he said, "I will escort you to your brother's house."

"I prefer my own escort, thank you." Her hand fluttered in pre-arranged signal and Gongyla disembarked.

Pittakos gaped, blinked, coughed then gaped again. Psappha stared. She had not expected this. Magnificent was too small a word. Gongyla strode down the gangway in full Lesbian military regalia, with slight, spectacular variations. Her greaves and breastplate were gold. They looked like the artisans had molded the metal to her body while still warm and allowed it to cool around every seductive curve. The sun's reflection on her face turned her cinnamon complexion to a polished cedar glow. A wide band of amethysts stretched across her forehead and disappeared into her mass of hair. She stopped, a few feet before she reached Psappha, and stood like Artemis awaiting the hunt, the tip of her long bow resting on the dock, the other tip half-hidden in the feather on her helmet.

With a slight enigmatic smile, she drew an arrow from her quiver, set it, drew the bow and let it snap. Psappha watched as the arrow snipped the line holding Pittakos's banner to the ornate sedan chair that stood waiting a few feet beyond the crowd.

So much for sedan chairs, Psappha thought as she took Gyla's arm. When they stepped forward, the crowd parted and Psappha wasn't sure which of them received the most attention.

Lycos followed on a chestnut stallion originally intended for one of Pittakos' honor guard. He too wore Lesbian armor complete with helmet and his own neatly trimmed red beard. His horse pranced nervously when he slowed beside them. Behind him, a wide-eyed Klies perched astride an amber filly waving grandly as if all of the excitement was for her alone.

Psappha skip-stepped to keep pace with Gongyla's easy stride, too intent on visions of her orchard to acknowledge the huzzas that followed her and her resplendent protector.

Everything seemed smaller, but no less beautiful, than she remembered. From the south beach, she ran ahead, tugging Gongyla's hand, drawing her along the winding footpath, while the others continued up the road. Walking through The Lady's Park, she could not help glancing about expecting to see a golden haired nymph dancing among trees that had just begun to bud. Festooned branches cast filigreed shadows over fragrant hyacinths. The culverts still trickled with remnants of melted snow.

The Lady's Temple drew the priestess of Cybele like iron to magnetite. Gyla took the tiered temple stairs two at a time. The temple guards nodded appreciatively and stepped back as she swung her quiver from her back and leaned it against the temple's natural wall. She removed her armor, revealing an ultra sheer short blouse above her abbreviated skirt. Psappha caught up with her as she was laying her breastplate and greaves on the floor of the portico.

Inside, the little girls, the Nymphs stopped their dance to ogle Gongyla as she passed. The pubescent Maidens sighed in admiration. Psappha noted that she knew none of them, which reminded her that, like her, her companions of old had graduated to the Mother chamber deeper inside the temple.

Gyla paused at the petal-portal to caress the smooth red clay with her fingertips. Her hair brushed across the perfect bud at its zenith as she bowed through to the musky chamber beyond. Taking a torch from the blush pink wall, she motioned Psappha through the next orifice. In the pear-shaped chamber, she chose the left opening as if by instinct. *Has she been in such a place before?*

Psappha had little time in which to wonder. It seemed only seconds before she fell to her knees at the center of the Crone Chamber. Gongyla did not. Instead, she scanned the room, placed her hand over her heart then extended it palm downward toward the Crone of Crones seated in her usual dark corner.

The holist among the women motioned Gyla to a seat beside her. Psappha had most anticipated this welcome. She had expected the Wise Ones to invite Gyla to take her place among them. *Just not so soon. I don't want to lose her to the temple.*

It was a full two hours later when they emerged from the temple and continued toward Eurigios' former home. Psappha climbed the rocky path up from the park with ease. Her legs were longer now. She felt as if she climbed Olympus. Her home was above.

Lycos waved excitedly as they breasted the hill. "The house is full," he shouted. "Larichos says if more come we will need a larger house. There are maidens everywhere. Some bossy female sent their servants elsewhere."

Praxinoa met them in the garden. The years had not been kind. Nevertheless, she had the strength to hug Psappha semi-breathless before she spoke. "It's not as confused as your flame-thatched man-servant thinks."

"Man-servant! I'll have you know I'm Psappha's personal business manager."

Psappha smiled. "Hush." He would not cow Praxinoa as Lyneachia. To Praxinoa, she said, "He's correct." Then, to Lycos she added, "Your duties have not changed, my friend, but Praxinoa will have precedence in all matters pertaining to household management. And she'll have charge of you," she added addressing Klies who was already in the garden surrounded by a bevy of pre-pubescent girls. "Now what's this about sending my student's servants away?"

"I sent the older maidens with their serving women to Larichos's grandfather's house up the hill. Their men and the married servants are comfortably situated in my late husband's house," Praxinoa explained. Psappha had forgotten the existence of Praxinoa's Lesbian husband, long dead before Psappha was born.

"You'll need more room soon, judging from the number of petitions coming in," Larichos said as he joined them

"I'll take care of those," said Lycos.

Larichos nodded. "Local maidens could come during the day, returning to their homes at night."

"Yes, of course," Psappha agreed. "Lycos, adjust their tuition accordingly."

"We'll still need more room," Praxinoa added.

"If we need it, we'll find it." That settled, Psappha took Gyla's hand and proceeded to show her the rest of her home. The house also seemed smaller but when they reached the nursery and she tried to sit in one of Larichos's chairs she understood the strangeness. The temple, the path, the house had not shrunk. She had grown, not much to be sure – just enough to be too wide for the tiny chair.

"I thought this would be suitable for your daughter," Praxinoa said from the doorway.

Klies squealed. "I can't sleep here. It's for babies!"

Psappha smiled at Praxinoa's familiar sniff.

"And who might you be, Young Miss?"

Klies drew herself up plunked her fists on her hips. "I'm a young woman."

Praxinoa looked perplexed. "Are you a Maiden already?"

"Well no," Klies admitted. "But…"

"But nothing, Young Miss. This will be your chamber."

"But…"

"But nothing," her mother echoed. "Come, Gyla, I have more houses to show you."

"But…."

Psappha kept walking as if she had not heard. She and Gongyla entered the chambers that had been her mother's and later hers for a little while. Unwelcome memories bloomed. She slumped onto the chaise and laid the back of her hand against her forehead in unconscious imitation.

"Headache?"

"No, my love, I'm just tired."

She barely had time to make herself comfortable before Klies came running in, dragging Praxinoa by the hand and followed by the rest of Psappha's entourage.

"Mo<u>ther</u>, this <u>woman</u> says I must do as she tells me." She dropped to her knees beside the chaise. "I never had to do what Lyneachia said unless I wanted to."

Psappha smiled and reached to smooth her daughter's undisciplined hair. "Lyneachia was less wise than Praxinoa. Praxinoa was companion to the grandmother for whom I named you. She tended me. She raised your uncle, Larichos alone. Of course you must do as she tells you."

Klies pulled away from her mother's soothing hand. "The daughter of Kerkolos of Andros takes no orders from slaves."

"Praxinoa was never a slave, Klies. She is the widow of an orphaned cousin of a cousin of your grandfather's, and has been part of this family for three generations. You need to learn what conduct is expected of a Lesbian aristocrat. There's no better teacher for that than Praxinoa. She'll teach you as she taught me." *With great difficulty*, she recalled, casting a tender glance at her aging nurse.

Klies frowned, an unanswered question in her angry eyes.

Psappha nodded. "Yes, willful one, I will do as Praxinoa advises and so will you."

"I don't need a nurse."

"We all need a nurse sometimes," Psappha said. "None of us ever gets so grown up we don't need someone, sometimes, to love us despite ourselves." She glanced toward Gyla then her gaze fell on the doors to what had been Eurigios's chamber. "Why are those doors closed? Lycos, I thought I told you both chambers were to be prepared, one for me, the other for Gyla."

"That's what I told the old witch," Lycos quickly deflected her displeasure.

"I prepared the gatehouse," Praxinoa said. "She is your guard is she not?"

"She is that and more. She will stay beside me." Catching an exchange of glances between Praxinoa and Larichos, she turned her irritated gaze on him. "Is this your doing?"

Larichos pouted. "Those are my rooms."

"You won't need them," Psappha said. "You're in charge of your grandfather's house. I need you there. I can't be in two places at once. Nor can Praxinoa. One of you will have to see to each. There's no one else I trust." Now, it was Lycos's turn to pout but Psappha continued to address her younger brother. "Mind you treat my pupils with respect."

Larichos's face brightened. The house up the hill was crammed with Maidens.

Psappha turned her attention to Lycos. "The gatehouse will be a fine place for you, my friend. You'll have all the privacy you need. You won't have to complain about our classes disturbing your work on the accounts. And think how convenient it will be for the handling of petitioners and tradesmen."

Mollified, Lycos blustered at Praxinoa. "Hop to it, woman. Have those doors opened at once."

"Open them yourself," said Praxinoa as she hustled Klies from the room. "You rest," she instructed Psappha as she followed Klies's defiant parade-of-one.

Lycos scrambled to open the doors and had an enjoyable few minutes ordering housemaids about before escaping by a different exit. He need not have hurried. Psappha had fallen asleep, fully clothed, on the chaise.

~ ~ ~

Three months later, Psappha looked upon the changes to her world and felt as if her soul might break free and fly off to Olympus at any moment. It was the thirtieth anniversary of her birth. Her school had survived the relocation beyond even Lycos' lofty dreams. Klies had grown as fond of Praxinoa as she, herself, had been. Each week brought more petitions from anxious fathers seeking to have their daughters admitted to Psappha's exalted circle. When

Larichos's grandfather's house overflowed, Psappha discovered that she owned the inlet where Alkaios had begun her wedding gift. There was more than enough gold to finish it far beyond its original plan.

A near perpendicular cliff bounded the inlet on three sides. There would be no need for gates. A small grove of The Lady's sacred olive trees struggled for survival at the very back of the sheltered inlet where only early morning sun could reach. Near what would become their kitchen, a tumble of buckets formed a creaking waterfall as ox-power turned the crank on a deep fresh-water well. The ruble of construction surrounded the well. When the house was finished, a goose-mowed lawn would lead down to a shallow half-moon of beach.

The entrance would be through a small villa on the bluff a short way from where Psappha sat strumming her lyre in the warm afternoon. Although she and Gongyla had allowed no male input on the design for the school, Lycos had designed his own villa.

The path to the beach was steep and treacherous. Eventually it would have stairs carved into the stone but, for the time being the workers used pulleys and rope to lower their materials and Psappha chose to watch from the bluff. The mid-summer breeze played hide and seek in the folds of her kiton. Below, in the secluded inlet south of The Lady's Park, local petitioners, too poor to pay their daughter's full tuition labored to build the school's future home. The criers called for teachers now, yet still more pupils came.

Gyla's going to have to leave off hunting with the foresters and help me with the school as she did in Syracuse. The thought saddened her. It had become impossible to imagine Gyla as anything but wild and free.

Evening shadows lengthened long before Gongyla sprinted toward her. Her brief kiton pressed against her as she loped along the edge of the bluff bow in one hand, a brace of bright-feathered birds in the other. When she reached Psappha, she tossed her bounty to the ground then leaned her bow next to the lyre. Gyla's free roaming had made her lovelier than Psappha had ever imagined she could become. Gazing up into dark, far-seeing eyes, she became impatient for the night.

Peggy Ullman Bell

[page deliberately left blank]

> "She was a form of life and light
> that, seen, became a part of sight
> and rose, where'er I turned mine eyes,
> The morning star of memory!"
> 'Lord Byron'

-- XX --

Lycos met them at the door to Eurigios's house. "There's a courtier waiting."

"Why didn't you have him leave a message?" Gyla asked.

"Never mind," said Psappha as she hurried past. She'd had her fill of courtiers. *I'll get rid of this one post haste.* She stopped at the entrance to the main hall, feeling suddenly as if she had stepped back in time. The courtier had his back to her. When he turned, she saw that only the uniform was the same; no greasy fingers and no lamb. This man gleamed with cleanliness as he bowed before her.

Psappha sensed Gyla behind her and was glad. She nodded politely to the courtier then settled herself into one of the chairs by the fire. She laughed at the expression that swept over his face as Gongyla took her place in the matching chair. "Well?"

The youth fumbled with his clothes, apparently searching for the scroll he held in his hand. He remembered where it was and handed it to Psappha while still keeping a wary eye on Gongyla. Psappha passed it to Gongyla. Lycos dismissed the courtier with a back-hand gesture.

"Damn," Gyla said after a moment's pause. "Will we never have done with that pig?" She handed the scroll to Psappha who took it between two fingers much as she might try to hold a tiny angry snake.

Psappha glanced at it, dropped it then marched to the sideboard and grabbing a flagon. She reached for the water, changed her mind, filled a goblet with wine and downed it. "You meet with him," she told Lycos. "It's your job to handle petitioners. Pittakos deserves no special treatment."

"That may be true," he said, "but you need to meet with him none the less."

"Perhaps," she said, "Perhaps tomorrow."

~ ~ ~

The sun was barely up when Psappha picked the scroll up from her dressing table, glared at it a moment then let it fall to the floor. "He's a plague," she grumbled, kicking the petition beneath the bed.

Gongyla turned Psappha toward the sheet of Phoenician glass that covered half of one wall. "Look," she commanded. "Is that Psappha, helpless orphan?"

What Psappha saw in the mirror bore little resemblance to what she saw in her heart. The woman in the glass looked confident, mature, the mother of a blossoming teenager, but, within herself, she was fifteen and frightened.

"You shouldn't need me to remind you who you are," Gongyla scolded. "You are The Poetess, The Teacher, respected throughout the world. Now -- Teacher, prepare to receive the pretender and, remember, my lady, Pittakos would not dare harm you. He is the usurper -- Not you. You are Psappha, daughter of Scamandronomos. The husband of Dracon's sister is beneath your concern."

~ ~ ~

It was late that afternoon before Pittakos stomped into the main hall. Psappha addressed him with exaggerated courtesy, making no effort to hide her revulsion. "You have orders for me, Tyrant?"

For the first time, Pittakos did not allow his focus to stray below her face. His growl dripped deference as he said, "I have a request."

"A request from a Tyrant is an order in effect, is it not? I heard that you have given new meaning to the word."

She had received him standing. Now, she motioned him to the only chair in the room, a low Egyptian affair intended for a menial. When he accepted it, she reclined on the chaise Gongyla had placed on the dais for her.

Pittakos squirmed as had been Gongyla's intent. "I do not come as Tyrant," he said. "I came today as a humble petitioner."

"Petitioners are Lycos's business. Were you afraid he would deny you? Have you some back-alley daughter you dare suggest for my group? Surely even you would not presume to that extent, a niece perhaps?" The connotation she placed on the word niece made it infinitely clear the word was not her first choice.

He stood to meet her challenge eye to eye. "Not a niece," he assured her, giving the word the same disparaging connotation. "My ward," he said, "an orphan more than worthy of your company. An exceedingly clever maiden," he concluded reflectively, "with a talent so great that I sometimes think she is Terpsichore and only pretends mortality to tease me."

"She must be quite special to have gained such praise from you while remaining a maiden. Unfortunately, I have no room for another pupil."

"Apparently I have not made myself clear. Atthis . . ."

Psappha trembled. Pictures flashed behind her eyes. *Golden Atthis!* The vision seared her brain. *Surely Pittakos' present ward can not be that same Atthis. She could not have remained maiden so long. Yet, he said she dances. Atthis was his ward. Atthis danced, like Terpsichore she danced. But maiden? After so many years?*

"Lady Psappha?"

"Excuse me, Pittakos. You were you saying?"

"I was saying, dear lady, that I was not suggesting The Lady Atthis as a pupil. I am suggesting her as an instructor."

The Lady Atthis! As an instructor? He presents a woman. But, of course. I was Klies's age when I left. But, a maiden? Such a beautiful girl? With no husband? It seemed impossible.

Pittakos continued unaware of her lapsed attention. "Her capabilities as a dancer would compliment your songs and add abundantly to the joys of your pupils."

Psappha wanted to refuse him on principle. However, since Lyneachia stayed behind in Syracuse, she missed watching her pupils dance. *And,* she reminded herself breathlessly, *it could be the same beautiful Atthis.*

"Very well," she said with an apparent calm, "send her to me. If she is as accomplished as you say, I will accept her." *You would accept the girl-child Atthis even if she could no longer dance a single step,* her conscience butted in.

After he left and she had consumed another goblet of wine to wash away his presence, she went out into the garden for a bit of fresh air.

Alone in her outdoor arbor-pavilion, Psappha closed her eyes and let her mind's eye gaze fondly on the girl-child Atthis. *Could she be?* She left the question dangling on the edge of nothing and allowed the buzzing of the bees to lull her into a peaceful doze. Listening to their droning, she imagined herself a dull brownish moth flitting from blossom to blossom, drinking ambrosia in the company of a glorious gold and blue butterfly.

"So, milady of the velvet voice, you have grown too famous to have time for poor petitioners?"

Psappha's eyes flew open. Her hand flew to her throat. The voice that he called velvet hid in the pit of her stomach. She rubbed her eyes with clenched fists in an effort to wipe out the apparition that strode toward her. Then, still not sure she wasn't dreaming, she gulped. He looked different yet the same. His milk-blue eyes were as full of mischief as ever. "What?" he teased. "Have you no song of welcome for your long lost betrothed?"

Psappha couldn't believe her senses. His voice was a little deeper, but so was hers. A thick reddish-blond beard covered most of his lower face. Through it, she caught a glimpse of the long jagged scar the storm-loosened spar had created on his left cheek. With a girlish squeal, she ran and threw herself into his arms, laughing and weeping for joy at the same time.

Alkaios caught her up, whirled and set her back on shaky feet, leaning over her until he unclasped her hands from behind his neck.

She grabbed both of his hands, and swung round and round with him in an improvised dance, her mind reeling in step. His gruff laughter blended with her chiming giggles as they high-stepped, circled, kicked and circled until they were both completely out of breath.

"Whew," he huffed, wiping his beaded brow with his thumbs. "This calls for a touch of the grape"

"Alkaios, Alkaios, the years have not changed you. You show up from Hades, not even a little bit drowned, and all you want is your wine-skin. Where have you been? I thought you dead!"

"And I you," he said. "But you're alive. How dared you be so sure that I was not? You didn't wait for me," he pouted comically.

"But, I saw you die," she protested belligerently. "I had…"

There was a rustling of leaves as Gongyla joined them.

"Gaea's blessing," Alkaios saluted. Gongyla scowled. Alkaios's flashed his winning smile. Gongyla glared. Alkaios glanced at the worried look on Psappha's face and grinned as Gongyla adjusted her stance to block his view. He winked at her, then, with arm extended palm upward in the ancient Cretan manner, he said, "Hail, oh Iphis."

~ ~ ~

Gongyla stayed mute through dinner and well into the early evening. Psappha could hardly contain her excitement. Her nerves crackled like the small logs in the fireplace. "How I've missed you faultless humor, 'Kios. Gyla, please stop scowling. Alkaios is my dearest friend from childhood."

"Childhood, 'S'pha?" Alkaios' eyes twinkled. "Where is the fine lady who became so upset at being called a child?"

"Oh, hush, Kios that was when I loved you."

"You don't love me? My life is worthless. I should have drowned after all." He grimaced at her with such a parody of grief that she bubbled with giggles.

They felt good the bubbles. She was tired of being serious.

"Kios, thou comedian, thank you. It's been too long since I've laughed so freely. Now tell us, what did happen to you? Where have you been?" She motioned him toward the chair opposite hers.

Gongyla's frown deepened. Alkaios smiled at her and pulled up a stool instead. He placed the stool at the third point in an imaginary triangle and her dark brows arched menacingly above penetrating onyx eyes. He watched her until she had seated herself in her usual chair. Then, he said, "For this we need refreshment."

He went to the sideboard and filled three goblets without even glancing toward the water. When he returned, he handed two of the goblets to Gongyla, granting her the privilege of serving Psappha. He settled on his stool, glass in hand with his long legs stretched toward the hearth. "I've been to Egypt and the continent," he said as much to Gongyla as to Psappha.

"Having assumed you were warming Poseidon's bed, imagine my surprise when I heard that Psappha of Lesbos was teaching Poetry in Syracuse. I would have jumped on the first ship available but there was the small matter of a little neighborhood war to be taken care of first. By the time that was finished, I heard you had returned to Mitylene so -- I petitioned Pittakos and here I am."

"You petitioned Pittakos? What happened?"

"He said, 'come home', of course -- else I'd be pining in some temple longing for you instead of sitting here with a broken heart."

"Be serious. What, exactly, did he say?"

"He said, 'come home,' and some nonsense about forgiveness being better than revenge. What does it matter? The important thing is, I'm here. Are you sure you don't love me?"

Before Psappha had time to comment, Klies joined them. Alkaios arched a brow. "My daughter Klies," Psappha said.

"May I go to the city with Larichos tomorrow?" Klies asked without acknowledging the introduction. "Lycos said to ask you."

"Did he say to ask me or did he say no?"

Klies' flinch betrayed her.

Psappha laughed. "So, little imp, Lycos said no and you wish me to over-ride his judgment. For shame, Klies. If Lycos said no, he had a reason."

"Please, Mother, Larichos is your brother. He wouldn't let anything happen to me. Lycos is a prissy old maid. He doesn't want me to go because Daphnos is going. He thinks I'm still in swaddling."

Her choice of words found echo in Psappha's memory. Alkaios chuckled. Psappha blushed. She knew the scene he was remembering. Not trusting her voice because of it, she nodded to Klies who ran out as if afraid her mother might change her mind.

"A fine little rabbit you have there."

Psappha shook her head. "No rabbit that one. She's as pampered as Cleopatra's cat. You must forgive her rudeness. She has seen no man except Lycos and eunuchs since she was a toddler."

"Lycos? Who is Lycos?"

Psappha shrugged. "Lycos is Lycos."

"Don't echo me, S'pha. Who is he?"

"You know who he is. He opened the gate for you."

"No one opened the gate for me. It was open. I just walked in."

"Then how did you know I wished to see no one?"

"There was a note on the gatepost. So, tell me who Lycos is and by what right does he dictate to your daughter?"

"You'll have to meet him to understand."

~ ~ ~

The next day, Alkaios remained at the guesthouse until after sunset. When he arrived at the main house, Psappha led him straight to the tiny room in the gatehouse where Lycos hunched over the household accounts. Without knocking, she barged in and demanded that he put his figures aside. "Come sup with a friend," she commanded.

Lycos brushed his fingers through his tousled red hair, pushed his chair back and turned wearily. "You know I don't like leaving my work to help entertain your guests." When he realized she was not alone he blushed vividly and began fumbling with his clothes.

Alkaios stared. Psappha eyed them both suspiciously. "Come, Lycos. We'll share wine before dinner."

Lycos had turned and shuffled his papers. "You go on. I've already sent word to have something brought to me here."

"I'll cancel that," she said. "You finish what you're doing. We'll see you at dinner." She turned to leave then stopped. "Klies will be accompanying Larichos tomorrow. She's too near grown to be confined."

"It's because she is nearly grown that she should be confined," Lycos said without turning around.

"There are no gynakia here."

"Then ask Praxinoa to go with them."

"Don't be stuffy, Lycos. Besides, Praxinoa is too old. She'd never keep up with them."

"Remind me sometime to ask Praxinoa if she knows why you refuse to discipline your child."

Psappha's ingrained hatred of confrontation stopped her from pushing the issue. Instead, she glanced at Alkaios, quickly shifting her gaze toward the door to indicate it was time for them to leave.

"I must apologize for Lycos," she said as they crossed the garden. "Please don't let his rudeness spoil your homecoming. I know better than to interrupt him. You will see at dinner that he can be a delightful companion when it pleases him. He isn't usually so churlish. He must have had something else on his mind."

"No doubt," Alkaios said. "I think I can explain…"

She cut him off. "Here we are," she said. They had reached the main hall. Moments later, just as she and he were comfortably seated and the wine had been served, Gongyla marched in, glanced at Alkaios who was sitting in her chair, then sat cross-legged, on the hearth and interrupted their conversation with "Will Lady Atthis be coming here?"

Psappha matched her gruff tone. "She will come for an interview. I will decide if she's to join us."

"I didn't know Atthis had returned from her sojourn in Naucratis," Alkaios commented gravely.

"You know her?" Gyla queried.

"Well," said Alkaios.

Psappha was too excited to question the tightness in his tone. The expression that had crossed his face at mention of Atthis had told her that yes this Atthis was, indeed, the same Atthis. "Do you think The Lady Atthis would accept a place here?"

"Atthis would be honored to be accepted here," he said.

"Hardly honored," Psappha said, overlooking his omission of the honorarium. "Would she be happy here, do you think, after her travels? We live a very simple life. It can be a dismal life for an attractive girl to live solely in the company of women."

"Atthis would consider this a perfect setting," he replied, drawing a sharp look from Gongyla.

Psappha squirmed in her chair. They seemed to be deep in a conversation in which she had no part, although neither of them uttered another word. They glanced at each other then eyed Psappha, rolled their eyes, made weird mouth noises then smiled like lifelong friends.

"What is it?" Psappha's discomfort forced her to sound pettish.

She got no answer. Gyla stood up and left the room. Moments later, she returned with an Egyptian chair to which Alkaios shifted as soon as she set it in place. "To Psappha," he said, raising his goblet.

"To Psappha," Gongyla echoed.

Psappha wasn't sure she liked their instant friendship.

"To friendship," 'Kios toasted Gyla as if he'd heard her thoughts.

"Friends?" Psappha tasted the word as she sipped her wine. "Yes," she decided. "We are friends now, Alkaios. Much has happened since we were pledged, much to change us both. Why is it that you never married? There must have been someone in all this time."

"I've been in exile, S'pha. Men without estates get few offers of marriage."

"Without marriage then," she teased. "Don't tell me you've been celibate all this time."

"Hardly. And you?" he added with a wink at Gongyla.

"We're talking about you." Psappha diverted the question. "Was there no one you wanted for your own?"

"Other than you, my lovely, there was only one, long ago before we . . ."

"Before we what, Alkaios?"

When he ignored her and pointedly munched an apple, she glanced at Gyla and realized she didn't want him to continue. "Do you think I should invite The Lady Atthis to join my staff?" she asked, reverting to her original topic.

"If you're sure you want her," he responded with a trace of tension in his voice.

"Would she accept?"

"She has no choice in the matter."

"No choice?"

"Not if her guardian wishes it. Obviously, his reasons for sending her away no longer apply. You and your school have turned fashion in her favor and Pittakos will follow fashion no matter where it leads."

That said, Psappha and Alkaios drank their wine in shared silence. Gongyla leaned down and kissed Psappha lightly on the cheek before she left them.

"Send more wine," Alkaios said, but Gongyla had already closed the door.

Psappha hurried to catch her, but, as she started to open the door, she heard voices and she stopped.

~ ~ ~

"Why do you slump so, Gentle Warrior?"

"Why are you here, Old Woman? It is late. You should be in your bed."

"This is a chair my bones are used to," Praxinoa told her. "Many nights, when Psappha's mother was alive, I never saw my bed. She was the demanding sort, Psappha's mother. Ever aware of her own importance."

"I thought you were Psappha's nurse," Gongyla said.

"That, too," Praxinoa said. "But, my Psappha was far less demanding than her mother. Never wanted a thing but her mother's love, that child," she said; her voice thick with sadness.

"Her mother did not love her?"

"Klies loved only Klies," Praxinoa told her tiredly. "Only Klies and perhaps her son. She doted on Charaxos. Spoiled him. I suppose that's why he couldn't stand it when she remarried. Went away right after that, he did. Hasn't been home since."

"He cared nothing for his sister?"

Praxinoa sighed. "Psappha was already promised to Alkaios. Her future was assured, or so they all thought. Too bad they never asked her. She'd have told them a thing or two, I'll warrant. Wanted nothing but to make her music, my Psappha. Had no use for marriage nor for men, even then. Don't look so surprised," she said. "Did you not wonder that I was not shocked to see you in her bed?"

"I did," Gongyla admitted.

"Well, Praxinoa always did know what was good for her Psappha."

~ ~ ~

"What's taking you so long, S'pha?"

Psappha pulled her ear away from the door. *How dare she say those things about my mother? None of it's true. If she weren't so old, I'd send her away for her lies.*

"S'pha?"

"I'm sorry, Kios. I'll be with you in a moment." Listening, hearing nothing, she eased the door the rest of the way open. Gongyla was nowhere in sight. Praxinoa looked up at her through sleepy eyes. "We need more wine," Psappha told her sharply. "See to it," she said as she slammed the door.

"Ouch! S'pha, take it easy on my head."

"Sorry, 'Kios."

When she returned to her chair, he said, "Do you remember what I said earlier about having someone in my life, though not a wife?"

Psappha nodded cautiously. "Atthis?"

"No, before that. During the retreat from Charchemish. Necho insisted each of us officers take a recruit under our wing for training. I was assigned a flame-crowned strippling from Leucos."

"Lycos?"

"That wasn't his name then but yes – maybe. It's hard to tell with that red bush on his face. But it would explain his rudeness."

"Did you treat him badly? Did you beat him?"

"No, Gentle-one, I loved him. I didn't beat him. Although he might have preferred that to what happened."

"Did he return your love?"

"Only in the way any youth loves his mentor, I thought. I didn't know. But it doesn't matter now, S'pha. I gave him reason to hate me." His voice was thick with guilt: His eyes, dark with pain. Psappha laid her palm on his knee in sympathy. He brushed it away and continued. "The army was bogged down. The only thing we had to fill the idle hours was gambling and our gold was soon gone. To keep playing, we wagered slaves. I ... I can't go on."

"What happened, 'Kios?"

"I can't tell you. It's too shameful."

"Where have I heard that before? Tell me. Lycos is very much alive."

Alkaios got up and refilled their goblets from the fourth flagon of wine. He swigged his on the way back to his chair. "I lost him on the turn of the dice. I know. Don't look at me like that. It was horrid of me I know, but I was drunk don't you see? Anyway, by the next morning he had vanished. Hades has no wrath like that of the fellow who'd won him. I nursed bruises for a month after but it didn't matter. I was glad he got away. I didn't want him to become a slave."

"He was free-born?"

"Yes."

"And you sold him?"

"I didn't sell him. I lost him."

"It's the same thing. He became a slave because of you. No wonder he didn't want to have supper with us. I'd be surprised if he didn't hate you."

Anger seemed to have cleared Alkaios' head. "The flaming fox couldn't hate anybody."

"What did you say?"

"I said the flaming fox couldn't hate anybody. What're you gaping at, S'pha?"

"The flaming fox," she said. "My little fox. Strange that we chose such similar names for him."

"Not so strange," he said, "considering that unruly mane of his."

Servants arrived with more wine and Psappha refilled the goblet he waved in her direction. After a moment, while he drained the goblet, she asked, "Is Lycos why you never married?"

"I never married because I was already married to my memory of you."

Psappha's flush of pleasure chilled when she saw merriment in his eyes. She made no move to refill his goblet or to stoke the dying fire.

"He still cares for you," she said after a time.

"Nah-h-h . . .," he yawned. "If he cared, he'd be here."

"How simple it must be to be a man," she said. "Lycos thinks like a woman and you obviously know nothing about women. If he did not care for you, the first thing he would do would be to flaunt his beauty before you to remind you of what you threw away. Beauty which -- in case you didn't notice -- has been heightened by maturity."

"I noticed," he admitted, pensively scratching his beard. "I noticed."

"If he cares, and I think he does," she continued, "giving you another chance to hurt him is the last thing he'd do. One's first is the hardest to forget," she added, secretly aware that she was speaking as much of herself as of Lycos. She felt a blush rising. *Is he remembering that he was my first?* She struggled for something to say, some way to explain to him that, although she loved him, she did not, could not love him in the way that she assumed he desired. *But, what is this with Lycos? Perhaps he does understand. We need to talk. How do I approach the subject?*

It didn't matter. Alkaios was asleep in Gongyla's chair.

> *"I loved thee, Atthis, long ago,*
> *"When our girlhood was all flowers."*
> *'Sappho'*

-- XXI --

A group of pupils clustered about Psappha, each with their personal lyre, most of which Gyla had carved for them the previous winter. Psappha could not help smiling at their perplexed expressions as they tried to copy her tune. Her fingers meandered at will, creating a unique melody that she would never quite duplicate because her attention was elsewhere. Nearly a year had passed since Pittakos presented his so-called request and yet Atthis had never come for an interview.

Not far from Psappha's tight little group, Klies, played handball on the green with Larichos and his friend Daphnos; with her skirt tucked into her girdle.

She's too old to be showing her ankles. If she is too old, then what, pray Hecate, am I?

The ball flew over Klies' head. She jumped for it, missed and fell laughing onto the grass. Daphnos snatched a handful of flowers and showered them over her.

In the midst of laughter, Psappha realized that her students no longer practiced their music. They watched the tableau on the lawn instead. She plucked her top string sharply and began the day's lesson again, this time giving it more careful attention.

Klies joined them dragging her uncle and his friend with her. She frowned when her mother yanked her skirt loose but she draped it demurely over her feet when she sat. Soon, her clear, sweet soprano blended and harmonized with her mother's rich contralto, adding swirls to the vibrant fullness of her mother's song. When they finished, Psappha ended the session and they all hurried down to the house. The nooning sun indicated the approach of story time.

Gongyla called from the opposite side of the garden where dozens of maidens had grouped themselves at her feet, avidly awaiting her latest story. All save Psappha joined them. She, too, loved Gyla's ability to weave elaborate tales, but she preferred to listen from the solitude of her arbor. As she listened, she closed her eyes.

The hum of Gongyla's monologue dwindled. Psappha noticed the silence and opened her eyes. A youngish woman knelt to touch the poppies along the path. Her long saffron colored hair fell forward to hide her face. Lycos stood behind her but Psappha paid him no heed. Her spirit reached to touch the veil of hair she saw as electrum sheen. The woman rose and Psappha sucked her breath.

What Psappha saw was beauty and perfection that filled her soul with song. *I thought Eros the best beloved offspring of Earth and Heaven. He shook my mind like the down-rushing wind that falls upon the oak trees.*

Remember, Atthis, how we came upon you in the park? Such an awkward, graceful child you were; gamboling among the trees like a spring fawn; so beautiful in you gangly grace. Even then, so early, you reflected the kiss of Terpsichore as you flitted on the grass. I remember well your flashing eyes as you peered at us from behind a bay tree. I felt so mature and grandly remote from you but my vagrant heart was already forfeit to that soul-eyed girl." We walked away from you but I carried the vision of you with me, unable to dispel the memory.

That time at the banquet my spirit was yours alone: A fair sight you were to see: I thought then I would come and speak to you, but you were fleet of foot and soon gone: I was so young then: So in love with love and beauty: Passion choked her voice as she said, "You wished to see me?"

Atthis shook her hair back from her shoulders and entered the arbor. Psappha saw her face -- the moon, with midnight in her eyes -- her smile -- the sun was shamed.

"Lady Psappha?"

Her voice fell on Psappha's ears like the whisper of a goddess. She extended a trembling hand, her voice lost beneath Eros' blinding fire. There was no further doubt. This fair young woman, warming her being with a radiant smile, was the golden girl-child, Atthis, grown and flowered into a magnificence of femininity. She wiped her palms on her skirt, forgetting her welcoming gesture.

Atthis frowned.

To Psappha, it was as if the sky had suddenly clouded over.

"Have I upset you, milady?"

"No," Psappha lied. "Please excuse me for my lack of hospitality."

"It is I who should apologize for coming upon you unannounced. The papyrus-pusher above said I was expected. I should have realized that you would not know the exact day of my arrival."

Gyla ducked into the arbor and took her place beside Psappha. "You were expected last year."

Atthis appraised her then returned her attention to Psappha. "My apologies, Lady Psappha, I only just yesterday, arrived in Mitylene. I had assumed my guardian would inform you as to when I was to dock. I should have remembered that Pittakos rarely troubles himself with decent amenities.

"I've been residing in Naucratis for several years, returning at my guardian's insistence, after he imposed upon you to consider me as a teacher for your illustrious coterie."

"You were ordered to come here?" Gyla asked.

Atthis ignored her and continued to address herself solely to Psappha. "There was no ship immediately available so one was dispatched for me. That's why it has taken me so long to present myself for your approval."

Gyla said, "There are ships available from Buto throughout the year."

Atthis cast Gyla a caustic glance, then addressed Psappha, "Would you like me to dance for you?"

Throughout her explanations, Atthis had held Psappha's eyes with her own. They seemed to bore into her, leaving her unsettled, exposed. The side-glance at Gyla had made her blink. The spell was broken.

"You have but to begin the music," Atthis said and Gongyla handed Psappha her lyre.

Practiced fingers found a melody. Her pupils arranged themselves in a large half-circle in front of her. Lycos, Larichos and Daphnos stood behind them while Praxinoa moved to Psappha's other side. Gongyla placed an arm on the back of the bench behind Psappha. On the third refrain, Atthis began to dance.

Psappha was certain that none of them had ever seen such dancing. She finished her tune with a crescendo flourish that Atthis translated into a pirouette that gracefully collapsed as the music rose. *Daughter of Pandion, heavenly swallow is she who swoops and swirls before me now.* Atthis finished cross-legged on the lawn with her head bowed between outstretched arms, her hair flared out over the grass. The song left a deafening silence in its wake. There was a distinct whoosh as the watchers remembered to breathe. Atthis raised her torso, extending open palms.

"Will you accept me, milady?"

Psappha nodded, unable to trust her voice. The students surrounded Atthis, competing for her attention, talking simultaneously and so fast, that no one could decipher their words. Atthis laughed and indicated that she would dance again.

"No," Psappha said. "The Lady Atthis is fatigued from her journey."

"I am never too tired to dance for lovely maidens."

Psappha said, "No. They'll see more dancing than they may want when they begin trying to learn the movements." Turning to Praxinoa, she said, "Have a chamber prepared."

"Next to yours?" Gongyla whispered.

"No, my love," Psappha responded without removing her attention from Praxinoa, "The one next to the old nursery." To Atthis, she said, "You may wish to use the former nursery for classes in inclement weather."

"I think I will come back and forth from the citadel if you don't mind. You seem overcrowded here."

Psappha felt the home she was so fond of diminish. "We can make you comfortable here," she said but her confidence had vanished.

"Perhaps when the new school is finished," Atthis said. Praxinoa sniffed haughtily and marched inside. Lycos and the boys followed. Atthis cast a slant-eyed smirk toward Gongyla that Psappha interpreted as a gracious smile.

"Tomorrow then," she said.

"Tomorrow."

When she had gone, the pupils drifted away by twos and threes. Klies responded to Praxinoa's call by stomping to the house and slamming the door behind her. Lycos returned to the gatehouse.

The instant they were alone, Gongyla pulled Psappha none too gently to her feet. "This dancer is the one you would have called to Iphis?"

Psappha refused to meet her stare.

"You love her," Gongyla said.

"No," Psappha said. "It's you I love."

"You answer too quickly. She's bewitched you with her dervish twirling."

Psappha hung her head. Desire and loyalty warred within. Behind her eyes, she still saw the girl-child Atthis dancing in the park. She looked up, letting her eyes wander over dark Amazon beauty, near strangling on confusion.

Gongyla laid a warming hand on her shoulder.

"Psappha, my precious Ianthe, I am your Iphis."

Psappha nodded then picked up her lyre and let Gyla lead her into the house.

~ ~ ~

Summer became, for Psappha, a theatrical spectacle, resplendent with music. The newness of the dance lessons wooed student attention from lyre, bow and grammar. Gyla found abundant time for hunting. Psappha dismissed her classes early and dreamed her afternoons away in the orchard overlooking the meadow that Atthis had chosen for a practice field.

She filled her mind with self-perfected images as she watched Atthis lead the maidens in intricate choreographs on the lawn with Klies echoing her every gesture. Observing them, Psappha remembered how she had ached to dance with another Klies. *How fine that would have been.*

Over time, she developed the habit of carrying a wax tablet and a stylus with her every day so she could compose lyrics while she watched. *No eyes have ever been so blessed. No happiness so joyful, no joy so sublime as to see each day thy beauty shimmering in my soul. To see thy hair of silver-embossed gold flow over shoulders molded of lily petals is to see the stars hide in shame as Atthis outshines their feeble light.*

The stylus broke and cut a jagged scar across her tablet. She rubbed it out then used a twig to continue writing. *Fires, sparked by thy alabaster beauty, inflame Psappha, thy slave, in unquenchable white heat. No water can cool the burning that must consume itself in matching fire: Fire that I shall one day kindle in thee.*

At night, after Gyla was asleep, she transposed the day's verses onto papyrus scrolls and locked them away from prying eyes in an inlaid Cretan box whose key she hid.

One day, when she seemed to be teaching chords to reluctant students, Psappha's attention strayed as usual, to where Atthis danced like a gold-crowned monarch butterfly. Near her, Gongyla instructed archery. Seeing the two of them so close, Psappha's heart felt a sundering wrench.

She was so intent on the dancing that she did not heed the dimming light. Nor did she let the jumble of voices beyond her arbor pull her attention from the object of her dreams. When the midday sun failed to add glimmer to Atthis' hair she left the arbor to discover that Helios had disappeared. Only a slim wing of brightness remained in his accustomed place.

Gongyla clustered her students around her. Atthis whirled to a stop, screaming in terror as the last of the bright orb disappeared. Psappha fell to her knees in fervent prayer. *Forgive thou me, oh blessed Olympians. Forgive thou me my vagrant desires. Blessed Mother, return thy shining son to the sky and I swear I will forever forsake that which I most desire.*

After one brief, painful glance skyward, Psappha kept her head down, her eyes tightly closed. She stood unmoving, not caring that her body ached from tension, certain that some worse catastrophe was due her. It seemed an eternity before she again felt Helios' warming caress on her back. Without raising her head, she cautiously opened her eyes to see the flowers in her basket, golden in the normal brightness of early afternoon.

Oh brilliant, brightly shining Helios, she prayed. *Blessed art thou in thy glory. Blessed be thy precious warmth. Blessed be thy holy mother. Queen of Heaven forsake me not again. Holy Mother, my vow to thee shall ever be my bond.*

~ ~ ~

Keeping her vow was far harder than Psappha might have supposed. She tossed endlessly while desire tore at her while Gyla slept soundly beside her. Awake, it was worse. Each morning she lay rigid in their bed, trying to block her agonized mind from visions of a dancing golden child -- Atthis -- so near -- so far -- so beautiful.

By the time the asters bloomed, the garden felt like the pit of Hades. The roses hung limp on thirsty branches and failed to supply relief from the heat. They shut out the relentless sun but they excluded the breeze as well.

Some of Psappha's misery was relieved when the dancers confined themselves to the coolness of the many-windowed nursery. However, as the summer grew hotter, Atthis started taking her advanced students to the inlet to follow dance lessons with a swim after the builders left for the day. The first time Psappha saw them strip and dash across the beach she decided Lycos needed help with the accounts. From then on, unless the weather was too bad for swimming or there were too many workmen on the beach for Atthis to take her pupils there Psappha spent most of her afternoons in the villa overlooking the inlet -- getting in Lycos's way.

By harvest time, he'd had enough. At his insistence, Psappha returned to observing the lessons from under her favorite tree. The succulent apples paled beside the beauty of intricate choreography upon the meadow between the orchard and the old house. Several of the maidens were good but Klies always stole the show.

Lycos joined Psappha in the orchard one late autumn afternoon, his hair hanging in damp tangles on his creased brow, a hint of silver accenting its fox-fur tint. Together they watched as the maidens wilted to the grass one after another, leaving the stage to Klies and Atthis.

Klies and Atthis swirled over the fallen leaves, approaching and retreating from one another like mating birds. Klies duplicated each move precisely, as beautiful as her namesake, inventing as she danced until it became difficult to tell who was the teacher and who the protégé.

Psappha's adoration of them both flooded her eyes and clouded her vision as she sang in rhythm with their dance. "Golden nymph beyond me in my garden, art thou the perfect apple hidden in the topmost bough that the gatherers missed as they passed? Nay, they did not miss thee -- they could not reach so high."

She wasn't sure which of the dancers inspired the lyric but when Klies relinquished the field to her teacher, Psappha continued to watch with avid interest.

Alkaios came to lounge on the grass beyond where Atthis gyrated. Her dance shifted as she focused her limpid attentions on him. Lycos took the lyre from Psappha's motionless hands and laid it on the ground at her feet.

"You want her," he said as he straightened up. "Why don't you take her?" When she did not answer, he said, "She follows Alkaios with her eyes."

"What bothers you, Little Fox, the fact that she watches him, or that he might look back with favor?"

Lycos retrieved the lyre and plucked aimlessly at its strings as if he had not heard her. No discernible melody came at first.

Gradually, the seemingly random notes evolved into a tune Psappha recognized as one Alkaios had used in his youth as a background to his love-lyrics.

Psappha cast him an incredulous glance. "You never told me that you played, much less that you knew Alkaios's music." She touched his arm and added, "I'm afraid, dear brother of my heart that we are more truly Ianthe and Hyacinthos than we have ever been before."

"I'm sure we are, Adelphi. Have you watched them together?"

"They've been together?"

"Not like that. He watches her dance and she watches him when he sings after supper. Soon they will catch each other's eyes. What then?"

"For someone who rejected his opportunity, you seem obsessed with watching. You don't need to settle for that, though I must or close my eyes. Atthis is forever lost to me."

"How can she be lost? You are The Poetess. You have but to ask and she would come to you. If not for Gongyla, she would probably have come without invitation."

"No, Little Fox. She would not come. She knows nothing of Iphis. Perhaps I could have taught her, but that is no longer possible."

"She needs no . . .," he began then appeared to change his mind. After a moment's reflection, he asked, "Why do you think it would be impossible?"

"I vowed to forsake my desire for her."

"Vowed? To whom? Gongyla?"

"No, dear friend, Gyla would never ask a sacrifice of me. I vowed to The Lady that I would forsake all thought of Atthis if she would return Helios's sacred light."

Lycos slumped disgustedly. "Psappha, Psappha," he said with more than usual impatience. "Whatever am I to do with you? Helios did not go away. Is that why you've been moping by yourself all these weeks? You should have told me. I've been teaching basic astronomy to the maidens ever since Selene, The Lady Moon passed between Helios and Earth and scared their silly heads to reeling. If I had known you thought there was something to be frightened of, I'd have instructed you as well. I never dreamed you didn't know. Much less that you were frightened enough to bind yourself with a foolish vow that I have no doubt you've broken daily in your lustful little heart. There was no reason for it."

"Reason or not, all knowing one, it's done."

~ ~ ~

Winter closed them in together. Cold winds and blowing snow seemed warm compared to the storm Psappha saw in Gongyla's eyes.

They lingered in the dining hall one night after the household had retired. Psappha sipped a third cup of wine, trying to ignore Gongyla's pacing.

Gongyla stalked like a trapped panther. Guttering candles spurted angrily in their smoke shroud before she finally pounced, yanking Psappha to her feet by the shoulders.

"If you want the shallow one, take her." Her voice rasped through clenched teeth, its normally warm tone lost.

Tears formed in Psappha's startled eyes. It had been a long time since anyone spoke to her in anger and never Gongyla. She stared through a fog of tears and wine until Gyla released her with a sigh.

"Why won't you take her?" Gongyla said. Her low sultry tone wrapped its usual magic cloak around Psappha.

"Everything seems so simple to you, thou splendid cat. Some things can't be had merely for the taking."

"And, some things can," Gongyla smiled wryly and pulled Psappha onto her lap.

Psappha burrowed her face into the niche beneath a firmly muscled shoulder. "You handle me easily enough, thou Amazon," she admitted. "But even thy strength would be taxed by Atthis. She may look no bigger than I, but Terpsichore has blessed her with a dancer's strength and agility. She is no wisp of air to be subdued by a raindrop."

"Must we talk on and on of Atthis?"

Her apparent boredom mystified Psappha. *Where has her jealousy gone? And why?*

"If you want her, take her," Gyla said. "Then perhaps we can forget about her, at least some of the time."

"I don't think I'll ever forget Atthis."

"I am not asking you to forget her, not now. I know you can't. You need to have her completely so we can get on with our lives without cluttering every conversation with your obsession for Atthis."

Psappha got up and walked away - confused. As usual, when there was something she didn't understand or didn't want to think about she picked up her lyre and let her mind retreat into music.

Gongyla cut softly into her thoughts. "Sing for her."

Psappha sighed. "If you only knew how I sing for her. The Lady must be weary of my songs. If I pray for her again, I fear The Lady will say, 'What is it that upsets you now, Psappha? Whom, now, must I tempt to give you her love?'"

"Why sing to The Lady? Will she quench your fires for you? Will she display your beautiful soul to Atthis' blind eyes?"

"The Lady has been good to me."

"The Lady has done nothing, my dove. The magnificence of thy poet's soul won thee thy glory. The fire of thy music keeps it bright."

"What has kept thee, thou patient warrior? You know how I burn for Atthis, yet you don't turn from me. Instead, you tell me to seek her out. Why?"

"I love you."

Unable to dredge up a response, Psappha fussed with the fire then retreated to a chaise and pulled her feet up under her. The flickering light dressed Gyla's face with shimmering chestnut highlights. She wore her usual inscrutable expression but her onyx eyes spoke volumes.

Gyla came and sat by her on the edge of the chaise. Psappha laid her palm on Gyla's pliant cheek. It looked to her like the wing of a dove spread against polished mahogany but Gyla's face was not wooden. She let her hand glide upward until her fingers disappeared amid tight curls that wound around them like The Lady's sacred snakes. "I'm sorry," she whispered, mystified by the pain of it.

"Don't be sorry, gentle bird. My love for you is my greatest treasure."

"How do you stand me? I am but a faithless slave to Aphrodite's fires."

"Psappha, you are my soul's mate. To live is to be near you. My joy is to serve you in whatever you need. I never pressed you for a fidelity you could not give. Faithfulness is empty if not freely offered. I'm happy being where I can help you gain whatever you desire."

Psappha dropped her eyes, shamed by Gongyla's selfless devotion. She resisted the fingers that tried to lift her chin.

"Don't turn from me because I love you, Psappha."

Psappha didn't speak. Anything she said could only hurt. Instead, she let Gyla fold her into a comfortable embrace. Lush lips whispered against her forehead. "Go to her then return to me, my love. Go to her but know I'm always here to shelter you with my life."

~ ~ ~

Psappha did not immediately follow Gyla's advice. Even after hearing much the same from Alkaios, she let days pass without approaching Atthis about anything not directly related to the school. Still, she never missed a chance to watch the dancers.

"Go to her," said Lycos, adding his voice to the others' but in a different tone. Lycos spoke with caution in his voice. "Your imagination needs a lesson in reality," he said. "Atthis isn't who you think she is."

[page deliberately left blank]

> *"A beautiful passionate body*
> *that never has ached with a heart!"*
> *'Algernon Charles Swineburne'*

-- XXII --

When most of the students had left for the winter, they moved to their new quarters below the villa. The house sat away from the inlet against a backdrop of olive trees. A sweeping goose-cropped lawn separated it from the shallow beach. An ox-powered pump stood near the kitchen.

Psappha had added a large pavilion for Atthis's classes. Atthis filled the adjacent apartment with enough trunks to hold the acquired wealth of a miser's lifetime. Psappha still didn't approach her as a lover but she did stop talking about her around Gongyla. Fortunately, they soon had other things to discuss.

The move was barely complete when Klies informed them there was double cause for celebration. "We must have a banquet!"

"We have no banquet hall," Psappha reminded her. The new school was a for-women-only compound with no facilities for entertaining. What little socializing might be required for business, Lycos could handle in his villa, but that wasn't large enough to accommodate a banquet as large as Klies's enthusiasm proposed. She made a mental note to ask him about a possible addition but Klies wasn't prepared to wait for that.

"Larichos has a hall," she said. "He won't mind. It's almost his idea."

"I haven't the strength for a banquet right now, Klies. Wait 'til we're settled in. I'll think about it then."

Klies disallowed her mother's inattention. She danced around Psappha insisting, "We have to have a banquet <u>now</u>!"

"Stop, Klies! You're making me dizzy. Why must we have a banquet? Wouldn't a simple supper suffice?"

"No-o-o," Klies insisted. "We have to have a banquet to announce my betrothal."

"Your <u>what</u>?"

"My betrothal."

"Who dared arrange a betrothal for you? You said Larichos? I'll have his head on a plate!"

Klies took hold of both her hands. "Don't blame Larichos, Mother. I'm arranging this myself."

"You're what? You're a child. Who is this seducer of children? I'll have him castrated."

Klies laughed. "Please settle down. He doesn't know about it yet. If there has been any crime, I have committed it. I love him. If you want to prosecute somebody, summon Eros before the magistrates. I'm not an infant, Mother. I'll pass my fifth Olympiad next summer. You've been too preoccupied to notice. I'm three years older than you were when Pittakos sent you into exile and I love him. I can neither work nor sleep for love of him. His beauty taunts me and, yes, I want to bear his children. Does that shock you?"

"No, dear, it doesn't shock me. If you marry, it's good to feel such things, but fiery feelings are not love. Love is more lasting than desire. No. Don't speak. I can see in your eyes that you will listen to nothing that might thwart your immediate wish to taste the fires of Aphrodite." *I'm the same.*

She didn't speak that thought aloud. She didn't need to. A sharp "Hurrumph" from the corner reminded her that it was obvious. Glancing toward the sound, she saw only Gyla's clearly-muscled back.

She smiled and returned her attention to Klies. "Who is this young man you intend to marry, although you've not yet informed him of his fate?"

"Daphnos," Klies said in a tone more suited to Apollo.

Psappha smiled. *Of course, I should have guessed. The many times he came here with Larichos, I should have known it was Klies who drew him. She was always with them. Years ago, I thought it amusing that she was so devoted to her uncle despite his mild disdain. Thou fool,* she chided herself. *Why haven't you been watching?*

She knew why but she chose not to admit it even to herself. She'd been neglectful of her daughter and she was ashamed. *Still, it could be worse. His family is noble enough in spite of their poverty. With industry, the union might eventually be blessed with some small measure of prosperity.*

Klies' impatience burst in. "Well?"

"Run tell Lycos we're having a party."

Klies was gone before Psappha could add a blessing.

Larichos warned Daphnos. His dumbstruck expression amused them all. There were man giggles in the shadows the day he rushed to propose.

The banquet soon followed. Before Psappha fully realized her baby girl had become a woman, she was too entangled in prenuptials to contemplate the repercussions.

Klies kept the entire household running in response to her brisk commands. Soon everything except her mother was ready for the wedding.

The wedding day dawned bright and clear. The streets outside were choked with people. Klies dripped in the center of Psappha's chamber, letting the holy water of her ritual bath dry on her lithe, dancer's body. A thoughtless, superstitious servant had told her that the first Klies who, at her second wedding had had her prenuptial bath water wiped away and had by so doing angered Hera who punished her by giving her a stillborn child. "Such disregard for tradition," the servant said, "May have been what increased the pain of her fourth appointment with Hera and thereby brought on her death."

"Hush!" The serving woman shrank from the anger in Psappha's eyes. "Take yourself elsewhere at once."

Klies waited impatiently while the maidens chittered around her, their arms laden with cambric and brocade, giving Psappha a headache with their clamor.

Lycos stood by with his paint pots like an artist waiting for apprentices to finish preparing his canvas. "Hurry, thou sluggards, her bridegroom will arrive before you get her dressed."

Four of the maidens rushed to the window to confirm his statement. Their delighted squeals brought Psappha, the rest of the maidens, and Klies, to peer over their shoulders at the spectacle below.

Klies pouted. "Oh, why must Larichos drive so slowly?"

Psappha surveyed her daughter from tip to toe. "It's a good thing for you that he does. Go. Allow the girls to dress you. Do you want to come down with chills on your wedding night? Go. Your bridegroom comes." She hurried her away with a bare-bottom swat then, as the disappointed bridesmaids groaned and followed. Psappha devoted her attention to the pageantry below.

It was hard to tell whether the prancing white mules drew a cart or a garden, so bedecked were they and their burden with boughs and blossoms. Psappha smiled. *Daphnos's father must have loaded every ship he owned with southern flowers.* There was no way he could have found so many on an island hurrying toward winter.

The cart stopped a few meters short of the gate and Daphnos hopped down from his fragrant perch. The populace lining the street chorused a ringing paean. Dancing children littered the ground before him with autumn leaves as he walked to the evergreen laden canopy where a sumptuous feast lay ready for him and his groomsmen. The bride and her bridesmaids would feast in Psappha's great hall before joining them.

Both banquets were nearly over before Psappha escorted her nervous daughter from the hall. Daphnos ran to meet them, pulling Klies gaily to the waiting cart amid mass ribaldry and laughter.

Psappha soon became breathless from the songs and jesting in the procession that followed them, but not so much so that her throbbing voice was indistinguishable from all others as they sang the bridal couple into the bridegroom's home with a rousing hymeneal. Nor was she too tired to lead the rest in a rollicking contest of flower throwing.

Psappha felt her heart lurch as Daphnos presented her daughter at the altar of the household gods. Tears dampened her lashes when his mother led Klies into the bedchamber, but her misted eyes cleared as she joined the singing outside the nuptial door. She, more than anyone, encouraged Daphnos when his friends escorted him to his bride, she whose voice was heard above all others as the songs and jests grew loud and bawdy. However, when Daphnos waved the stained linen for all to see, only Psappha's voice was missing from the resultant cheer.

Gongyla took her hand and led her back through the quiet streets. They paused only to burn the wedding sheet on The Lady's altar. The temple was deserted. As was the great hall when they reached it, but Psappha soon realized that only the crowd was gone. The hall slumbered in shambles as if mourning the ribald throng so recently departed. However, when her eyes adjusted to the dimness, Psappha saw that her friends and the members of her household had returned before them.

Through a curtain of stale smoke from guttered candles, she saw Lycos sleeping near the hearth. Approaching him, she heard Alkaios singing plaintively in the near corner. Atthis sat at his elbow, seemingly entranced. Psappha settled into her usual chair and sipped the wine Gongyla brought her, trying to think of Kerkolos, of her wedding, of Klies' birth, Klies' face when last she saw it, both happy and frightened, but all she really thought of was Atthis dancing in the park. Watching her now enthralled by Alkaios was more than her longing heart could bear. Like a shade, she slipped from the great hall and hastened to the garden.

"Why run, Adelphi? There's no escape."

"Lycos! I thought you were asleep. Why did you follow me? Don't you know I want to be alone?"

"You want to be alone right now about as much as Klies does."

"They'll be happy," she said when they reached the roses.

"Atthis and Alkaios?"

"Them too, I suppose, I was thinking of Klies and Daphnos." He didn't even pretend to believe her. "I feel so alone," she said.

"You have Gongyla," he reminded her. "Do you remember the night Klies was born?"

Psappha gave him a wry smile. "I was rather busy."

"So you were. It was a remarkable sight. Gongyla..."

"I remember," she said dismissively; her attention taken by Atthis who passed them unnoticing with Alkaios in tow. The Lady Moon slid behind a lonely cloud. Psappha squeezed the hand holding hers. The cloud passed. They could see Atthis sitting on the grass, Alkaios' head resting in her lap.

Psappha's tongue drove into the roof of her mouth as if to lock the pounding of her heart from her ringing ears. Her jaw ached from holding her breath lest an explosion from her lungs betray their watching.

Lycos tugged at her hand and they slipped away. At her door, he lightly kissed her cheek. She saw the desolation in his eyes through the tears in her own.

Inside her chamber, Psappha rushed blindly to her couch and her lyre, her precious, comforting lyre. Her heart throbbed in her music; the words clear in her mind as she played.

"Peer of the gods he seems as he sits close beside thee listening to thy sweet voice and lovely laughter. My heart trembles. My muse deserts me. My tongue is broken. Seeing you blinds my eyes. My ears roar. Sweat invades my clothing. My being quakes with tremors and the fluids of my vessel pour. I am paler than

the dry grass upon which you lie. Death rides near but I must lack. I must endure for Klies's sake. Oh, Helios, release thou me from my foolish vow."

She had barely finished committing the song to papyrus when she heard Gongyla's throaty laugh in the adjoining room. She quickly placed the verse in her little locked box, not expecting to hear Lycos's familiar chuckle. "…Atthis made Dracon's sister look like an uninitiated maiden," he said. *Liar!* Psappha thought as she flopped onto the bed and covered her head with a pillow.

~ ~ ~

Late autumn storms threatened the next day. Psappha's old chambers seemed a prison of frustration as forbidden thoughts clamored for fulfillment. The unseasonable cold ignored her braziers, chilling her flesh beyond bearing in sharp contrast to fires within.

It was too much. She forsook her solitude and went to join Gongyla in the main hall where she huddled as near as was safe to the fire, which crackled dangerously as the door burst open.

Alkaios stumbled in on a gust of wind, looking like a pile of ruffled fur. His great, imported, bearskin robe covered him to the eyes. It filled the chair where he tossed it, overflowing onto the floor as he stepped briskly to the hearth in a vain attempt to warm his hands. "What a magnificent day to decide to go to Egypt," he announced, rubbing his hands together. "A pity I can't leave at once. I'd welcome the desert sun right now."

"Egypt? But that's so far! If you would travel, why not to Crete, or Syracuse?" Psappha asked. "You could use my house there. What would you do in Egypt?"

"Fight, of course, and make love. The only two things I'm good at."

"You have your music," Atthis put in.

How did I not see her sitting there so close to him?

"My music's a diversion at best," Alkaios said. "Compared to Psappha I have no talent."

Psappha prepared to demure but Alkaios shook his head. He plopped his lean frame onto a couch, stretched his long legs, crossed his ankles and clasped his hands behind his head. "Lesbos is much too tame since old Crack-toes turned into the people's pet. Egypt's interesting. There's nothing like a merry little war to shore up the ravages of boredom." He winked at Gyla.

She grinned. "If you crave excitement so badly, go demand that Boreas stop his blustering and let autumn stay a little longer."

"I've already done that. He laughed at me. Can't you hear him?" Together, they drowned the wind god's laughter with their own.

Atthis moved to a stool at his side. He absentmindedly rested his hand on her hair. "Will you miss me, Androgyn?"

Atthis' eyes darkened at the label. Gongyla smiled and Psappha frowned at her own confusion.

Atthis spoke with firm politeness. "Of course I'll miss you, Alkaios. We will all miss your music."

"And your insane sense of humor," Psappha put in, thinking of the odd appellation with which he had tagged Atthis.

"Yeah," said Larichos. "Who will tempt laughter if you go?"

Alkaios's face stayed stern as he studied each of them in turn, then he broke into a broad grin. "You need my sense of something, S'pha. You seem to have misplaced your own. The mischief in this room would send the God of Ridicule into a spasm."

Psappha jumped to her feet. "What do you mean I have no sense?"

"Sit down," Lycos said. "You look like a ruffled goose with your wings propped on your hips like that."

"I have a better present for you this time," Alkaios said.

She blushed and let her hands fall to her sides. She remembered the tiny statuette, and her reaction to it. Embarrassed, she resumed her seat.

"Will we see you again before you sail?" Gongyla asked.

Alkaios gave her a rueful smile. "I think not. The mountain trails will soon close. If I go overland, I can embark from Eresus and not have to dally in every port along the coast. The bread ships sail straight to Egypt."

Gongyla raised her goblet to him. "May Poseidon carry you safely on his back and may The Lady Cybele greet thee with kindness."

"Thank you, Priestess." He held his goblet for Atthis to fill and took the flagon from her when she would have returned it to the sideboard. "Don't look so sad, S'pha. I'm leaving you a present and, when I return, Gyla, I'll bring you something from the caravans. You can carve the little trinket for Klies that we discussed." Turning to Larichos, he said. "You want some fun? Come with me. I'll find you a good commander." Lycos sneered. Alkaios's grin turned sheepish. "If you ever change your mind, little fox, let me know." Then, turning his attention to Psappha he said, "You're missing all the points, aren't you little purple-eyes? It serves you right you know. Write me a song sometime when you get out of the clouds of your mind long enough to see what's right before your pretty little nose. As for you, androgyn, may you get what you're after without causing too much damage."

Atthis glared at him then moved her stool across the room.

Alkaios grinned wider. "Tell me, S'pha, when next I visit, what can I bring that would set your frigid little heart aflutter?"

"Bring yourself, dear friend, and may Apollo bring you fair weather."

"May Eros smile on you," Atthis added from the hearth.

"And on you, Androgyn. Come, walk with me." He bowed to Gongyla then grinned at Psappha. "On you, I am sure he shall grin most satisfactorily." Retrieving his vast robe, he strode toward the door, beckoning Atthis and whispering to her as he walked.

"Alkaios wait," Psappha called. "Don't leave without telling me what you mean. Why should Eros grin at me? What present do you leave?"

"Ask Iphis," he said over his shoulder before they disappeared in a flurry of flying leaves. Gongyla bolted the door behind them.

She didn't need to slam the bar so hard. "We'll be staying over," she told Larichos.

"Sure," he agreed. "No problem. Go ahead and stay in here a while. I only had one bed warmed and I'm going to be in it in about five seconds."

When he was gone, Lycos stifled a yawn, drained his goblet and left as well.

Gyla returned to the fire and reclined on the couch Alkaios had just vacated. Psappha watched her stretch her lithe form, cross her ankles and clasp her hands behind her head in delicious duplication of Alkaios's pose. On her, it looked seductive rather than arrogant. Her breasts strained the seams of her doeskins. The wind howled through cracks unnoticed in the summer.

Psappha wrapped her robe tighter. Gongyla showed no sign that she knew the wind existed. She uncoiled from the couch and took her bow from the wall, flexing the string before bracing her rear against a table to begin polishing the bow with a length of chamois.

"He means nothing to her," she said after a time.

"How do you know?" Psappha scoffed. "She is always at his side."

"His genius draws her. She follows him as a daughter. She never knew her father, did she?"

"N-n-no . . . ." Psappha said through chattering teeth.

"I thought so. She . . . Psappha, you're freezing!" She whipped the cover off a couch, tossed it over Psappha's lap and reached for the wood box. "Is there no way to warm this mausoleum?" she grumbled, as she stoked the fire. "One day I will take you to my green land where you will never be cold again."

When she had the fire roaring to her satisfaction, she knelt to remove Psappha's slippers then rubbed the tiny feet between her strong, hunter's hands. Looking up, she asked, "Why haven't you taken her?"

"I can't," Psappha whispered.

"You must. I'm weary of your mooning. If you don't take her soon I'll take her for you."

Psappha balled her fists and beat a tattoo on Gongyla's shoulders. "You stay away from her!" Then, barely audibly, she added, "Even if I could take her, I don't know how."

Gongyla chuckled and pulled her tiny adversary down onto the fur hearthrug, giving her a very un-motherly kiss. "Then I will teach you," she murmured, but she didn't get the chance. A persistent knock upon the inner door interrupted them.

"Come," Psappha called.

A student, Timas, a sparkling bubble of mischief from Phokaea stuck her head into the room and said "The Lady Atthis wants you in the nursery. They're dancing a story, milady. Do come."

~ ~ ~

Atthis wore her hair pulled back and twisted into a coil at the base of her neck, forcing her chin to a regal height. Her pale gown matched her hair, causing Psappha to think of rich cream touched with peach blossoms as she and Gongyla settled together upon a pile of cushions. Several Maidens crowded around them. Psappha lent close concentration to the posturing Nymphs surrounding Atthis.

The story evolved into a fluttering tableau involving a masquerade. Psappha could tell it was a typical deception of the Gods but she was not sure which one. Atthis danced the part of innocence. When she had been dramatically subdued, she glided over to Psappha and parodied a sweeping bow. "Did you enjoy the dance, Lady Psappha?"

"It was beautiful, Lady Atthis, as are all your dances."

"Thank you, milady, I choreographed the dance for you. Alkaios said you would appreciate it. My dancing it for you is the present he mentioned."

"What is the story?" Timas blurted.

Atthis turned to her. *Like a gentle goddess granting a favor to a beloved child.*

Atthis spoke to Timas; her eyes remained focused on Psappha. "It is the story of a cruel and vicious man," she said. "A man who forced his wife to vow that, if the child she carried was born female it would be given to Death. The -- "

A thousand rumblings of Zeus roared in Psappha's brain. *Oh, Alkaios, dear, demented demon, with what parting gift of furies hast thou furnished me?*

~ ~ ~

Psappha and Gongyla sipped after dinner wine as the storm threatened their candles. Gongyla shuttered the windows while Psappha guarded the flickering light. "What am I going to do," she asked when Gongyla returned to the hearth.

"Go to her."

"I can't," Psappha protested weekly. She slumped onto the edge of the hearth, elbows on her knees, her face hidden in her hands.

Gongyla persisted. "Go to her or send her away."

Psappha's head jolted up. "What are you saying? I can't send her away. I'd rather let Helios's light die in the sky."

"Then go to her, or I will. I won't stand by and watch you burn for her any longer. Go to her or let me go to her or find me a ship to Syracuse. I've had enough of holy rivals."

Psappha glared at her, her eyes brimming with panic. *Send Atthis away? Lose Gongyla? No!* "All right," she said, "Since you insist, I'll go to her. Just remember it's your idea."

"Here," Gyla said, offering a fresh goblet. "Have another cup before you go."

Psappha quaffed the wine and snatched up a lamp before she had time to change her mind. As the light passed Gongyla's face, the war of emotion she saw in the tender warrior's eyes seemed but a small echo of her own.

Fear and desire burned her soul. All the years that she had yearned to teach Atthis the wonders of Iphis blended into a tapestry of emotion that threatened to strangle her. "I won't go."

"You will or I promise I'll leave you at the slightest mention of her name."

Psappha dared not look back. The wind in the corridor heckled her as she walked to Atthis' chambers. It darted around her reluctant feet, lapping at the shutters, throwing raindrops against the side of the house. Her lamp cast a tiny circle on the tiles as her buskins whispered across them. She had often used this corridor to reach the kitchen but tonight it seemed to stretch with each forward step.

Her knock on Atthis' door resounded in the echoing silence. It went unanswered. Psappha knocked again, louder.

"Enter."

Psappha's heart caught in her throat.

"Enter," the call came again.

The latch felt cold in her hand. Slowly she squeaked the door open.

"Psappha! Come. Share my fire." Atthis huddled under eastern silk coverlets, the light dimmer than her smile, the fire cooler than her voice in spite of its red glow.

Psappha's spinning soul refused to submit to direction. Her knees felt weak. Numbly, she dragged a chair to the hearth, placing it opposite the chaise upon which Atthis was enthroned.

"Will you share wine with me, Psappha?"

I'll share my life, Psappha thought, but all she managed was a timid smile. Atthis nodded then rang the tiny serving bell at her side.

Gongyla did not knock. She marched in with the serving table balanced on one hand. There was hatred in Atthis' eyes. *What am I doing here? Atthis knows nothing of the gentleness behind Gyla's carved cedar mask.*

Gyla, my love, I don't want this any more. "Please join us," she invited nervously. "I'll have my wine un-watered. Atthis?"

Atthis nodded.

Gyla grinned as, with one hand, she lifted the mate to Psappha's Egyptian chair and swung it into position between them, setting the small table beside it with her other hand. Seated, her back to the fire, she filled three goblets. "The choreography for the story of Iphis and Ianthe must have been very difficult," she said. "It is a familiar tale in my country."

"I thought it might be," Atthis countered icily.

"I assume it is also well known to you?"

"The dance of Iphis has been part of my repertoire for many years."

Gongyla's cool laugh was as nothing Psappha had ever heard.

"By Thalia, Gongyla, why are you acting so strangely? Have you changed your mind?"

"Not at all." Gongyla upended her goblet before placing it beside the others on the table. She handed a brimming portion to Psappha, another to Atthis then she rose and melted into the darkness beyond the reach of the firelight. Haunting laughter trailed behind her as the door creaked shut.

"How much do you know of Iphis?" Psappha asked after she downed her wine. It had an odd, acrid taste but the warm echo of Gongyla's fingers on the goblet abated whatever caution she might have felt.

Atthis reached for the flagon, refilling her cup and Psappha's while gazing at her curiously through her lashes. "I know the temple well," she said.

Her satiny tone shot through Psappha like lava. She struggled for breath. Her eyes burned into Atthis', their question blazing. She surveyed the much beloved face. Her gaze fell on the throbbing pulse-beat clearly visible on Atthis' throat. *Is that my answer? Oh, Aphrodite, thou deceptive porna, have you been mocking me? Have I wasted years in aching, fruitless dreams when I had but to reach out to claim that which I most desire? Oh, Helios, Selene, thou fickle fiends, you have robbed me of so much priceless time with your games of hide and seek.*

Atthis brushed her coverlets aside and stood, nude except for a span of saffron clothe twined and tied around her loins.

Oh, Sweet Aphrodite, Psappha prayed. *My soul is in danger. Not even on Olympus is there fitting match for the beauty that stands before me now.*

Atthis began to sway slowly, as if listening to the beat of some hidden music. Her body glowed in the dim firelight. Psappha could see the rhythmic beat of her heart beneath the rise and fall of pale breasts half-hidden in trailing silver-gold tresses.

Heaven poses before me on ivory toes, Psappha silently composed. *Oh, insipid songs I've sung to beauty without imagining such quality as this. To call up every word I've ever heard would only serve to prove how impoverished language is. For the glory that is Atthis, I must find a new word.*

The unheard beat increased in tempo. Atthis depicted first a flower slowly unfolding, a leaf tossed in the wind, a snake giving homage to the sky then searching garden paths as she slithered ever closer to Psappha's tingling toes.

Psappha's mind conjured remembrances of a childhood garden. She welcomed innocence, pure and beautiful. She reached out her hand, desire driving her beyond caution, wine coursing through distended veins.

Silently, Atthis took her hand and led her to the voluptuous bed, maneuvered her onto it and began exploring her mouth with her own.

No! This isn't the way it's supposed to happen! I'm supposed to be the teacher here.

Atthis urged her back against the cushions, her hips undulating expertly, her tongue demanding entry.

No! I must be Iphis. I've waited for it for too long. This woman is not my beloved Atthis. This woman is cruel. Her touch is painful. This is not love, she realized at last. *Whatever it was I thought I wanted this isn't it.*

The realization came too late. Her traitorous body responded to Atthis' experienced hands. She thought fleetingly of Gongyla's patient expertise then gave herself over to the demands of postponed desire -- consummate skill -- and the tingling spell of tainted wine.

[page deliberately left blank]

> "Still from the fount of joy's delicious springs,
> Some bitter o'er the flowers
> its bubbling venom flings."
> 'Lord Byron'

-- XXIII --

Psappha awoke in the room she had planned for Klies. She hadn't wanted to remain with Atthis nor was she ready to face Gongyla. Disillusion cut deep. *Lycos warned me.* Her head pounded. Her tongue tasted copper-plated. *The world is full of traitors. What was it 'Kios called her? Androgyn! Was I deaf as well as blind? I should have....*

The rasp of raised voices in the hallway drew her from her cocoon of covers. The sound of Atthis' voice stopped her at the door.

"Out of my way you miscarriage of a mangy jungle she-cat. You drugged the wine!" Atthis' accusation grated through the carved panels.

No wonder the Gods are raging in my head.

"You heathen bitch," Atthis shrieked, "If you didn't want me to have her, why'd you leave her with me?"

"She wanted you," Gyla's familiar tone sounded nearer the door.

"I need no drugs," Atthis said. "My skills are great when I choose to use them."

Gongyla chuckled. *Indeed,* Psappha thought, pushing the memory away.

"She still thought of you as an innocent girl," Gongyla continued. "Did you cure her of the notion?"

"Move!"

The latch clicked and Psappha backed away from the door. Atthis rushed into the room and Psappha for the first time saw a tall, rather ordinary woman in a stark white peplos and skirt whose sole distinction was her swinging, professional-dancer's gait. Gongyla followed looking unrepentant.

"You drugged the wine?" Psappha asked.

"I wanted you to learn the truth," Gongyla said.

"The truth is that the night was everything I've ever dreamed it would be," she lied, casting a broad smile toward Atthis.

Atthis smiled sweetly at Gongyla.

Gongyla frowned.

"Next time, I'll drink none of your concoctions," Psappha told her. "Because of that, I've forgotten all that came after the dancing." Sudden anger on top of her disappointment made each lie easier than the last. "But, I know it was perfect," she added spitefully. "What made you think drugs were necessary?"

"It was a mistake."

"Indeed," said Atthis. Psappha waved them both away.

~ ~ ~

Throughout the winter, Psappha continued her deception. Atthis shared her bed while she ignored Gongyla, ashamed to face her but too proud to admit her error. In the night, she added guilt-ridden verses to her collection of hidden poems.

In my loneliness, I feel her kitten fingers on my breast and wonder what sweet fragrance tempts me now. I feel your web entrap me, as my fingers tangle in your raven hair. My lips reach, dry and flaking, to taste her pungent flavors and wander, oh so lightly, across the ebon satin of your thighs.

With each passing moment, I can hear your languid whisper, 'Let me love you, My Lady.' And gently did you carry me, on waves of sensation, to volcanic peaks of feeling then tenderly escort me safely down, while all the while I watched her dance behind my eyes.

Tomorrow is as nothing. Yesterday is gone. There is only here and now and dreaming to fill my empty hours. Though people crowd around me, demanding my attention, I still float, within my soul, into your arms. She is. I am. We are. All else is mere charade. Why was I not born singly, like others that I know? Duality lies heavy on my soul.

Spring brought the laughter of the maidens, providing a cheerful contrast to the silence of their teachers. Summer danced by on wary feet. When the heat of the season grew uncomfortable, Psappha decided to take the girls to Mt. Olympia. Daphnos was at sea, leaving Klies free to accompany them. It would be cooler at the mountain resort. *What good is wealth without a way to spend it?*

From the top of Olympia, they could see the entire island at once. Psappha loved it almost as much as she loved Mitylene. She left the girls to their own devices and she wiled away the daylight hours sitting under a huge pine. If she was quiet enough, deer came to play nearby as she gazed past rolling pastures over the tops of absurd plane trees to Mitylene and beyond to the cities of Aeolia across the water.

Gongyla thrived on the majesty of Olympia, but Atthis was quick to tire of the mountain.

Psappha opened her shutters one cool, bright morning and stood quietly for several minutes to watch a pair of squirrels argue over a pinecone. Still sleepy, she returned to bed, snuggling deeply, hiding her eyes from Helios' glare. She could hear Klies and the girls chattering in the kitchen below. Just as she was falling back to sleep, her covers were snatched from her grasp. She blinked as Atthis bent over her to tease her nose with her hair.

"Psappha, I swear I shall stop loving you. Get up for our sake. Unleash your beloved strength from the bed." Psappha grabbed her covers and rolled over. "Do get up, Psappha, and bathe. I'll have Klies bring your saffron blouse and purple dress. Come, beloved, and stand like a spotless lily beside the pool, sweet with the beauty with which you drive everybody mad."

Psappha sat up grudgingly. As she stepped from her bed, Atthis called to the others from her door. "Praxinoa, roast some chestnuts so I can make the girls a proper breakfast. The Gods have granted us a favor. This very day, Psappha, the most marvelous of women, has promised to go back with us to Mitylene, the loveliest of cities."

Psappha didn't have the heart to contradict her.

~ ~ ~

They returned to find that another school was to open, drawing many of their students with its newness. When bubbly Timas told them she was transferring, Psappha spoke angrily to cover her pain. "Why do you wish to leave us, Timas? This woman you would follow is a peasant without breeding enough to hide her feet." The instant she spoke, she regretted her tone.

Timas' eyes brimmed with tears. "I do not wish to leave, miladies, but my father insists. It is the fashion. Andromeda has won fame of sorts and her assistant, Gorgo, with her family heritage -- not so exalted as yours, milady Psappha, but important in my father's business. Please give me your blessings. I do not want to go."

Timas' tears were hard to watch. She was not the first whose parent followed fashion blindly. Psappha placed her hands on Timas' young shoulders. "My blessings, Timas. Return to us."

"Oh, I will, milady. My father thinks you old fashioned, but I will change his mind over the winter. Next season I will return to you or I will go no more to school."

When they were again alone,

Psappha told Gongyla, "I begin to grow tired of Gorgo."

"Fashions change, Psappha."

"I know they do. But so quickly? And to turn so far against us? How can anyone consider Andromeda and her kennel, which she calls a school, superior to our teaching the virtues of grace and discretion? How can it be that fidelity can pass out of style? Perhaps if I chased the young women around the gardens like the lascivious Gorgo we could be fashionable again."

"You underestimate yourself," Atthis scoffed. "You would have to do little chasing. Now that Andromeda and Gorgo have made Iphis fashionable on Lesbos, our girls make it obvious that they adore you. They would happily compete for your favor. But, don't you so much as wink at one of them or your voice of angels will ring from a badly battered face."

Psappha stayed Gongyla with a glance. "Why, Atthis," she said with teasing innocence. "Should I sit idly by while our best pupils desert us for the promiscuous Andromeda? Wouldn't it be simpler to seduce a few to keep them hoping?"

She ducked to avoid a flying flowerpot.

~ ~ ~

Their pupils arrived with spring, although not as many as before. Andromeda's school flourished. It was not long before Pittakos ordered Atthis to the new, more stylish establishment. He too followed fashion. Atthis did not seem to mind. Apparently, Psappha's feigned affection was not enough to keep her loyal and Psappha, acting out of instinct, decried her leaving.

"I'm a ward of the city," she said. "I must go. Pittakos insists."

"Oh, damn Pittakos! Must he forever be a stone under my foot? You will not go. I won't let you."

"As a ward of the Tyrant, I am subject to his will."

"Tell Pittakos you want to be released. He can't force you to do his bidding then. We've lost many of our pupils, but not all. We need you here. If more pupils leave us, I'll accept writing commissions.

"No," Gongyla said. "You hate confining your muse to other people's ideas."

"I can do it," Psappha insisted. "Tell her not to go. Why should she? Andromeda couldn't dance if Eros himself did the piping."

"Psappha," Atthis argued, "I must remain a ward of the city until I marry. To do otherwise would bring disgrace. Iphis may rule fashion, but men rule politics and marriage is the essence of politics. Why must you be so irrational about this? I'll be in the city. You'll be able to see me. Many of our girls are studying with Gorgo. I'll be able to look after them."

"You want to go," Psappha said without inflection. All teasing, all pleading had left her voice and she felt inexplicably relieved.

"Psappha, I swear it is against my will that I leave you," Atthis said, sounding as insincere as a Phoenician trying to make a sale.

"You want to go, thou deceitful witch," Psappha snapped at her, reinforcing her charade. "Have you forgotten what we've had? There is no hill, no sacred grove or stream we haven't visited together. Will you think of us when you go there with her? Will someone else now bedeck your hair, as Klies did, with wreaths of roses and violets? Will Gorgo drape your neck with garlands of a hundred flowers? Will you lie in Andromeda's arms and perfume your body with royal perfumes? We gave you all that a fastidious Ionian might desire, and yet you choose to leave us."

Psappha's throat was raw. She had sung so many paeans to this woman she was embarrassed by their number.

"I do not want to leave you, but I must," Atthis claimed.

"You want to go," Psappha repeated tonelessly.

"All right -- All right -- thou child! I want to go."

"Then go, thou bitch! Go to this cow who calls herself a woman! Go, and be quick, thou faithless sow! Thou sluttish she-goat! Go! Go, I say, thou shameless porna! Go, and return no more to me!"

~ ~ ~

Without Atthis and still ashamed to admit her lies to Gyla, Psappha wandered the city, her remaining pupils trailing like tinted ducklings. Each day she passed by the house of Andromeda. Each night she sat behind closed doors, pouring her memories onto scrolls, which she locked away from prying eyes. The beauty of the city eluded her; once beloved sounds clanged in her ears. The combined odors and fragrances stank. Her sadness slowed her steps as she put aside all memory of their disappointing night together; all visions of Atthis as she really was. Instead, she tortured herself with longing for the little sister of her dreams; the little sister, who didn't exist, had never existed except in her own pubescent dreams. Every day, when she returned from the city, she led her students through the park, imagining that she saw the girl-child Atthis dancing there.

The scrolls mounted in the locked chest. Bits and pieces of her being flowed from her stylus like blood from her wounded heart. As was her habit, as she wrote, she spoke her verses in her mind. *When I looked at you, it seemed to me that Hermione was never such as Atthis is. Only Helen could I liken unto you, never an ordinary girl. Oh, Atthis, I rendered your beauty the sacrifice of all my thoughts. I worshiped you with all my senses. Love, the limb-loosener shook me. Love, that creature fatal, bittersweet, Love is a weaver of fictions, a bringer of pain. You've come to hate the thought of Psappha and run off to Andromeda instead.*

The stylus broke in her hand. As she searched for another, she heard Gongyla moving around in the next room. She glanced over her shoulder to assure herself that she had securely bolted the intervening doors then, picking up a fresh stylus, she began again. *Ah, Atthis, dear seductress – it was not I who changed.*

The lamp flickered and went out. Psappha looked up from her tablet, surprised to see that it was no longer dark. Sunshine slipped in between the drapes. Walking stiffly to the window, she watched the maidens practice with their bows, assuming Gongyla was with them. When she pulled the drapes back a little, she saw Klies surrounded by another group of girls, on the far side of the garden. *It's nice to have her here to teach while her husband is at sea.*

A knock on her door startled her. "One moment please." She slipped her tablet and stylus beneath her bed. She would transcribe the poem to papyrus later then lock the scroll in her secret place. "Come," she called when she had securely hidden the poem.

Praxinoa's smile was almost as wide as the tray she carried, until she saw Psappha's face. A concerned frown immediately replaced her smile. "You haven't slept," she accused as she put the tray on the bedside table. "You've been writing all night again. This must stop. You have neglected the students for weeks. They deserve better. Come. Sit. Eat. I'll prepare a bath for you. When you've finished, you will go and teach your pupils. It's time to put this incessant grieving behind you."

It isn't grief, it's guilt. She had long since forgiven Gongyla but she couldn't forgive herself. She longed to tell someone where her heart lay but Praxinoa would scold her foolishness and Psappha felt too drained to argue. Instead, she sat and tried to eat the breakfast Praxinoa had prepared for her. When she finished, she went to the bath, numbly letting her old nurse take charge of her as if she were a babe in swaddling. The steamy, scented water, combined with Praxinoa's skillful hands, eased a season's worth of tension from her aching body and touched the tender edges of her soul.

After the bath, Psappha stood still while Praxinoa patted her dry, wrapped her in a fresh kiton and led her through the corridors, across the garden and into the trellised arbor where delighted pupils immediately surrounded her. She could no longer permit herself to ignore them even at the cost of facing Gongyla's forbidding scowl.

Taking up her lyre, she began to sing -- old songs, written long ago. The new ones would remain safely locked away to be brought out from time to time to ease her heart and mind -- but only when she was alone.

~ ~ ~

Psappha closed herself into her solitary world again as soon as the last of the pupils left for the winter. She had gotten through the remainder of the summer by taking one day at a time, by rote. Now the garden stood bare and empty. The thread of her life grew thin. Snow clouds seemed to hover over her loneliness like vultures over the dying carcass of Earth. Her muse deserted her as though she were an upended flask of wine, its contents spilled, wasted to the last drop. The price of pride weighed heavy on her mind.

I'll go to Gyla, she decided. *As soon as I can, I'll go to her. Sacrificing happiness to salvage pride is too high price to pay.* A good thought but she'd waited too long. Her frail body rebelled against her neglect. She lost strength with each passing day. Autumn chill and false summer heat brought fever. She could not rise from her couch. Eleven

Olympiads had come and gone since first she walked on toddling toes through the halls of her father's house. Now, she was too sick to walk, too tired to care. Light faded to one infinitesimal spark of imagined bliss. From the void, she heard someone call her name.

Psappha clung to that tenacious thread. *Who calls me? Aphrodite, my queen,* she prayed, *am I at last to have some rest? Poseidon, my father, I am too far from the sea.* She heard her name as if through a tunnel. *Who calls?* She fought against the fog. *I don't dare cheat Poseidon,* she thought. *My life is his to take. I cannot lie here like some base-born drudge and die. He would make me wander forever between never and naught. His kingdom is mine by right but I daren't arrive unbidden. I have to hang on 'til he claims me.*

Deep within her mind, Psappha clutched at visions of a huntress poised with arrow fledged. The heat of her desire permeated every particle of her being. She saw Gyla climbing from the sea. She reached for her. She fell, plunging into cold and clammy water. She shivered, falling deeper into Poseidon's dark domain, then floating upward toward Helios, burning from the nearness of his light. Inch by agonizing inch, the curtain of delirium parted. She heard her name through agonies of fire and ice. With what remained of her strength, she willed her eyes to open and saw Gyla's precious face.

Her lovely eyes shone like the moon appearing after a wildly raging storm. Seeing her, Psappha realized who it was who called her from Hades' slimy grasp. She reached and Gyla's hand met hers halfway. She pressed it to her heart. She looked for Gyla's other hand and felt a soft damp clothe upon her forehead. Slowly and with confidence renewed, she drifted into peaceful, dreamless sleep.

~ ~ ~

Psappha's strength gradually returned, as much a result of Praxinoa's fine cooking as from any will on her part. From thin barley gruel to thick rabbit stew, she could measure her recovery by the dishes with which her old nurse tempted her appetite. She was devouring an offering of thick mutton swimming in garlic sauce when she heard a timid tapping on her door.

"Enter," she called.

Lycos peeked in tentatively. "Well, little sister," he chirped. "You seem to have found a respectable appetite at last." Pulling up a lady's chair, he waited for her to finish her breakfast before he spoke again. "Your brother is in Egypt."

"Larichos?" She was puzzled. *Have I been ill so long that Larichos has left the island without my knowing?*

"Not Larichos," Lycos assured her. "Isn't he still with Pittakos?"

"I don't know. Since Daphnos took Klies to his family home, I haven't seen Larichos. Perhaps when she gets here he'll come. Did I tell you Klies was coming for a visit?"

Lycos abandoned the delicate chair and perched on the edge of her bed. "I doubt Larichos will come here to see Klies since he couldn't drag himself away from the palace revels to visit you, though he knew how sick you were; nor could she for that matter. Why is she coming now that you're so much better? Has something happened to Daphnos?"

"No. She's lonely and unhappy with him at sea. There're only two women in the household and Klies fares badly with her mother-in-law, since there is still no grandchild, so she asked to spend the summer here. "If Larichos is not in Egypt, who is?"

"Charaxos."

"Charaxos? I'd nearly forgotten I had another brother it's been so long since I've seen him. How is it that you know where he is when I don't?"

His grin threatened to stab both his ears. "The first ship of the season brought a letter from Alkaios."

"How is he?" she asked politely, as if she did not already know from the look on his face.

"He's fine," he chortled. "He's helped a score of maidens pay their dues to the Goddess and is happily looking forward to the summer campaign against the Persians. He says that the busiest

Temple of the Goddess in Naucratis so he spent the winter there. That's where he found Charaxos."

"At the Temple? Does Charaxos, also, frequent temple gardens or is it as a merchant that he chose Naucratis?"

Lycos fidgeted. "Neither, I'm afraid. He's a merchant all right, but it isn't trade that keeps him in Naucratis."

"If not trade, and not maidens sacrificing their maidenheads in the temple gardens, what holds him?"

"A rose."

"There are roses in Mitylene."

"Ah, yes," he agreed, his eyes full of mischief. "But no mere rose equals Doricha*, the Rose of Naucratis. She shines above them all."

"So," she mused aloud, "it is a lady that entices my wandering brother."

"Not a lady, Psappha, a courtesan."

"Charaxos of Mitylene consorts with pornas?" She tried to get up as she spoke but he restrained her with a smile.

"No, Psappha. Doricha is too renowned to be considered a porna."

Psappha sniffed stubbornly. "She sounds expensive. My meandering brother will find himself well plucked from the ministrations of such a one. Our father's pride must have bypassed him."

"Oh, he's proud enough," Lycos said. "Alkaios wrote that he struts about Naucratis like a rooster and well he might. The Rose is desired by kings."

"Stop talking like a cupbearer. The merely desirable acquire no claim to station. A porna -- is a porna -- is a porna no matter reputation or gender." She smiled when he assumed a properly chastised demeanor.

---

* Doricha (door-RICH-ah)

"Alkaios did say that Charaxos is often short of pocket," he offered.

"The cost of trinkets runs high."

"How about your trinket, Adelphi? Has she not cost thee dearly enough?"

"She has cost me nothing but my dreams, dear friend. I am alone because of my own foolishness."

"You've never been alone, Adelphi. I'm here and I'm not the only one. Have you forgotten that the school will reopen soon? And, Klies is coming. And, you have Gongyla despite how you've treated her."

Psappha shook her head. "She'll never forgive me."

"She already has. You must forgive yourself. Be brave, Adelphi. Admit your mistake and forgive yourself."

"My courage shrinks with the years, old friend."

"The years are not so many."

"Dear, sweet Little Fox, perhaps I should not trust you with my accounts if you can't add better than that. I've placed the rods on my dedication shrine forty-four times and must soon do so again."

"Your Lady of a Thousand Names must love you dearly, Adelphi. The years have left no mark."

"Not where it shows," she patted his hand. "Not where it shows."

> *"Indeed the Idols I have loved so long*
> *Have done my credit in this world much wrong,*
> *Have drowned my glory in a shallow cup,*
> *And sold my reputation for a song."*
>   *'Omar Khayyám'*

-- XXIV --

From a pallet in the olive grove, Psappha watched the leaves unfolding on the trees. A squirrel gazed down at her questioningly, scolded her then skittered away. A minute bird worked at a flower near her feet. Helios' kiss upon her cheek found firm, sweet flesh amid her silver-stranded hair. From the house, delicious kitchen aromas wafted on a swirling breeze. Her pupils' hushed voices soothed her loneliness. She summoned them with a gesture. They hurried to her and settled, petal-fashion, on the ground. The essence of fresh-crushed mint caressed her nose as they sat down.

Others both new and returning had replaced those few students who had followed Atthis to the new school. Psappha smiled and sighed when met by Timas's happy smile.

"Please sing for us, milady. I fought so hard to be allowed back."

Psappha started to decline, but the girl's expression disallowed it. When Praxinoa appeared with her lyre and an armload of cushions for her back, she sat up and reached for the instrument. With stiff, un-practiced hands, she tested the strings. Familiar melodies found their way to her fingertips, chords followed. She played song after song, but she did not sing. She closed her eyes and let the music paint kaleidoscopic memories on the inside of her eyelids. Gyla, sweet shadow, patient, loving, constant, guardian spirit -- Kerkolos, his tender understanding covering her in the protection of a gentle man's love -- Klies, her fairy daughter dancing on the stage of her mind, lighting all around her with laughter -- Lycos, her echo, little-red-fox-turned-silver, her twin in all save birth – 'Kios in martial splendor, his mocking grin a constant challenge – and there was Atthis, sheathed in memory – Atthis the moon of her life and Gyla her guiding star. As she played, she saw them all, behind her eyes.

~ ~ ~

Lycos pushed the scrolls to the back of his worktable and swung his chair around. He had been rattling on about accounts and purchases without realizing she wasn't listening. Psappha had something else on her mind and when she tired of waiting, she swept styluses and scrolls from his desk to the floor. "Psappha! Where is your mind? We must go over these notes. You have to approve the expenditures."

"They're approved," she said. "Just tell me if we have enough in the coffers for a trip to Naucratis." She snickered at his incredulous expression. "Don't you want to see Kios, Little Fox?"

"Of course I want to see Alkaios, but you've only been up and about for a few weeks. You aren't strong enough for such a journey."

"I'll decide what I'm strong enough for. Can we afford it?"

"What about the students? Much as I'd like to see Alkaios, we can't close the school in the middle of the season."

"The school will be fine. Timas can conduct most of the classes and Klies can teach the dance."

"That's another thing," he vacillated. "Klies just got here. Surely you want to visit with her."

"No," she shook her head. "She's changed. I don't know her any more. She's become avaricious and seems to have lost her understanding of the language, at least as far as her mother is concerned. She won't miss me as long as she can play mistress of the house. I've decided to go to Naucratis. Someone needs to talk to

Charaxos and remind him who he is and Gyla wants to show me where she's from."

"I'll make the arrangements."

~ ~ ~

Klies made an excellent teacher. She led the maidens in the intricate patterns she had learned from Atthis, inventing new ones as she danced, enjoying her power and elevated status. Psappha smiled approvingly as she passed. In the great room, one of Gongyla's assistants supervised a writing class. In the kitchen, Gyla demonstrated the proper method of preparing rabbit pelts for clothing.

"Ho, Psappha," Lycos called from the villa when she stepped outside. "We have passage on the new moon tide. Will you be ready by then?"

Before she could answer him, Gongyla appeared at her elbow. "You're going away?"

"We're going away, grumpy one. We're going to Egypt. Perhaps, after I've brought my brother to heel, you can show me your precious green land."

Psappha waved to Lycos, nodded emphatically in response to his querying gestures, and continued toward the orchard, an echo of Gyla's pleased smile on her face.

~ ~ ~

All of Psappha's trunks were packed. A small pile of items that had not fit into the sea chests lay on her bed. She searched the room with her eyes, looking for a container. The chest that held her commissioned writings was too large and too full. Behind it was the small, carved Cretan box in which she had locked her odes to Atthis. Rising from the edge of her bed, she went to her dressing table for her teak jewel box. Turning it over, she flicked the hidden catch with her thumb and lifted the tiny key from its secret place and smiled., remembering Klies, before she was old enough for braids, rapturously trying on all of her jewels, then crying suddenly, in fear of punishment, when the bottom of the box popped open. *She thought she broke it.* She remembered comforting the child by letting her pick up the little key and fit it back into its snug compartment.

Lycos burst into the room unannounced, waving a scroll, a dozen or so others tucked under his elbow. "This is the best piece you've ever published," he declared without preamble. "These, too, are good," he added, indicating the other scrolls. "Why weren't they given to me for release like all your others?"

Noting his petulance, she made haste to placate him. "Don't be silly," she said, snatching the scroll from his hand. "You know I authorize no publication except through you."

Psappha snatched the scroll and began to read. "Peer of the gods he appears to me ...." The words swam before her eyes. "Where did you get this?"

"In the marketplace," he pouted. "I bought a copy of each one. I think that one is the best, but you should have trusted them to me."

"I trusted them to no one. These were not written for publication."

The tiny key was still in her hand. Her fingers fumbled the lock on the Cretan box. It was empty. The precious private odes were gone. She slumped to the floor, squatting like a discarded doll. "How could she do this to me?"

"Who?"

Her mind fought against the evidence. *She wouldn't hurt me. Not intentionally. Not for mere gold. There must be someone else.* Gyla! Her mind clutched the name. *Only Gongyla knew where I kept the key*, she hastily convinced herself. "Gyla has sold my reputation," she said.

"There must be a mistake," Lycos protested. "Gongyla would never do anything against your wishes; certainly nothing that could hurt you, although these are more likely to enhance your reputation than harm it. These are good. Your best so far. They'll add great esteem to your name."

Psappha was not mollified. She had passed disappointment, disillusion and heartbreak and was building an unhealthy anger against the one person she knew would never hurt her. "She was jealous of Atthis," she added to the argument she was having with herself.

Lycos disagreed. "Gongyla was never jealous of Atthis."

"She was," Psappha insisted. "That's why she stole the odes and exposed my naked soul to the world."

"Gongyla was never jealous of Atthis," he repeated. "Be reasonable, Adelphi. If she was jealous, why did she send you in to Atthis in the first place? And why would she wait until after Atthis was gone to get her revenge?"

Psappha refused to listen. To do so would require accepting a harsher truth. A truth her mother's heart was unprepared to see. "It was Gyla," she stated, in a tone that broached no further discussion.

"There must be someone else," Lycos persisted. "Think, Psappha. Who else knew about that key?" When she refused to look at him, he stroked his chin a moment, then he smiled. "The copiers know who they bought them from. I'll go ask them. They'll prove it wasn't Gongyla."

"No!" She stopped his move toward the door with something akin to fear in her eyes. "Don't ask them. It was Gongyla."

"But . . .?"

"No."

Lycos dropped his hands to his sides and stared at her as she went through the door ahead of him.

"Don't follow me," she said. She didn't know exactly where she was going. Out! Out was all she knew. The house no longer felt safe to her. She hurried through the corridor toward the light, seeking sanctuary in the garden. Tears blinded her eyes. She did not see Klies until she bumped into her, nearly knocking her down. She flashed her daughter an automatic smile then bolted through the portal.

Gongyla came from the archery range to greet her with a warm smile. The smile disintegrated when she saw Psappha's tears. Her eyes filled with concern.

"Who has hurt thee?"

Psappha recoiled from the tender touch upon her arm. "Don't touch me, thou traitorous bitch."

Gongyla took hold of the hand that would have swatted her aside. "What is it? You know I could never betray you." She kissed the palm of the captive hand. "What do you imagine I've done?"

Psappha jerked her hand free. "I imagine nothing, thou jealous she-cat. You know what you did, thou slithering cobra. It will please me well if I never lay eyes on thee again. Get out of my way, thou whelp of a jungle cur."

Shoving Gongyla away, Psappha raced across the beach and around the bottom of the southern bluff with the sparkle of Klies' laughter ringing behind her like the taunt of a thousand harpies.

Book Four

PSAPPHA

Peggy Ullman Bell

[page deliberately left blank]

Sappho Sings

> *"I'll publish right or wrong:*
> *Fools are my theme, let satire be my song."*
> *'Lord Byron'*

-- XXV --

Psappha rushed past the abutment then southward along unfamiliar beach. Sand crabs scurried to avoid her sandals. Gulls invented script on the sky. Poseidon whispered his love to the shore. The rising evening breeze kissed her hair, sensuously unfurling her braids. *How futile, how sterile the kiss of the wind*, she thought, reaching as if to gather it to her aching heart.

Looking at nothing, Psappha stumbled through the sand, tripping over rocks. Seaweed entangled her ankles like snakes. She paid no mind to the young angler who stared at her over his net as she passed. A ragged goat trace led her to the top of the bluff where she stood, entranced, contemplating Poseidon's frothy pounding on its base, impervious of the spray, which soaked her dress.

Oh, dear Lady, why hast thou chastised me so? Has my crime been to love too much? Have I offended some other, by my devotion to you? Has Artemis grown jealous of my faith and chosen to punish me? Does Apollo desert me because Artemis guarded me? Will she desert me now that my unbridled tongue has wronged her servant? Shall I now, at last, go to my father, Poseidon? Oh, wondrous Lady, desert me not on my journey.

The edge of the precipice beckoned her. Shame and disillusion ravaged her spirit. Step by step, staring inward at a dream, she walked toward blessed oblivion. Suddenly, strong hands snatched her from Poseidon's siren call. Her mind continued on to nothingness.

~ ~ ~

Psappha regained consciousness as strong arms deposited her on cool sand. Her eyes blinked open. A young man hovered over her, a sunlight halo obscuring her view of his face. *Alkaios? No. Alkaios is no longer youthful.* In form, he reminded her of Kerkolos. *But Kerkolos is long dead.* She shivered. *Could Charon be so beautiful? Has he dumped me here on the sand because I came to Styx without his penny?* A crab, angry at having his front door blocked by her body, proved to her with his pincers that she was not ready for Hades just yet.

"Are you all right?"

"I'm fine," she said and, to prove it, she rolled onto her side and tried to get up. His helping hand beneath her elbow reminded her of Gongyla and she flinched. He led her to a small cave. A glowing fire-ring welcomed them. He wrapped her in fleece. She sat cross-legged on warmed sand and studied his youthful face. He had full lips that tipped upward as he added twigs to the coals. The fire-glow danced over near perfect features and seemed to seek out the small scar that bisected his left brow. *Gyla's is on the right.* Behind him, stalactites twinkled like orange icicles while, all around them, stalagmites absorbed heat from the rekindled fire and transferred it to Psappha's chilled bones. She clutched the lambskin and edged nearer the crackling driftwood before venturing, "Who are you?"

"Phaeon*," he answered simply.

The pink line through his brow lent a slightly demonic aspect to his face. Psappha scooted back. The lambskin slid off and under her as she moved. His stare made her instantly aware of the thinness of her kiton; a garment never intended for outdoor wear. She lowered her lashes and observed him through them.

He knelt and concentrated on the fire. His old-gold hair lay in loose waves on his shoulders. His upper body gave him the

---

* Phaeon [FAY'on]

appearance of a rower, but unlike Kerkolos, his legs were as sinewy and straight as a marathon runner's. She wanted to touch him, to let the power of his beauty drive away shame and loneliness.

As if he sensed her need, Phaeon came to her. Psappha lifted her hands and watched them disappear in his. Her heart fluttered like that of a trapped bird, afraid to stay, yet more afraid to flee. He urged her to her feet. Standing close to him, she ran her fingers over his smooth chest and upward to trace the faint laugh-lines beside his mouth. Her tentative fingers wandered downward toward each other, tracing his square jaw in passing. For reasons she did not bother to decipher, she let him lower her to the warm sand floor of the cave.

Her kiton whispered its consent as he whisked it away. Her nostrils flared as he tossed his loincloth after it. Her tongue flicked over her parched lips. She sucked in his scent as if to absorb his power, but absorption was not enough, her spirit demanded power of its own. Summoning all of her strength, she shoved him onto his back and mounted him before he had time to protest. His insolent grin as he folded his hands behind his head assured her that no protest would be forthcoming. Using him to crowd Gongyla from her mind, she rode him with the zeal of a battle-bound Spartan.

~ ~ ~

It was three days before they took time to talk. They lived on fish and wine, and the wonder of Eros gone mad as she tried to let Phaeon's enthusiasm drive Iphis from her mind.

The morning of the fourth day dawned with soft, summer rain drawing a shimmering curtain over the mouth of the cave. Psappha rolled toward the fire, propped her head with her fist and gazed sleepily at the nude image of Adonis that was Phaeon preparing their breakfast in the flat clay pot nestled among the flames.

Psappha stretched then sat up to brush sand from her breasts. "Will it rain all day?" Her voice seemed to hang in the air like the smoke tendrils rising from the cookery.

"Does it matter?" The scent of savory sauce wafted by her nose as Phaeon stirred the fish.

"Not really, I suppose, but I must see to my home eventually. There are some there who will be worried." She frowned as she visualized those she thought would not. Her frown deepened as he turned concerned eyes toward her. "No, no, beloved, do not look at me so. I will not stay away. The school will run quite well without me."

"School? What school?"

"You don't know who I am?"

He grinned. "You are Selene come down from the sky to taste of mortal bitchery."

She chuckled. "Ah, yes, you know who I am. Who I am here with you, but you, who know me so well, must know who others think I am." The perplexed expression on his unschooled face made her giggle with pleasure. "I am who I am, thou delightful. I am who you think I am, and I am also Psappha, The Poetess, and, for a little time, I must be about my business. Close thy beautiful mouth before thee catches flies."

"But -- but . . ."

"But -- but . . .," she teased, throwing off the rest of her coverings to go to him and tousle his hair. "Art thou a goat that thou wilt 'but' me so?"

"But, I know of you. I've heard your poems throughout the city. Why is The Illustrious Psappha here -- with me?" He pulled away from her touch. "The Poetess is not for the likes of me," he said, wrapping himself in the loincloth that had lain unheeded for days.

She yanked it off him. "What is this? We are as we are. Nothing is changed, thou stallion. I must go for a time, but the day will not end before I am back here in thy wondrous arms." To accent her words, she encircled his thick neck with her arms and twisted her fingers firmly into his hair, molding her body to his.

Phaeon loosened her hands with his and tossed her onto the sand. Later, she explained why she had gone to the bluff. To her surprise, he laughed at her sad tale.

"Why art thou grinning like a thieving cat?" she snapped. "Haven't I just told you that my soul is exposed to the jests of the mob?"

"What you said is that your odes are putting gold in someone's purse. It had better stop raining soon before you loose more to the thief." He laughed at the glare she gave him.

"I didn't want them published, thou buffoon. I didn't want to advertise my pain. Can't you understand that?"

"No. I fight old man Poseidon like a slave and live in a hole in a hill. All you have to do is scratch some pretty words in wax and you're Midas. If I were you, I'd be scratching day and night. What you need to do now is see how many more you can write." He smacked her bottom as if to hurry her on her way.

~ ~ ~

It was late afternoon before Psappha reached the secluded inlet. She hurried to her house. Once there, she went directly to her chambers, wanting to collect her thoughts before facing anyone. Her time with Phaeon had heightened her sense of guilt. The pain of betrayal had lessened. She was prepared to apologize but the traitor remained to be dealt with.

The sound of a scuffle in the corridor pulled her from her reverie. She turned in time to see Lycos thrust Klies through her doorway. "What is the meaning of this?" she demanded. "Lycos, you overstep yourself. Take your hands off my daughter."

Instead of letting Klies go, Lycos gripped both of her shoulders and propelled her toward Psappha. "Tell her," he commanded.

"Tell me what?" Psappha knew what, but she didn't want to hear. She took her daughter protectively into her arms and stroked her golden hair.

"Tell her," Lycos grated between clenched teeth.

Klies sobbed against her mother's breast.

Lycos ripped her from Psappha's embrace and shook her. "Stop your make-believe blubbering, you thankless whelp. Tell your mother the truth!"

Psappha pummeled him with her fists. "How dare you? Let go of her! Stand back, damn you!"

Lycos let go of Klies and stepped back with sympathy in his eyes for Psappha. For Klies he had only contempt as he positioned himself between her and the door, daring her to try to leave. "She sold your scrolls, Adelphi."

Psappha could see that her lack of surprise jolted him. He made no effort to hide his disgust. She flinched from his accusing scowl and turned an unreadable gaze upon her daughter. "Why, Klies?"

"Why not?" Klies shrugged. "Why should you lose students to Andromeda because people think you old fashioned? Those lyrics prove you are a greater priestess of Iphis than she or Gordo could ever be. Lycos is turning away new, and returning, applicants already. Ask him. You are more famous now than ever. Pittakos will have to let Atthis return and the gold from the sale of the odes will buy Daphnos a ship of his own. Your daughter will wear purple again. Your coffers will not hold your gold, nor mine."

"The poems were mine. You had no right to profit from them, nor will you. From this day forth not a dram of gold will pass from my hand to yours or your husband's."

Klies looked at her askance then darted from the room, shoving Lycos vindictively out of her way.

Psappha made no move to follow her. Another thought had intervened. "Gongyla," she whispered and would have gone to her had the look in Lycos' eyes forbidden it. She withdrew her hands, twisting them together painfully behind her back. "I should have listened to you. How could I have let myself accuse her?"

"You managed," he said curtly. He cupped her chin with his hand, lifting it to gaze deeply into her veiled eyes. "I warned you to beware. Now your foolishness has cost you more than you can afford to pay."

"I must go to her. I must make her forgive me. What can I say to her?"

"Nothing."

"Nothing? Have you lost your senses? I have to apologize."

"Gongyla is gone, Adelphi. She took the ship we all planned to take to Egypt." She eyed him askance. He shook his head sadly, "She'll come back."

"Not unless I ask her, and I can't. You don't know the terrible things I said to her."

"I know what you said to her, and why. She told me. She understood. Send for her, or better still, go to her. She wants you."

"I can't."

"You mean you won't. Send for her," he repeated as he turned away.

Psappha closed her eyes. She didn't want to see him leave. His sadness was harder to bear than his well-earned scorn. "Oh, Gyla," she moaned, collapsing on the bed the instant he left. *What have I done? I'll never see you again and I might as well be dead.*

She heard Phaeon whistle to her from beyond the garden, but she did not go.

~ ~ ~

Klies was right. Publication of the love poems turned the tide of fashion in her favor; Atthis' arrival came as no surprise. Psappha didn't ask if Atthis came to stay, she didn't care. Out of habit, she showered her with presents. When Lycos complained of the cost, she wrote for publication. "Why not?" Klies had said. *Why not, indeed? What does it matter? The world puts value on my simple words. Why shouldn't I? No amount of anger will change Klies; Gyla has taken herself beyond my reach, and Atthis?* She shrugged as she chose a fresh wax tablet.

"Why does the daughter of Pandion, the heavenly swallow, weary me?" she mumbled as she wrote, puzzling over each word. Writing deliberately for the public without a pre-arranged commission was different from anything she had ever done. The poem refused to behave.

Laying her stylus aside, she studied her reflection in the mirror. *Once there was beauty there and I thought thee ugly*, she told the womanly face that stared back at her. *How blind I was. I am grown old without my notice. And, Atthis?* She tried to picture Atthis as she had seen her earlier that day. She couldn't. Her mind showed her only remembered visions. *I love the child*, she realized, *but the child no longer exists. Did she ever truly exist? Except within my stubborn mind?* She looked again at the first lines of the poem. *It's true*, she decided. *I have grown tired of Atthis. I was a child in love with a child. I refused to see the woman we'd both become.*

Her awakened consciousness shouted of other things that she had refused to see. She slammed the door on Wisdom and grabbed an empty scroll upon which she transcribed an edited version of an old refrain.

"Remember, Atthis, when I first saw you. You ran in beauty, strong and young, your golden hair a glory in the sun. Truly, I drank that beauty with my soul. The man with me thought me a poor walking-companion, so lost was I in the magic of your spell.

"Those times I walked with my friends, in the city, I passed your dwelling. Sometimes, I scarcely heard them. My spirit was yours alone. I thought, then, I would come and speak to you, but you were fleet of foot and soon gone. A fair sight it was to see you. I was so young then, so in love with love and life and beauty.

"I remember, Atthis, how we came upon you in The Lady's park. Such an awkward, graceful child you were, gamboling among the trees like a spring fawn, so beautiful in your gangly elegance. Even then, you reflected the kiss of Terpsichore as you flitted upon the grass. I remember well your startled flashing eyes as you peered at us from behind a bay tree.

"I felt so mature and grandly remote from you, but my vagrant heart was already forfeit to that soul-eyed girl. We walked away from you, but my thoughts stayed behind. I carried the vision of your darling face with me, completely unable to dispel the memory." *There,* she thought. *Let Lycos publish <u>that</u>.*

Having been committed to papyrus, the memory was gone. At last, she knew Atthis as a dream of her own invention. *And, Alkaios? He, too, was a fantasy lover, a convenient tool of my self-education. And, Kerkolos? No dream he, and yet no true reality, a symbol, perhaps, of what society deemed right and respectable, a husband and an unexpectedly proficient lover. And, Gyla? Gyla is gone more surely than Kerkolos.*

Enough! She concentrated on the nightingale outside her window.

Phaeon's whistle imitated the bird's song. Her feet forgot their years. She ran from memories, from emptiness, her hair flying free the way he liked it.

Phaeon descended the path ahead of her, perhaps thinking she was not coming. Psappha saw him standing by the cleft in the bluff as she turned onto the beach. Kicking off her sandals, she ran along the waterline, dark hair and diaphanous purple kiton waving like battle flags behind her, unmindful of Poseidon's impending bout with Zeus.

Closeted in Phaeon's snug cave, they ignored the angry Gods. Zeus's lightning bolts and Poseidon's pounding surf were as nothing compared to the throbbing fury of their mating. The hours danced, the minutes sang, the seconds cried because they lived so briefly. The storm without could not outlive the storm within. Stars filled a cloudless sky to wink at Eros' victory over Melpomene.

Dawn watched Psappha climb up from the beach each morning. Sunset welcomed her back.

[page deliberately left blank]

> "Men err who say the Muses are nine . . .
> How careless! Behold!.
> Sappho of Lesbos ... the tenth."
> 'Plato'

-- XXVI --

Summer faded into autumn. One by one, the maidens called farewell from the decks of homebound ships. Though most of them traveled on the black, tri-masted ships of Tyre, some chose the lesser, brighter crafts of their native lands. Psappha was not sad to see them go. Their presence reminded her of Gyla's absence. *Oh, sweet Melpomymnia gentle-hearted muse of sorrow, why can't I cry? Where are your tears now, dear muse, tears that flowed so freely for a fool? I loved her more than gods allow and now I've driven her away. What bitter gall remains of the horror I bestowed upon her leaving. Such bitter webs deception weaves. My eyes are dry and barren. Grief and guilt have imprisoned my tears. My soul retches, but my eyes cannot spew it forth.*

Life still flowed warmly in her veins. She was loath to waste a moment of it.

The last pupil embarked on a dreary, threatening day. Psappha sent her chair home empty, choosing to walk in spite of the turbulent sky. It began to rain as she neared the fork in the road. Without conscious thought, she reversed her steps. Going neither home nor into the park, she walked south through the downpour, south to Phaeon.

The cave was musty, damp and empty. The coals were cold. She could see his squat boat tied to its boulder nearby.

Psappha gathered driftwood from deep inside the cavern and laid a fresh fire. It soon cracked and sparked, sending smoke-curls to form a backdrop for the sheet of rainwater cascading over the mouth of her sanctuary. Shivering, she wrapped herself in a lambskin and lay down on the warming sand, next to the fire pit.

She awoke alone. The rain had stopped. Phaeon had not come. Clasping the fleece around her shoulders, she went onto the bright beach. *He wouldn't expect me here in the middle of the day*, she reasoned. *Perhaps he went to call me from the house.* She smiled. For the next few months, the time of day would not matter. Her pupils had left her for the winter. She didn't need to return to the house 'til spring.

Content with the knowledge that Phaeon was safe else the boat would not be here, she followed the waterline farther south. About a league beyond the cave, past an outcropping bluff, a stout cabin hugged the incurving base of a cliff. She could see a man mortaring thick limestone in the chill sunlight. She was almost upon him before he heard her and looked up. She yelped a happy huzzah and ran toward the cheery cottage.

"Oh -- Phaeon -- Phaeon -- it's beautiful." She collided with him, laughing, covering his sweat-glistened chest with kisses.

"Hold." He struggled to free himself. "It's only a cabin. Did you expect to spend the winter nights in the cave?"

She nodded, not ready to tell him it would be more than just nights.

"You would. But, I won't let you." He lifted her hair away from her face and kissed her forehead. "My grand lady of the silver tongue," he said, "ready to shiver in a cave like a fishwife. Well," he asserted, "a house is what you deserve and a house -- such as it is -- is what you shall have." Taking her hand, he ducked through the low doorway.

The inside walls glowed with whitewash. A wide, hand-hewn bed filled one corner, smelling sweetly of dried seaweed and thyme. Against the back wall, he had built a small writing table. It, together with its stool, invited her to work if she wished. The fireplace filled the entire remaining wall. An angora goatskin lay on the stone hearth. In the corner, behind the door, a shelf held Phaeon's cooking brazier. Several cupboards decorated the wall above it. A polished table flanked by a pair of worn Egyptian chairs occupied the center.

"It's beautiful," she exclaimed.

"It's warm," he said.

"It's beautiful." She pulled him onto the crackly bed.

"It may be," he teased. "If you'll let me up from here so I can finish it."

"Oh, bother," she mumbled against his neck. "Finish it later."

~ ~ ~

The Island slumbered in winter's vice. Psappha snuggled into the crook of Phaeon's arm, listening to the waves sloshing on the beach outside. Last night's fire slept under warm ashes, giving off little heat, making her grateful for the thick, down coverlet she had brought from the house on the hill. The rhythmic rise and fall of his chest under her ear lulled her into the euphoric haze between waking and sleeping. The knock on the door seemed a part of her dream. When it was repeated, louder, more insistent, she swung her feet over the edge of the bed and reached for her rabbit-skin cape. Clutching it close, she stumbled across the cold floor and cracked the door open.

Klies pushed past her, azure eyes widening as their gaze fell on Phaeon, nude and uncovered on the tousled bed. Psappha pulled the displaced coverlet over him then glared at her daughter.

"I had to come," Klies whined. "My friends snicker behind their hands when your name is mentioned. The way you are carrying on with that uncouth barbarian has all of Lesbos laughing."

The uncouth barbarian was awake and grinning, leaning on one elbow, watching them. "Psappha, my love," he requested with a suppressed chuckle. "Hand me my clothes and I'll build The Lady Klies a proper fire."

Psappha quickly gathered his garments from where he'd dropped them the night before then hurried to toss them at him. Seeing Klies' obvious interest in the activity beneath the down, she took her arm and turned her away. "You dare to come here to hurt me by saying I am a reproach to you?"

"What else could I do but come here and insist that you be more discrete? Your fame is great. No one of your stature can flaunt unfashionable conduct without reproach."

The admiration in Klies' eyes as she watched Phaeon putting logs on the fire told Psappha that her impertinent daughter would not mind appearing foolhardy for such as him.

"Everyone laughs at you," Klies continued. "They deride me. They even question my birth."

"Is it my reputation you would protect, Klies or your own? What did Daphnos say about your coming here?"

"Nothing."

"Nothing? That surprises me. He struck me as a sensible young man."

"He isn't sensible at all," Klies complained. "He won't let me buy him a ship and he insists on living in the new city among a bunch of merchants."

"Might I remind you, young woman, that your father was a merchant?"

"Of course," Klies said. "But, he was rich. I will not live in dirty little alleys when I can live above it all unless, of course, your shameful behavior forces me to leave your lovely new house."

The little cottage suddenly seemed unbearably warm. Psappha threw off the skins, too angry to care if Klies was shocked to discover that her mother was nude without them. She accepted the admiration in Phaeon's eyes as she dropped a thin wool kiton over her head. Then she reached for the wrap Klies had scornfully tossed onto the little table and held it toward her arrogant daughter. "I'm not inclined to ignore the bad temper of youth, Klies."

Catching a glimpse of Phaeon's grin, she winked at him, letting him know she felt her own display of temper justified. "I haven't forgotten the extent of your treachery, Klies. I know what to expect from you so you'd best mend your ways and be careful. I am easygoing but I've power enough, still, to chastise you severely." With that, she shoved the purple wrap that she had paid for into Klies' reluctant hands and opened the door for her. When Klies would have said more, Psappha pushed her outside, latching the portal behind her.

"Suppose I tumble your high-nosed offspring in the sand?" Phaeon teased. "That would make her forget about what people say." The twinkle in his eye did not protect him from having his hair pulled.

They tangled on the rug and the aftertaste of Klies' visit was soon lost in the scuffle.

~ ~ ~

For the first time in her life, Psappha hated spring. Spring meant she must return to the school each morning. Lycos's villa now presided over her home in the inlet, a huddle of guesthouses, workrooms and outbuildings plus the two original houses on the bluff. Though Psappha reportedly reigned over the entirety, her select group had grown to such proportions that now there were as many instructors as there had once been students. She could not get used to passing young women in the corridors or on the lawns or beach whose names she did not know. She rarely heard the familiar Adelphi in the halls. Few retained the temerity to address The Poetess at all.

It was shortly after the vernal equinox when a message from Lycos interrupted her crowded lonely day with a summons to the villa. If Lycos's note hadn't identified her visitor, Psappha wouldn't have recognized him. More than eight Olympiads had passed since last she saw her elder brother.

Charaxos's dissipated appearance repelled her. His eyes looked peeled. Tiny capillaries traced jagged lines across the sallow yellow of his eyeballs as if to draw attention to the grotesque, dilated pupils. A typical Sybarite's paunch lopped over his girdle. He looked to her like an overage eunuch. His aspect repulsed all that was female in her.

"Charaxos do sit down," she said. "You look like you're about to have apoplexy."

He strode back and forth before her. "You must stop seeing him," he sputtered.

"Stop seeing whom?" Psappha replied with feigned confusion.

"This fisher person you've been snuggling up to. It's scandalous, Psappha. You are not some farmer's daughter to have your actions go unnoticed, word of your behavior travels fast and far. Everyone in Naucratis speaks of it. At great personal sacrifice, I took the first ship out of the Nile to come here and save your reputation from yourself. You must stop seeing him."

"By whose dictates, Charaxos? Surely not yours."

"Yes, by Zeus, by my order, Psappha. By my authority as senior male member of our family, I forbid you to go to him again."

"You forbid, Charaxos? I think you know what you can do with your pompous authority. If you ever had any authority over me, which you did not, you forfeited it long ago."

"It is beneath the dignity of the House of Scamandronomos for your name to be linked to that of a fisherman," he said, "a fisherman whom you flaunt like a prize, according to Klies."

Psappha chuckled through a sardonic smile. "Klies thinks he's a prize does she? That doesn't surprise me. But she was wrong to complain to you. Look around you, Charaxos. The House of Scamandronomos is in Old Mitylene. This is the house of Psappha, The Poetess, The Lady of Lesbos if you will. Lycos tells me some call me The Lesbian in foreign cities, as if there is no other. Is that what they say in Naucratis? Is your porna jealous of your sister's fame? Have your peccadilloes lost the public's attention? Is that what brings you here to try to lord it over me?"

She took a breath and cocked a brow at him. The twinge of guilt she felt as his face reddened was not enough to slow her anger. "How dare you come here after a lifetime of neglect and presume to dictate to me, Charaxos? Where were you when our mother died? Chasing pornas, I've no doubt. All Aegea has laughed at your antics, yet you dare to question my decorum. So what if Phaeon catches fish for a living. He at least has a respectable occupation. How much better that than your notorious Rose?"

His bulbous face purpled. "I won't have you use that tone with me, Psappha. You must not see him again or I'll cease to support your disobedience."

Psappha laughed. Her laughter rose like leaves caught in a whirlwind. When it subsided, she asked, "What tone would you have me use, thou fool? The God of Ridicule cannot devise enough barbs to hurl at your folly. You won't support?" Her laugh was not pleasant. "You haven't supported me in all the years since our mother died. What familial monies your debauchery left you are as a mustard seed compared to the harvest of wealth I've earned without your patronage. I wouldn't be surprised but what my reputation enhanced your ability to keep up with your porna's demands." She turned away in disgust.

He stepped in front of her, his opium-ravaged eyes pleading. "You can't intend to sanctify this outrageous relationship," he sputtered. "Even our rash ancestress, Ariadne, chose a king upon whom to bestow her favors. You can't mean to impose a base-born man on our great tradition."

"Great tradition? Which great tradition, Charaxos, the stupid princess who got herself puffed up and abandoned, or the foolish king murdered by his own adulterous wife? Our entire aristocracy is descended from an army of idiots who fought a ten year war to preserve the honor of a woman who had happily sacrificed it to a beautiful young man rather than waste her own youth and beauty on an impotent ass. Take your great tradition, your orders and your over-indulged appetites back to your porna and try to convince her of your illustrious heritage after your money runs out. The only tradition she understands is the sacrifice in the temple garden. Go!" She pointed toward the door. "Go, I tell you! Go, and trouble me no more. I'll marry, or not marry, whom and when I choose. What I do with my life is no concern of yours."

He hesitated, shuffling his feet. "I should at least stay for your birthday."

"My birthday has not concerned you in thirty-three years, Charaxos. You left before my sixth. Please just go. Stop by Lycos's office on your way out. I'll instruct him to give you a small purse. You'll need it for your porna and your pipes."

~ ~ ~

With Gongyla gone, their home on the beach stifled Psappha but nothing, not Phaeon or her embarrassing elder brother could lessen her love for the orchard of her childhood. Blossoms scented the air. Yellow-green grass beneath her favorite tree welcomed her. The herbs growing amidst it accented the pleasant sensation with their fragrance.

Psappha no sooner got her dress arranged around her feet than she saw Lycos dragging toward her, squinting from the setting sun. He reclined on the ground beside her, chewing on a blade of mint until her questioning eyes insisted that he say what he had come to say.

"You should release him, Adelphi."

"Not you, too, Lycos. I thought you would understand and want me happy."

"I do understand. Better than you do, perhaps. Forgive me, sweet sister, but have you thought of the future?"

"What of the future? Isn't today enough? I'm not alone, Lycos. You know what that means to me. I never need be alone again. Phaeon will see to that."

"Will you marry him?"

"I might."

"You don't love him." His level gaze left her no chance to deny it.

"I love him -- as much as I can."

"Is that enough, Adelphi?"

"Phaeon thinks so."

"For now," he allowed. "But what of the future? He's young, Psappha. He has many years to live. Isn't he entitled to all of them? Shouldn't he raise sons of his loins to bring comfort to his later years? You're no longer a girl, Adelphi. Your years of bearing are past. True, you are as beautiful as ever. More beautiful, I think, but the years will not always be so kind."

"You talk as if I were halfway to my bier. I am at the height of my powers as a woman. Were I any younger, I could not begin to match Phaeon's prowess as a lover."

"That may also be true, Adelphi, but he is in the full flush of youth. My years are as yours and it has been a while since I stopped counting silver strands in my hair. What of Phaeon's love when the years make their tardy mark on you?"

"I'll blow out the candles," she countered, but it didn't divert him.

"He deserves children. You must free him."

"I know, Lycos. I know . . ."

"Now, Psappha, don't put it off. The longer you postpone it the harder it will be on him. He truly loves you."

Peggy Ullman Bell

[page deliberately left blank]

> *"Fare thee well! and if forever,*
> *still forever, fare thee well."*
> 'Lord Byron'

-- XXVII --

Sand invaded her sandals. She took them off and continued south. Her white, funereal kiton flared behind her, billowing with warm salt air. His boat bobbed on the water near the cave.

Psappha undid her braids as she walked; letting fawn-red waves spill down over her back. Phaeon stood thigh-deep in water washing his nets. She waved to him as she stepped onto the beach. *Once more, my love, and then goodbye,* she promised herself as he stepped ashore to welcome her.

The night combined all that was rich and vibrant in their relationship. Youth mated Pleasure and learned. In the morning, she told him it was over. Her eyes brimmed with tears as she said, "Don't love me, Phaeon. I'm like Poseidon's Ocean. You've floated safely on my surface for a while but you want to plunge too deep. There are tides and currents in my depths that will drown you and I – I do not wish for you to die."

"You will marry me," he said.

"No, no, my love, that won't do. If my breasts were still capable of giving suck, and my womb were able to bear children, I would not hesitate, but would come running to be your bride. But age is already writing on my face and Hera hastens not to fly to me with her gift of pain. You must find a lovely daughter of Illustrious Aphrodite and take her swiftly for your own. I'll go again among the maidens and you'll come and regale us with tales of her of the violet-scented breast and golden tresses."

"You're talking rot, Psappha. You're beautiful. I want to marry you. Your body is rich in treasures. I love you and I'll have no other for my bride."

"If you love me, Phaeon, choose a more youthful companion for your bed. I couldn't endure being married to a young man," she lied. "I'm too old."

"No!" He crushed her to him as if to snatch her from the cool morning and return to the heat of the night. She pulled away. "Psappha." He groaned and dropped to his knees on the hard, dirt floor.

The pain in his eyes almost changed her mind. She stared beyond him, filing memories in a back corner of her mind. There stood the bed upon which they'd invented magic, the sweet table whereon he'd tempted other appetites, the hearth where blazing logs had failed to compete with the raging fires they created between them, the goatskin that had welcomed their wrestling.

Psappha shook her head, clearing it and her eyes. She ran her fingers through his tousled hair. "Stand up, fair youth, and look me in the face as friend to friend," she said, speaking in formal lyric form to dull the pain. "Unveil the beauty that is in your eyes, Phaeon. Our time has been a beautiful time but I, you must know, love delicate living. For me, the desire for richness and beauty is as strong as the desire for the sun."

She could see her lie reflected in his eyes, but she continued, unheeding. "I could not forsake luxury for the life you lead and you, my darling, are too proud to accept my bounty. It's best we part. To go on any longer would tarnish that glory which has been ours." He made no move to stop her as she opened the door for the last time. In parting, she whispered, "Goodbye my brave and beautiful dolphin. May you ever sleep in the bosom of a tender companion."

She stumbled, walking away. She squared her shoulders and went on, not looking back.

~ ~ ~

Psappha hissed and sputtered at words in the wax. Each time she thought she had the epic poem going the way she wanted it the characters got obstinate and refused to behave with any sensible degree of predictability. Thoroughly frustrated, she threw the tablet into the fire where it hissed and sputtered right back at her.

She shoved the pile of blank scrolls off her worktable and took up another tablet. There would be time, and more, to transcribe yesterday's work onto papyrus later. She felt as if she had nothing but time. The school functioned smoothly under alumna teachers. Lycos and his assistants entertained her numerous, celebrated guests.

Dreaded evening came upon her unaware. She flinched as a bird-mocking whistle pierced the sunset, soft as the rising wind that whispered goodnight to the day, calling her to the scorching pleasure that was Phaeon -- but she knew she dared not go.

She clenched her stylus, broke it, reached for another, broke it, threw it aside and picked up another as the birdcall faded with the light. A soft tap on her door told her it was time to put her work aside and join the household at dinner. She ignored it.

Praxinoa entered with her supper and a lamp. The lamp cast a moonlight glow on Psappha's tablet. Words, which had been eluding her for hours, now flowed onto her tablet. *Know you not that age has wrinkled my skin and my hair has turned from dark to white? Surely as Starry Night follows Rose-armed Dawn and brings darkness to the ends of the earth, so Death tracks every living thing, and catches it in the end.*

She wrote of him in long impassioned verses. She wrote of how Endymion attracted the attention of the Lady Moon as she passed him while he slept. With her stylus, she told of how Selene peeked into the cave on Mount Latmos and about the beautiful youth sleeping there who enthralled her. From deep in her tortured soul, she brought forth the tale of how the Lady Moon kept Endymion asleep, eternally young, to enjoy his slumbering love which, alone, was capable of warming her ethereal heart, arousing, with her kisses, his dreaming passions.

The ache of frustrated passion stole all other appetites. She would see Phaeon again, but she would not stay with him. *For his sake, that cannot be.*

Resentfully, she tossed the tablet aside.

"Why do you torture yourself so, Psappha?"

Psappha jumped. She had forgotten she wasn't alone.

"Put aside thoughts of past lovers," Praxinoa said. "What is over, is over, there is no profit in wallowing in it. Maidens crowd your garden, Psappha. There is one, Gyrinna*, a dusky beauty from the birthplace of the Nile, who always gazes at you with adoring eyes."

Released from the throes of reflection by the possibility of fulfillment, Psappha noticed that the light was wavering. Praxinoa swayed unsteadily. "You're ill," she admonished, urging her to a chair. "You should have sent someone else."

"No one else could get you to slow down and eat."

"Nor can you, old friend. I have no appetite for food. And you, you need to be in bed."

"After you eat the supper I brought you."

"Now," Psappha said after she had succumbed to Praxinoa's blackmail. "The tray's empty. Now, get you gone and don't leave your bed until you're fit."

"I'm not too ill to serve thee," Praxinoa countered through a cough.

"You must go at once and rest," Psappha said.

Although it was mid-summer, a damp chill seeped in as her old nurse left. *How long before this unseasonable weather draws off all her strength?*

Hours later, her hand aching from rapid and constant writing, she walked through dark, empty corridors to the student's quarters.

Gyrinna welcomed her, not as a teacher, but as a woman, full-blooded, passionate and alone.

---

* Gyrinna (guy-reen-ah)

Once again, expected innocence proved to be elusion. Gyrinna, like Atthis, was well schooled in the Rites of Iphis and determined to teach her teacher what she knew but this time Psappha no longer cared. She allowed no nagging memory to mar her joy as Gyrinna stroked her flesh, tracing erotic nerves to their source, whispering her need at the temple gates with silent syllables schooled in splendor and yet Psappha felt cheated once again.

~ ~ ~

The slow creaking of the cog-wheel over the well, the slosh of the water as it tumbled from the pots, the murmuring of the well-man coaxing the ox around its hoof-cut path, and the raucous shrill squabbling of small territorial birds combined to pull Psappha from her dreams of verdant jungles into cool, bright morning.

When she was dressed, she snatched a pomegranate from the bowl by her bed, carried it to the window where she ripped it open, picked out the blood red kernels with her teeth and spit the seeds onto the ground outside for the birds to find.

Beyond the grounds, she could see the twin harbors of Mitylene. A lone trader rocked at anchor near the estuary. She spun away from the view, tossed the remainder of the pomegranate into the slop-jar by her door, walked gingerly on fresh washed tiles in the corridor, waved a cheery "good morning" to the gardener. Still wearing her slick indoor slippers, she slipped and scrambled up carved steps and pounded on the villa door. "Lycos! You're sleeping my life away! Get up! Unleash yourself from that bed."

Through the tiny octagonal glass in the door, she saw Lycos stumble from his alcove, rumpled and bleary-eyed.

"Come, thou sluggard, open this door!"

"Damn, Psappha, what are you doing here at this hour? You know I work most of the night."

The minute he let her in, she said, "Start packing. We're going to Africa. Arrange immediate passage for me, yourself and Praxinoa."

"What will I tell your guests?"

"I don't care a fig what you tell them. Tell them Pharaoh needs a hymeneal for the sister he didn't marry and he insists I sing it to her personally. Tell them I'm going to get gardening advice from Nebuchadnezzar. I don't care what you tell them. Just get us on a ship!"

She allowed him no time for protests. She left as abruptly as she had come.

Back at the main house, she dispatched a messenger with passage money, gave Praxinoa's substitute enough instructions to keep her busy past nightfall and then hurried to the oven-dried room behind the kitchen. She found her old nurse shivering in swelter. "We're going to Egypt," she announced. "On the way we'll visit your home."

"I have no home," Praxinoa murmured. "Israel is no more. My people have been carried out of their land to serve pagan masters." She covered a racking cough with her hand. "I'm sorry," she said when it stilled. "I forgot you're not of my faith."

Psappha seated herself on the edge of the narrow cot. For the first time, in a long time, she looked closely at the woman who had warmed the fringes of her life for so many years. Praxinoa's once olive skin was sallow, her raven hair had grown silver without notice.

How could I have been so unobservant? Psappha chastised herself. Taking an emaciated hand into hers she said, "Perhaps your God is also one of mine. Aren't He and Zeus, when he's on his best behavior, much the same?"

The pained, disapproving expression in Praxinoa's eyes forbid pursuit of the subject so Psappha tried a different approach in search of a smile. "Once, long ago, I heard a girl with doves in her voice tell of a rash young man. Tell me, Praxinoa, do you recall what Gyla said about what happened to him?"

Praxinoa's disease-ravaged face brightened as she recited the tale of the traveler's homecoming.

"When the young man returned from his journey, he found that his father had died and left all that he owned to a slave. The only inheritance left to him was the choice of a single item from the estate, nothing more. The young man thought and grieved. He prayed long and loud for guidance. 'Which one thing should I choose,' he asked, but the Goddess left the choice to him."

"What did he choose?" Psappha's delight with the faint sparkle of amusement in Praxinoa's eyes made her want to delay the story's end.

"He chose the slave, of course. The young man's father was very wise. If he had left the inheritance to his son, who was absent, the slave would surely have squandered it. Thinking it his own, he guarded it well."

"Very clever," Psappha observed. "It is said that cleverness is the childhood of wisdom. A young man with so clever a father must have become very wise as he grew older."

Praxinoa sighed. "No," she said. "According to Gongyla he did not. Cleverness is also the childhood of avarice. The young man grew old, but he did not grow wise. Few people do." She studied Psappha's face a moment, and then went on. "The older the young man got, the more selfish he became. One day he went to an oracle who told him that all he had would one day belong to his neighbor."

"How could that be?"

"The oracle did not say. So, the young man, now old, made up his mind to thwart her prophesy. He took all that he owned to the market and sold it. With the gold he received, he bought a huge diamond, which he had sewn onto his turban. 'Now,' he thought. 'The poor man cannot steal my wealth.'" The volume of Praxinoa's voice fell off as the sentence ended. Her eyes drifted shut.

"But, the oracle said his neighbor would one day own it," Psappha prompted.

"And, so he did. One day the rich old man went down by the sea. A strong wind came and blew his turban far out into the water. 'Well,' he thought. 'The oracle was wrong,' he gloated. 'The poor man did not get it after all.' A few days later, as the poor man's wife cleaned a large fish he had netted, she found the diamond inside."

Psappha smiled. "His just due, I'm sure." Her chuckle died unborn as racking coughs besieged Praxinoa. Psappha knelt and gathered her into her arms as if to delay the progress of illness with the warmth of love.

When the spasm subsided, Praxinoa pulled her coverings tighter although the tiny room beside the kitchen was excessively warm. "You have been foolish, like the young man," she said. "You've squandered your love on the unworthy and let your child squander what is rightfully yours, but, at least, you need not worry about the penalties of avarice."

"Perhaps I do,* Psappha protested. "There is a thing I dearly covet, yet dare not hope to own."

"How can that be, Psappha? You have wealth beyond a Sybarites dreams. Your fame is greater than any woman dares to hope."

"That is the problem, old friend. 'Greater than any woman dares hope.' I dare to hope for more. My wealth and fame are trifles as long as those whose esteem I most value have no thought for my work. No matter how great my school becomes, nor how widely read my lyrics, I remain a woman and, as such, must remain outside The League of Poets.

"I enjoy the gold my work has brought me, but I desire a greater compensation."

Seeing that her paltry complaint added to the pain in Praxinoa's eyes, she cursed the fate that ordered destruction of so beautiful a spirit. "I am going to Egypt where it's warm and you must come with me."

Praxinoa rewarded her with a cautious smile. "Why, Psappha? Why do you want to leave your home? Why now, when if you wait a few months it will be winter and your time will be your own for months?"

"Because of winter, I suppose. Because Lesbian winters are cold. Because I am alone in a crowd of women, and it doesn't please me."

"What about Gyrinna?"

"She'll not miss me," Psappha answered, unsurprised that Praxinoa knew all of what passed in the night. "I have given her what she wanted of me. She'll use the knowledge well I'm sure. I planned a journey to Egypt some time ago. There's no need to postpone it any longer."

"You've seen your brother," Praxinoa said. "Must you travel so far to see him again? Or, is there a bigger reason?"

"Your health is reason enough," Psappha said, refusing to give her the admission she knew she sought. "You'll feel much better in the dryness of Valley of the Nile."

"I'll feel better in my grave, Psappha. I'll not see another spring in this life."

"Hush. Don't speak of it. We're going to Egypt where you'll drink sunshine and nectar. The life-giving juices of Apollo's fruit will soon have you up and bossing me about as always."

"Don't delude yourself, Psappha. No amount of sunshine, nor any fruit of your multiple gods, can change God's will. I will go with you, if it makes you happy, but, before I do, I would have your promise."

"Anything," Psappha agreed. "What is your wish?"

"You must swear to me, by whatever power most binds you, that, when my numbered days are gone, you will not burn my body on a bier."

"Hush," Psappha tried to insist. "Your days are far from over. You will tend the Nymphs again." Even as she spoke, she knew she hoped in vain. The light in Praxinoa's eyes was growing dim.

"I'll tend no more children," Praxinoa said without remorse. "Promise me," she repeated. "You must have my body prepared in the manner of the Egyptians and taken to Ashkelon. From there, what is left of my family can take it to Bethlehem. With my spirit gone, they'll be free to place my body in the sepulcher of my father. He can no longer deny me then. Promise me."

"By the thousand names of The Lady and by all her myriad of godly children, I swear it."

"By one," Praxinoa insisted.

Psappha nodded and thought carefully. *By whatever power most binds you,* Praxinoa had said. *By what power am I most bound? By Aphrodite? No. She is too fickle. By Apollo? No. His gift of words and music come only on his whim. Zeus? No. He belongs to foolish warmongers. Poseidon? No. He will claim me when it suits him, but he helps me only if he chooses. Hera? No. She has no further need of me. My days of blood and babes are behind me.*

Is there no god who has proved faithful, she wondered, *no goddess who has not abandoned me in the hour of my need?* She smiled into Praxinoa's tired eyes. "By The Lady Artemis, I swear it," she crooned. "By Artemis, dark shadow of Musicos, who blessed me greatly, although her earthly image is now lost to me. It wasn't her fault I squandered her gift."

Praxinoa rewarded her vow with a wan smile then let her lashes fall.

Psappha kissed her drawn forehead and determined to hasten their departure to warmer climes.

As she left, the sound of muffled weeping attracted her attention. Following it to a corner of the kitchen she found Anaktoria* a fleet-footed maiden of Lydia, hunched in a corner, crying. Kneeling beside her, she placed the girl's raven-tressed head on her shoulder. "What is it, child that brings tears to your lovely eyes?"

"Oh, my lady, I must leave thee." Anaktoria's dark eyes swam in tears.

"But, sweet nymph, that's no cause for weeping. Of course you must go, later, as you always do at the end of the season, before winter bolts the harbor doors with ice, to return on the first breath of spring."

---

* Anaktoria (Ann-ak-TOR-rhea)

"No, my lady, I must leave now. I can't stay the summer. My father has ordered that I sail at once."

Taking Anaktoria by the shoulders, Psappha held her away from her and brushed her straight, jet hair from her tear-streaked face. "It will be all right, Anaktoria. I won't be here in any case. Master Lycos, Praxinoa and I are sailing to Egypt with the new moon. Perhaps we can come visit you on our way home. Would you like that?" To her dismay, Anaktoria began to sob. Psappha again held her tightly. When, after several minutes, the girl's tears didn't subside, she loosened her embrace, grasped the girl's shoulders and shook her. "Stop this, Anaktoria. Stop crying and tell me what's wrong."

Anaktoria snuffled, sniffled and tossed her head as if to shake off her tears. Her hair fell behind her shoulders like a dark cape. "You cannot visit me, milady. I go to the Temple."

Psappha felt as if a falling tree had struck her down. "No! You can't! Cybele would not demand the sacrifice of such beauty as yours to the sterile life of a priestess. Surely the knife would break before it could stop the flow of your beautiful seed."

"Not the priesthood, milady, though I would prefer it. I must go, within the month, to the sacred garden of Ishtar to await the purchaser of my maidenhead."

Despite the relief she felt in knowing the lovely child would not to be sterilized, Psappha tasted gall. *Men joking about the Temple gardens is one thing, having one of my lovelies trapped by the barbarous custom is quite another.* Angry tears filled her eyes.

Anaktoria saw them and began to cry again.

Psappha quickly dammed her tears, composed her face and forced her rage to subside. *There's nothing I can do.* She recalled Alkaios's latest letter. *He said something about saving plain maidens from months of futile waiting. But Anaktoria is lovely. She will not have long to wait. Some man with a hefty purse will purchase her maidenhead without delay. But there's a better way.*

She took both of the child's hands in hers, and made her tone as comforting as possible as she said, "I swear to you, Anaktoria, that although I, like you, had but one virginity, I did not fear that threshold beyond which The Lady bid me cast it away."

"But you knew to whom you would cast it," Anaktoria sniffed.

Psappha smiled, remembering. "Yes. I knew, and so shall you. I've heard that lovers can arrange to meet in the Temple garden on the night of the sacrifice to keep strangers from tasting beloved fruit. It will be so with you."

"My lover can never be my husband."

"So much sweeter will be the sacrifice," Psappha soothed. "Could you give a more precious gift to one who will see you wed to another?"

"My lover doesn't need a maidenhead, milady. She's not yet lost her own."

Psappha hastened to cover her mistake. *I have failed this tender creature in not preparing her for the outer world of marriage and men. My students must learn to thrive in whatever environment The Fates chose for them. This cannot happen again. I will never again assume that my darlings come to me with previously learned lessons. I must somehow teach them all that they need to know.* But, resolutions for the future did nothing about the immediate problem. She searched her mind and found no ready answers. *There is not enough time. Or is there?* "Could you give yourself to a man you know?"

"If I must give myself to a man at all, it would be better if I knew him. But, I know no men, milady."

"I'll send a message to your father at once," Psappha informed her. "If he'll permit you to travel with us, I'll take you to the Temple of Astarte in Naucratis. Don't look so bleak. He won't mind. The temple in Naucratis is older and grander than the one in Sardis. Your father will feel honored. Besides, even if he minds, what can he do after the fact? We'll be in Naucratis before my message reaches him."

"How will I suffer the touch of any man after I have lain in my lover's arms and known the joy's of The Lady's true mating?"

"The man I would have thee meet in the gardens is a true and tender friend, Anaktoria. He'll teach you that Eros has another face which smiles as kindly as the side you've already seen."

"But, even if what you say is true, milady, and I do not doubt you, the wedding will follow. How will I suffer the touch of the unknown man my parents have chosen as my husband?"

"I did not go to my marriage bed in purity, little one, and yet I swear to you that night was sweet enough to me and neither have you anything to fear."

"Can the night be sweet without love, milady?"

"It may not be without love, dark flower. Aphrodite, like Eros, has many faces. You will be astonished at silver-throated Hera. She is not miserly with her gifts. Have no fear, my child. Lord Alkaios is the gentlest of lovers. I'll take you to him."

"Can Aleta* come too? Her time in the temple gardens will come soon. Perhaps we could share the sacrificial night."

---

* Aleta (ah-LEE-tah)

[page deliberately left blank]

> "Oh! that the desert were my dwelling place,
> With one fair spirit for my minister,
> That I might all forget the human race,
> And, hating no one, love but only her!
> *'Lord Byron'*

-- XXVIII --

The ship lay becalmed off the coast of Phoenicia. Less than a shadow of its former self, the once great seafaring confederation sprawled like the recalcitrant slave it had become. High on a seaside promontory, the Temple of Ishtar reminded Psappha of Anaktoria and others who, like her, had sacrificed their pride to the devil-goddess of Babylon. The sight of Tyre, her double-glory tarnished but undaunted, made her think of Dido's peninsula.

It had been years since Carthage had crossed her mind. *Or, has it been?* Soft words echoed in her memory. *'A green land, beyond a white land beyond the land of the Carthaginians.' Ah, but, Gyla, my sweet, sweet love, I cannot see so far*, she thought as she squinted eyes swollen from sleepless nights and tears.

Praxinoa lay close to death in a dank lower cabin next to the one occupied by Anaktoria and Aleta. Psappha took a deep, sustaining breath of salty air then left the railing to return below deck.

The cabin was silent. No blood-spotted cough disturbed Praxinoa's sleep. "Will she wake?"

"She'll come around," Lycos assured her sadly. "She may not wish to, but she will, at least for a while."

"What do you mean, not want to? Praxinoa loves life as Poseidon loves the shore."

"I've seen this sickness before, Adelphi. It is not a pleasant way to die." Praxinoa moaned fretfully. Lycos filled a spoon with the elixir Psappha had extorted from The Lady's Crones before they sailed. He dribbled as much of it as he could into Praxinoa's half-opened mouth then grabbed a shallow bowl and held it beneath her cheek as the coughing, choking, bloody flux began again.

Psappha nudged him aside. Taking some of the elixir into her mouth, she placed her lips on Praxinoa's and let the potion flow, from her tongue, into her old nurse's constricted throat. She laid her cheek against the almost imperceptible pulse in Praxinoa's limp wrist and felt a silent scream rise. *Where is nameless, useless One God with whom your parents punished you, Beloved? Why does he let The Fates treat thee so cruelly? Why must you die? Why not me? I've wasted the love they gave me all because of a foolish obsession. Why can't I be the one to die? Why didn't Phaeon let me fall from that cliff? All I brought him was pain. All I bring anyone is pain.*

Great, wracking sobs tore at her until the sleep of exhaustion claimed her.

Lycos did not wake her when Praxinoa's faltering heartbeat stopped.

~ ~ ~

The lighter that would carry Praxinoa's body on the first leg of its journey to Bethlehem bobbed against the hull. Psappha's knuckles were white upon the railing. She was glad that the Port of Joppa had no docking facilities. This was the doorway to Praxinoa's ancestral homeland and Psappha felt as excluded from it, as Praxinoa had believed herself to be.

Praxinoa had told Psappha enough about her family, and her father, for her to know she would only make things awkward with her presence. Hired mourners, faithful to the One God, would accompany the body to its final resting place. She watched the western sky change to an excitement of color, recalling all that she could remember of Praxinoa, letting memory fill yet another void in her life. She was relieved to hear the clatter of the rising anchor-chain. When the long oars finally dipped into the cerulean water, she turned her back on Praxinoa's harsh holy land whispering, "May your next life bring you greater joy. May your One God be enough to grant thee all the happiness you deserve."

~ ~ ~

Psappha stayed in her cabin throughout the journey from Joppa to Pharos, withstanding all of Lycos's coaxing. Her grief overshadowed whatever desire had summoned her hence. She had no desire to meet the infamous Doricha, Rose of Naucratis or to argue further with Charaxos. She let the others disembark without her. When, near sunset, the crewmembers eyed her resentfully, she decided she could delay their pleasures no longer and allowed the revel-bound seamen to row her ashore.

Once aboard the tender, she cordoned a place for herself among the amphoras. An obstinate glare was enough to insure her privacy. She wanted to remain as alone as she felt. She wanted to wallow in her grief until it seared her soul and cauterized its gaping wound.

Getting directions to her brother's house proved easy. Lycos met her in the doorway.

"Doricha is here," he whispered. "Atthis is with her."

"What is she doing here?"

Before he could answer, Atthis welcomed her and bade her enter as if it was she and not Doricha who was mistress of the household. She led them to the great hall where Doricha lounged on an ornate couch, her ginger hair splayed on the cushions. Charaxos lolled on the couch opposite sucking his pipe like a pleased potentate. The look that passed between Doricha and Atthis left no doubt that they knew each other more than well.

To what inglorious trust has Doricha this second time come round? Psappha wondered. *First Charaxos, now Atthis?* She whirled away, bumping into Lycos who followed her outside. "We will sail at once," she said. "I will not stay in the same house with pornas."

"There is no ship," Atthis said from the doorway. "You will have to winter here."

"You may winter here, not I. The harbor overflows with ships."

"None will leave port this late in the season except those who hug the coast plying their trade with the Ionians."

"One of those will do. Lycos, send word to the harbor that The Poetess desires passage on the next vessel leaving port."

He did not budge. "I'll not sail on some tadpole trader. They're dangerous."

"Stay, if you wish. The pornas should make you perfect company."

"You wrong her," Lycos said. "Doricha was never a porna by choice. She was sold by Iadmon* against her will."

"She has done no entertaining of that sort since I purchased her and set her free," Charaxos said as he joined them.

"She hasn't needed to," Psappha countered. "You've purchased her retirement at great expense to both of us I'm sure. Lycos, just how much have I paid for my brother's whore?"

"Psappha! You are my only sister and I love you. But I'll not have you ranting on my doorstep."

"Better your doorstep than within your brothel."

"Silence!" He cast an embarrassed glance at the gathering crowd.

Lycos tugged at her arm. "All right, Little Fox. I'll say no more. We'll go."

"No, you won't," Charaxos sputtered. "You will not shame me by refusing my hospitality."

"I can add no shame to your tarnished reputation, Charaxos, only to my own. I will not share a roof with your harlot and her paramour." She turned to go.

"No," he stopped her with a whisper. His face had turned a mottled scarlet.

---

* Iadmon (eye-add-mon)

"Charaxos," she said softly. "I cannot stay here. When, if ever, you learn where true values lie, come to me." She nodded to Atthis who shook her head.

"I'll stay here," Atthis said. "Doricha is expecting a guest and has asked my assistance."

Psappha sniffed. "Of course and, Charaxos, will you stay to watch?" He cringed from her sneer.

"You're wrong, Psappha. The guest Doricha hopes for is not that sort. It is rumored that Solon may stop here on his current tour."

Psappha scoffed. "You've kissed the God of Darkness if you think the world's greatest statesman will visit stoop to visiting the infamous Rose of Naucratis. It almost makes me pity you. For all her airs," she said without apology, "your precious Doricha is a porna. If she hadn't bewitched you, she'd be walking the streets leaving 'follow me' footprints in the dust."

Charaxos' face turned crimson with rage.

Atthis came to his rescue. "She loves him."

"She loves his gold; as you'll learn to your sorrow, Charaxos, when your money runs out."

"She's good to him," Atthis persisted.

"You are under her spell yourself," Psappha said despite Lycos's attempts to silence her. "Was your taste so completely shaken by your affair with Gorgo that you can no longer judge food from garbage? Or, have you always preferred gutter twat?" Atthis' blow grazed her cheek. She lunged, then stopped mid-stride, threw back her head and laughed. "Stay with your porna, Atthis. 'Tis more than you deserve."

She pushed through the gathered onlookers, frowning at Lycos when he caught up with her. "I thought I sent you to find us a ship."

"We don't need a ship, Adelphi. We can winter with Alkaios."

~ ~ ~

Alkaios's quarters outside of Naucratis were sufficient if not ample. Psappha's room provided a marvelous view of the delta.

With Alkaios' good humor to brace her flagging spirits, she filled tablets faster than Lycos could get the finished poems copied and aboard the coastal vessels for distribution.

"Dark Cybelean warrior, in some distant land . . . ," he read from the latest one. ". . . remembering the magic of the night." He mumbled under his breath for a few lines, then exclaimed, "This is wonderful, Adelphi. The best of the lot."

"It's a poem, nothing more," she said, not wishing to discuss it.

"Is it?" Alkaios asked from the chaise near the fire.

Psappha frowned. "Hello, Kios. Don't you have something to do? What of Anaktoria and Aleta? Isn't it time they reported to the temple?"

"All taken care of," he said as he stretched his long frame and clasped his hands above his head. "They went last night."

"Are they all right? Were you able to protect them from strangers?"

"They protected each other. With a little help from Gongyla."

"Gyla's here? Where?"

"Easy, little one. She's gone. But she left behind a little gift for Klies that we thought Anaktoria and Aleta could put to more immediate use."

"What?"

"I'll let them tell you. They asked to be alone for now. They'll explain it all tomorrow."

"They're here?"

"Yes."

"Both of them?"

"Yes."

"How?"

"I'll let them explain that too. Don't worry, S'pha. And don't work too hard."

"You're the one who works too hard," she said. "Doing nothing at all has got to be a strain."

He awarded her with an insolent grin. "Not at all," he said, "but watching you work is. I think what you need is a long slow trip. In fact, I have just the thing in mind."

"Oh, you do, do you?" She mocked his impish grin. "Are you trying to get rid of me?"

"Never." He sat up and studied her face intently. When she caught him at it, he veiled his eyes and said, "You're a bright light in a dark, drunken tunnel, S'pha. My poor poems sparkle with reflected genius whenever you're near."

"You overdo your flattery, Kios. I think you have some mysterious motive for your sudden suggestion."

"You wound me, S'pha." He emphasized his statement with a hand fluttering over his heart. "Come, dear friend. Help me empty another flagon. You've scratched enough sad epics for today."

"Have I become a burden to you, with my brooding? Is that why you want me to leave?"

"You're as burdensome as an empty vat at a Dionysia," he responded.

"Empty?"

"Aye, Psapph'. Your cup is empty. The poems thou art producing so prolifically are but dregs of a once rich brew. Clear thy fire-shooting eyes, velvet-voiced one. Thy talent turns lowly dregs into ambrosia, but you are capable of challenging the Muses."

He refilled her goblet, while letting her know by his expression that he had not strayed from his analogy. "I want you to take the island route to Mitylene."

When she would have protested, he stayed her with an upheld palm and a shake of his head. "Visit the temples and gardens, S'pha. Refill your spirit with beauty and light. By the time you reach Lesbos, things will be better for you. I promise."

"What makes you an authority on my fate?"

"The gods whisper to me," he teased, refusing to be serious another moment. Instead, he became playfully argumentative and continued in that vein long after Lycos returned from the copiers.

The three of them reviewed old arguments, instigated new ones and drank their way through several more flagons. They exhausted subjects and themselves, waxing profound and prophetic into the morning hours.

Lycos had long since curled into a sleeping ball on the hearth when Psappha took exception to Alkaios' opinion of the Trojan War. "You're a greater fool than I thought, you insufferable sot. Do you actually believe that men fought for ten years over nothing more than a faithless wife? Look at the story! What do you have? As men tell it, you have supposedly intelligent men, of all cities, dying to defend the honor of one minor king who was not man enough to keep his wife at home, while quarreling among themselves for the privilege of despoiling women other men thought they owned. I tell you, Helen was a woman in love, nothing more. Menelaus and his greedy brother wanted control of the Hellespont and used her as an excuse, as if men ever need an excuse for their bloodthirsty games of grab and grovel."

"Surely you aren't saying that Helen had no part in it," Alkaios slurred.

"Of course she had a part," Psappha admitted, accenting with a wave of her arm that sent wine slopping onto the hearth without her notice. "Of course she had a part, but who are we to say what that part was? Who are we to judge her? Who are we to pretend to know what those who knew her thought of her? History is a plague if you take it without question.

"Homer was a man, or men, no one is sure. What can a man know of a woman's mind? Can you, claim to comprehend the many facets of mine? No. Of course, you can't. Nor I yours, but I ask you, 'Kios, how might the story read if written by a woman's hand. How would the years of battle sound if told by Helen or Klytemnestra? What might Penelope have had to say about Odysseus' adventures? In her version, might not her troubles exceed his in import? History is written, and oft revised, by men, Alkaios, and men, when it comes to their precious honor, are unmitigated fools."

"Ah, S'pha, you make me glad I'm dishonorable." Four empty flagons flanked the one with which he had originated the discussion. Now, he brought it full circle. "You need to sail away from this den of fools, S'pha. Lycos! Wake up! Find Psappha a berth on an island hopper."

"There is only one fool here, 'Kios. If we go, you will be all alone here, with only your cellar for company."

"Lycos will stay with me, won't you, Little Fox? I have work for him to do."

"No, 'Kios, I won't leave without him."

"I'll come in the spring," said Lycos, rubbing his eyes. "You could do with some time alone."

"Aye," Alkaios said. "There is work to be done."

Psappha knew she had lost and still she argued. "You said I worked too hard."

"Aye," Alkaios toasted her with yet another flagon, "you do. But I have other work for Lycos."

"What are you plotting . . . ?" she asked. She received a brimming goblet in reply.

~ ~ ~

Psappha's temples throbbed as she wandered into Alkaios's shaded garden the next morning. Servants brought breakfast but in deference to her aggravated innards, she didn't eat. Fortunately, Alkaios brought wine when he joined her. She was nursing a goblet and her head when the girls joined them.

They came hand in hand, leaned down together and kissed Alkaios on opposite cheeks without letting go of one another. They then raised their linked hands, walked to a nearby bench, perched together on its edge and shined smug smiles at Psappha.

"It appears you've gained admirers, 'Kios."

"Not I. I think their smiles are for Gongyla."

"Gyla again. What's going on, "Kios? You told me Gongyla's gone."

"She is, S'pha. But she gave the girls something before she left for Thebes."

"She's in Thebes?"

"Across the river from it last I heard. She said she wanted to see the female pharaoh's temple."

"Oh wonderful," Anaktoria exclaimed. Then to Aleta she said, "Let's go to Thebes."

"You'll do no such thing," Psappha said. It was obvious they were stalling but Psappha did not intend to track Gongyla down. She'd managed to resign herself to the fact that, if Gyla could forgive her, she'd have already come home. "Hatshepsut's temple will have to wait. I promised your fathers I'd see that you got home as soon as you finished your business in the temple gardens."

The girls giggled at mention of the temple gardens.

Psappha arched a brow. "I would have thought your sojourn in the temple gardens would have been a more sobering experience." Again, they giggled. "What is the magical something that has the two of you smiling so smugly? What happened? Were both of your fees paid by so exceptional a lover that there's nothing about the sacrifice to sadden you?"

"Oh, yes," they piped in unison. "Oh, yes." They giggled. Alkaios was also grinning broadly.

"Well," Psappha injected impatiently. "Tell me so I can laugh too. I need some humor in my life."

"We went to the temple," Anaktoria said.

"And the fees were paid," chimed Aleta.

"And we hid in the bushes." Anaktoria giggled.

"And we made the sacrifice," said Aleta with an adoring glance at Anaktoria.

"But how," asked Psappha more curious than ever. "Who managed to find you in the bushes? Alkaios?"

"Don't look at me," he said. "I wasn't there."

"Then who? Who broke thy maidenheads?"

"Not who," said Anaktoria.

"Not who," Aleta echoed.

"Not who. What," they said together.

"Stop this! I don't like being teased," Psappha groused. "Stop this nonsensical snickering and tell me straight out. How did you manage the sacrifice?"

"With Lady Gongyla's present. Wait. We'll show you."

They ran from the garden in giggling tandem and returned scarce moment's later carrying a tiny sarcophagus.

Psappha turned the foot long casket over in her hands, examining the carvings. *Yes. It could be Gyla's work.* The image on the lid was a fine rendition of the Cretan Ophidia, arms and body entwined by snakes, hands folded over her personal altar.

"Open it." Anaktoria giggled.

Aleta gazed at her with her heart in her eyes. Then to Psappha she said, "Yes. Open it milady."

Their close scrutiny made Psappha uncomfortable. All eyes focused on her face as she searched for the catch. When she found it, she opened the lid only far enough to see the purple velvet lining. She felt weird. It was after all, regardless of size, a container for the dead.

"Open it all the way," Aleta encouraged.

Psappha raised the carved lid slowly. Inside, on a bed of plush royal purple velvet, laid an exquisite ivory olisbo*. Now it was Psappha's turn to laugh. *Would that she had left me one of these. Think of all the trouble it might have saved.*

~ ~ ~

Psappha was still smiling when she hobbled from dock to deck the next morning. Later, in her cabin, after seeing the girls to theirs, she unrolled the bundle Lycos had thrust upon her at the last minute and smiled to find two flagons of wine. When her stomach stopped

---

* olisbo (dildo)

trying to trade places with her brain, she realized that Alkaios had gotten her onto the boat without revealing his reason for doing so. She had no idea what chicanery he was up to and her head hurt too much to care.

The maidens enjoyed their reprieve from matchmakers as the squat trader rolled and rocked from port to port. Upon arrival at Aleta's home on Cyprus, they learned that Lycos had arranged for Aleta to marry the eldest son of Alyattes, King of Lydia. Anaktoria was to be given to him as well, instead of to the half-brother to whom she had been promised."

"It's wonderful news," Anaktoria said. All the sadness had vanished from her face.

"I don't want to marry," Aleta whispered.

"We must marry," Anaktoria soothed. "You knew that. This way we'll still be together."

"I was hoping," Aleta whispered.

"And your hopes have been answered, my love. Prince Croesus has more wives and courtesans than Solomon. He'll never notice us! We could die untouched by man."

Thank you, my foxy friend.

~ ~ ~

With the ship to herself, Psappha passed the time in endless games of sennet with the Samosan captain. When they reached the Ionian Dodecapolis*, she indulged herself with brief shopping sprees in several ports while the little ship exchanged cargos. The diversion soon grew tedious. By the time they reached Samos, she was more than happy to accept the captain's invitation to linger a while at his home. Samos sounded to her like a fine place to break the protracted journey and she welcomed the chance to keep her feet on solid ground.

The little red ship nestled with its fellows in their homeport, bobbing impudently close to wintering Carthaginian triremes.

---

* Dodecapolis (a group [in this case a coastal string] of twelve cities)

Smaller craft scurried over the placid water. Behind the Acropolis, the island rose in tiers like an amphitheater designed for the Immortals.

Psappha lingered on Samos longer than she had intended. This time, she was in no hurry to reach Mitylene. To get away from the captain's harried wife, she spent as much time as possible wandering the countryside. It was several weeks before she realized that the woman's antipathy stemmed from jealousy. Psappha chastised herself for not noticing that she, too, would have liked to roam the island, but they both knew she would die in the arms of her grandchildren with the desire unfulfilled.

Soon freedom for women will be a memory, she mourned, thinking of the countries she had visited and those students had described. *I pray the memory does not fade completely.* The woman's fate, and that of so many of her former students saddened her, making her finally hungry for Mitylene and the free-spirited Lesbian maidens who had not yet felt the restrictions of a true gynakeon.

Arrangements made, Psappha went on one last tour of the rocky island. Her gown caught on some brambles beside the well-worn path. She yanked it loose and continued up-hill unperturbed. At a gurgling spring, she perched on a rock and removed her sandals. A few paces farther on, she tied her kiton up like a girl's then climbed toward the Temple of Hera on the crest.

White columns pointed to the red-tiled roof like virgin fingers reaching for the blood of womanhood. The huge statue of Hera wore a high, basket-like headdress over a marriage veil. In Her extended hands, she held ancient betrothal scarves. Someone had piled roses around the statue's feet.

Oh, Queenly Hera, Psappha prayed. *Take present shape beside me, down from my dreams in that beautiful form which once appeared at the summons of kings, the sons of Atreus, who, when they had brought to an end the destruction of Troy set out hither from the river Scamander. They were unable to win home and were obliged to entreat Thee, and fertile Zeus.*

Now, I, Psappha, daughter of Scamandronomos beseech Thee, Lady, that, as in the past, so again may I do things pure and beautiful among the maids of Mitylene whom so often I have taught to sing and dance at Thy festivals -- and, even as the sons of Atreus, by grace of Thee and Thy fellow gods, set out from Troy, so in prayer I, daughter of the Illian heir Scamandronomos, entreat Thee, Hera, protect thou me on this my returning journey to the pure and beautiful island Thee found for him.

She was reluctant to leave the temple grounds. All the flowers she loved were there, their beauty unexcelled by the flamboyance of Hera's birds. The bold peacocks screeched their dominion over beds of heavy-scented herbs and roses, sounding like laboring women in the throes of The Goddess' appointed rounds. Psappha watched their courting rituals until Helios rode low over the sea.

Upon her return to the ship captain's home, the path she chose took her along the top of the island. Pausing on a rough outcrop, she imagined that, if she looked long enough and hard enough, she would see Lesbos -- thirty miles distant, beyond Chios and the Erythrae* peninsula.

A rocky promontory farther along offered a better view and although she knew she would see naught but water, she headed toward it. She heard voices and she stopped. A gathering of women, out of doors, on Samos and most of the places she had visited was rare enough to make her hide, lest her unexpected presence frighten them.

They danced around a huge crystal that centuries of caresses had worn smooth. A stubborn lump stuck in Psappha's throat as she watched a pageant unfold. Their paeans to The Mother sent shivers to her soul. The priestess separated herself from the worshipers and strode to lands edge, the jewels on her long cape shimmered as she walked. Her crown looked like pink-gold in the sunset. Two of the women left the shrine and followed her. Together, they removed the crown and placed it ceremonially on the lush ground.

---

* Erythrae (ur-rhee-thray)

The myriad of tightly woven braids upon the woman's head reminded Psappha of Medusa's legend. *Of course,* she thought, *Medusa was but a jungle queen in braids who defeated some great army. Her power alone would be enough to set the men struggling for supernatural explanations.*

The women reached as one to lift away the priestess's velvet cape. When they stepped back, Psappha gasped. *Beautiful, beloved - strong and free,* she composed within her mind. *Beautiful, beloved - strong and free - I see my perfected self in thee.*

Tall, true Amazonian - willow bending in the wind. Unbroken, unflinching -- the willow leans to kiss sweet Earth from which she springs; roots tied to bosom, reaching for clouds - resilient, firm. Oh, how my adoring heart sings:

Exultant is my song, Oh, willow, exultant is my song. Life blows thunder yet you, my beloved, reach enveloping branches -- sanctuary -- willow tall and softly whispers acceptance, love, the siren's call.

"Are we not sisters after all?" she whispered.

Like a graceful black swan, the Nubian priestess dove into the cerulean foam below.

Psappha stopped a sob with her fist.

Peggy Ullman Bell

[page deliberately left blank]

> *"All who joy would win must share it,*
> *happiness was born a twin."*
> 'Lord Byron'

-- XXIX --

Psappha couldn't get off Samos fast enough. She booked passage on a fishing boat to Chios where she found lodging at a local winery, got maudlin drunk over an ode to the peacock priestess and stayed that way for days. Everywhere she looked, she saw reminders of Gongyla and every time she did, she reached for another flagon.

After a while, she ran out of pocket gold. Her erstwhile proprietor poured her onto a ship bound for Lesbos. "This is the Illustrious Psappha," she heard him tell the seaman who had carried her aboard. "When she wakes up, she'll consider this a kindness."

It took the little island trader about a week to reach Mitylene. Lycos had arrived before her. He greeted her with a letter he had brought from Alkaios.

"A word once sent abroad flies irrevocably," she read. "Whatever Providence bestows upon you, receive it with a thankful heart. Do not defer the joys of life while you build yourself a monument more lasting than bronze. I, Alkaios, will one day fade from memory but what is best of Psappha shall live beyond the pyre." She read it again to herself and then she shrugged. "Whatever does he mean by all of that?"

"You'll see," Lycos smiled mysteriously. "But it could have something to do with this." He handed her a fine Athenian scroll.

She perused it then exclaimed, "This says Solon of Athens wants to meet me. Is it real?"

Lycos studied the scroll she returned to him. "Looks real enough to me."

As days grew into weeks and nothing happened, Psappha decided missive had been some bored scribe's bad joke. Each day brought more messages from travelers hoping to find welcome in the house of The Poetess. Lycos unrolled each one with an air of expectation. Alkaios, he told her, was in Syracuse. She assumed Lycos watched for another letter from him and she let him screen all incoming correspondence while she divided her time between administering her school and her work. She read only those queries which he insisted she must, and she resented every interruption and tried to ignore him.

Ancient Rules of hospitality would not allow her to ignore her duty. Custom demanded that she appear in the great hall every evening. It was there that she permitted Lycos to press correspondence upon her. The pretense of reading allowed her to be present and absent at the same time. Sometimes she sat for long moments tapping her palm with a scroll as if deep in thought.

She posed thus now, but she had read the scroll -- twice. A broad smile teased the corners of her mouth. *Charaxos is coming home! Alone! The prodigal returns!* She gloried in the thought, happy for the first time on months. *Golden Nereids*, she prayed, her elation subdued by caution. *Grant my brother's safe return, I beseech thee, that his desire may be fulfilled, and that, undoing in every way his former mistakes, he may become a joy to his friends and a sorrow to his enemies, so that we may be shamed before no one.*

May he desire to hold his sister in due honor, Golden Ones. And, may he find a desirable wife among decent young women.

Having finished her prayers, Psappha laid the scroll on the table with a contented smile. Then she scowled and stabbed the contents of her platter. As she conveyed the filled blade to her lips, she didn't bother to squelch disgruntled thoughts. Instead, she savored them for later transcription. *As for you, Doricha, you obscene and evil bitch with your nose set to the ground, may you go off and do your hunting elsewhere! What a wonderful poem that's going to make.*

Amusement restored, she signaled for her tablet and stylus so she could note the beginnings of Doricha's poem before it got away. That done, she turned her attention to a nearby discussion.

The animated conversation centered upon a dignified, silver-haired gentleman with a clear, cultured voice. He criticized a new play by Stesichorus* Tisias that concerned a maiden so virtuous she chose Death rather than lose her maidenhead unmarried. Psappha could not help laughing. "An interesting premise, milord, she said as she interrupted. "Interesting," she emphasized, "Interesting but unlikely."

"You do not find the theme believable, milady?"

"Not in the least, milord." Psappha noted that his eyes sparked with humor at the prospect of debate. She imagined that hers were the same. "Maidenhood is a commodity of value only to proprietary males. A healthy young female might consider an intact hymen more of a burden than a virtue."

"Did you find it so, milady?" The stranger's magnetic eyes twinkled.

Psappha smiled, meeting his challenge directly. "I am a daughter of The Lady, milord. The disposal of my maidenhead was, rightly, a choice I reserved for myself."

"A most remarkable accomplishment for a gynakeoni," he conceded.

"Perhaps, milord, since men consider gynakeoni little better than animals, caged for their exclusive enjoyment and profit. But, there are no gynakia on Lesbos. Lesbian men are still wise enough to know that a caged beast eats many trainers before it is subdued."

He glanced at the stunned expressions on some of the faces around him and he chuckled, a warm, musical ripple. Then, he raised

---

* Stesichorus (chorusmaster)

his goblet. "I salute thee, milady, you have made my argument. Gentlemen? A toast to . . . ?"

"Your hostess, milord." Psappha grinned. "I am pleased to welcome to my home a man who recognizes gynakia for the absurdities they are."

"Greetings, Most Illustrious Psappha, I should have recognized you by your irrefutable logic. Accept, dear lady, a toast to thy brilliant mind. Alkaios did not exaggerate. Solon of Athens hails thee, oh Poetess."

Psappha's hand rose, reflexively, as far as her waist before she gulped her surprise and willed her fist to lay quiet at her side rather than stuff itself into a gaping mouth, which she somehow willed to stay closed.

"Forgive me, Master Solon," she said after a second's hesitation. "I should have welcomed you at my gate." She cast an angry gaze around the crowded hall in search of Lycos. She spotted him near a Theban courtier and beckoned him to her side. "How is it, thou donkey, that I was not told of so venerable a guest?"

Rather than appearing chastised, Lycos stole furtive glances toward the entrance. To Psappha, he looked more like a fox than ever; a wily fox with his ear cocked for the bay of the hounds.

"Lycos, I asked you a question."

"He didn't tell you because I didn't tell him," Solon said softly.

Psappha scrutinized the elder statesman's face. *Of course*, she mused, *he would not wish to be the center of attention.* "Please allow me to welcome you properly now, Master Solon. I am grateful for the opportunity to entertain you."

"And I, Lady Psappha, am grateful for the opportunity to converse with you. Your fame is more far-reaching than you know."

"Not far-reaching enough, I'm afraid."

"What more do you want, Illustrious Lady?"

"Nothing a woman can attain in a world being taken over by gynakia. You mentioned Alkaios. The honor I desire is one he can achieve. Are you familiar with his poetry, milord?"

Before he could respond, the ringing of a sistrum* halted all conversation. Lycos, looking suspiciously unsurprised, lifted his hand and the musicians struck up a flourish. Servants quickly drew back the couches to make room for a troop of nude Cybelean temple dancers. The priestesses twirled and stamped to the rhythm of brass castanets. Their breasts swayed, their bellies rolled, the coins on their collars and belts jingled in time with a distant drum. A flute sounded from beyond the entrance and the dancers undulated to its wail like fascinated snakes. A gong reverberated beyond the door and the dancers wilted to the floor in a graceful semicircle, their heads toward the open door, their noses pressed to the tiles.

Clouds of colored smoke filled the entrance. All present drew breath as one.

Only Lycos could arrange such wonder on short notice, Psappha marveled. Thinking the spectacle an extravaganza for Solon's benefit, she rewarded Lycos with a broad smile of forgiveness. He grinned back at her like a boastful child with yet another surprise up his sleeve.

The High Priestess of Cybele stepped from amidst the smoke. A magnificence of opulence, heavy gold chains hung in swags on her forehead in front of an opaque veil. Their ends, which hung in shimmering ribbons on either side of her hidden face, reached to and below the layers upon layers of golden coins that dressed the shoulders of her jewel-encrusted, purple and scarlet cape. Pearl-dressed saffron satin slippers peeked from beneath her cloak.

Psappha heard Lycos chuckle as the last wisps of smoke drifted away. Her heart thumped red behind her eyes. The room took on a rosy glow as a dark hand extended from the folds of the High Priestess's cape. Her throat locked and she could not speak. Every hair, every capillary on her skin ached to be touched. A pulsating tremor began deep in her gut, flowing lava-hot to her personal temple where it vibrated like a purring leopard. She blinked. She

---

* sistrum (musical instrument resembling a small tambourine with a handle)

stared then blinked again. Within her mind, a song took wings. *Aphrodite, thou marvelous, thou wondrous purveyor of a thousand dreams, she comes! Hold back my tongue, thou Harpies. Don't let my words destroy me again.*

Gongyla studied her from behind her veil with a serene, tender smile then she snapped her many-ringed fingers and the dance resumed. Under cover of inattention, they left the hall.

~ ~ ~

The door to the adjacent chamber stood ajar as if Lycos had anticipated Gongyla's return. Light from tall candles danced like fireflies on ceremonial finery. Psappha waved her servants away. She ached to serve Gyla herself.

When they had gone, she reached beneath Gyla's heavy collar and pushed the magnificence of brocade from her shoulders. It fell in an undignified heap on the floor.

Gongyla did not move. Perfect emerald scarabs held her pearl-encrusted outer kiton. Psappha worked at them impatiently until, at last, one after the other, they came free and got tossed aside to lose themselves beneath the bed. Soon, the diaphanous saffron under-gown also drifted floor-ward, covering the temple robe like summer sunshine on a bed of many-colored flowers.

Gyla removed her headdress and her veil. Psappha forgot to breathe. Fragile silver chains of infinitesimal flowers lay upon dark braids like garlands. She reached. The proud head bent to meet her hands. She twined her fingers in the tiny links and lifted them away like a monarch's crown. Now only the wide collar adorned chestnut-warm flesh as if its row upon row of shimmering coins were part of Gyla's supple body.

Psappha became effusive against her will. Afraid to speak and yet unable to keep silent she whispered, "Oh, my beloved. Thou art a wonder to behold. There exudes from thee a regal light. Thy beauty glows forth from thine accepting eyes. Thou hast forgiven me. Thou art kindness incarnate. Thou art creation. Thy love empowers me. It spills forth to touch and caress everything around thee. Thou art my life, my love. Thou art love."

Gyla shushed her with a smile. With the gentlest of winks, she released the catch on her collar and cast it aside as if weightless. Then, she strode to the bed, stretched upon it like a lithe cat and beckoned Psappha with sultry eyes and seductive smile. "Do you still wish to play Iphis?"

Psappha's garments flew from her like leaves caught by an autumn wind. She scattered them behind her as she crossed the room. Her body trembled as she perched on the edge of the mattress and tucked chilled feet close to the hot moistness beneath her hips. She reached, with feather touch, to trace Gyla's ageless brow. Tentative fingertips followed the tiny crease of eyelid, brushed over glistening lashes that framed olive-centered, misty, almond eyes. They drifted from high cheekbone to firm jaw. They roamed beyond the cup of ear to caress pierced lobes and tenderly remove the diamonds that dangled from them. They drifted, petal soft, down gentle curve of throat then like twin brushes, they painted invisible swirls on pulsating breasts. An impudent gleam filled Psappha's eyes as she flicked up-tilted nipples turned black with passion.

Gyla didn't commandeer her passion. Instead, she lay still except for impassioned breathing while Psappha's hands molded lush contours between damp palms. Here hands flowed over sloping hips to taut thighs as if of their own volition. They traveled across and upward to the fragrant altar and paused there like pilgrims at Delphi awaiting the Oracle's divination.

Psappha's too-long-lonely eyes followed the journey of her hands. Their eyes met. Psappha plunged soul-forward into humid jungle pools as seductive as the river Styx. The map her hands had drawn became the guideline for thirsty lips and tongue. Avid hunger hardly recognized 'til now, found at last its only nourishment. The consummate divinity of Iphis became the only reality, devotion the only instruction as Psappha's silent tongue spoke the love so long denied her.

Gongyla mirrored Psappha's every gesture, echoed each caress. Barriers ripped and vanished. Iphis met Iphis in a coalescence of image and reflection. Shadow and substance blended, melded – into a completion of itself.

~ ~ ~

Psappha woke the next morning with her lips, her soul, her taste buds infinitely addicted to the narcotic intoxication of The Lady's sacred nectar and her world abundant with birdsong that seemed as nothing compared with the singing in her veins. Years had fallen from her spirit. Youth filled her body with music. *Today I am born, Sweet Aphrodite. Long have I found fault with thee, when the crime was my own blind stubbornness.*

Rising early, as was her habit, she cut her feelings into wax. *Sweet longing permeates the soul as summer dances into fall on satin-clad feet: How dear to have a friend with whom to walk and talk through breezy easy autumn days: To dream and scheme of winter warmed by friendly fire and sweetmeats roasting, goblets toasting: Karmic twins entwined in magic.*

Laying tablet and stylus aside, she returned to the massive bed and snuggled into Gyla's gathering arms. Her contented smile found answer on welcoming luxuriant lips temptingly close to her own. Psappha tested their texture. She found them full and warm as never before. The wonder she had so long accepted as her due was at last a gift she'd won. Her spirit cried for all the wasted years, but only for an instant. *This is no time for recriminations, even self-deserved,* she thought as she again mapped Gyla's precious body with her lips.

> *"Come daughter come*
> *full and spilling come to the feast and*
> *sit down at the table heaped with honey*
> *and hollyhocks squashes and pomegranates*
> *small furry animal stumbling through apples.*
>
> *After all the work and waiting*
> *after all the fear and sorrow*
> *come dear hurry*
> *come*
> *full and spilling*
> *run laughing to the feast."*
> *'Sonia Johnson'*

-- XXX --

Three months flew by on satin feet with only Lycos noticing there was no further word from Alkaios. Syracuse was too far away from where Psappha and Gongyla dwelt for them to give it any consideration. They forgot all but each other until the morning a summons from Lycos called them to the villa. His office smelled of lamp oil and tablet wax.

Psappha fidgeted on what should have been a comfortable bench. "If he wished to see us, he could at least be prompt."

Gyla draped an arm along the top of the bench behind her and tweaked her opposite ear. Psappha wiggled into a more comfortable position, rested her cheek in the crook of Gyla's shoulder and sighed, resigning herself to wait.

Her wait was brief. Lycos burst in, scurried directly to his accounting table, sent tablets and scrolls in a dozen directions, found the missive he searched for and handed it to Psappha. "You should have responded to this days ago."

"I'm sure she would have," Gyla said, "had she not had better things to do."

"Hush!" Psappha unrolled the scroll, scanned it, re-rolled it, blinked, unrolled it and read it through with amazement.

"Conference of Poets . . . Syracuse . . . The Illustrious Psappha . . . invitation . . . member...," she mumbled incoherently. The words blurred before her eyes.

"It's true, Adelphi," Lycos beamed. "Note the signet."

Gongyla took the message from Psappha's trembling hands and read it aloud.

"The servants of the Muses have, this second year of the fifty-third Olympiad, chosen to admit to their Conference of Poets, held each year in Syracuse, The Illustrious Psappha of Lesbos, known to many as The Poetess. We, therefore, send forth this invitation that she meet with us there and become, if she chooses, a member of our League." Re-rolling the scroll, Gongyla tapped it in her palm, her eyes wet with pride. The signet pressed into the wax was the seal of Solon of Athens leaving no doubt as to the scrolls authenticity.

Psappha was dumbstruck.

"You will go," Gyla decided for her.

"I will go nowhere without you."

"We'll all go," Lycos chirped. "I wouldn't miss this for anything. They have never invited a woman before, Adelphi. Do you realize what an honor this is?"

"Of course, I realize it, you goose. What do you think I've been aiming toward most of my life?"

"Me, I thought," Gongyla teased. Their combined laughter must have given the gods a merry chuckle.

~ ~ ~

Lycos made sure that word of the unprecedented invitation spread over the entire island. All of Lesbian society wanted to honor her with a banquet. Since Psappha would not permit Pittakos to profit from her fame, she refused him and therefore couldn't possibly accept any others. No matter how many banquet invitations came, they attended none. Instead, they held constant audience until moments before they sailed.

Psappha and Gongyla passed the first leg of the journey perfecting the bonding of midnight and noon, Artemis and Aoede, one hundred leagues of sipping the intoxication of Io's blessing; uninterrupted passion in Poseidon's tender care.

~ ~ ~

The ship bumped against the docks. Awakened by the cacophony of the wharf, Psappha wondered, *Can we be at Kenchreai* so soon? Wasn't it just yesterday we sailed from Mitylene?* She tickled Gyla awake and was dressed, and on deck before her champion got her eyes completely open. Word of the honor soon to be bestowed upon her had preceded them. She clung to the railing with one hand while waving to the welcoming throng with the other, swelling with pride as much from having Gyla at her side as from the fact that the Corinthians sang chorus after chorus from her own books.

"If this is your reception among strangers," Lycos commented as he joined them. "What's it going to be like in Syracuse where your odyssey began?"

Psappha had no idea. Psappha, The Poetess, the inventor of words was speechless. She ran down the gangway and bumped into a sedan chair. She refused to release Gyla's hand so they shared the chair that was quickly born away from the docks. Lycos led the merry crowd that followed, serenading them both with many of Psappha's own rollicking and bawdy hymeneals.

The procession halted in the center of the Agora. The chair was set down and Psappha stepped from it to stand breathless with wonder at the beauty of the Acrocorinth, across and above the Agora to the south. She looked forward to the darkness of night when,

---

* Kenchreai (KENCH-ray-i) ancient Corinthian port.

reportedly, the lights of the sacred citadel resembled the windows of heaven.

Apollo's temple stood high above them on a sacred pinnacle reached by seemingly endless stairs. Psappha reverently removed her sandals and tugged at Gongyla's hand. The marble felt warm beneath her feet. The crowd came in whispers behind them as they climbed.

Treading humbly upon the garden of the Gods, Psappha paused and looked down upon the twin ports of Kenchreai, gateway to the Aegean and Lechaeon across the isthmus, gateway to the Adriatic. The view was incredible. Nothing interfered.

Nearer at hand, down a short flight of rock-cut steps, lay the sacred Glauki* spring. As they approached it, Gongyla reminded them of the story of Medea's gift to her husband's second wife. The bridal garments had burst into flames and Glauki had plunged into the waters of the spring, thereby giving it its name.

Standing before Apollo's temple, surveying the myriad scenes below, Psappha felt as if she stood on the doorstep of Olympus with the world of men at her feet, which in her deepest heart is exactly where she stood. *Oh dear Lady of a Thousand Names, look upon thy daughter now, on the doorstep of thy brilliant son with the fulfillment of all I desire in hand.*

She squeezed Gongyla's fingers then continued.

Oh, father Poseidon, many times I've cursed thy children for stealing my beautiful ones. Forgive thine errant daughter for the shortness of my sight. I didn't know, nor understand, where lay my perfect blend. It was for this that you let Kerkolos snatch me from your embrace all those years ago. Carry me yet a little farther, Great Ocean, for I go to claim a hard-won glory. The poets of Hellas have deigned to number me among their own.

They strolled away from the temple hand in hand with Lycos following, hustling to keep up. Psappha chose to descend the western slope. Part way down, her eyes rested on the series of cave-like reservoirs, with their marble facade and portico that held the

---

* Glauki (GLOU-key)

sacred water of the spring Pirene*. They munched honey cakes and watched old men at their games while Psappha tried to remember how the spring got its name. She could not.

"The spring is named for the nymph, Pirene," one of the old men told her. "Fair Artemis killed her child by accident and here is where she spilled her grief."

"It is said Pegasus was conceived here when his mother lapped Pirene's tears," another added. Psappha smiled her thanks then left them to their gaming and continued down to the Agora.

The crowd followed her quietly until she reached the white road to Lechaeon, from which they were to sail for Syracuse. There, they lined the shoulders of the paving and sang her along with their cheers.

Sacred prostitutes watched her approach from the entrance to the Temple of Aphrodite ahead. In the haze of her happiness, Psappha allowed herself to appreciate their collective beauty. *Some of these may have once been my students.* The thought made her smile and nod to the holy priestesses. At their behest, she followed them inside and prostrated herself before the statue of Aphrodite.

Hearing a familiar voice behind her, she rose. The adoration in her eyes did not change as she turned them from Aphrodite to Gyla. "Let's not go directly to Syracuse," she suggested. "Let's visit the Oracle at Delphi first. It isn't far."

"I've no wish to consult the oracle of Apollo," Gyla grumbled.

"The oracle doesn't get her wisdom from Apollo," Psappha argued. "Nor from Dionysus who currently shares the sanctuary. The Pythia's prophesies come from their Lady Mother, who was there before they were born. Wouldn't you like to have her word on our future?"

"Isn't it better to let The Fates weave their webs in secret?" Lycos asked.

---

* Pirene (Pie-REEN)

"No," Psappha insisted. "I've made too many stupid mistakes. I want to know what lies ahead."

Contrary to Psappha's assumption, the way to Delphi was long and arduous. As they approached the Oracle's cave, Gongyla gazed longingly toward the Gulf of Corinth beyond the fertile valley of the Pleistos. *If she looks hard enough, she'll imagine tigers stalking through the grass.* Psappha thought as she led the way to the fountain of Castalia.

"You don't need to drink from here," Lycos said. "The gift of poetry you have is more than enchanted water could bestow."

Psappha laughed. "Perhaps to your prejudiced ear, my friend, but it pays to accept every gift the gods may choose to offer."

The mouth of the ancient Oracle's cave loomed before her and she wasn't sure she wanted to enter after all. Sacred smoke wafted from it to insult her nostrils. She would have run had not Gongyla's tall form and firmly planted feet stood in her way. "'We're here and here I'll stay until you've finished."

"I'll wait with her," Lycos said. He looked pale.

Embarrassed by her own trepidation after having been the one to demand they come here, Psappha inched forward as her spirit rushed from The Mother's presence to cower in the far corners of her mind. Inside the cave, the acrid stench of burning hemp stung her eyes. She stared in dismay as priestesses swayed before her. *Or is it I who sways?*

When, at last, the Pythia came, Psappha could not understand a word. An assistant hurried her to the exit the instant the Oracle left. "Here is your future, she said, handing Psappha a tiny scroll. Psappha thanked her groggily and ran into Gongyla's waiting arms.

"What did she say," Lycos asked.

"I don't know. Here. You read it." She hid her face against Gyla's breast has he unrolled the tiny scroll.

"You shall lie soon and long in the arms of your strongest and most constant protector," he said.

"She said I shall lie long in your arms, Beloved," Psappha interpreted.

Gyla frowned. "Are you sure? Oracles are often riddles. I suspect a different meaning."

Psappha shook her head. "There was nothing ominous. She said I'd lie long in the arms of my strongest and most constant protector. Whom else could she possibly have meant?"

"There was nothing more?"

Lycos shook his head.

Psappha snatched the scroll from his hand and scanned it. "There's nothing more," she said. "But, she did say it would be soon, and it shall be if you will stop dawdling and hasten with me to our cabin."

~ ~ ~

Psappha lounged in a deck chair. Gyla climbed to the lookout atop the main mast. Moments later, she descended like a swooping gull to lash the water near where a dolphin played in the wake. Psappha remembered how it once frightened her to see The African float downward from her lofty perch but she had learned to take pride in the oarsmen's admiring gasps. To her eyes, Gyla was lovelier in her natural finery than Hera's sacred peacocks. Nude, except for a covering of olive oil, she was more graceful than The Lady's swans.

When Gyla returned to the deck, Psappha brushed droplets from her arm and leaned away. "Stand back, you gorgeous fool, you're drenching me with your drippings." Her pulse fluttered as high, cone-shaped breasts quivered with laughter mere inches from her nose. A flash of ivory, in startling contrast to full, sensuous lips, brought scorching juices to her temple. Twinkling black eyes evoked wild, mindless yearning. Psappha's flesh screamed its craving while her spirit wept from an excess of tenderness. Her muse hid from a love too great for her songs to describe.

~ ~ ~

Psappha sat determinedly at her table every day, when she would much rather have been on deck watching Gyla swim. Yet, her tablets remained empty. The proper ode for the Conference would not come. She stormed around the rocking cubical, each false start more frustrating than the one before it. The close air grew warmer with every passing hour. She could hear the oarsmen's respectful "Ah-h-h," every time Gongyla dove.

Psappha hurled her stylus at the bulkhead. The tablet followed. After another "Ah-h-h," from the deck, she stiffened her shoulders, retrieved her tablet, found a fresh stylus and attacked her task with renewed determination. *The sooner you get this done. The sooner you too can enjoy the journey.*

Each line came in bits and pieces. *Like a festering tooth from an old man's mouth.*

A momentary break in the rhythm of the oars distracted her. In her mind's eye, she could see Gyla plummet from her rookery into the foaming wake. "Be still my heart," she chided. Thus self-disciplined, her reluctant talent tried once more to answer her direction. She scratched letters into the tablet almost as fast as she could think.

For me you cannot throw out, in rapid, hymn-spurting inspiration, an Adonis song, which in beauty of style shall please the Goddesses. Dishonoring Desire and heart-conquering Aphrodite have made you speechless. Brain-destroying Peitho, from her flagon of gold has poured her sweet nectar upon your wits.

Hither to me now, tender Graces and lovely-haired Muses. Hither now once more to Psappha sweet rose-armed Graces. Come hither, daughters of Zeus, that I may once more, on the morrow, create again a lyric worthy of thy love.

Once before, you honored me by giving me your own song for my own. Hither again, thou lovely ones. Arise, once more, my lute divine, and make thyself my voice. Make my song reflect thy glory so that when I die I'll never be forgotten.

She laid the tablet with her private collection and took up another. One by one the words for her acceptance speech appeared, as if by another's hand, upon the wax. Toward the end, she sounded them out in her mind, savoring their effect. *You dishonor the good gifts of the muses, my friends, when you say, 'We will crown you, dear Psappha, the best player of the clear sweet lyre.'*

~ ~ ~

Dawn had not yet penetrated their cabin. Psappha and Gongyla faced one another across a lamp lit breakfast table. Psappha smiled as watered wine turned her chunk of Eresian barley bread passionate pink. It was a small matter of personal pride to her that Eresos, so famous for the whiteness of its bread was also the city of her birth. She never mentioned it. To mention it would evoke conversation of that early exile and of too many other things she didn't care to discuss. A clatter on the deck outside interrupted her thoughts.

Gyla looked up from the apple she was eating. "It's just the water casks, my love. They'll be loaded into cargo nets and lowered into lighters that'll be rowed ashore where the crew will fill the casks with fresh water."

Psappha nodded. "I've heard it said that the water here is sweeter than that of Korfu, though it seems a waste to make an extra stop."

"Stopping at Leucos isn't extra," Gyla explained. "According to the captain, we won't dock at Korfu. Instead, he said we'd wait offshore until others join us for the crossing of the narrows. An oarsman told me the narrows are too treacherous to risk alone. There'd be no one there to rescue us if the ship went down. He said he and others in the crew welcomed their sojourn here. They want to sacrifice to Apollo in hopes of safer passage."

"There's a temple here?"

"No not a temple. Only a small shrine, but it will do. Finish your breakfast and we'll go on deck to see."

"I'm finished." Psappha pushed her chair back and went around the table. "I've no desire to see anything other than thee," she murmured against the nape of Gyla's neck. "Can't we stay inside a little longer?"

Gongyla reached around, took Psappha by the waist and pulled her into her lap, gave her a brief kiss then pushed her gently away. "We'll have a lifetime for that," she said as she got up and opened the door. "Come. We'll have years in which to hide in the warmth of our light. We'll never be parted again."

Psappha's face clouded.

"No," Gongyla assured her, "not even then. The Lady would not be so cruel. We'll be together through a thousand lifetimes, as we were meant to be."

"Don't speak of it. You'll tempt the Gods. They think Death is a misfortune, else they would have died."

"If The Lady's multiple children are not already seething with jealousy, nothing I say will rile them. Now come."

Psappha stepped across the threshold, stopped, and backed into the cabin. "I don't want to go out there. That cliff crouches like a hungry vulture."

"It is only an island eaten by Poseidon," Gongyla insisted. "See," she said, displaying her half-eaten apple. Taking a huge bite, she completed the indented circle around the core. "The waterline is here - at the center. Poseidon's waves have whittled it away. At the top is the precipice you see and there's a matching outcrop beneath the waterline – just like my apple. There's no danger unless some fool dives head first from one into the other. In that case, they'd end with a head like a dropped melon. You don't plan to do that do you?"

Psappha shook her head and laughed. Yet, when Gyla propelled her onto the deck, she still felt a deepening sense of foreboding with the jagged promontory overhead and the diminishing depth beneath. The ship snuggled into the cutout like a duckling nestled beneath its mother's wing but Psappha did not feel safe. She burrowed into Gongyla's protective embrace and watched, with one eye, as the cumbersome water-boats shuttled back and forth from ship to shore. A contingent of scrubbed oarsmen scrambled over the side and into a small skiff. Curiosity overruled apprehension. She approached the rail. "Where are they going?"

"To the shrine, see -- there," Gyla pointed skyward to where Psappha saw a bit of roof above the sharp edge of the projecting cliff.

Psappha impulsively ran back into their cabin and snatched up a copy of the Ode to Apollo she had finally completed for the Conference. With it in hand, she returned to Gyla only to grab her hand and lead her across the deck to the swinging, rope ladder.

"What's this?" Gyla teased. "A moment ago you were trembling now, all of a sudden, you're a nimble goat ready to climb to the top of the world."

Psappha chuckled at the mischief in Gyla's dark eyes, but she refused the bait. "I want to thank Apollo for lending me his gift of song. I wasn't ready at Corinth. Come with me."

"Not I, Little Love. I'll stay here and worship wind and water."

"Please, Gyla, I don't want to go alone."

"You aren't alone. You'll never be alone again. Wherever you are, I will be. Wherever you go, I go also, if only in spirit. We are one, you and I. I'll always watch over you. My heart is ever with you and I'll never be far away. Go, nightingale, bestow your gifts upon thy God, then hasten to me and we will honor The Mother together."

~ ~ ~

The freshet-carved path up from the indented waterline was almost vertical and slippery with moss. Psappha stepped with care. She wound her way around fallen rocks and through strange succulent plants, her newest poem clutched in one tight fist. She stumbled often in the shadowed water-cut. She fought for breath as she ascended a sharp curve. Then, she blinked as brightness surrounded her.

She slumped onto a marble bench to catch her breath, fanning herself with the scroll, admiring the gulls as they skimmed among tumbling clouds. The shrine gleamed upon flat flowered lawns. The grasses waved in the gentle salt breeze. After a moment, she continued toward it. Her step quickened as she approached the altar. Time seemed nonexistent as she approached the roofless shrine.

Knees on the grooved penitent's stone, she recited, "Golden Apollo, beloved son of She Who Is, hark to my words. I bring thee gratitude for thy revealing light. Great has been thy gift to me, Oh Apollo. Truly, thou hast sent thy sister, Artemis, to be my companion. No grander gift could I have dared expect, yet in thy benevolence thou hast deigned to grant another.

"Long have thy lyrics filled my mind and flowed through me to thy sacred lyre, yet my hope to be considered equal to those of thy servants most highly praised seemed futile. Yet, this also, Oh Bountiful Musicos, thou hast seen fit to grant me. I offer thanks, Oh Wondrous Apollo, that in this world of men, Psappha of Lesbos shall wear honor. Many praises shall I sing to thee, Phoebos. The Lesbian bears, for thee, a grateful heart."

She left the poem on the altar stone and then, with a silent *thank you* to Alkaios, *beloved meddler*, she strolled from the sanctuary.

At land's end, she stretched her arms to encompass the bay below and called out, "Blessed art thou, Father of Ocean. Once more, you carry your hereditary daughter in thy gentle arms. I go to claim an honor of which I have too long dreamed. My heart is full, Earthshaker. All my prayers, both great and small have been granted. No mortal could imagine more than that which now is mine. There is no glory left for me to acquire, save immortality. With The Lady's blessing and with thine, thy divine nephew's gift of songs has earned me even that. The great poets of Hellas wish to number Psappha among their own. My songs will live after me, Father. The Poetess hails thy holy name."

Shading her eyes, she surveyed her surroundings. The cerulean sea mirrored the iridescent sky. She felt as if she could embrace The Queen of Heaven by merely extending her arms.

Lady of the pure and beautiful, I thank you above all others. Always you sent them forth with blessings for thy never humble daughter. The wonder is that you never forsook me, Blessed Lady, though I know I tried your patience more than once. Mother you were and Mother you remain – blessed above all others. All hail to thee, My Lady of Ten Thousand Names.

Gulls circled and dove to squabble over escapees from a sailor's net. Psappha leaned forward to gaze down into the inlet. The view made her dizzy. From the top of the jutting precipice, the ship looked like a toy in a tub. Directly below the overhang, Gyla climbed the mast for another dive. As she climbed, she looked up and waved.

Earth sighed. To Psappha, Earth's groan, as she repulsed Poseidon's onslaught, sounded like the melodious harmony of the planets rolling through the universe. She raised her fingers to her lips and blew Gyla a kiss.

Earth trembled. Psappha dug her toes into the turf. The rhythmic slosh of Ocean's heartbeat rose to a crescendo as Poseidon hammered at the time-worn wall of rock. Gyla stood in the lookout on the mainmast below, poised for another dive.

Earth shivered. Waves gathered themselves into a fist to strike a crushing blow at the concave wall. The ship wallowed and tipped. The overhang trembled. The edge upon which she stood tilted and fell. Her scream rent the air as Gyla's supple body sliced the waves. The last thing they heard was Earth's agony as the rest of the precipice ripped free, turned over in midair and crushed them both beneath, leaving Apollo's little shrine with its marble toes sticking out over the edge of a fresh cut cliff.

Helios hid his face behind dark clouds and wept.

Velvet-voiced Psappha would sing no more among the maids of Mitylene.

[page deliberately left blank]

Sappho Sings

Excerpt from The Life of Greece *by Will Durant
Simon & Schuster, N.Y., 1939.*

Above the Ionian Dodecapolis lay the twelve cities of mainland Aeolia, settled by Aeolians and Achaeans from northern Greece soon after the fall of Troy opened Asia Plinor to Greek immigration. Most of these cities were small, and played a modest role in history; but the Aeolian isle of Lesbos rivaled the Ionian centers in wealth, refinement and literary genius....

"Sappho was a marvelous woman," said Strabo, "for in all the time of which we have record I do not know of any woman who could rival her even in a slight degree in the matter of poetry." As the ancients meant Homer when they said The Poet, so all the Greek world knew whom men signified when they spoke of The Poetess.

Psappha, as she called herself in her soft Aeolian dialect, was born at Eresus, on Lesbos, ...Pittacus, fearing her maturing pen, banished her...she married a rich merchant of Andros; some years later she writes, "I have a little daughter, like a golden flower..."

After five years of exile she returned to Lesbos and became a leader of the island's society and intellect ... Eager for an active life, she opened a school for young women, to whom she taught poetry, music, and dancing; it was the first 'finishing school' in history....

Her verse was collected into nine books, of some twelve-hundred(sic) lines, six-hundred survive, seldom continuous.

In the year 1073, of our era, the poetry of Sappho and Alcaeus was publicly burned by ecclesiastical authorities in Constantinople and Rome (sic).

Then, in 1897, Grenfell and Hunt discovered ... coffins of paper-mache, in whose making certain scraps of old books had been used; and on some of these scraps were some poems of Sappho....

In truth, we do not know when she died or how; we know only that she left a vivid memory of passionate poetry, and grace.

[page deliberately left blank]

Made in the USA